MW01264760

ANONYMOUS
HEROES

A Sam Richards Thriller

JOSEPH R. RITCHIE

Anonymous Heroes
A Sam Richards Thriller
Joseph R. Ritchie
Enrichment Press

Published by Enrichment Press, St. Louis, MO
Copyright ©2020 Joseph R. Ritchie
All rights reserved.

No part of this publication may be reproduced, stored in a retrieval system, or transmitted in any form or by any means, electronic, mechanical, photocopying, recording, scanning, or otherwise, except as permitted under Section 107 or 108 of the 1976 United States Copyright Act, without the prior written permission of the Publisher. Requests to the Publisher for permission should be addressed to Permissions Department, Enrichment Press, Jrmdosu@gmail.com.

Limit of Liability/Disclaimer of Warranty: While the publisher and author have used their best efforts in preparing this book, they make no representations or warranties with respect to the accuracy or completeness of the contents of this book and specifically disclaim any implied warranties of merchantability or fitness for a particular purpose. No warranty may be created or extended by sales representatives or written sales materials. The advice and strategies contained herein may not be suitable for your situation. You should consult with a professional where appropriate. Neither the publisher nor author shall be liable for any loss of profit or any other commercial damages, including but not limited to special, incidental, consequential, or other damages.

Names, characters, businesses, places, events and incidents are either the products of the author's imagination or used in a fictitious manner. Any resemblance to actual persons, living or dead, or actual events is purely coincidental.

Editor: Dorothy Zemach. dorothyzemach.com

Cover and Interior design: Davis Creative, DavisCreative.com

Library of Congress Cataloging-in-Publication Data

Library of Congress Control Number: 2020921526

Joseph R. Ritchie

Anonymous Heroes

ISBN: 978-1-7321143-0-2 (paperback)
       978-1-7321143-5-7 (hardback)
       978-1-7321143-4-0 (ebook)

Library of Congress subject headings:

    1. FIC031090 FICTION / Thrillers / Terrorism 2. FIC031050 FICTION / Thrillers / Military 3. FIC031060 FICTION / Thrillers / Political

2020

*To my loving wife for her
patience and encouragement
and
To the brave men and women who
selflessly protect this great nation*

Prologue: Present Day

The evening heat made the jungle excessively steamy, and Sam Richards' camouflaged body was soaked with sweat. He had been waiting in this position for the last twelve hours, hoping that the intelligence he had obtained from his source would prove to be accurate. Ever since he'd been told that the leaders of the largest drug cartels in the world, along with the scumbags who deal in human trafficking, had planned a meeting, he and his team had been stoked. This evening's mission would, without question, be the Trust's greatest success so far. During the last two years he'd been working with the Trust, their missions had delivered a positive affect on the less fortunate around the world, but tonight would be a transforming moment. The hope was that tonight's intervention might curtail criminal drug activities for many years, resulting in the drug cartels waging internal battles for power. Their focus, at least for a while, would be drawn away from their illicit activities that ruined innocent lives every day. Of course, Sam knew that it was foolish to think that the world would ever be completely rid of evil like these monsters. But for now, he had to be content that tonight's mission would be a positive ripple and make a notable difference in the world *today*.

He had remained focused while waiting, but it was inevitable that his mind would periodically wander. His thoughts were filled with the events that had led to these criminals scheduling a face-to-face meeting with each other. These hoodlums didn't schedule regular get-togethers like one might see in legitimate business. But Sam and his team had disrupted each dirtbag's cash flow through a series of attacks in order to drive the message home to these assholes—someone was seriously trying to shut them down. After years of lame attempts by the U.S. and various Central American governments to do the same, the negative effect on the cartels achieved by Sam and his men over a brief period was without precedent.

At first, the cartel leaders thought that a competitor had begun this war, and they had attacked each other mercilessly. All the while, Sam and the Trust had observed from the background more criminal-on-criminal violence than they had ever hoped to see. It was satisfying to have evil men killing each other, instead of the innocents who often became collateral damage during their drug dealings.

It had been relatively easy for Sam and his team to follow the drug runners as they pushed their poison toward the growing, insatiable appetite of the American population. They operated with little concern that police or government officials would engage them. It was disgusting to Sam that the U.S. had the means to shut it all down, but because of "political concern," they did not take the battle to these dirtbags in their own country before they could arrive in the U.S. It was the ability to act without these constraints that had first attracted Sam to the Trust.

Over the last month, the Team had succeeded in disturbing cartel business by using a few well-placed explosives. The result had wreaked havoc, and more importantly, spread fear through the ranks of the cartels' soldiers. Sam had been able to accomplish this with his usual detachment, but keeping this separate mindset was becoming harder and harder for him. Ridding the world of heinous individuals wasn't difficult for Sam and his colleagues, but how could anyone forget the faces of teenage girls being smuggled for sex slavery, or families ripped apart as children were taken forcefully from their parents' arms? Helping innocents was what he lived for, but the seemingly endless depth of evil in the world was taking an emotional toll. He really wasn't sure how much longer he could do this. He had always truly believed that there were times when good people were justified in killing bad people. This belief was what he clung to as he continued his work.

A loud noise brought him back from his reflection. He shook his head to clear the thoughts of sadness and anger, and saw that the entire cartel assembly had finally arrived. Before him were some of the worst villains in this part of the world, responsible for untold depravities against those unable to defend themselves. He checked the detonator, and the light was green. Using the information provided by his source, who had confirmed the meeting location, he and his team had been able to plant more than enough explosives before the criminals had arrived. He pushed the detonator, and watched the entire area vaporize. This form of execution was certainly more humane than what these bastards did to defenseless, innocent people. In his mind, he knew that the world was now a better place; but, as usual, he worried (just a little) about the disposition of his soul.

PART ONE:

Ten Years Prior

Chapter 1

It was the beginning of fall quarter, and Sam was walking to class with a fraternity brother when he noticed the brunette bombshell walking with several of her friends. He was in his final year at Ohio State, but he hadn't seen this girl before. This was an advantage of such a large school—there were more pretty women than one could ever possibly hope to meet. This girl must not be in a sorority, he thought, because he had probably met most of those girls at any one of the many social activities hosted by his fraternity. He was known somewhat as a player, but he remembered all the women he met, and they would all say that Sam treated them wonderfully, and that he was open and honest with them. He just wasn't one to stay with the same gal. He hadn't found anyone that could keep his interest for very long. However, he was immediately mesmerized by this girl; something was different about her. Their eyes met for a brief moment; however, the connection was interrupted by some idiot who leaned in and started talking to her. Sam broke away and continued on to his religion class but was unable to get the image of the girl out of his mind. He found his way to his seat and waited for class to begin.

Sam had been looking forward to his final year of college, but had yet to determine what he was going to do once he graduated. A Philosophy and Religious Studies degree was somewhat limited in its options, and he really didn't think he wanted to go to grad school. He really enjoyed the writing and the debates that had gone along with his studies the last four years, but he was ready to be done with school. His parents had supported his choice and had been nothing but a source of encouragement. Well, certainly his Mom had been. He could still remember his Dad's look of bemusement when he announced his choice of studies. It wasn't exactly disappointment, but more one of surprise. His father had not pushed him to follow in his footsteps and become a physician, but his Dad had hoped that Sam would make a career choice with better economic security.

Sam had been fortunate to grow up with the advantages that wealth can bring. He had been to many places, and had had many experiences in his young life that many would never experience in a lifetime. Sam warmly remembered one of the sayings his Dad had told him at sixteen, when Sam was excited to pick out his own car. When he told his father his vehicle choices, his dad had simply smiled and shook his head, saying, "Son, as a father I will strive forever to give you what you need, but not always what you want." He ended up getting a great car, and it was much later before Sam understood his father's words: that there is certainly a difference between "want" and "need" in a person's life. His parents had grown up in middle class homes, and while trying to better their children's lives, they had not wanted to produce spoiled brats. Their parenting technique had always centered on being grateful for what you have, while realizing that what you do have does not make the person. As Sam matured, he appreciated his parents' philosophies more and more.

❋ ❋ ❋

The sound of the bell snapped him back to the present. He looked around at the people in this upper level class, noting the usual students who were also in the same major. Almost all of them had their plans after graduation wrapped up—grad school, law school, or the like. However, today he was shocked to see among those students the very same brunette he had seen outside. Who was she, and what was she doing in this class? It was all he could do to concentrate on anything the professor said during the next hour. When the class was over, he decided that he needed to approach her.

Over the next several days, they spent time talking to one another after class. There was an obvious, mutual attraction. Soon, they were spending time together studying at night. Sam was really falling for this gal; he'd even stopped going to fraternity parties so he could be with Mariah. His friends were amazed at the change in his behavior—the former player was completely engrossed in one woman. They spent countless hours together, getting to know one another and talking about their dreams.

Sam learned that Mariah had transferred to Ohio State for her final two years from a small community college in Dayton, Ohio. She was pursuing a degree in social work, and her goal was to "save the less fortunate." Her parents were from less than ordinary means, and she had witnessed personally the daily struggles of the economically challenged. Sam characterized her parents as hippies, and told Mariah she was their "flower" child. Mariah knew she couldn't change everything in the world, but she felt that she still could change what was immediately around her for the better. As they became closer, Sam would tease her about this, and challenge her goals.

"What difference can one person really make?" Sam asked.

Mariah responded, "Have you ever heard the story of the starfish?"

"Say what?" said Sam, with a look of confusion.

With a furrowed brow, Mariah told the story. "Once after a great storm, there were hundreds of starfish washed up on shore. An old man was slowly walking the beach, and as he did so, every few paces he would pick up a starfish and throw it back into the sea. He did this until it was too dark to see. There were countless starfish still on the beach when he quit. But for the ones he threw in the ocean, this one man made all the difference in the world."

It was then that Sam knew he loved her. He told her so, and from then on they were almost inseparable. Fall quarter ended, and over winter break they visited each other's homes. Sam's parents had never seen him this way with a woman. Instead of his usual, measured aloofness, he was constantly attentive to Mariah. They were amazed at their son's behavior. Mariah's parents weren't quite the hippies that Sam had envisioned. They were compassionate, caring people, not unlike his own parents. They, too, could tell that Sam was deeply in love with their daughter.

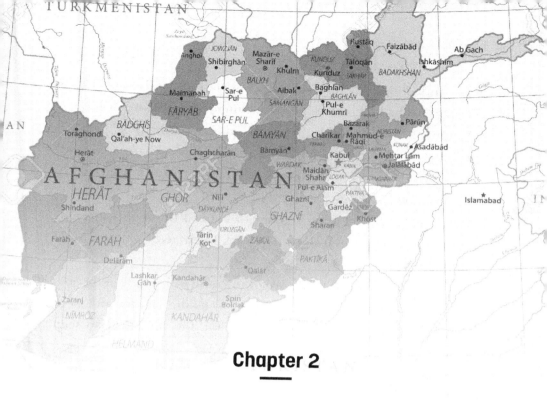

Chapter 2

Sam could not believe that he was now sitting at a table in the Bamyan Province of Afghanistan waiting to have dinner with Mariah. He laughed as he recalled Mariah's excitement at the opportunity to volunteer abroad through school for an entire quarter. He would never forget their conversation and his reaction to her telling him.

"I have wonderful news," Mariah had said excitedly. "I have an opportunity to travel on a school-sponsored building project in a third-world country for all of spring quarter."

She was near tears with excitement. She had done multiple missions with her church for short periods, but nothing close to the ten weeks that an entire school quarter offered. Sam was outwardly smiling, but inwardly he was crushed, selfishly thinking of the time apart from her.

"That's great," he'd said, "but that's a long time to be in a backward place." Sam had never experienced a mission, and except for once as a little kid, his "camping" had consisted of the five-star resorts that his parents had taken him and his younger sister to on vacation.

Mariah had just laughed and poked him hard in the ribs. "I guess a prince like you couldn't hack a trip like that," she mockingly answered.

"Would you want me to come?" he'd asked, unsure what his response would be if she were really asking.

"Of course! How else am I going to know if the man I love has what it takes to put up with the kind of work I want to do with my life?" Mariah had explained.

He was glad now that he'd agreed to come with her. The people in this area of Afghanistan were referred to as the Hazara and were Shia Muslims. In the weeks since their arrival, the students had seen the gratefulness of their hosts. The Hazara were anti-Taliban; they'd been the target of several massacres in the late 1990's at the hands of the Taliban, so they were very grateful to the Americans for what they had done to push the Taliban back. These Afghanis were good people, and Sam couldn't wait to share his experiences with friends and family back home, especially his somewhat narrow-minded father, who thought that every Muslim was probably a terrorist.

Mariah soon joined him, hand-in-hand with an eight-year-old local girl who had immediately latched on to her. One of their local hosts was also with her. Mariah's eyes contained the same excitement they'd had on the day she told him the news of this trip.

"How was the afternoon?" asked Sam.

"Fantastic," she said, pointing to the host. "Jaleel and I have been helping at the Bamyan Maternity Waiting Home. That place has done an amazing job reducing childbirth deaths for mothers. We take so much for granted in the U.S."

"No doubt this trip has shown that to be the case for me, Mariah. I have to admit that the main reason I decided to come was to be with you and get to know you better. But I now understand your enthusiasm for trying to change the world for the better with actions. I'm so glad I came."

He took her hand into his.

Suddenly, his world turned upside down. Sam's moment with Mariah was interrupted by gunfire and screams in the distance. Before anyone could react, the doors opened, and men with AK-47s burst in screaming at them. One of the orderlies from the hospital reacted by jumping out of his chair, and he was immediately shot. Hysteria ensued, but the group quickly became silent when the presumed leader fired into the ceiling.

"Silence," the man screamed in perfect English. Sam guessed that he was probably in his mid-twenties and had been educated in the West. He carried himself differently from the others, and the men constantly looked to him for their next command. "You are now political prisoners, and if you wish to live, you will follow my orders."

At that point, the local host and one of the doctors in the hospital started yelling at the terrorist leader in their native tongue. After listening calmly to the verbal barrage with a smirk on his face, he slowly walked over to them and simply shot the doctor between the eyes, then hit the Afghani host across the head with his rifle butt. Whimpers and sobs echoed throughout the room.

"Any more questions?" the terrorist asked. "I didn't think so. You will remain here until our demands are met. Whether you live or die now depends on your government's next actions. Your lives are really in their hands, not mine."

They were separated into groups and blindfolded. Fortunately, Sam had grabbed Mariah's hand and was able to keep her by his side. She was remarkably calm; certainly much more than Sam. All Sam could think about was the U.S. government's stance of not negotiating with terrorists.

On the other side of the world, the President had just been awakened by his Chief of Staff.

"Sir, we have bad news out of Afghanistan. A group of terrorists has taken some American hostages in the Bamyan province. Seems a group of college kids has been there six weeks or so helping out the locals. We've known about these college groups going there, and to date, haven't had anything more serious happen to them than a sprained ankle. Our closest troops passed along the information after demands were received from the terrorists."

"What are the demands, Mr. Michaels?" asked the president.

"The immediate release of specific prisoners in Guantanamo, along with 25 million cash, a million for each student," responded the Chief of Staff. "Since we don't negotiate with terrorists, they won't see a penny of cash, let alone expect you to release prisoners."

"Tell that to their parents," President Collins said with a sigh. "Who in the hell allowed these kids to go there in the first place?"

"Essentially, you did, sir. It was part of your platform during the election campaign. Remember, you talked about extending American good will through private citizens, rather than through the uniforms of the military." Michaels had never expressed it, but thought at the time that this had been wishful thinking on the part of the President and an unattainable goal.

"So, the media will perceive this as my fault? My memory is that our leadership thought that it was top-notch idea," said the President. "Tell the military we have to get those kids out of there ASAP!"

"Yes, sir, but it won't be easy. As you've been drawing down the military, we don't have any close assets, and the area is pretty remote," Michaels pointed out.

The President was already worrying about the political fallout and its effect on his upcoming re-election. The economy was terrible, and even though his administration had killed a few high-profile terrorists, many still thought that the President was soft on terror.

Meanwhile, local American military assets had dispatched an Air Force drone to try to get visual reconnaissance on the village. The local Afghani military had passed the news of the hostage taking to U.S. officials who, in turn, had run it up the chain-of-command. That was how it had caught the eye of U.S. Navy Lieutenant Commander Patrick Hughes, the current commanding officer of the United States Naval Special Warfare Development Group, commonly known as DEVGRU, and informally known as Seal Team Six.

This situation cried out for his team's expertise. If he could only get involved before some civilian knucklehead made the wrong decision, or worse yet, before a local group tried to intervene, Hughes thought he might be able to bring those kids home without loss of life. Of course, he wasn't talking about the bad guys. His team would rid the world of any terrorist they encountered. He and his men had been in the area for many months, assisting locals when needed, and were standing ready in case there was further need of their expertise. Seal Team Six had been responsible for the killing of bin Laden years before, and they had recently re-deployed to the region. While there, they had disposed of many terrorist leaders. It was fortuitous that they had not returned to the U.S.

Chapter 3

The students' hysteria had somewhat subsided, but the fear was certainly palpable. The terrorists had asserted their dominance, and had shown that they had no concerns with taking human life. Sam could see ten armed terrorists in the room. They wore no masks, apparently unconcerned about anyone seeing their faces.

The leader who spoke perfect English gave orders to his men in their native language. Some of the orders were easy to understand by watching the actions of the men, such as barricading doors, and positioning guards about the few windows that the small building possessed. In one corner, a video camera had been set up, and this had sent a shock of fear throughout the group. Every American has seen the videos produced by terrorists that ended with the death of some poor soul. Sam wondered if anyone in the U.S. had any idea about their situation. He also couldn't stop himself from seeing his father's worried look when he'd told him of the trip. This was exactly what Dad had been afraid of.

Khalid Ali watched his group of men go about their tasks. He wasn't sure how much time they had, but knew that the taking of these hostages had been coordinated with their demands being dropped off simultaneously at the closest U.S. facility. His comrades should be arriving with trucks to move these people away from this site in about four hours. Once done, they could hide in areas more familiar to all of them, making it nearly impossible for them to be found. He could not understand his superiors blowing the element of surprise by informing the U.S. immediately of their demands. When he'd pointed out this tactical error to the old men organizing the mission, he had been nearly punished for insubordination.

It was proof that the Americans' success in killing senior Al-Qaeda officials was working to some degree. Men of similar age, though not similar intelligence, were replacing some of the leadership, and many of his contemporaries were noticing their ineptitude. Khalid was part of a younger, even more ruthless group that was preparing to displace these idiots. Meanwhile, he, his younger brother, and the rest of the group were not ready for martyrdom. Although the others could certainly meet Allah if they wished, Khalid was going to ensure that he and his brother met no such fate.

The plan was to get the hostages on the trucks and into the hands of the next group, so that he and his men could live to fight another day. He had been chosen because of his flawless English that had been perfected while attending school in the U.S. His father's position with the Pakistani military had taken him and his family to the U.S. for three years. He and his brother had never fit in, though. They made no real friends, and felt the local U.S. Muslims they met were traitors for having become so Westernized. He had been disgusted with what he had seen and experienced, and upon returning home, he and his brother had decided to take up arms against the West and had joined al-Qaeda. Soon, they'd fostered friendships with those their own age who were ready to repeat acts similar to the events of 9/11.

Khalid Ali had been informed by his superior that it was time to make a movie. The set was prepared, and the script had been written during the terrorists' planning sessions. It was time for the world to see their demands, and to know that the humiliation of Americans who were in this part of the world was never going to end. He randomly chose a student and one of the local hosts. Resistance was met by violent beatings to the brave but foolish friends who tried to intervene.

"Enough," Khalid screamed, "or you will all die."

It was heartbreaking, but what could any of them do? Sure, they outnumbered the terrorists, but what defense could they mount against all of the machine guns? Sam had never felt more helpless and was overtaken by shame. He was thankful that he and Mariah had not been chosen, but at the same time, he was riddled with guilt. He wanted to act, but knew it would mean instant death. Tears of anger and frustration filled his eyes. Mariah picked up on his emotions and squeezed his hand.

"It'll be okay," she said. "Just please don't do anything stupid."

"Mariah, you might be the next one chosen. I couldn't stand by and let that happen. I'd rather die than see them kill you."

The two who had been chosen were placed before the camera. On either side was a guard wearing a mask and carrying an AK-47. The leader, Khalid Ali, was not wearing a mask, and had begun to rant incessantly into the camera. One of the local hosts who was sitting by Sam and Mariah was quietly translating for them.

"'We are tired of Americans in our countries. It is time for you to leave. If you do not, we will hunt you down and kill you all, no matter how long it takes.'"

Khalid was spewing his hatred and enjoying every moment of it. He was carrying a dagger, which he nonchalantly tossed from one hand to the other.

The translation went on: "'Your arrogance is laughable. You now foolishly send children here, thinking you have made this country your own. We have given you a list of our brothers to be released from Guantanamo prison in exchange for the infidels we now have in our possession. To show our seriousness....'"

Sam no longer needed the translation as he saw the throat of one of his fellow students slit in front of them all. Gasping and crying ensued. Sam started to get up, but Mariah and the host held him down. One of the students closer to the movie set had reacted the same, getting up to launch himself at Khalid. But before he was even close, the leader raised a gun and shot the student.

"Perhaps now you will understand our resolve. But let us not forget our so-called Afghan brothers who aid and abet our enemy. They, too, will meet with a similar fate."

With that, Khalid slashed the throat of the local host. It was mind-numbing to them all. Sam could see the looks on his friends' faces. They were lost, hopeless, and beaten. No one even attempted to make eye contact with anyone else.

The terrorists had broadcast the video live, knowing that U.S. intelligence would be monitoring the situation. President Collins and his staff witnessed the live images. His advisors were all looking to the President for his response. His expression was exactly like that of the hostages—he appeared lost.

Chapter 4

Lieutenant Commander Hughes thought that someone had read his mind; the call came from his superiors only thirty minutes after he himself had seen the flash message sent to Washington. He called for Chief Petty Officer Hernandez.

"This has to be some sort of record for a response, Chief, or maybe the political figures haven't yet caught wind of the situation. If we can act quickly and decisively, without any delays for political input, we can rescue those kids."

"Roger that, boss. The world would have a lot fewer enemies of America if we didn't have to wait on their input."

Hughes had been given orders to proceed to the area to gather intel and plan for a hostage rescue. However, he was not to engage the terrorists until he had an "okay" from Command.

"Chief, alert the team to be ready to move, and that this is not an exercise. Inform them that the lives of Americans about the same age as them are at stake."

"Copy that, Commander."

His team was made up of consummate professionals, but LCDR Hughes knew that telling them that they were going after Americans would sharpen their focus and readiness even more.

At the same time as the President and his staff viewed the video, LCDR Hughes and his men saw the event. However, their reaction was different. Their eyes conveyed a calm focus of knowing what needed to be done. With that look, the eight men loaded onto their Blackhawk helicopter, the same silent design that had become public knowledge when one had been lost during the bin Laden raid.

The team made their way toward the location in silence. Battle-tested and ready for anything, the group had eliminated many terrorists and performed rescue missions in the past. Yet this was the first time that they would be going after American civilians.

Hughes briefed them again on the specifics of the building and shared what he knew from the drone reconnaissance. There were at least a dozen men surrounding the building, but the number of terrorists inside was anyone's guess. Hughes and Chief Petty Officer Hernandez formulated a plan to overtake the terrorists outside with as much stealth as possible. They were armed with various weapons, but the HK MP5SD machine gun was the perfect weapon for secrecy and suppressed fire. Their training, weaponry, and experience should win the day for them. After eliminating the individuals outside in silence, they would then be in position to breach the building.

"Gentlemen, we're about an hour out. It looks like we have more company—Command has a drone showing trucks heading to our destination."

"They could be friendlies," replied Hernandez.

"Copy that, Chief, though that's not necessarily a good thing. I'm not so sure we want Afghan Army troops in our way. If the trucks are empty, then they're going to be used to transport hostages. If they're not friendlies, then it's a shitload of more terrorists. Ask Command if they have any info."

"Roger that."

Khalid Ali had just received a transmission from the trucks. They were about sixty minutes away from their location. They had made excellent time. Khalid was thankful, as he was anxious to leave the area and get to more familiar surroundings. He knew that once they were able to hide in the hills, it would be nearly impossible for any rescue mission to be successful. As it was, Khalid was fairly certain that no serious resistance could be organized by the locals—or for that matter, anyone else—in the four hours total that they'd been in this location. Maybe the stupid old men who were running this mission weren't so dumb after all. He told the other three terrorists inside the building about the trucks' location, and then passed the word to his brother outside, who was with the largest group of men.

LCDR Hughes had been informed that the trucks were not part of any local rescue effort. That meant there were probably more terrorists in those vehicles, and they were planning on transporting the hostages somewhere else. If the trucks were full, that could mean as many as thirty more bad guys. Hughes informed Command of his thoughts. He and Chief Petty Officer Hernandez then focused themselves on coming up with the best way to deal with those trucks. Now that the trucks were close, taking them out either with guns or missiles would alert the group holding the hostages.

"Commander, I have an idea about how to handle those trucks."

"Let's hear it."

Hernandez proceeded to outline his plan. It would require unbelievable precision on both the part of the pilot and the SEAL Team. The timing would also have to be perfect. As they agreed on the plan and finished the briefing with the rest of the team, Command had informed Hughes of their own plan.

"Alpha 1, let the trucks arrive at the building. Our analysts feel the trucks are coming to transport the hostages. You are to follow those trucks to a suspected terrorist base. We'll then dispatch additional troops to eradicate the terrorists and their base."

"Sir, it's like they don't care about those kids," grumbled Hernandez. "We're good, but if those trucks fill up with hostages, I don't think we can do much without significant loss of life."

"Agreed, Chief. Command's plan is reckless and foolhardy. This could not be the idea of Admiral Thorbahn; it has to be coming from someone above him," stated Hughes.

Either way, Hughes would have to make a decision quickly.

It was actually Chief of Staff Michaels' idea to follow the terrorists once they started to transport the hostages. Everyone in the room agreed that the trucks were probably for transport and not for bringing more terrorists. But the military leaders in the room were wholeheartedly against allowing the students to get on the trucks. They had pleaded with President Collins to allow Hughes and his men act according to the situation in the field to prevent the students from boarding those trucks, because the longer they were in the hands of terrorists, the more likely that there would be more videos. In the end, Michaels had convinced the President to follow the group once they were in the trucks.

"Mr. President, neither I nor anyone else wearing a uniform in this room will take the fall for this plan if it goes poorly," said Joint

Chief of Staff Chairman Tankersley. "Rolling the dice with those kids' lives is not what we should be doing."

"Your objection is noted. And you certainly will not take the credit when it goes perfectly," replied the Chief of Staff angrily.

Joint Chief Tankersley calmly responded, "That's the difference between those of us in uniform and those of you in a suit. We don't give a shit about the credit or the political gain—we just want to bring those American kids home safe, and rid the world of bad guys. It's that plain and simple. Let us do our job and stay the hell out of our way."

"That's enough! We'll have Lieutenant Commander Hughes and his men follow the trucks and plan for a rescue when they reach their destination. It'll be a huge victory for us if we take out more terrorist leadership," was the President's response.

General Tankersley and his fellow military Chiefs of Staff made eye contact, knowing the incredible gamble that the President was taking with American civilian lives. He knew LCDR Hughes, and hoped that he would act best according to the situation in the field. That was all that any of the military men in the room wanted—to allow the men on the ground to react to the situation as they felt best.

Chapter 5

The decision was passed down the chain. After voicing his disagreement with the plan, Admiral Thorbahn had passed the message to LCDR Hughes as instructed, but his heart was heavy. He could tell how shocked Hughes was by the orders. The time was quickly coming when Hughes would have no choice but to allow the trucks to get to the hostages. If they were going to take the trucks and the terrorists simultaneously, they would have to act soon. Hughes made his own decision.

"I'm sorry, Command, your last transmission was garbled. Say again, what are the orders?" Hughes calmly spoke into the radio.

On the helicopter and back at Command, those who were listening were now smiling. They knew damn well what Hughes was doing. Thorbahn repeated the orders, and again Hughes responded, "I'm having trouble hearing you, but I think you said proceed best as situation dictates. Roger that." With that, Hughes and Hernandez readied their men to carry out their own plan.

The building where the students were being held backed up to a cliff that fell off sharply from the back of the building. The terrorists had placed their guards in a semi-circle around the front and the sides of the building, apparently feeling it made sense that the rear would be safe from any rescue attempt. The fifteen or so terrorists were arrogantly strolling around the front of the building. The winding road leading up to the front was easy to view for a significant distance, so the terrorists were confident that any rescue attempt would easily be spotted and certainly turned back. Essentially they had the high ground; all access was from the front.

Inside the building, four guards watched the students while Khalid Ali fidgeted and waited to hear from the trucks. He knew that their vulnerability would lessen once they were on those trucks heading for safer grounds.

LCDR Hughes briefed his men again on the timing of their assault. It was critical that the trucks be taken out at the very same time the building was breached. In the short time they had gathered intelligence on the building, he had noticed only occasional radio use by the terrorists. Hughes' plan was to drop in behind the building and below the cliff with his men, rappel down from the chopper to a ledge below the top of the cliff, and then climb up the cliff to the building. Being below the top of the ledge would further dampen any noise from the helicopter.

He would then have the pilot and his navigator sweep ahead to take out the trucks with missiles after getting the signal that the hostiles outside the building had been neutralized. The "silent" Blackhawk helicopter would allow them to get close without being heard, and the pilot would keep the chopper below the clifftop to prevent being seen.

This stealth Blackhawk was a definite game-changer when it came to raids like the one they were attempting tonight. The suppressed MP-5s would enable the assault on the exterior guards to also be quiet. Hopefully, the sound of dead terrorists falling to the ground would not be heard inside.

If all went well, at the same exact time the trucks were blown up, LCDR Hughes and his men would then enter the building and neutralize whatever terrorists they encountered. The SEALs were relying on a split-second period of confusion when the terrorists would all turn toward the doorway to see the source of the explosion. Typically in such a situation, civilians would cower or draw back when an explosion occurred, while combatants would look to explore the noise. Hopefully, this would enable his men to identify and neutralize the bad guys.

Khalid radioed his brother. "Faheem, the trucks are about 30 minutes away."

"I see their headlights. Nothing else happening out here."

"Excellent. Come inside I want to speak to you privately."

"On my way, brother."

"Faheem, my brother, you're holding up well. It won't be long until your first mission is complete, and we'll be honored for our actions. We must continue to be diligent in our attention, for I fear that there will be some attempt by the Americans to stop us."

Faheem responded, "I would welcome such foolishness and cherish the chance to kill American soldiers."

Khalid was proud of his fifteen-year-old brother, but also knew inside that the young man was very nervous.

"Faheem, you and I are not going to become martyrs today. I want you by my side until the trucks arrive. If something should go wrong, stay with me. I've located a hidden exit that will allow us to leave unnoticed should the need arrive."

Faheem was confused. "What could happen? What about our brothers?" he asked.

"I am your brother, Faheem. The others do not matter."

At the same time Faheem's face contorted from his brother's words, an incredible explosion emanated from what seemed to be right outside the door. Throughout the building, the different reactions by the combatants and hostages happened simultaneously.

As expected, screams from the hostages filled the air. Sam instinctually covered Mariah with his own body. Khalid tried to grab his brother as he was running to the escape exit he had found, but Faheem pushed him away and headed toward the main door.

LCDR Hughes had given the signal to the pilot to hit the trucks immediately after his men had finished the precision killing of the terrorists outside the building. Simultaneously, Chief Petty Officer Hernandez and three others entered the building, unsure of the resistance that they would encounter or the position of the hostages. It was chaos for everyone else, but not for these brave American soldiers; their countless hours of training, and the prior experience of battle, slowed time down and gave them a clarity that they used to their advantage. They surveyed the room, identified the hostiles, and neutralized them without a single return rifle shot.

Khalid turned back from the hidden entryway and saw the Americans take down his comrades. He nearly screamed as his brother was shot. Frozen in rage, he saw the American commander enter the room. As Khalid turned down the exit tunnel, he saw his brother moving. He was alive! Faheem was sitting up, and was pointing his rifle at the American commander!

"Allahu Akbar," Faheem screamed.

It reminded Sam of the fast-paced action of a lacrosse game. As a player, he had been gifted to see the game slowed down, and was always able to react faster than others could. Similarly, he was now able to follow the present action as it was occurring. The American soldiers had entered the room and taken out the terrorists before they'd even had a chance to raise their AK-47s. Sam heard the bullet hit the terrorist standing right in front of him. The man dropped his rifle as he nearly fell on top of Sam and Mariah. He was amazed at the quickness of the soldiers. They were calm and efficient along with having amazing speed. Something stirred inside him as he was witnessing this event. Sam recognized the leadership in the eyes of the man who next entered the room.

Out of his peripheral vision, Sam also noticed movement from one of the terrorists that had been shot. The soldiers had not noticed this individual, as they were securing the other fallen terrorists. The terrorist was raising his rifle. Before Sam could think, he jumped up, grabbed the rifle in front of him, and pointed it at the terrorist. He pulled the trigger as he heard the boy shout something he thought he had heard before.

LCDR Hughes heard the shout and turned to see the rifle pointed at him. A split second later, he heard the sound of an AK-47. But just as he expected to be hit with gunfire, he saw the person holding the gun pointed at him recoil as bullets ripped across his chest.

The smile that had started on Khalid's face changed to one of horror as his brother was shot to pieces. He fought to hold back his anguish as he turned to run down the tunnel. However, before he left, he burned the image of the man who had killed his brother to memory. He would never forget that face.

Chief Petty Officer Hernandez and his men turned to respond to the gunfire.

"Stand down," he yelled.

He had immediately processed that this was a student holding the gun, and he had just shot the terrorist aiming at LCDR Hughes.

Sam was shaking. He dropped the rifle and fell to his knees, emptying his stomach contents. Mariah had witnessed the entire scene and immediately ran to Sam's side. She held his shaking body to her own while she whispered words of comfort into his ear.

"Young man, I am Lieutenant Commander Patrick Hughes of the United States Navy, SEAL Team Six. Your actions were unbelievably brave. Not to mention, you just saved my life."

Sam looked up at the smiling face of the American and took his extended hand.

"No big deal," was all Sam could manage.

LCDR Hughes chuckled as he pulled him to his feet while the other soldiers patted him on the back like he was one of their own. Mariah hugged him tightly as the rest of the room was doing the same with the person closest to them.

The next several hours were a blur. As the students left the building, they saw the dead terrorists strewn across the grounds. Sam could not believe that the soldiers had killed all those men while no one inside had heard gunshots or screams. Local troops and American Army liaison officers arrived to take the students to the airport for a flight to safer surroundings. The SEALs handled the two fallen students gently and respectfully as they placed them in body bags. As the students boarded the vehicles, they also saw the burned-out trucks that had been the source of the explosions. LCDR Hughes waved to Sam as he and his men boarded the helicopter. The students had hardly been able to express their thanks before the soldiers had left. They all could see the pride on the soldiers' faces. and Sam thought he had noticed that some were near tears. He understood why—LCDR Hughes had confided to Sam that this was the first time that they had been tasked with the rescue of American civilians. He had also told Sam that when word of the rescue leaked out to the world, no one would know the identity of the rescuers. It was their job to do what they had done, but it was not part of the job to bask in the glory they so richly deserved. Along with gratitude toward the SEAL team, Sam was also filled with pride and thankfulness that the United States had people like these men committed to fighting tyranny and terrorism.

As Mariah rested her head on Sam's shoulder during the flight home, he contemplated the events of the trip, its ending, and his future. He had really never known what his focus was going to be, deciding on grad school simply because he didn't know what else to do. Also, he could be close to Mariah as she finished her last year of studies. But it was now clear to him what he wanted to do. He knew in his heart that while he wasn't making a decision based on the present circumstances, something that had been stirring in him had been triggered by these events. He had always wanted to help others and make a difference, but he never knew how he would achieve this desire. That is, until now.

Sam wanted to become a Navy SEAL.

Chapter 6

Khalid made his way to the hidden camp. He was in no mood for the questions that would be asked of him by his superiors. The mission had been a total failure. More importantly, his younger brother was dead at the hands of the Americans. If it took him the rest of his life, he would avenge Faheem's death. He would never forget the face of the man who took his brother's life; now revenge would become his only goal.

Departing from the local camp, Khalid then made his way to a larger camp on the Afghanistan-Pakistan border. He was relatively close to his parent's home in Islamabad. He would have to inform his parents about Faheem's death, a prospect he dreaded. His father was no fan of the West, ever since arriving back in Pakistan after their three years in America, but he had strongly disagreed with Khalid's decision to join Al-Qaeda. Khalid would be blamed for his brother's death; the parting words from his parents had been "Faheem's life is your responsibility."

It had been about six months since he had last talked to his parents. His father had taken a position in Kashmir, defending that region from Indian aggression. The area had recently seen an increase in the number of skirmishes between the two countries.

"Mother, it's good to hear your voice,"

His statement was met with silence. As he was about to say something, his mother finally responded.

"A lot has happened since we last spoke. I reached out to the emergency number you gave me months ago, but it never picked up."

"I'm sorry, mother, that line was compromised. Why did you reach out?"

"Your father is dead. I buried him without you and your brother."

Khalid fell to his knees. He had been dreading this call to give the news about Faheem; but now he would have to give his mother more bad news.

"What happened?"

"Your father was transferred from his Kashmir Command to the Afghanistan border. He was working to eradicate terrorist camps in that area. Ironic, since his two sons are al-Qaeda."

"Mother, he has no love for the Americans."

"And neither do I, Khalid. Anyway, he was killed by an American drone—they've ruled it 'friendly fire.'"

Khalid was shaking with anger. The U.S. was responsible for the death of his brother *and* father. He couldn't speak; he could only scream from pent-up rage mixed with guttural pain. He had been broken. He now knew that religion was not the basis for his revenge; it was the drive to avenge their deaths no matter what. The United States needed to pay for their arrogance and for the many deaths that they had caused in this region.

Khalid would make them pay or die trying.

PART TWO:

Five Years Later

Chapter 7

Lieutenant Sam Richards was daydreaming as he and his team made their way back to Virginia Beach. He was looking forward to getting back to Little Creek Naval Amphibious Base and seeing Mariah. The last five years had been wonderful. He had joined the Navy, and thanks to Lieutenant Commander Hughes, was fast-tracked into SEAL training after receiving his commission as an officer. That had taken some doing, since he had not been in ROTC as an undergraduate at Ohio State. But he had excelled during Officer Training School, and proven Hughes correct that he had the "right stuff" to become a SEAL. All of his instructors had knowledge of his actions during the rescue by LCDR Hughes and his men, and while remaining objective, inside their hearts they were all pulling for his success. He had amazed his instructors at the Great Lakes SEAL Preparatory Class. He was a natural when it came to understanding tactics of Special Operations.

From there it had been off to the Navy Special Warfare Training Center at Coronado, California, for Basic Underwater Demolition/SEAL training (BUD/S). The six months of rigorous training had been the hardest task of Sam's life. Some of the instructors at BUD/S weren't happy that Sam had been chosen for SEAL training so early after joining the Navy, and those individuals had been harder on Sam than they usually were with a new recruit. But again, Sam's performance silenced any doubters. He earned the respect of those around him quickly, and those same individuals who'd ridden him hard were the first to congratulate Sam when he set new records during Hell Week.

After completing his training, Sam had been assigned to his first 36-month sea tour. During that time, he had spent every moment of leave with Mariah. Their love had grown intensely, and had survived the separation that his career entailed. They had discovered that the hostage experience had given them a certain clarity about life usually only seen by older individuals.

Two years after Mariah's graduation, they married. She went to work for the Red Cross, planning and participating in activities home and abroad. The two of them had similar goals, but were on opposite sides of the spectrum in the ways in which they helped others and tried to improve the world. At times, Mariah was helping those in war-torn areas. At first, Sam had not told her that some of those areas were the very same areas where SEALs had gone in and taken out enemy leadership in order to improve the lives of those being oppressed. But as time went on, he shared many details with her, as she could listen and help him deal with the psychological turmoil that went with his job. Every one of his SEAL teammates always commented on how "together" Sam was; little did they know that it was his wife's counseling that kept him that way.

Sam was brought back to the present when Chief Petty Officer Douglas Sawyer yelled at him, "There's no place like home, huh, Lieutenant? Bet you can't wait to see that wife of yours. I keep waiting for you to tell me she's expecting nine months after one of these return trips home."

"We all can't be as fertile as you and Cathy, Chief," was Sam's reply.

Sawyer had touched upon a subject that he and Mariah spent a lot of time discussing. They had now been married four years and were getting browbeaten by family and friends about starting a family. But how could they do so? Sam was deployed for long periods of time, and Mariah was still traveling as well. If they had a child, it would mean big changes to both of their careers. They both wanted children, but they weren't sure how they would juggle a family with other commitments. Mariah wanted to continue traveling with the Red Cross, and Sam would continue to be gone for long periods during deployments. As it was, he had been gone four months on this deployment.

As they disembarked from the ship, he could see his team and the other sailors running to their loved ones. Sam saw Mariah talking to Chief Petty Officer Sawyer's wife. Just as Sam and his men spent a ton of time together, so did the wives and girlfriends. It was a bond that was unbreakable. As Sam and Sawyer made their way to their ladies, Doug's three children came running to him. Cathy was waving at her husband and Sam, but Mariah kept her back to them. Just as Sam was about to reach out and grab her arm, Mariah turned, and the unmistakable bump of a pregnant belly met him.

"What the hell?" Sam stammered. He then recovered from his surprise and grinned. "Looks like someone's been hitting the beer hard since I've been gone."

Mariah smacked him on the arm and said, "I thought you'd be more surprised. I didn't tell you because I wanted to see your face.

You were surprised for like, maybe, two seconds; then you recover and insult me!"

Sam grabbed her and hugged her tight. "This is the best news ever. Do you know if it's a boy or a girl? What are we going to do? How are we going to handle a baby in our lives?"

Mariah calmly replied, "No, I don't know the sex—I was waiting for you to come home before finding out. What do you mean, what are we going to do? We, obviously, are having a baby."

"I know that, but...."

Sam was cut off by Mariah's reply. "We can talk about it when we get home."

With that, they said good-bye to Chief Sawyer and his family.

Chapter 8

When they got home, Sam and Mariah did what they always did when one of them returned after being gone for a while—they got reacquainted with each other's naked body. After the lovemaking, Sam told Mariah about his mission and the good he felt about what he and his men had accomplished. The mission had been to deploy into Uganda and help regional forces deal with trying to eradicate the Lord's Resistance Army (LRA). This group was responsible for the rape, kidnapping, and murder of many innocent people. Sam and his team had helped organize local militia and had been making headway toward the goal of eliminating these thugs.

"These poor people have been defenseless against the LRA. We just want to give them a chance to protect themselves. If my team were allowed to engage the enemy, we could change the whole landscape for the better."

"Who's stopping you?" asked Mariah.

"Politicians, babe. We aren't allowed to engage unless it's self-defense. I know that the U.S. can't police the world, but if we're going to be somewhere, don't handcuff us."

"That is frustrating. Maybe you can think of a work-around—use the self-defense thing to your advantage."

He kissed her, rubbed her pregnant belly, and said, "Beautiful and smart. Thanks for listening, babe. I'm sorry I talked for so long. That stuff isn't important now. We're going to start a family!"

Sam had tears welling up as he looked into the eyes of the person that meant more to him than anyone else in the world. He was wondering if he could love a child as much as Mariah.

"Don't say that," Mariah responded, "of course that stuff is important. Even more so if we're going to bring our own child into this world. Don't ever forget our promise to each other to try and help those less fortunate; the poor and oppressed people who can't help themselves. What you do in the military has a positive affect every time you accomplish your mission. What I do in the Red Cross helps those with immediate needs. Although we go into an area and leave after the work is done, the lives we help are better from the work we've done. Don't ever forget that."

Sam was grinning. He loved it when she got worked up over this topic. Her furrowed brow and her purposeful speech were amazing turn-ons for him. Mariah sensed this as she ran her hand down Sam's stomach and felt his excitement, and she started to giggle.

"You did that on purpose, to get me riled up. How could I forget the affect it has on you? You're incorrigible." She started to say more, but then Sam was kissing her.

"I love you so much," was what he said as he gently entered her.

The next morning they lounged around, basking in each other's presence. Suddenly Mariah got serious. "I have the solution to what you said at the airport. Do you remember, Sam?" He nodded yes, and Mariah continued. "The Red Cross has offered me a position that's more of a management position. It doesn't require much travel, so it's perfect for raising a family."

Sam looked at her. "Won't you miss going to see the people you help, and being there in person as it happens?"

"Sure, at first I will. But I want a family," Mariah offered. "I've already traveled more than I ever thought I would. Maybe I'll travel again, maybe I won't. But having this child and starting our family is my new adventure. Besides, I'll still get to hear about your exploits when you come home."

"Maybe it's time I tone down those escapades," was Sam's response. "I don't like being away for long periods as it is, but now, it will be even worse with a child. I think I need to change that. I could apply for a SEAL teaching position, or I could leave the Navy after this tour is completed."

In a serious tone, Mariah responded, "You do that only if you want to. I'm proud of what you do, and that will never change. But sure, I want you around more."

Sam knew he was blessed to have Mariah. She was so supportive of his career and was his therapist in a sense as well. Every time he returned from a mission he would tell her the details that haunted him about his work. It wasn't the justified killing that bothered him; it was the seemingly endless human cruelty that he witnessed that cut to his core. Man's inhumanity to man was rampant where he and his men were told to go, and he was continuously amazed at the degree of pure evil that existed. Just when he thought he had seen everything, a new situation would be worse than the last.

In the beginning, the missions he completed were satisfying because he felt that his team's accomplishments had made a huge difference to those they helped. The missions were clean and straightforward—take out these bad guys so that a good thing could happen to people. Recently, however, it seemed that the rules of engagement had been changed. The ability to use necessary force was being replaced with only acting in self-defense. It put more risk on him and his team when they were forced to be reactionary rather than on the offensive.

The recent mission he had just returned from was a perfect example: there were evil men raping, killing, and stealing from their own countrymen, and the local governments were powerless. Sure, it was a good idea to help train the local police to use military tactics to deal with their oppressors, but why not allow U.S. forces to also engage and eliminate those criminals? Sam felt that the U.S. had always been a great country because it helped the less fortunate, especially those being bullied by evil forces. He was grateful for the opportunities he had been given, but this recent mission was not an example of what he wanted to do with his elite fighting force. Unfortunately, he and his men would be returning to Uganda in a few weeks.

During their leave, Sam and his men settled into a nice routine. They would train, work out, and socialize together. Everyone was either married or had a girlfriend, and the ladies were as close-knit as the men. It was often hard for warriors like Sam to assimilate into the civilian world. The problems that were so important to his civilian acquaintances were nothing but simple inconveniences to him. Likewise, civilians didn't understand what people like Sam did, nor why they did it. As a consequence, SEALs were a close group even during noncombat times.

Sam and Mariah spent as much time together as they could. Mariah had a great boss that supported her need for time off whenever

Sam was home from a mission, and the two of them did what every couple did—eat out, go to movies, take walks, and love each other. The highlight of the time home was going to the obstetrician with Mariah. She was four months along, and all was going well. She had felt great the entire time. They were both excited to welcome a child that they had been trying to conceive for a long time. The ultrasound showed a healthy, growing little girl. Sam put a picture of the ultrasound in his wallet to take when he deployed. Life was good, and both of them were thankful for their blessings.

But, as always, Sam's duty called, and it was time for him and his team to return to Uganda.

Chapter 9

His men were professionals, and upon their return to Uganda, they focused on the task at hand. There were a total of fifty American soldiers training the local forces, but it seemed that little headway was being made. It wasn't that the locals weren't willing to learn or lacked the necessary skills; they were simply fearful of the Lord's Resistance Army. All of them had felt the sting of the LRA, and they simply felt that they were powerless to change their situation. Sam and his men were cheerleaders as well as instructors to these men. He genuinely liked these people, and it was important to him that his team be successful in teaching them how to protect themselves.

The days consisted of teaching the local men how to use the weapons they possessed to their best advantage. Sam's group would also teach them how to set up defensive perimeters in case the LRA was going to attack their villages. Similarly, basics of rescue operations were explained. Finally, offensive strategies to take the fight to the enemy were also emphasized. Many of the men they trained were beginning to see that they could defend themselves. Their confidence was growing, and this was very satisfying to Sam and his men. They were changing their attitude from being docile to being appropriately responsive in combat training situations.

Sam and his team were stationed outside Arua, Uganda. This location gave them access to eastern Congo, southern Sudan, and northern Uganda. Villagers from all three countries would come to train with the American soldiers. Usually, when they returned to their homes, a few of the American military would accompany them and supervise activities for a period of time. This served a twofold purpose: 1) an opportunity to help with real missions, and, 2) the opportunity to gather intelligence on the Lord's Resistance Army.

Sam and his team were set to travel with the next graduating class to an area of the southern part of Sudan. The LRA had been particularly brutal in this area, and it was reported that their leadership resided there as well. Sam was excited to possibly engage these troops, and potentially even capture their leader, Joseph Kony. This common criminal had been running free for far too long. The raping, pillaging, and kidnapping that his group had been subjecting the locals to with impunity needed to cease. This was a mission that Sam believed in fully, down to his soul. He was always ready to battle for the underdog and the oppressed; this mission definitely fit the bill.

Sam and his team had met many villagers and their families. Everyone he met told him endless stories of oppression, mutilation, and murder. Now was the time to act and take these criminals down. Unfortunately, his orders were very clear: they were only allowed to engage in self-defense, and they could not participate in any offensive missions.

Only a civilian who had never experienced combat could come up with such a stupid rule of engagement (ROE).

"Sir, the men have concerns about what happened while we were home," stated Chief Petty Officer Sawyer.

"You're talking about the Army Special Forces guy, Chief?"

"Affirmative."

"I know that group's leader. He's a good man. He told me that the ROEs had been pounded into his head so much that he waited too long to fight back. He's messed up now; thinks it's his fault he lost two guys."

"It's amazing more men weren't killed," replied Sawyer.

"Copy that, Chief, but don't worry—if faced with a similar scenario, the ROEs are gone. There's no way in hell that I will allow that to happen—anytime, anywhere. These guys are common thugs, evil pricks that need a tremendous ass kicking. And we're just the guys to make that happen. I hope the opportunity presents itself."

"Hooyah! The boys will be glad to hear that."

Following the death of the American Special Forces, Joseph Kony had told his men that the American government was comprised of cowards, and that the soldiers sent to Africa were no match for them. He told his thugs that the reason the Americans did not engage with them was out of fear, and his warriors believed him. They operated without fear of repercussions from the American forces. Despite this rhetoric, there had been no changes to the rules of engagement by the U.S. military brass.

That exact scenario did not take long to come to fruition. Sam and his team had been given orders to head to Western Equatoria, South Sudan, with a group of villagers whom they'd trained. This area had shown promise as a hiding spot for the leadership of the LRA, and it was also very close to where the deaths of American Special Forces had taken place. Sam's mission was to accompany his trainees back to their villages and to search for any LRA bases. This intelligence would then be passed on to the Sudan government. The American-trained villagers would then either engage on their own or along with Sudanese soldiers. Of course, this depended upon whether any Sudanese troops happened to be in the area. This was rarely the case, so Sam and his men expected that their trainees would be acting alone.

Chapter 10

Kony was a genius at escape and evasion. He had been hunted for nearly twenty years and had never been caught. In 1994, the Sudanese government had attempted to wipe out the LRA and failed. Operation Iron Fist was launched by Uganda in 2002 to kill and capture Kony and the Lord's Liberation Army, but instead, nearly 2 million Ugandans became displaced from their homes. The International Criminal Court issued arrest warrants for Kony and other leaders in 2005. Uganda attempted to make peace with the LRA in 2008, but during the negotiations Kony continued to launch raids into Sudan, Uganda, and the Congo. In 2008, a poorly planned offensive by those three governments along with U.S. support destroyed many bases, but failed to capture any of its leadership. It was probably a combination of luck and skill that had allowed the LRA to continue to survive. However, now the

United States had invested in the use of elite soldiers to train the locals. Hopefully, this would change the fortunes of Kony and his men.

❖ ❖ ❖

Lieutenant Commander Sam Richards and Chief Petty Officer Doug Sawyer headed out to Sudan with the other six SEALs comprising their team, along with about fifty trained Sudanese who would be returning to their homes. They would arrive just before daybreak, and the trip would not take long. They would rest during the day, and then begin night searches in the jungle for evidence of LRA camps. The dense landscape made reconnaissance a daunting task, and the lack of any air or satellite support was also a disadvantage. Despite the negatives, the group was upbeat and confident about their mission.

They were only minutes from the Sudanese village when they heard the sound of gunfire—the unmistakable rapid staccato of machine gun fire could be heard over the sound of the transport trucks returning the soldiers home. Similarly, screams of death were becoming more and more prominent. The men they had trained were barely able to keep it together. Sam and the rest of the SEALs tried to calm them, but it was a losing battle. Instead of stopping the trucks and advancing on foot to hide their arrival, the truck drivers drove directly into the village. It was total chaos from that point on—the men jumped out, and instead of forming up into their teams, they immediately ran to their homes to protect their families. The LRA forces were more experienced and had no loved ones in the area, so they began picking off the men one by one as they began their retreat.

The few trainees who had listened to Sam were now organizing a defensive posture, and they began returning fire on the Lord's Resistance Army. They inflicted casualties on the LRA, and this hastened the LRA's retreat from the village. Sam and his men witnessed the frenzy with shock and frustration. All the training had mostly been for naught;

the first interaction with the enemy was looking like a total clusterfuck. Sam now knew why Kony had been so successful over the years: the ferocity and barbarity of his raids had instilled a fear in the local people that contributed to their helplessness.

The SEALs began securing the area. Each SEAL took a few trainees and began looking for any LRA who might have become separated from the other soldiers. Chief Petty Officer Sawyer ran into some of the trainees who had jumped off the truck to get to their homes. They were hacking an LRA soldier with their machetes when he discovered them.

"Stop," Sawyer screamed. "What are you doing?"

"We are doing to him what they have done to our village," one of them responded.

Sam had heard Sawyer's voice and saw the carnage. About five of the Sudanese had hacked a man to pieces and were about to start on another man.

"Don't do it. Don't become like them. Be human," Sawyer was pleading with the men.

Most of the men fell to their knees, tears streaming down their cheeks. But Sam could see that one man was choosing not to listen. The bloodlust in his eyes was unmistakable. He was squeezing the machete handle so tight that he was shaking. Sam recognized the man and knew him by name.

"Samir, please listen," Sam softly spoke to him. "This man doesn't deserve to live. He certainly deserves a punishment similar to what he inflicted on your people. But do you really want to do that? Could you live with that vision in your mind the rest of your life? Think it through. I won't stop you if that's your choice. But you're better then this evil man; you're not like him."

"Maybe I should become like him. Maybe all of my people should," Samir shouted.

He had pressed the machete to the man's throat. Sawyer was close enough to neutralize Samir, but Sam had waved him off.

"They've butchered us for too long. We need to do the same to them."

"Go ahead, then," Sam responded. "Become a butcher and throw your soul away. Your action will haunt you the rest of your life. Because you are not a butcher, you're a good man, better than this scumbag."

Samir fell to his knees, dropping the machete. He looked up at Sam with incredible sadness and pleaded, "Please help us stop this madness."

Sam was struggling to keep his own emotions under control. He felt this man's pain, and Sam wanted in all his heart to put an end to the atrocities. He nodded to Samir and stepped forward to deliver a ferocious blow to the LRA soldier's face. The man screamed in pain as his nose shattered.

"Chief Sawyer," Sam said, loud enough for all to hear who had just witnessed the exchange between him and Samir, "secure this piece of shit and prepare him for questioning."

"My pleasure," was Sawyer's response.

The LRA soldier had regained his confidence now that the threat of being hacked to death had been eliminated by the American soldier.

He actually laughed as he said to Sam, "You'll do nothing to me. Your rules prevent you from torturing me. You're weak. You try to train these weaklings to fight us, while you hide in the jungle." He spat at Sam.

The SEALs were stung by the man's comments, although they were essentially true. The LRA soldier had pretty much stated the current rules of engagement. Sam noticed his men's expressions. They all had the same look, and their eyes revealed a sense of frustration and defeat.

"Well, today must be my lucky day, and the beginning of your worst day," Sam said slowly and coolly. "The rules have changed, and today is the first day of open season for Navy SEALs to hunt and kill members of the Lord's Resistance Army."

"Hooyah!" was the response of Sam's team.

Chapter 11

The LRA soldier was correct. The politicians had made rules similar to those that had been in place during the Iraq war and now were in place in Afghanistan. U.S. soldiers could not engage the enemy unless they were absolutely certain the people that they encountered were hostiles, and in many cases, they could only engage after being fired upon. As a consequence, many American lives were lost, or soldiers injured, because it was often late in the encounter before there was certainty of who the actual enemy was. There were even cases where U.S. soldiers were brought up on charges of murder because it was felt that they had not adhered to these rules.

Certain media outlets and politicians were always ready to broadcast these events. Sam and every other soldier serving in the U.S. military knew that, unfortunately, in war, there would always be mistakes and innocent lives lost as a result of collateral damage. When terrorists disguised themselves as local villagers, the risk of collateral damage was even higher. The U.S. fighting man or woman was more concerned with the loss of innocent life than any other fighting force in the world. To be handcuffed by those rules diminished their effectiveness and put them in more harm's way than could be justified. Any country that didn't understand that there would be some unavoidable loss of innocent life during war shouldn't go to war.

Sam was not alone in his utter disgust and frustration with the men and women outside the military who made these rules despite them never having any military experience. What was worse, the terrorists knew about the rules of engagement and used it to their advantage. That was the reason Sam had spoken to the captured LRA soldier—the rules were now different for Sam after witnessing the massacre of the villagers during his group's arrival.

Navy SEALs, trained in interrogation techniques, did not take long to get useful information from their captive. They learned that many of the Lord's Resistance Army leaders were camped in hiding not too far from their current location. If this information was correct, LCDR Sam Richards and his SEAL team could change the course of affairs in this region in a positive direction.

"Chief Petty Officer Sawyer, let's gather some more intel about this location and plan a visit to these scumbags," directed Sam. "We'll set out at nightfall, SEAL team only."

"Aye, aye," Sawyer responded.

The Chief and the rest of the team were fired-up over their leader's decision.

The site of the terrorists' camp was not a great distance from Sam and his team's current location, but it would take several hours to reach, due to the density of the jungle and the paucity of roads. The prisoner's description of the camp location showed that it backed up to a river.

The LRA apparently used the river for transport, and felt it probably also offered safety from any assault. This, however, was the very side of the camp that the SEALs would take to approach. It was a type of entry that was second nature to them. It would be nice to use a tactic that was near and dear to any SEAL; the water was a "happy place" for them.

LCDR Richards briefed his team.

"Once there, we'll break up into teams of two. I'll take Petty Officer Wilhelm and go to the north side of the camp. Chief Petty Officer Sawyer will take Durrant and cover the south side. Petty Officers Kerney and MacLeod will go to the east side. The other team will stay at the river and sabotage any boats they see. Sawyer and Durrant will survey the camp from the south, while Wilhelm and I will do the same from the north. Our goal is to take out the entire camp. Our arrival time should be late, so I would hope that only sentries will be awake. If that's the case, it should be no problem to plant explosives during our little stroll through the camp. Once Sawyer and I are done with our walks, we'll head back to the north and south perimeters. When we're in place, we'll detonate the explosives, and then each team will advance toward the middle of the camp and eliminate any hostile they encounter. Pretty simple, really." Sam grinned.

Sam's remarks were met with a chorus of "Copy that" and "Hooyah."

The team was marked with camouflage paint that made them black as the night but also had an ingredient that made it easy for them to spot each other with their night vision goggles. When viewed through the goggles, the paint made the individual glow like Casper the Ghost. Their individual communication systems (comms) allowed them to talk in whispers and keep each other apprised about their progress and location.

Sam was correct in his assumption. The security was weak when they arrived at 3 am, and the walk around and through the camp was easier than expected, even by SEAL standards. They had quietly taken out the guards and planted enough explosives to level the few huts and structures in the camp. Sam and his team felt no remorse about killing these men. They had recently killed American soldiers as well as murdered, mutilated, and raped the innocent people of this region. A killing blow to the Lord's Resistance Army was long overdue. This night raid was finally taking the fight to the enemy and delivering justice. Nor was Sam worried about the repercussions of his actions. He knew his team was taking a chance, but they had all discussed this mission, and the eight-man team was unanimous in going forward.

The explosions brought daylight to the jungle. Sam and his team waited for the fires to die down, and then advanced on the camp. With surgical precision, they eliminated any man left alive. The whole ordeal was over very quickly, and the SEALs had not even suffered a scratch. In that short period of time, Sam's team did more to hurt the LRA than had been done since their reign of terror started many years ago. It was a perfect example of focused, unrestricted, total punishment delivered to a deserving enemy, and an example of what the American military could accomplish if allowed to do its job fully. Sam wished all of his fellow soldiers could use their skills to this same extent when called upon to perform their duty.

The team was silent as they made their way back to the village where they'd arrived just twenty-four hours ago. When they were close, Sam radioed to Command that they had found an LRA camp presumed to contain most of the leadership. He was told by Command that his group should note the location of the LRA camp and wait for support.

"Not necessary," was LCDR Richards' reply. "The camp has been neutralized. Request investigation team to identify dead hostiles."

"This is Colonel DeHart of the U.S. Army. By whose authority did you attack that camp?"

Sam's reply was priceless and brought chuckles from his men. "By the authority of the Navy SEAL creed—we train for war, and fight to win; we stand ready to bring the full spectrum of combat power to bear in order to achieve our mission."

"That's not good enough," was the Colonel's response.

Sam couldn't resist. "Say again, Command? Last transmission sounded like *great stuff!*"

With that, LCDR Richards silenced the radio. His team was in hysterics. Sam figured there would be hell to pay for his actions, but he really didn't give a shit. The mission had been to eradicate the LRA, and his men had done a great service to the world by tonight's actions. If the brass didn't see it that way, then it might be time for him to move on to something else.

Chapter 12

The local U.S. Command did indeed send an investigation team to the coordinates that the SEALs had radioed to them. They found an area with no standing buildings and a lot of dead bodies. A quick count showed more than 150 dead LRA soldiers, with more probably incinerated by the blasts. The forensics team went about their investigation. Bodies were laid out and pictures were taken of faces to run through facial recognition programs. Hopefully, this method would quickly identify many of the soldiers. Fingerprints and DNA would also be obtained to try to put a name to the bodies. The hope was that they would be able to identify many of the LRA leadership among the dead.

The story of how a single SEAL team had punished the LRA was quickly spreading through the villages of the Congo, Sudan, and Uganda. In large cities, people were taking to the streets in jubilation. The crowds were waving American flags and singing "God Bless America."

Outside the small bases where U.S. soldiers were training locals, there were crowds of well-wishers shouting "USA, USA!" The crowd wanted to personally thank the U.S. soldiers who had made this wonderful moment possible. It was a celebration of immense size. It seemed that the locals somehow knew that Joseph Kony would be among the dead.

Colonel DeHart and his staff met LCDR Sam Richards and his men at the village.

In his Texas drawl, DeHart spoke. "Son, what you and your men accomplished was a thing of beauty, but you've put me in a real pickle. I'm struggling with the best way to report this to the Pentagon. Should I tell them that an American SEAL team took out more than 150 soldiers by themselves, when we've been told to only engage the LRA in self-defense? Or should I report that they were simply observers, and that locally trained soldiers did this? The only problem with that is the brass won't believe that there were no trainee casualties."

The Colonel's aide then spoke. "Sir, it seems that the Pentagon already knows it was our SEAL team. Apparently, the Sudanese president called the White House to thank the U.S. for stepping up their involvement."

"Well, that's just dandy," replied DeHart. "I guess I'll leave it to the civilians to spin this event and explain it to the media. One thing's for sure, Richards—you're on your own. I wish you luck."

"I didn't expect your support, Colonel," was Sam's reply. "I knew damn well that if I called the location in to you, I would have been told to stand down. Keeping you out of it will protect you from any repercussions. It was a decision made by me and me alone. It was long overdue for those bastards to receive a dose of what they'd given to these people. We've all seen the carnage that the LRA inflicts on villages. Have you ever seen all four extremities hacked off of a child? It was time for payback. Actually, we were more merciful than they ever were—we eliminated them in their sleep."

Chief Petty Officer Sawyer spoke up. "Sir, I also helped in the decision to go in." In quick succession, the rest of the team began saying the same thing to Colonel Miller.

"Quiet," yelled DeHart. "You SEALs are un-fucking-believable. I thank God that you and I are on the same team. While I can't publicly condone your actions, I respect the hell out of you and your men, Lieutenant Commander Richards. I'll support you as much as I can."

With that, the Colonel and his aides paraded back to command. The interaction had gone better than Sam had expected.

Sam turned to his team. "Gentlemen, the mission was my decision. I order you to tell that to anyone who asks. Is that clear?" There was no response. "I said, is that clear?"

"Aye, aye," was the weak response.

By late afternoon, the investigators reported that Joseph Kony was indeed among the dead. In fact, every LRA leader that the Pentagon was aware of had perished at the hands of Sam and his men. The news was announced to the public, and the locals elevated their celebration. People were crying with joy in the streets. Chants of "No more Kony, no more LRA" were heard everywhere. The government leaders of the Congo, Sudan, and Uganda made announcements on radio and TV. Everyone was vocalizing praise and gratitude towards the United States. It was a great feeling for Sam and his men to see television images of local people supporting the United States. Sam was filled with a sense of pride as he thought about what he and his team had accomplished. The feeling came from knowing that they'd changed the world for the better. He and his team didn't want medals or recognition; they'd gotten all the reward they needed by eliminating Kony and his evil men. They had done the right thing!

Chapter 13

The SEALs were immediately called back to Virginia. The mission debriefing was going to take place at their home command. Sam knew he had pissed off the politicians, but thought that the military leadership would outwardly display displeasure but inwardly be okay with his actions. He and his team were scheduled to meet with their commanders the next morning. Sam had reminded his men that their answers should be consistent—it was his decision to eliminate Kony and his men in the camp; they had just been following his orders.

The panel that debriefed Sam consisted of three admirals. As well, there were various captains sitting in the back of the room. Sam realized this meeting was different from others he'd experienced, but he hadn't expected the panel to consist of officers with such high ranks. He was not concerned; however, the whole scenario felt "off."

"LCDR Richards, my name is Admiral Thompson. This is Admiral Peterson and Admiral Andrews. We've been tasked with giving a recommendation on your future in the Navy."

"I suspected that was the case when I saw all the rank in the room," smiled Sam. "I figured this was not a congratulatory meeting regarding the actions of my team, who acted under my orders."

Admiral Thompson went on. "Son, this type of meeting is unprecedented for the Navy. The military is responding to pressure from politicians who are going crazy over what happened. Our efforts to explain to them that locally trained soldiers carried out the raid with your help have failed. The world knows that eight U.S. Navy SEALs killed almost two hundred men without suffering a scratch. I want you to know that we're all very proud of you and your men. The world is a better place with those men gone. The governments of many African nations are praising the United States. The world is flying American flags instead of burning them. However, as much as this helps you, the politicians don't agree with your actions. They're claiming that we can't control our troops, and are calling for us to make an example of you and your men. None of us in this room are happy about where we're sitting right now. Do you have any thoughts?"

First Sam asked, "Are we being recorded? Are my statements going to be read to some politician, leaked to the media, or show up on the Internet?"

"No," Admiral Thompson quickly said. "You have my word."

"In that case, I have something to say. My men had nothing to do with the decision to raid that camp. Like good soldiers, they followed my orders. They correctly pointed out to me that the rules of engagement did not allow us to attack the Lord's Resistance Army except in self-defense. That being said, my team should not be subjected to any disciplinary action, but honored for their courage and flawless execution of the mission in question. My decision to eliminate Kony and his men <u>was</u> based on self-defense. We were going to have to engage those men sooner or later. Just a week before, the Army lost two Special Forces soldiers because they adhered to the very rules that handcuffed them and cost them their lives. So, in self-defense, I elected to kill Kony and his men. I would do it again. I'm tired of being put in positions where I have to perform at a level below my best. That's when people get killed. It seems that politicians who have no clue about combat are deciding military doctrine. How can any of you put up with that shit?"

"Easy, son," said Thompson.

"Sir, with all due respect, what we do in the field is not easy. The rules now in place make it even harder to perform our jobs. When we become afraid to execute our missions because of what a group of politicians think back home, we'll lose the lives of valuable soldiers. If these same politicians don't want to get involved in situations where things can go wrong, then they need to keep us the hell out of those places. Combat is either all-in or all-out."

Admiral Thompson responded softly, "Unfortunately, that's not our reality."

"It *has* to be my reality," said Sam, "and, all due respect, it should be yours too. You should take a firm stand and educate politicians about how they're handcuffing your soldiers. By refusing to do so, then you have to accept accountability as well for the loss of U.S. soldiers. And if top military leadership can't educate politicians to do the right thing, then it will never be a reality. And if that's the case, then I'm out, Admiral."

The entire room went silent, shocked by Sam's last statement.

Admiral Thompson quickly replied, "Commander Richards, it is not our intention to recommend that you be discharged from the Navy, even despite your last statement. This event is just another shit-storm that will blow over and soon be forgotten. We'd already decided before this meeting began that we'd recommend a token disciplinary action against you. Soon, life will return to what it was before."

Sam stood up and headed toward the doors. Turning back, he responded, "That's bullshit, and I can't live with that. A disciplinary action for doing my job? I don't want life to 'return to what it was before' because being a handcuffed SEAL sucks. That shouldn't be 'normal.' What about the next time? What a great example to our soldiers! If this is now the status quo, I can't continue to serve. It would be against everything I stand for. And you should all be ashamed that you don't have the balls to say the same thing."

Jaws were hanging open as he left the room.

Mariah was waiting for him as he came out. She could see the anger and frustration in his eyes, but she kept silent until Sam spoke.

"That went well," he laughed. "I tried to implement your idea of a 'work-around' to explain my decision. But I don't think they bought it."

He was incredibly calm for someone who had just resigned from a career that he loved more than anything else in this world except for the very pregnant woman in front of him now. But that had always been his style. He wasn't quitting the Navy; the Navy had quit him.

Mariah gave Sam his space as they headed home. When they arrived, Sam related the specifics of the meeting. As always, he had already told her the details of the mission and what his team had done to Kony and his men.

"I'm out, Mariah. I can't stand it anymore. We go to places, and we could make huge changes that would improve the lives of people. Yet politicians who are too worried about so-called 'political correctness' and who don't trust us to follow the law place unnecessary burdens on us. Before our last mission, two Special Forces soldiers lost their lives because they hesitated to engage the enemy. There's an underlying fear that we, the soldiers, will face bullshit charges of murder if we deviate from the rules of engagement. It's happened before. I will not be responsible for the loss of a man's life because of this fear. I'm also not going to risk facing charges and put anyone through some charade of a trial. So, excuse me, but fuck the politicians and the military brass who are too impotent to take a stand for their troops."

"You'll get no argument from me, Sam. I truly understand your feelings. I don't want you at a disadvantage when deploying to bad places. As a soldier, you're asked to go to places where no one else dares to go. You're asked to carry out missions sometimes not knowing the real reason why. But you knew *that* going into the military. Is there anything else that's driving these feelings?"

Sam thought for a while. "Maybe. Before, it was just you and me, but now we'll be three. I have never been careless on missions, but always had a sense of confidence that somehow I was protected. It was always worth the risk to get the job done. Now, the bullshit rules that are in place no longer make the risks acceptable, not when we're starting a family. Don't get me wrong; if the reasons for our missions were transparent and we had no restrictions to get the job done, then I wouldn't leave the Navy. But currently, in the military, that's no longer the case."

Mariah responded, "Babe, I'm all for you staying out of harm's way. But you *are* making a difference in this world. The elimination of the LRA was a good thing. Maybe you can somehow do the same thing in a different way."

"So beautiful and so smart," smiled Sam. "Maybe there is another way. But for now, all that matters is that we're going to have this baby soon!"

Sam's decision to leave the Navy did not go unnoticed in the close-knit world of Special Operators. The Navy approved his request for an honorable discharge. If they hadn't, Sam had said he was prepared to grant interviews to the press and tell the world about his missions. Of course it was just a bluff; Sam would never betray his oath of secrecy. Fortunately, the Navy had not pressed the issue. The news of Sam's resignation rippled through the Special Forces community as well as the Intelligence world. Those who did not know the whole story thought Sam was probably just another SEAL who had served his time and was ready to move on to something else. The few who knew the truth, and his character, respected him for his actions and his words during his investigation. They hoped that leadership would listen and act accordingly to change the way that the U.S. chose to enter conflicts. Certainly, no one was holding his or her breath—the same politicians and media were still running the show. Unless there was a total change in the way elected officials steered military rules of engagement, it would be just more of the same bullshit.

Chapter 14

Mariah and Sam settled into a new lifestyle that neither had ever expected. Sam was at home, while Mariah worked for the Red Cross headquarters in Washington, D.C. She was enjoying her work as a planner and administrator, though she missed the fieldwork. Her true passion was to be with the people who needed help, and she relished the gratitude that they conveyed. This feeling of enjoyment that occurred after helping someone had always remained the same for her, ever since she had gone on church missions with her parents as a little girl. Mariah lived to serve and always would. Now at the end of her pregnancy, she was looking forward to the new chapter in her life.

Sam had settled into a routine that was similar to when he came back from a mission. He would wake up with Mariah, they would enjoy breakfast together, and then piddle around for a while. He would begin with his coffee and newspaper. He then went for his daily five-mile run, followed by an hour workout with weights. In the Navy, he would then hook up with his old team to train together. This had consisted of weights, self-defense sparring, and firearms training. Sam was having a difficult time now adjusting to the loss of contact with other men who shared this common bond. He continued the same type of training to stay focused, but he was now doing it alone. He'd always been independent, and perhaps a bit of a loner, but had always had his team or other SEALs in which to confide. It was a huge difference for him.

Mariah had noticed his uneasiness when they went to her Red Cross fundraisers. Sam would smile and be charming with the people they spoke to at these events. But small talk was not his forte, and he had nothing in common with these people. Mariah could see the sadness and frustration in his eyes as people asked him questions about his Naval career. Sometimes she saw anger as well. At the last event they'd attended, Sam had tried to resist the urge to pummel two husbands of her coworkers, but the situation had gotten out of hand. These individuals had for some reason felt that Sam's service was a waste of his life, and as taxpayers, of their money. They were both trust-fund babies and had never worked a day in their lives. Unfortunately for them, his effort to resist his urges had failed.

"What is it that you do exactly?" one had started. "I mean, with all the smart bombs and drones, isn't your type of soldier obsolete?"

"Exactly," said the other. "And why do we hold on to the idea that America needs to police everyone else and get involved in other countries' business?"

Back to the first guy. "I mean, really, who even cares about those people and places anyway?"

Sam was silent as the conversation between the two men continued. They were escalating their ignorant drivel, and the people standing around them had started to take notice. They rambled on incessantly. Sam just stood there and absorbed the verbal blows. It was all he could do to stop himself from throwing these jokers out the window. Finally, he'd had enough and was ready to move on.

"Nice talking to you, fellas. Sounds like you have the world all figured out," Sam said as he turned to go.

Unfortunately, one of the imbeciles made a comment loud enough for the room to hear—"That guy is a moron. I bet he wasn't discharged from the Navy, but was either kicked out or quit because he's a pussy."

The focus of the entire event now turned to Sam and the two men. Even Mariah had heard their last comment from across the room, and she started to make her way to Sam so that the two of them could leave. Sam could see the worried look on her face as he made eye contact with her. He winked to show her that he was okay, about the same time the other genius opened his mouth. They just couldn't let it go.

"No shit. How he got that smoking hot babe to marry him is a mystery to me. I'll bet she got knocked up by someone else while he was out playing soldier."

They both went into hysterics. The room was dead silent at this point.

Still looking at Mariah, Sam stopped dead in his tracks. She cringed and mouthed to him, "Sam, no."

Sam just shrugged his shoulders and did an about face.

"You two are out of line. I stood here and listened to your sanctimonious bullshit about how you could change the world. But now you just made it personal by insulting my wife and me. You owe us both an apology."

"You're fucking crazy, asshole. We don't apologize to anybody. Sorry if the truth hurts," was one's reply.

It was the second one's statement that did them both in.

"There's really nothing a quitter like you can do about it anyway. "

It was at that moment that Mariah began running across the room to try to get to Sam. She knew those words would put him over the top. It was quite the sight to see a full-term pregnant woman trying to sprint toward her husband while wearing a formal maternity dress. The room was murmuring. Many watching had yelled for the two men to shut up, but the men had been ignored them.

"Sorry, fellas, but you brought this upon yourselves. You two remind me of some of the scumbags I've had to put down. Fortunately for you, I'm only going to maim you."

Mariah heard this, and this time she screamed out loud, "Sam, no!"

Sam stepped toward one man and with a simple kick, crumpled his knee, causing ligament damage that would take surgery and lengthy rehab to fix. The man immediately fell and was writhing on the floor. Sam turned to the other man.

"You sonuvabitch!" he yelled, as he tried to throw a punch at Sam.

Sam simply sidestepped the blow, grabbed the man's arm, and spun him around. He applied pressure until his wrist snapped. Those close to the altercation could hear the sound of the bones breaking. The man joined his partner's shrieking with his own screams. The whole thing was over in probably twenty seconds.

But Sam wasn't quite finished. "Now that I have your attention, you can listen to me. This country has a long history of standing up for those who cannot stand up for themselves. My predecessors in the military made sacrifices so this country could be the greatest in the world. Their actions secured the freedom and the way of life we now enjoy. In some sick sense, perhaps they were too successful, if it created ungrateful, unproductive scum like you two. That generation of warriors sheds tears when they hear the likes of you. My generation of American soldier continues to try to perpetuate the tradition of helping the less fortunate. In Iraq, we took down a brutal dictator who gassed his own countrymen. In Afghanistan, we obliterated the Taliban and fought Al-Qaeda, who was responsible for training terrorists that flew suicide planes into our buildings and who have disfigured women. If the media didn't distort the truth, and the civilians running this country would just listen to the military, we could eliminate most of the injustices in the world today."

"Fuck you, man," was the only reply from one of the men on the ground.

Sam just shook his head, while the rest of the room applauded him.

Sam turned to see Mariah. "I am truly sorry, babe. I listened to their shit as long as I could. I think it's time to go."

Mariah was about to open her mouth, but her boss spoke first.

"Don't sweat it, Sam," was his response. "We've been listening to those two dickwads spout their bullshit rhetoric for years. For some reason, they think that wealth entitles them to be immune to anyone else who states an oppositional opinion. We all have your back. But you should probably take that beautiful wife of yours home."

Mariah spoke up next "Thanks, John, but Sam needs to take me to the hospital first… because my water just broke."

Sam was almost in a panic at Mariah's words.

"Easy, cowboy," Mariah's best work friend Teresa said to Sam. "Lee and I will go with you to the hospital."

Sam was immediately grateful. Teresa and Lee Manna had been good friends to Mariah whenever Sam had been gone on deployments. They had a couple of kids of their own, and Sam and Mariah had grown close to them. Lee had become a great substitute to the emptiness he felt from leaving the male camaraderie of his SEAL team, and he was also funny as hell.

As they got their coats and were heading to the elevator, Lee snapped Sam out of his anxiety by saying, "Bro, for someone who just made it look simple to kick two guys' asses, you sure are acting like a sissy."

Mariah spoke next, "Lee, he just panics over things that are out of his control. Maybe someone should be shooting bullets over our heads to calm you down, honey."

Sam's anxiety broke. "You guys are merciless!" The four of them laughed together as they got into the car.

Gracie Elizabeth Richards came into the world at 1:23 am, weighing six pounds ten ounces. Mom and baby had no problems, but Dad was a basket case the entire time. Sam might have been as worn out as Mariah from all the pacing and worry during the time leading up to Gracie's birth. Mariah had really breezed through the delivery, and had helped Sam more than he had helped her. During labor, Mariah had laughed more than once to see this tough-guy SEAL with multiple combat experiences brought to his knees by the process of childbirth.

The two had become three, and they were lying together on the hospital bed. Mariah teased Sam and said, "I think I found your kryptonite. You were kind of a mess during Gracie's delivery."

"I know," was Sam's reply. "It's hard to give up control and feel helpless about the situation. But now that I've done it, I'll have no problem next time."

Mariah laughed and replied, "Whoa, big boy. Let me catch my breath."

"Look at her, babe—she's perfect. When you do this kind of work, you can't just stop at one." Sam kissed them both and continued, "I'll give you some time to catch your breath, but then, watch out!"

Sam was experiencing a new feeling. He'd thought that his life with Mariah could not get any better, but with the arrival of Gracie, it did. The next morning, they made phone calls to family and friends to share the news, and over the next month, they received visits from many of these same people. His former SEAL team came to see their fearless leader deal with a dirty diaper. They all commented about how relaxed and happy Sam seemed.

Mariah and Sam settled into a wonderful routine. Mariah was on maternity leave, and with Sam still in limbo about his work future, the three of them were together 24/7. When Mariah was able to go back to the gym, they would take Gracie. They strolled through parks together and would fall asleep for a nap in the afternoons. Life was unbelievably simple and good.

Unfortunately, the day came when Mariah had to return to work. After all, one of them had to pay the bills. Sam became Mr. Mom, and he relished his new role. Of course, he knew it was only a short-term plan, but he was determined to enjoy it while he could. He continued his schedule prior to Gracie's arrival—doing his daily five miles with her in a running stroller, and then hitting the gym with his daughter in tow. The gals that he and Mariah had met at the gym were in awe of Sam's skills with the baby. He would leave her in her car seat and then move her from workout station to station, making her smile between sets of exercises. He even continued to go to the firing range. He would put earplugs and a headset on her while she watched her father keep his shooting skills. Sam noticed that she didn't event flinch during his range time. Of course, he knew it was because of the ear protection, but he liked to think that it was from genetics.

Chapter 15

One afternoon, Sam and Gracie were returning from running an errand when they were met in the driveway by a black sedan. Sam immediately noticed the government-issue plates and intuitively assumed a defensive posture, parking away from the sedan. He quickly exited his car, brandishing his H & K U.S. SOCOM (Heckler and Koch Special Ops Command) .45 caliber handgun.

The man emerging from the sedan quickly raised his hands and spoke, "Whoa, Sam, my name is Marvin Royster, and I just want to talk. I'm with the CIA." He smiled and added, "I bet that baby is better protected than the President's kids."

Sam retained his defensive stance while he asked, "Let me see your credentials."

Royster produced them, confirming what he had said. He was indeed from the CIA, but he had neglected to say he was a Deputy Director (DCI) and the Director of the National Clandestine Service (NCS). Formerly the Directorate of Operations, the NCS had been created after 9/11 as an effort to improve coordination between intelligence services. Sam had worked in coordination with this entity on several missions, and he now relaxed and handed the man back his credentials. He retrieved Gracie from the car and held her in his arms.

"Sorry about the gun, but old habits are hard to break."

Royster surprised Sam with his response. "That's actually what I'd like to talk to you about, Sam. I'll get to the point: we followed your career in the SEALs, and we want you to come work for us."

Sam was quick to reply. "If you know anything about my departure from the Navy, then you also know that I'm done working for a government that handcuffs its soldiers. Talk to any of the Admirals who were in my last mission debriefing, and they can give you the more detailed statement that I gave when I left. Now, if you'll excuse me, my daughter is hungry, and she can get cranky like me when she's pissed."

Royster replied as Sam turned away, "I know all about your last mission, and I know what you said at the hearings, because I was there. I share your opinion and also left the Navy because of the same sentiment. I just want a moment of your time to hear my offer."

Sam was now intrigued. "Come on in, then, and we'll talk while I feed Gracie."

"She's beautiful, Sam." Royster went on, "Cherish these days, as they'll go by quick. Mine are now in high school and hardly have any time for me."

Sam learned that Royster had been one of the captains sitting in the back of the room during his Naval hearing. Soon after Sam's speech and subsequent departure from the Navy, former Navy Captain Marvin Royster had accepted a position as Director of the National Clandestine Services (D/NCS). He had been in Navy Intelligence his whole career. Toward the end, he was frustrated by the restrictions politicians had placed on his operatives.

Specifically, Royster wanted Sam to come work for the Special Activities Division (SAD), considered one of the most mysterious branches of operatives in the world. As Sam was well aware, this was a highly classified group of Tier 1 special operators, and only the most elite, skilled, and decorated soldiers were considered for SAD recruitment. They didn't wear anything that would associate them with the U.S., and if captured, it was highly likely that the U.S. government would deny knowing of their involvement. Sam knew that this group had broad responsibilities and mission-types, rumored to also include assassinations. Sam had worked with these guys on several joint missions as a SEAL.

"I need a man like you. We think alike and want the same thing. Together, we can continue the fight to rid this world of bad people and protect this country's interests. I know that's what you want, Sam. You can't do it working for some security company babysitting celebrities."

"Come on, Captain," Sam retorted. "We both know there are similar political constraints on your actions."

"Call me Marvin, Sam. Yes, we have constraints; but not many."

Royster went on to deliver a convincing argument to Sam as to why this was the case. He shared with Sam classified information about several missions that had been very successful. Sam knew of the missions but was not aware of which branch of the government had executed them. A "moment" of Sam's time lasted several hours as Royster gave him detailed descriptions of their missions and successes.

"Tell you what, Marvin. Let me think about it and get back to you. Of course, I need to discuss this with my wife. You probably know that she works for the Red Cross. She's been sitting behind a desk since Gracie was born, but now she has a chance to get back in the field for a couple of months. And with me being unemployed, the three of us are going on the mission together."

"I know all about Mariah's and your upcoming support mission to the hurricane victims in Haiti. Those poor people are just getting out from under the earthquake tragedy, and now this. How about you give me your decision when you get back, Sam?"

"Marvin, I see you're well informed. It's a deal. I'll let you know when we return from Haiti."

Chapter 16

Mariah was excited about the upcoming mission. Sam had decided to tell her about his job offer sometime after their arrival and after they were settled. Not only was Mariah ready to get back into the field, but she was also taking Gracie and Sam with her for her first trip. Their pediatrician was fine with Gracie traveling as long as they were careful about what she ate and drank. Cholera was probably the greatest health risk, but this concern was minimal where they were going. There were American doctors at their location, and they weren't that far away from Miami, Florida, in case there were some sort of a disaster. Both Sam and Mariah were used to having medical contingency plans for themselves, but it was different also planning for your own child. They realized from now on they would always have to think beyond themselves, a feeling that was both new and exciting.

The most recent earthquake had wreaked havoc on Haiti, and the Red Cross had never left after the event. They had made great progress in assisting people back into homes. Fortunately, the recent hurricane had not caused a tremendous increase in the number of homeless. The major effect had been to disable much of the water purification systems, as well as interrupt the food supply to a large number of people. Mariah was heading a group that specialized in logistics and food distribution. Her team was set to mobilize local charity groups to assist in getting food and water to people until the normal supply chains could be reopened.

Sam's job was simple—primarily take care of both his girls, but also enjoy a mission that didn't entail killing bad people. His plan was to meander over the countryside with Gracie while Mariah was working. They would spend their evenings together as a family. Of course, Sam also was planning to volunteer his sweat to help with any physical tasks they needed.

They arrived in Port-au-Prince, where they would be staying for most of the month. Mariah would be touring various locations away from the capital where she and her team were responsible for coordinating the delivery of supplying life-sustaining food. The quarters the Red Cross workers would be sharing were very generous. Their group was housed together in one large building. Sam, Mariah, and Gracie had their own room that was more than large enough.

Mariah and her group immediately went to work. They reviewed the areas they would be supplying, and set about planning routes to deliver the goods. They inventoried the supplies they'd already brought and set up a means to receive new deliveries from the airport. They met with other Red Cross workers who had been there since the earthquake to get an idea about the quality and quantity of local help.

A troubling observation had become apparent in the last several months. Namely, there were groups that had been ambushing supply trucks and had started a black market for these stolen goods, which they would turn around and sell back for a profit to the needy people the Red Cross had identified. The attacks and thefts had been on a steady rise. The local police had turned a blind eye, and many suspected that they were participating in the thefts.

It was sad enough that individuals would take advantage of the kindness of the Red Cross, but it was pure evil that they would then make a profit off their unfortunate fellow countrymen who were barely hanging on to their lives. The American government had been made aware of the thievery and was planning on eventually sending a small contingent of National Guard troops. The recent hurricane hopefully would accelerate the timetable for the troops to arrive.

Over the next two weeks, Sam and Gracie enjoyed their tours of the countryside. With a vehicle at their disposal, they covered a tremendous amount of the country. Sam was impressed with the will of the people to overcome the disasters that had befallen their country. They were very friendly and readily accepted Sam and Gracie wherever they went. However, Sam had noted the lack of supplies coming into many of the small villages. Red Cross goods were clearly marked and were usually readily apparent, and he knew that with the arrival of Mariah's group, supplies were flowing like never before. When he asked the villagers where all the supplies were being kept, he was met with silence. Their smiles would disappear. When he pressed for an answer, they simply walked away.

It was during a return to Port-au-Prince from one of these villages that Sam discovered the reason for the paucity of supplies. He and Gracie came upon a supply truck with four flat tires. As Sam approached, he also noticed that one of the men was flat on his back with the others attending to him.

"Are you guys okay?" Sam asked. He could now see that the man was bleeding from his head. "What happened?"

"We were attacked and our supplies taken," one of the aide workers explained.

"How?"

"Two trucks sandwiched us in between them and forced us to stop. Guys with guns surrounded us while others loaded our stuff onto their truck. Robert here tried to stop them, and they smacked him on the head."

"It's a wonder they didn't kill him. Has this happened before?"

"Oh, yes. And it's becoming more and more common. After the hurricane, desperate people would steal from us, but before it was always from our warehouses, and at night."

"But recently there have been other attacks like this, in broad daylight?"

"Yes, although no one's been hurt before. We think gangs are to blame. The attacks have become well-organized."

"I'll call for some help. I'm so sorry."

As he and Gracie made their way back to Port-au-Prince, Sam was sickened by yet another example of man's inhumanity to man. This was the evil in the world that he longed to help eradicate. These types of injustices seemed to be inescapable wherever he went.

Mariah was waiting for them when they returned. "You had a long day. How was your trip?" she asked.

Sam then told her about what they had come across on their return journey.

"I was going to warn you about that this morning," Mariah said, "but you and Gracie had already left. We got briefed this morning about the increased theft of our supplies. The American government has been made aware, and they'll probably be sending a small group of National Guardsmen. They think it's a small gang that's responsible."

Sam replied, "I got the feeling from the men I met on the road that this may be more than just a small gang. They've been hit several times, and they know other aid workers whose trucks were ambushed. What seems to be a common link is that the thieves are well armed and very organized. The attacks are happening in broad daylight, and it almost seems that the attackers know exactly where and when the supply trucks are leaving. Mariah, that sounds like an inside job."

"Sam… I know that look. We're only here for another few weeks or so. You are my guest during that time. Let the local authorities handle this problem. You should just enjoy the time with Gracie and me." Mariah had a hard time looking Sam in the eye as she said this.

"OK, babe, you know that's some serious bullshit you're spewing. This is a crime against those who are helpless. In my opinion, someone with authority is using their position to pull off these attacks, steal the supplies, and then sell them for a profit. It's corruption, and it's evil, plain and simple."

Mariah replied, "You're probably right, Sam. But you're a civilian now and all by yourself. What do you think it is you could do?"

Sam was smirking. "Probably nothing much," he said with a wink. "Can I have your permission to gather some intelligence on these guys? I want to see where this leads. I'll pass the info along to the proper people. Babe, this what I do—no one will even know."

He was smiling at her now with those irresistible eyes she had fallen for the very first time she had seen them.

"Damn you, Sam. You're incorrigible. You know I'll feel guilty if I say no. Just promise me there won't be any violence."

"Sweetie, violence begets violence. I promise you that my violence would only be in self-defense. Besides, I don't have any weapons. They won't even see me while I'm gathering intel. Just promise me that you won't say a word to anyone."

Mariah responded, "You think someone in the Red Cross could be involved?"

"Probably not. But they may be talking to someone with the local authorities, who then uses the information. I'll keep you informed of everything I find out. Trust me, babe—this is the right thing to do."

Chapter 17

Sam strategized on the best way to gather information on the group responsible. He knew he needed to follow a group of thieves after they stole some supplies. He would then see where they went and what they did after acquiring the goods. The only problem was that working alone meant he had no ability to cover all of the delivery routes. It would probably come down to dumb luck at being in the right place at the right time. He set about reviewing the previous theft locations to see if there was a trend in time and location for these occurrences.

There weren't that many routes out of Port-au-Prince for the Red Cross trucks to travel in making their deliveries. It didn't take long to see that about half of the thefts took place on route 2, which went north of the city, and the other thefts on route 101, which went east. The thefts were always on one of these routes, and always 5-10 miles from the capital. Right in the center of the thefts was Bel Air, one of the worst slums of Port-au-Prince, known for its crime and violence. It was often the launching point of many political demonstrations and had been the worst hit area of Port-au-Prince by the recent earthquake. Sam felt this was probably the best bet on a location for a group of thugs to make their headquarters.

He decided that he would focus his attention on that area rather than blindly hope to be around one of the thefts on the road. He planned to perform his reconnaissance from midnight to 6 am; that way he wouldn't take any time away from being with Mariah and Gracie. He was used to working with minimal sleep, and besides, he could always nap with Gracie in the afternoon.

He didn't think it would take long to find the individuals responsible. Some of the drivers who had been robbed by these thugs agreed with Sam's logic about the home base being in the slums of Bel Air. Sam didn't share any other details of his plans with those he talked to, for fear that maybe someone driving for the Red Cross might be working for the thieves.

Sam began the next day. He told Mariah that he would be back by the time she and Gracie were awake. He made his way to Bel Air and found that the community was even more unfavorable than he'd expected. In fact, the slums were by far the worst he had ever seen. He had been to some really bad places during his time in the SEALs, but this place was the shittiest hellhole he had ever encountered. Most of the buildings were still in shambles from one or more of the previous earthquakes. A tremendous number of tents had been set up by families, and over time these had become permanent residences. Trash was scattered haphazardly on the sides of the streets. The combined aroma of trash with the stench of body odor was a new scent for Sam. He tried to characterize the appearance of this place and decided that it reminded him of a war-torn area that had been partially rebuilt. However, the vast number of people living in an area being rebuilt was not typical of war zones.

The human activity was minimal at this early hour. Sam had little trouble meandering through the streets without being seen. He was dressed in all dark clothing and had blacked out his white skin. He had gathered info from Red Cross locals about the layout of the area, and with this information, he had planned a grid search to uncover the thugs' headquarters. He suspected that any organization responsible for thefts would be using one of the remaining buildings still standing after the earthquake and hurricane. If correct, this supposition would save Sam an enormous amount of time.

Sure enough, on only the third day of visiting the area, Sam found a large warehouse that was bustling with activity at 5 am, and he could easily see the Red Cross markings on boxes that were meticulously lined up in the building. Sam was appalled at the amount of stolen goods. It was obvious that this group had been stealing for some time, probably going back to earlier earthquake missions of the Red Cross. The activity Sam was witnessing included the stacking of incoming goods as well as the loading of trucks for presumed deliveries. He watched for a while, and then did a survey of the building, noting the entries and exits.

Sam was about to make his way back to where he'd hidden his jeep when he noticed a large car approaching the building. He couldn't believe how out-of-place the vehicle appeared in these slums. Intrigued, he made his way closer to check out this new arrival. Even with his binoculars he could clearly make out the vehicle and was slack-jawed at the sight—he was staring at a '61 convertible Cadillac Eldorado. It was in mint condition. Only someone with money and power would dare drive a vehicle like that through these slums. There were two passengers in the front and two in the rear. Activity came to a standstill as the vehicle drove up and stopped. He could see by the expressions and demeanor of the men who had been working that the occupants of the car were both feared and respected.

Sunrise was only moments away, and Sam knew that he needed to get going before his anonymity was ruined by the oncoming dawn. However, he needed to identify these four people. He switched from his binoculars to the telephoto lens on his camera. He just needed a few more moments to snap pictures of these guys, and then he would bolt. His opportunity came when the car drove into the building. The improved lighting was all Sam needed. The subjects also cooperated by turning toward his position as they exited the car. He snapped his pictures and then made a quick egress from the area.

When he returned to their room, Sam found Gracie and Mariah about to leave. He was about two hours later than he had been the previous two mornings, and he could see by the expression on Mariah's pretty face that she was pissed.

"Sorry babe, I didn't mean to be this late, but I made some great progress."

Before Sam could continue his story, Mariah began to speak. "This is ridiculous, Sam. What exactly do you think you can do about these thefts? The US government plans on sending some troops to accompany our deliveries. Once that occurs, everything will be better."

"I hear you, Mariah, but believe it or not, I found the location of these thugs' headquarters. I also think I got some pictures of their leadership. I was planning on sending the pictures to a friend of mine to see if he can ID any of them. I'm just getting advanced intel for the incoming team. As a matter of fact, I'm done with my little morning missions. It's cool, babe."

Mariah gave Sam one of those "yeah right" looks. "Well, I've got to get to work. I thought Gracie could hang out in the day-care area for a few hours."

"That would be great," Sam responded. "That would give me time to upload the pictures. How about I pick her up at lunchtime and we all grab a bite to eat?"

He was giving her his most charming look of contrition. Gracie was laughing at her father, which only made Mariah laugh.

"You are hopeless," was Mariah's reply.

Chapter 18

Sam uploaded the pictures onto his computer. He accessed local newspapers and media to see if he could identify any of the four men he had seen, and about shit himself when he saw that one of the men was the Mayor of Port-au-Prince and another was the Chief of Police. He made no progress with the other two. This had now turned into a conspiracy of corruption that involved two of the most powerful people in the area. Sam decided it was time to call his new CIA buddy to let him know what he had found.

When Director Royster picked up the phone, the first words out of his mouth were, "I knew you couldn't resist my offer, Sam. When do you want to start?"

Sam laughed. "I'm still in Haiti, sir. And I am continuing to consider your offer."

"It will be the best job you ever have, Sam," was Royster's reply. "If you're not calling about that, then why do I have the pleasure of talking to you?"

Sam explained the situation in Haiti and the thefts of Red Cross supplies by local punks. He went on to share the intel he had gathered. "I've identified two of the people involved in the leadership—the Mayor and the Chief of Police for Port-au-Prince. I have pictures of two others that I'd like to send to you for identification."

"What happened to this being a little R and R with the family? I hate to say 'I told you so,' but you're a natural for the job we discussed."

" Yeah, well, shit seems to follow me."

Marv laughed. "Send me the uploads and I'll see what I can find out. I recently became aware of the theft problem down there. It's the President's plan to send a small contingent of troops down there to act as security for the convoys. Of course, that will take some time. In the meantime, I'm sure the trucks will continue to be hit."

"Copy that, Captain. After finishing my recon, I've promised my wife to stay out of it. Besides, I have no weapons."

"Tell you what, Sam. There's a diplomatic flight every week for Embassy needs. I'll include a little package for you. It will be there just in case the need arises. I'll give you the name of my contact at the embassy after I respond to your upload."

"Now you're just tempting me to do something," laughed Sam. "Mariah will kill me if I get involved. But that's good to know."

Royster was laughing. "Not my intent to entice you, Sam. I'll be in touch."

Sam shared with Mariah the identities of the two leaders he had seen at the large warehouse. He also told her of his conversation with the Director of the National Clandestine Services (D/NCS), Marvin Royster. He left out the part about the package that would be arriving at the embassy for a "just in case" scenario, but he did take the opportunity to tell her about his job offer.

"Marvin was at my Navy hearing. He knows how I feel about the constraints placed on soldiers, which could jeopardize the lives of those involved. His section deals with similar types of problems that we dealt with in the SEALs, but they go about it in a more covert way. I'm considering saying yes, but only with your permission."

Mariah replied, "Sam, helping people who are oppressed and in need is in your blood. On our college trip, I knew that was the case after our first week in Afghanistan, when I saw on your face the joy of helping others. Our experience with the terrorists showed you the direction you wanted to go to give that help. You're the unsung hero, the knight in shining armor, and you're damn good at it. The government has trained you with a skillset that few have. I say if it's what you want, then go kick ass and help those who can't defend themselves."

Sam was near tears. He couldn't believe how well his wife understood him and supported him. They were truly soul mates. He grabbed her and held her close. "God, I love you more than anything, Mariah. I can't believe I'm so lucky."

"Hooyah," was Mariah's response.

Sam just shook his head at her.

Sam and his family only had three weeks left in Haiti. He and Gracie spent the days together while Mariah worked, and they all found time together in the evenings. This had been their routine since arriving in Haiti. Sam's previous intel missions hadn't even changed their schedule. Sam was completely relaxed and enjoying every single minute with his two favorite girls. It was five days before he heard from Royster about the pictures he had sent to him.

"Sam, I have the identities of the other two guys. One is a Haitian army colonel, and the other is a local gang leader."

"So, in summary, the Mayor, the Chief of Police, an army colonel, and a gang leader are working together to sell stolen Red Cross supplies to unfortunate people still recovering from an earthquake and a recent hurricane," Sam said. "Those guys are true scumbags."

"Agreed," said Royster. "By the way, the package will be arriving tomorrow. So, what are you going to do?"

"I don't know. If Mariah is okay with it, I guess I could tag along with one of the convoys and protect it. Obviously, I can't travel with all of them. Who knows how deep the corruption goes?"

"Tell you what," said Royster, "I'm going to give this information to one of my reporter contacts, who then can write a story. At least it may put some pressure on the government to send those troops sooner. It's better than nothing."

Sam replied, "That's a good idea. But I sure wish I had my team down here. Eight SEALs could make this whole issue go away very quickly."

"Copy that, Sam. Let me know if I can do anything else. Talk to you soon," Royster said, and hung up.

Sam made his way to the US Embassy a couple of days later to pick up the package. Marvin Royster had sent Sam a variety of weapons, including a sniper rifle, an MP5, a trusted H and K 45, and a few explosives. The contents were a SEAL's dream. He went through the guns, cleaned them, and thanked the Embassy marine that Royster had told him to contact. He would allow Sam to access and take the weapons whenever he wished.

Over the next couple of weeks, about one out of every three convoys was hit. The other two would make their destinations and deliver supplies to poor people barely hanging on. Fortunately, the trucks that were assaulted rarely sustained any injuries to the men on those missions. Sam took some consolation in that but felt helpless just the same. He was struggling to remain on the sideline. Mariah reminded him that they were still doing a tremendous amount of good, and Sam would just smile at her and control his rage by working out and sweating.

Royster's reporter friend broke the story in the *Washington Post.* The article mentioned the four leaders involved and called for immediate U.S. action to stop the thefts. Royster told Sam that a House Representative had demanded a Congressional inquiry. This pressure would be helpful in pushing up the deployment of National Guardsmen.

Then, five days before Mariah and Sam were scheduled to leave, things changed. Usually about four or five deliveries were made by the Red Cross each day. On this particular day, however, six convoys went out with a major amount of supplies, and thieves hit every single convoy. Moreover, this time there was loss of life—both men in each convoy had been killed execution-style, and twelve Red Cross workers had been murdered delivering supplies to half-starving Haitians. This was a complete change in tactics from the prior thefts.

Mariah told Sam that the Red Cross had decided to suspend their deliveries until troops arrived to protect them. She could see the frustration and anger in Sam's face.

"I can't take this any more, babe," said Sam. "They must be reacting to the article in the *Post* or making one last big score. The four leaders have disappeared since that article was written. They know that the local authorities can't do anything to stop them. I know the location of their operation. So, the Red Cross stops its deliveries, as they should, hoping troops will be coming soon to guard the convoys. Meanwhile, innocent Haitians who can't afford to buy goods on the black market starve to death. That's bullshit. Fuck that!"

"What could you do, Sam?" Mariah stated.

"I could try to give this country some hope by ridding their world of these intimidators. These scumbags don't deserve to live. In a crooked country like Haiti, if they were caught and taken to trial, any thought of justice is a pipe dream. I'm sorry, Mariah, but these men need to be put down like rabid dogs. Their deaths would be righteous kills."

"Sam, you don't have the means to pull that off, and you're all alone. It's a terrible situation, but troops will be here soon."

He then told her about the weapons that had been sent to the Embassy.

"I could do a lot of damage to their operations, and probably slow them down until troops came. Their arrival has been pushed up because of the recent deaths."

"No one can know it was you, Sam. If the Red Cross had any connection to something like that, it would hurt their neutrality and cause an international incident," Mariah stated.

"Everyone knows that any reprisal against this gang would be from someone associated with the U.S., not the Red Cross, so there would be no connection. Besides that, these guys will never know who hit them. This is what I do, and I'm very good at it."

"I know you are, babe. Oh Sam, I feel terrible for saying this, but go for it. But, please, be careful."

Chapter 19

After retrieving what he needed from the Embassy, Sam made his way to the warehouse around 2 am. Royster had included night-vision goggles, so it was much easier to get closer to the building with a much lower risk of being seen. The security was weak, so Sam was able to make his way around the perimeter of the warehouse. As he did so, he planted explosives that he could remotely detonate. He then made his way into the building and did the same. He also put listening devices in the building so that he might hear any conversations. Royster had even sent a telephoto video camera, so Sam could record both the audio and video of any meeting. After he completed these tasks, he found a perch, sat with his sniper rifle, and waited. This was a classic SEAL mission—get behind enemy lines, wreak havoc, get out without a trace, a similar tactic to that he and his team had used to eliminate Joseph Kony and his men as his final act as a Navy SEAL.

Sam waited throughout the night. At first there was minimal activity, then more and more men kept arriving. They arrived in cars that they would park some distance away, and then they would walk the rest of the way to the warehouse. There were about twenty-five men just loitering around the opening to the warehouse, smoking and talking. Something big had to be planned. At 5 am, the Cadillac Eldorado pulled up with the four ringleaders. Sam had earbuds in so he could hear the upcoming conversation, and he had his video camera ready.

The Haitian army colonel spoke first. "In about two hours, army trucks will be arriving to move these supplies to another location. This position has been compromised. You will all help with the loading and unloading."

"Not until we're paid," said one of the men. "My family is in great need of the money you promised."

The colonel replied, "You'll will be paid at the other location."

As the colonel began to speak again, the man spoke a second time. "I don't believe you. I want my money now."

The Colonel scratched his chin, then walked up to the man, pulled out a gun, and shot him in the face. "Does anyone else feel the same way?"

Sam had been recording the entire incident. It was apparent to him that this was the time to act. He readied his sniper rifle and visualized in his mind what it would involve to take headshots of the four leaders. It would be tough to get all four men with the required half-second between shots. In his mind, he prioritized the order: colonel, Chief of Police, gang leader, Mayor. He figured that he would first kill those most experienced at hearing the sound of gunfire. He assumed that the Mayor would probably freeze. The colonel would probably be the fastest to look for cover. The four targets were helping him by standing side by side, facing their workers.

Sam went over the upcoming scenario in his head, visualizing the kills, the explosions, and his escape. This would all occur within several seconds. Sam was hopeful that after his four main targets were taken out, the rest of the men would scatter like roaches. He had the feeling that these were just desperate men just trying to look out for their families, not soldiers ready to fight. However, if they saw Sam and were hostile, he would have to take them out with the explosives before they could retaliate against him.

Without hesitation or remorse, Sam pulled the trigger, and successfully completed the four headshots. His sniper instructor would have been impressed. There was momentary confusion on the workers' faces, and then, sure enough, they scrambled away as fast as they could. When he was sure all of the men had left, he quickly and quietly retrieved the explosives and equipment. No sense blowing up all the Red Cross supplies needed by the poor people whom these four dead shitheads had been stealing from. An anonymous tip to the Red Cross about stolen supplies found in a warehouse would be easy to arrange.

The following day, the press corps reported the story, both locally and across the hemisphere. Video recordings of the previous meetings and the colonel shooting a man somehow made their way to social media. Reports went on to say that the Mayor, the chief of police, an army colonel, and a local gang leader had died by gunshot wounds to the head. The article detailed the Red Cross supplies that were in the building, and it finished by speculating that a rival gang was probably responsible for the killings, although no group had claimed responsibility. This assumption was hardly believable, and none of the men seen running away in the video had come forward to tell what had happened. No one could understand why, if it were a rival gang, the supplies had been left. The event remained a mystery; however, there were a few SEALs who knew Sam was in Haiti with his wife, and they simply smiled, knowing that he had to be involved.

Soon thereafter, the Red Cross resumed its humanitarian mission. U.S. National Guard troops arrived to accompany deliveries, and the convoys delivered supplies without a hitch. People in desperate need of food and drink were once again replenished with the basic staples. Those people receiving the supplies were grateful to whoever had stepped in and done something to help them. The morale of the country took a turn for the better. However, the locals were beyond angry that their own government had failed to stop the robberies.

Mariah, Gracie, and Sam made their way back home several days later. Mariah did not struggle with what her husband had done. She knew Sam was a good man, and she shared his belief in helping those could not help themselves. However, she did struggle with the lack of guilt she felt about the deaths of the four men.

"Sam, shouldn't I feel bad about what happened to those four thieves?"

"Why, babe? Guilt is nothing more than an emotion that comes from a feeling of doing something wrong. I did nothing wrong—the killings were morally justified and performed in the self-defense of the Haitian people."

"I don't know, Sam. That sounds very convenient."

"Are you kidding me? Those fools declared war on the Red Cross when they killed 12 aid workers. It won't keep me up at night."

Morally, Mariah knew Sam was right; but spiritually, she worried about their souls. Sam went on to tell her that the actual Hebrew translation from the Ten Commandments was "Thou shall not murder," not "Thou shall not kill," as commonly referenced. Murder was the killing of someone without justification, as Sam reminded her, and he only killed when it was morally justified or in self-defense. He quoted Ecclesiastes 3:8: "There is a time to love and a time to hate, a time for war and a time for peace." He didn't kill for pleasure or for gain, but to eliminate evil men who oppressed others.

Many would say that what Sam had done in Haiti was consistent with vigilantism—taking the law into one's own hands and attempting to effect justice according to one's personal understanding of right and wrong. While in the military, he and his team had done many of the same types of missions. They would go into an area where oppression existed, and they would, in fact, dispense "justice." Their actions were sanctioned by the U.S. government, and by the government of the nation in which those missions occurred. Similar to the early days of the Wild West in the United States, these Third World countries did not have the organization or the ability to enforce the Rule of Law. Sam had simply done the same in Haiti. It was a fine moral line, but Sam was comfortable with his actions. To him, there was no question of what had been right and what had been wrong in Haiti.

Chapter 20

Upon their return, Sam contacted Marvin Royster and informed him that he wanted to talk more about his offer.

"I'm glad you called, Sam. But first, tell me about the events in Haiti. Other than me and my man at the Embassy, no one in the U.S. Government knows of your involvement in the affair. However, those who knew you were in-country do have some suspicions of your involvement, especially since no one has come forward claiming responsibility. I simply tell people it must have been an anonymous hero. Only with your permission would I ever tell another soul," said Marvin.

Sam could read people's character, and he knew Royster was sincere. He went on to tell him the particulars of the morning, which had put an end to the abuse of the Haitian people by the four dead dirtbags in charge. Then the two of them planned to meet the next day in person to discuss the details of what Royster needed from Sam.

As soon as they sat down for the meeting, Royster got right to the point. "So, what can I do to get you to join our work here at the CIA?"

"Start with a job description, and then tell me why the constraints are different than those I had as a SEAL," Sam replied.

The Director of the National Clandestine Service then began a long description of what Sam's role would be. Sam would report only to Royster or the Director of the CIA. His missions could be very defined, or they could be very broad. He could be working independently, or be leading others. It might involve helping local groups who were fighting governments that were interested in undermining U.S. interests. He could be coordinating and leading a team of men to take out terrorists abroad. It might involve assassinations of individuals responsible for actions, or their support of those actions, that were responsible for the loss of American lives.

Sam listened intently and only interrupted Royster when he had a particular question.

"Sounds like you want James Bond, not me," laughed Sam. "My Dad and I loved to watch those movies when I was a kid. He, in turn, had watched them with my grandfather when he was a kid."

Marvin laughed too. "Yes, I guess it does. But you're better than that. Your SEAL file and your mission results are better than anyone's I've ever seen. Add Haiti to your resume. I'm not just blowing smoke up your ass, that's the truth. Not to use a cliché, but your country needs men like you, Sam."

"I'm flattered, Marvin, I really am, and I like what I hear, but I still want to know why there aren't the same constraints as there were in the SEALs. I think I know the answer, but I want to hear you say it."

Marvin replied, "This is truly the part I hate, Sam. The constraints are different because you aren't wearing a uniform when you work. As an agent of the CIA, the U.S. government can take a position of deniability should you get caught. Depending on the circumstances, the government may push to the fullest to get you back. Conversely, if it's not in the best interest of the U.S. government, they may choose to sacrifice you. That's the main reason that there are stars on the wall at Langley, not names for fallen heroes. The ability to have deniability leads to fewer constraints."

"That's what I figured. I understand the risks and the reason for the policy. But I'm not sure if I could abide by that rule if one of my men were caught during a mission that I was leading. You need to know up front that I would probably ignore any order to stand down if I felt that I could recover someone that you want to sacrifice."

Marvin looked Sam squarely in the eye and told him, "Sam, I would never want to sacrifice someone, but my boss, the Director, and his boss, the President, might have to make that decision. You have my word as a fellow Navy Officer and SEAL that I don't agree with that policy and would also disregard it to save a man's life."

"You were a SEAL? I thought you told me you had been Navy Intelligence your whole career."

"I came out of ROTC and went to SEAL training. I made it through, but after a year it became evident to me and the Navy that I had better abilities in the intel field. I made the change and rose through the ranks. After experiencing similar episodes of feeling limited, like you did with Kony, I retired and came to the CIA."

"Well, hell, Marvin, you should have told me that you were a SEAL at the beginning. I knew there was a reason I felt comfortable with you. I'm all in."

"Hooyah!" was Marvin's reply.

Chapter 21

Khalid sat in the early morning, sipping tea and reflecting on the past several years. He had gone from a low point after the death of his brother and father, withstanding the ridicule of his superiors after his failure, to becoming an al-Qaeda Special Operations Unit Commander. He had regained the old men's trust, succeeding numerous times in disrupting the Americans in Afghanistan. His current location in the Kandahar province, along the border with Pakistan, had allowed him to occasionally make his way to Islamabad to see his mother. Ever since the death of her husband, she had embraced Khalid's association with al-Qaeda. Her rage, coupled with his own, continued to motivate him. His thoughts were interrupted by his second-in-command.

"Khalid, preparations have been completed in London."

"Excellent, Jamal. Are we sure the martyrs continue to be willing?"

"Absolutely. Their recruitment was easy; there are many followers there who want to do their part."

"I know that the Pakistani trio will finish the task—I recruited them myself. Are you sure about the Jamaican convert?"

"I am. His belief is beyond doubt."

"We shall see," said Khalid. "I only wish this was an attack on the Americans."

"I understand, Khalid. Your hatred of them goes beyond that of any of the rest of us—I sense primarily because of your personal pain. I beg you to keep your perspective."

"What do you know of my pain, Jamal? Until you have lost what I've lost, you know nothing."

"I beg your forgiveness, Khalid, I meant no disrespect. Take some solace that the G8 conference is occurring in Scotland as we proceed. Their proximity will show them that no one is safe from our reach."

"Hmm, I'll try to put that in 'perspective,'" Khalid replied with sarcasm.

Jamal nodded at his commander, then excused himself. Khalid's increased narrowing tunnel vision for "Americans-only" might become a problem. He wondered if he needed to consider conveying his thoughts to someone above Khalid.

❊ ❊ ❊

Mohammed Khan, Shehzad Tanweer, and Hasib Hussain had just left their meeting, having reviewed and finalized their individual duties. Each of them was ready. They jumped into their rental car, left Leeds, and made their way to Luton to meet up with the fourth member of the group, Germaine Lindsay. The three Pakistanis were impressed with the Jamaican's zealotry. They said their hellos and boarded the train for London.

❊ ❊ ❊

It was a beautiful July morning in London as Patricia was waiting at the King's Cross St. Pancras Station. She was excited to get the day over with; she was ready for the three-day weekend with her boyfriend. She was sure this would be the weekend that he would propose to her.

John was brooding about the fight that he and his wife had that morning while waiting at the Liverpool St. Station. For the life of him, he couldn't understand his wife's position on immigration. She was passionate about the U.K. becoming a refuge for displaced people, especially Muslims. It seemed that that the latest terrorist attack had only been a few years ago, and John felt that letting more Muslims into the country was the stupidest idea in the world. But he decided that when he got to work, he would call her to say, "I love you."

Michael wished that he had stayed home that day. He had been up most of the night throwing up and running to the bathroom, and the thought of being nice all day to tourists coming in from Heathrow almost made him throw up again while waiting for the Underground. He usually made the short walk from his apartment near Edgware Station to Paddington Station, but he felt that he needed to save as much energy as he could in order to endure the workday.

Jane and George Peters had finally made it to London. Having recently retired, George had started planning this trip a year ago. It had been forty years since he and his wife had honeymooned in London. George had digitalized all the pictures they had taken as newlyweds, and the couple was excited to compare them to the same places all these years later. They were riding on the double decker bus, enjoying the morning, awaiting their stop at Tavistock Square. There, they would recreate the picture from forty years ago in front of St. Pancras Church. He couldn't wait to post the two pictures on Facebook, a skill he had recently learned from his granddaughter.

❊ ❊ ❊

"Allah be with you," Mohammed said to the other three. "Today, we become martyrs in the fight against Western tyranny, joining many of our brothers in Paradise."

The four men hugged one another, and then Khan, Tanweer, and Lindsay entered the tube station at King's Cross Station, where the three men would board separate trains. After saying his goodbyes, Hussain, the youngest at 18 years old, left them and made his way to the bus stop.

Shehzad Tanweer, aged 22, who lived with his parents, had allowed those waiting at the Liverpool Station to board the train. His detonation killed him and seven others. John never got the chance to tell his wife "I love you" after their argument. An investment banker who survived would be blinded in one eye from a fragment of Tanweer's shin bone.

The ringleader, Mohammad Khan, age 30, had earlier left his wife and young child at home. Instead of going to the school where he worked that morning, he detonated his suicide vest after the subway train had left Edgware Station. If poor, sick Michael had walked to work like usual, he would not have died along with Khan and six others. A construction manager who lost both of his legs in the attack would later describe seeing Khan's arm move quickly and then a "big, white flash."

The Jamaican, Germaine Lindsay, was 19, with a young son and a pregnant wife. His was the third bomb to be detonated in a train, one minute after leaving King's Cross Station on its way to Russell Square. Patricia would never get to know of her boyfriend's intentions or start a family of her own. She, Lindsay, and 25 others would die. One survivor thought that she was having a heart attack when the bomb exploded. She passed out, then awoke to discover both of her lower limbs were badly injured. She somehow had the wherewithal to use her scarf as a tourniquet around each leg. She lost her legs, but her actions saved her life.

Finally, Hasib Hussain detonated his suicide bomb on the top of the double decker bus as he sat behind Jane and George Peters. The three of them, along with 11 others, were killed by the cowardly act. Hussain's detonation was an hour after the others, and mobile phone records would later show he had tried to contact the other three bombers. The bus exploded in front of the headquarters of the British Medical Association, where a conference was being held. Dozens of physicians poured from the building to start first aid. One survivor remembered not sitting by the bomber because his rucksack had taken up both seats.

Fifty-two innocents were killed and 700 were injured as a result of the first Islamic terrorist suicide attack in London. The city had been chosen for a reason—an estimated 3 million people rode the London Underground every day, and another 6.5 million used the city's bus system.

Jamal reported the results of the attacks to Khalid. "All four bombers were successful. We have brought the war to the infidels in London. Allahu Akbar."

"Indeed," was Khalid's simple reply.

PART THREE:

Present Day

Chapter 22

Sam began his career with the CIA by meeting with the Director, Robert "Buck" Ritchie. The Director assured Sam that there would be less interference from politics working for the CIA than there had been in the military. The leader of the Agency reiterated everything that Marv had told him previously. The Director seemed genuine and purposeful, and he put Sam at ease as he discussed policies and procedures. Unlike other jobs, when joining the CIA, one didn't go down to Human Resources and get a welcome package outlining the job description.

After this initial meeting, Sam then spent the next several weeks acquiring documents for aliases he might need to use as well as methods to access funds when necessary. He also attended numerous briefings and read many memos explaining the role of the CIA and the Clandestine Service in various parts of the world. Sam was impressed with the anonymous services by the CIA that had been provided in some of the same areas that Sam had been deployed to as a SEAL. He met many people who would support him—some in person, such as other agents like himself as well as administrative people and others by reviewing their pictures and dossiers on the computer. It was somewhat overwhelming, but he knew that he was getting an overview of the big picture. As missions were prepared, the specifics needed would be easy to grasp. He also knew that his role would mostly involve specific, focused projects and missions.

Mariah would always ask Sam about his day when he arrived home.

"Well, I don't think the CIA is going to work out. I didn't tell you, but I've been interviewing for other jobs as well. I'm happy to report that the winner is Guardian Security. They've offered me an executive position, and I accepted."

"What?"

"Check it out—here's my new badge. And, oh, check out these pictures of my new corner office. It's going to be awesome."

Mariah stood slack-jawed, then furrowed her brow in confusion as Sam went on incessantly. Finally, as Sam stopped to take a breath, Mariah had a chance to say something.

"I didn't even know you were entertaining such an offer. All I've heard is how excited you were to get back into a job that allows you to protect our nation and the world from those set on dispensing misery to others. Where did this come from?"

"Don't you think that mindset is really naïve and too idealistic? I was fooling myself into believing that I could make that much of a difference," was Sam's response.

Mariah had been standing at the counter and holding Gracie, but she couldn't help but sit down. She couldn't believe what she was hearing. For that matter, she could barely register in her mind the words he had just said. It took her several minutes before she could look at him. When she did, Sam was beaming.

"Psych," was his response. "That story is my cover, so you can tell everyone something about what I do for a living instead of saying I'm a spy. Gotcha!" Sam was rolling with laughter.

"You asshole," Mariah shot back. "You think you're real funny, don't you? I was thinking of how I was going to have to leave you because you were going soft on me. Gracie and I were out the door." She was smiling at Sam.

"Ouch," said Sam. "I'm offended you said that."

"Well, I guess we wouldn't really leave," she said with a smile.

"Not that part," Sam replied, smiling in return, "I'm talking about the soft part. As a matter of fact, why don't we put Gracie down for a nap and I'll show you just how soft I am for you!"

He grabbed them both and hugged tightly.

"Seriously, though, before you show me that," winked Mariah, "tell me more about the organization."

"Really? Well, let me read something from the CIA website. I'm warning you, its wordy. You and Gracie both might fall asleep as I'm reading it."

"Well, catch us if we do and start falling."

"OK." Sam emphasized taking a deep breath, then began: "The Central Intelligence Agency's mission is 'To preempt threats and further U.S. national security objectives by collecting intelligence that matters, producing objective all-source analysis, conducting effective covert action as directed by the President, and safeguarding the secrets that help keep our Nation safe. The National Clandestine Service (NCS) serves as the clandestine arm of the Central Intelligence Agency (CIA) and is the national authority for the coordination, deconfliction, and evaluation of clandestine operations across the Intelligence Community of the United States.'"

"Wow, that is a mouthful.

"Uh, that's what she said."

"Jesus, someone is horny. Settle down. I have some more questions."

"Sorry, babe," Sam grinned. "Hit me with those questions."

"So, you'll go to Langley every day."

"Yes and no. I'll drive to an office in McLean, Virginia, then take an underground tunnel to Langley. That's why I've been leaving in workout clothes. I run there instead of using the golf carts, then shower and change. It's a new world, Mariah. In the SEALS, we were the hammer that delivered the blow based on orders from above. Now I'm taking part in the decisions, the plans, as well as the execution. I'm seeing the big picture from the beginning. I am so stoked to get back in the game."

"I can see that, Sam. Now, wasn't that worth the wait?"

Chapter 23

The current crisis in Venezuela would be the setting for Sam's first CIA mission. The country was a powder keg under the current President. Sam had learned from the briefings that Venezuela had once been the richest country in South America, but starting with the election of Hugo Chavez in 1999, the government proceeded to undermine their own economic success. Prior to Chavez becoming president, Venezuela had supported American strategic interests, but upon him taking office, the country became an adversary of the United States. This attitude was highlighted in a speech given to the United Nations in 2006, when Chavez called President George Bush the "devil" and accused the United States of "exploitation and pillaging of the peoples of the world."

Sam's intel briefings discussed how Chavez had linked the Venezuelan economy solely to the exportation of oil, and the current President had continued this policy when he narrowly won presidency after Chavez's death. As oil prices declined, the economy continued to collapse, causing severe hyperinflation, leading to mass poverty and political unrest. The crisis led to a mass exodus of approximately 4 million Venezuelans. In January 2019, the opposition leader declared himself acting president, only 2 weeks after his adversary had won "re-election." The United States recognized the opposition leader as the President of Venezuela and provided some support.

U.S. sanctions against Venezuela further crippled its economy. Sanctions could put pressure on the government and lead to citizens becoming disgruntled, hopefully helping to incite change. However, government leadership rarely suffered, as they continued to drive their fancy cars and pad their bank accounts. The CIA's involvement in Venezuela was meant to facilitate regime change to allow the opposition to succeed. U.S. interests in Venezuela involved the demise of a socialist republic and eliminating their alliance with Russia and Iran, as well as securing access to the vast oil reserves. However, Sam's first mission involved a completely different area of concern altogether—a horrible humanitarian crisis.

Royster explained to Sam that with the massive departure of so many Venezuelans, many of those people were at high risk of becoming victims of human trafficking. The refugees entered host countries with no money, no possessions, and no jobs. Exploitation began with the promise of finding economic improvement and instilling a false sense of hope to the victims. Although low on the list of CIA priorities, D/NCS Royster explained to Sam that they thought it was important enough to formulate a mission to try to dissuade these traffickers, and hopefully drastically reduce the number of victims.

A positive outcome to that mission would be looked on favorably by the people of Venezuela and further trust in the United States' offer to help its citizens. The CIA Director thought that this task was impossible, but gave Royster the approval to begin his effort. Royster, in turn, felt that this mission was a good starting point for Sam to get his feet wet. He had also convinced the Director that this could also be a source of good press for CIA involvement in the area, something that was always needed at home.

When Royster briefed Sam and his ten-person team, he was excited about the opportunity, although he agreed with the Director about their ability to make a difference. The task seemed daunting, but Sam welcomed the challenge—any good cause to operate and use his skills, was his mantra.

The Venezuelan government would be of no assistance, so Sam's plan involved using Non-Government Organizations (NGOs) as a cover to gather local intelligence on the groups responsible, the major routes of migration of refugees, and the techniques employed by these various trafficking groups. Of course, none of those organizations would openly help the CIA, as the plan called not for the arrest but the elimination of the main players responsible. Sam would have his team covertly attach themselves to various NGOs, as they were charitable organizations that wanted no ties to the U.S. government. It was the hope that by beginning a mass removal of these criminals, momentum might change in the favor of these NGOs and improve the chances of the noble work they were doing. Sam and his team considered their task to level the playing field, so that the NGOs could be more successful.

Sam came home that evening and told Mariah that he was going to deploy with the CIA within a week's time. He told her the plan, even though he was breaking his top-secret status by doing so. He had decided that she needed to know his missions not only for her to have some small peace of mind by knowing his location, but also so he could hear her opinion about the purpose of his missions. It was what he had done while a SEAL, and he wasn't going to stop confiding in her now.

"Wow, what a gallant cause. I'm really surprised that the CIA has any interest at all in human trafficking," was her reply. "So, I guess if this is successful, the CIA will find some way of leaking their humanitarian victory to the rest of the world."

"That is correct—*when* the plan works. And why so condescending? We can always use the positive press to help win the hearts and minds of the people," responded Sam with a sheepish grin.

"You sound like an aspiring politician," she said, as she simulated vomiting.

"That really hurts," Sam replied, as he withdrew the imaginary knife from his back.

"Are you guys fighting?" Gracie shouted as she came into the room.

"Never!" Sam replied. "Mommy was just saying how smart I am."

He lifted his three-year-old and winked at Mariah, who once again had resorted to fake puking, while laughing at Sam.

"Is that true, Mommy?" Gracie asked.

"Absolutely. Let's get you to bed, baby," Mariah said with a gigantic smile. "And then Daddy has some wonderful things to do... I mean, say to me."

Sam mouthed a big "YES" back to Mariah before he kissed Gracie good night and swaggered back to their bedroom.

Sam and his team departed for Caracas three days later.

Chapter 24

After arriving at the CIA safe house, Sam made plans to quickly get his people in place as undercover agents. The first phase of his plan was to attach 2-person teams to five different NGOs: Anti-Slavery International, Shared Hope International, EPCAT International, and other similar ones. They would act as volunteers and gather intel on the traffickers and their routes. By working as fellow volunteers for several weeks, Sam hoped that enough information could be obtained to carry out the second phase—the elimination of a large group of traffickers.

It was paramount that his teams not jeopardize the activities of these volunteer groups by becoming identified as CIA operatives. But if they could eliminate enough traffickers and disrupt current activity, the result would allow the NGOs to work more effectively. Taking the fight to these shitbags would also help to deter continued trafficking. Sam realized that total elimination would be difficult, because in his experience, evil would continue to try to raise its ugly head. Evil could be pervasive, scattering like cockroaches when threatened, only to return when the threat left. Sam's hope was that by delivering enough pain to the traffickers, some deterrence would follow.

It became clear after a very short time that the traffickers' organization was better than expected. With little fear of interference by Venezuelan authorities, the traffickers had no concern about the consequence of their actions. Therefore, they were very organized, if predictable, in their methods. The habitual tactics employed by the traffickers would work to the advantage of Sam's team.

It did not take long to identify the main players and their egress routes out of Venezuela into neighboring Latin American countries. It was also fairly easy to identify the major recruiters who would deceive the refugees about getting them jobs, setting them up with new housing, medical care, and other benefits in Columbia or another country. The NGOs had been doing their best to educate people regarding the misinformation, but their efforts were falling short.

Several factors had been found to lessen the risk of individuals falling prey to traffickers. First, if Venezuelans had safe and legal pathways to enter host countries, they were less likely to fall into the hands of traffickers. Second, regularizing the status of Venezuelans already within a host country was vital if victims were going to feel safe in reporting incidents of trafficking to the authorities. Third, without the right to work, displaced Venezuelans were at a higher risk of falling prey to exploitative situations in order to survive financially. If refugees worked with the NGOs, the risk of falling prey to traffickers was markedly reduced. So by reducing the number of major traffickers, the NGOs groups would have a better chance of success.

Sam and his team met to discuss their progress gathering intel the past ten days.

"There doesn't seem to be much variation to the traffickers' operation," began Sam. "I'm comfortable with going operational."

"Agreed," replied a team member. "They use the same pick-up sites around the city, then transport to the same areas on the border. I've worked undercover at these sites, so I can tell you—our pleas for people not to get on the trucks fall on deaf ears."

"It's the hopelessness. These victims fool themselves into believing that although they're leaving with traffickers, that anything is better than staying."

"Exactly. And after they're on the trucks, they're restrained and guarded by the armed thugs."

Sam continued. "The guards have nothing to fear from the police, and the Venezuelan government doesn't care. The traffickers just get ballsier; they feel they can get away with anything. Let me tell you my plan to change things up for these assholes."

Sam explained that in order to minimize collateral damage, he'd decided to engage the trucks along the road during the journey from the urban collection point to the border. There were plenty of points that would allow a safe ambush by combining sniper coverage with assault teams. The initial interdiction was to take place that evening, and the entire 10-person team would be along for the first encounter. Sam wanted overwhelming force available for this index contact. He was fortunate to have two team members who had been part of his SEAL team: former Petty Officers Steve Durrant and Paul Kerney had come on board shortly after they'd heard their former "boss" had done the same. Sam had trained hard with all of his new team, but having shared live-fire experience with Durrant and Kerney was very comforting to him.

"Alpha 2, do you copy?" said Sam through his Comms.

"Alpha 4 and I are in position with clear view of road. I can see your location through my NGVs,", replied Durrant. "It's pretty hard to miss Alpha 3's backside."

The entire team chuckled, and Sam was thankful for Durrant's nonchalant remark to relax the team. Many on the team had yet to experience a combat-type mission.

"Can you see what I'm doing now?" responded Alpha 3 (Kerney), as he flipped Durrant the middle finger.

Nothing had changed between those two best friends, noted Sam.

Sam had situated two observers on either side of the road five hundred yards ahead of him and the rest of the team. They would signal when, and how many, trucks were coming. He then had staggered the rest of the team, alternating them on either side of the road, to cover both sides of the approaching vehicle once it stopped. They had placed spike strips to flatten the largest of tires, as well as explosives to take out the vehicles if necessary. The explosives, if used, would require perfect timing in order to prevent collateral damage. The plan called for Durrant and the other sniper to take out the driver along with anyone riding shotgun, then the spike strips would do their job and bring the vehicle to a halt. The remainder of the team would then engage the vehicles and eliminate any other hostiles who were in the trucks.

"Alpha 1, this is Alpha 10. Two transport trucks heading your way. Say again, two tango trucks."

"Copy that, 10," replied Sam. "It's show time, Alpha team."

The plan went off without a single problem. Durrant and the other sniper took out the drivers and front-seat passengers of each vehicle right before they hit the spike strips, which then caused the vehicles to slow to a stop. Armed gunmen sitting in the back of the transports were put down as soon as they revealed themselves. The entire event took less than 30 seconds. The plan was flawless. The traffickers had never expected to encounter any form of resistance on their way to the border.

The hardest part of the operation came as the team cleared the trucks of any hidden armed men. The first truck contained young women only; the second contained children. The look of fear and anguish on their faces would be imprinted on the brains of the Alpha team members forever. One of the Spanish-speaking team members was able to obtain formation from several of the young women. They told Sam that after meeting at the departure point with their families, they had been separated from their parents, who were told at gunpoint to leave or they would be shot. The same was done to the children in the second truck. Many of the young women were actually older sisters to some of those children. There were nearly 60 young Venezuelans in the two trucks, and most were sobbing. The word was quickly spread among them that they were now safe and that they would be taken back to their parents.

Sam and his team had their debriefing along with D/NCS Royster on a secure video conference call. They were happy with the result, but certainly it was difficult to process some of their emotions. Kerney and Durrant had seen it all during their time as SEALs, but this was the first operational experience for many of the young team members. The CIA Director had signed off on Royster's idea of attacking human traffickers, but certainly not with the use of experienced agents needed elsewhere, so Sam had been given green agents to train. He was okay with that, as long as he had Kerney and Durrant. Together, the three of them had trained the team hard and were confident in their abilities prior to the operation. Now, those young agents had their first operational mission under their belt.

"What we did tonight was prevent the sex trafficking and probable slavery of nearly 60 lives," Sam told the team. "You should feel happy about that. Eliminating the scum that were on the scene tonight was just icing on the cake. This is new to most of you, but understand that because of us, those children are reunited with their parents and will live another day. Sure, their circumstances haven't changed, but at least now the aid agencies have a chance to get them out of the country the proper way. Little by little, as we continue this work, hope may become more of a reality to these people. Hope can snowball and change the morale of all who cling to it. The bigger picture in Venezuela is out of our hands, but we can make a difference for the people we meet and help."

The response was a smattering of "copy that" and high-fives amongst the team. Sam could see the pride in the young agents' faces.

Over the next several weeks, the team split up into smaller groups to continue to disrupt the traffickers. They had many similar missions like the first encounter, but also took the fight to the traffickers at their meeting points in the urban areas. The team also ventured into host countries to follow the traffickers to their leadership. They were relentless in their pursuit of those scumbags. The elimination of the leadership assholes helped to further impair the flow of trafficking.

The outcome was better than expected. The NGOs were now better able to educate and place refugees in a safe fashion. Word on the street spread quickly about these "guardian angels," which, in turn, helped to instill hope for the oppressed Venezuelan people.

"Great work, Sam," Royster said over the Sat phone. "We didn't really deny our involvement to the press. One reporter from a newspaper that normally isn't very sympathetic, to say the least, even wrote that 'If the CIA was involved, it was an excellent use of its resources."

"Just like you planned, Marv. You can feel it here, too. The fact that America cares about Venezuelan citizens has given them some hope."

"What do you think about me pulling you out? I'll leave Kerney and Durrant to supervise the young agents for a while longer."

"Up to you, but I don't mind staying. It's gratifying work."

"I need you here. Time to get your opinion about a new problem."

"Copy that," Sam replied. "Seems there's no shortage of problems."

"Sadly, my inbox is always full, Sam."

Mariah and Gracie met Sam at Dulles International Airport. The reunion was sweeter than ever, as it was the longest he had been away since Gracie was born.

"Daddy, I missed you so much!" yelled Gracie. "You were gone a long time. Did you sell a lot of security stuff?"

Sam winked at Mariah as he picked his daughter up into his arms. Gracie only knew that her father worked for Guardian Security.

"Even the papers wrote about your sales success," added Mariah with a grin. "We sure are proud of your hard work, babe."

Sam had tears in his eyes as he hugged his little girl. Through her, he could see the faces of the young children they had rescued, and he could not comprehend the pain of the parents whose children were lost forever.

"We did okay, we did okay," responded Sam quietly, as he buried his head into Mariah's neck to hide his sobs from his daughter.

Chapter 25

Since the failed kidnapping attempt of the American students, during which Faheem had been killed by of one of the students, Khalid Ali had devoted his life to continuing the war on the West in any manner he could. Along with the London bombings, he had commanded other successful operations.

He had continued his association with al-Qaeda, but also had participated in ISIS activities as well. While both groups shared the goal of establishing an Islamic Caliphate, they approached the goal with different strategies, and with differing degrees of success. Al-Qaeda had responded to the instability in the Middle East by attempting to soften its image. The group specifically instructed its affiliates to situate themselves in local conflicts and to slow down the implementation of sharia law. ISIS, on the other hand, focused on seizing territory and violently disrupting state-building efforts. By the close of 2017, al-Qaeda's rebranding had successfully allowed the group to expand its footprint in a number of Middle Eastern civil wars, although at the cost of its central authority. ISIS, meanwhile, had lost most of its territory but retained the ideological strength to inspire attacks abroad.

Khalid considered himself a free agent to any cause that harmed Western interests. The deaths of his brother and father had continued to unceasingly drive his rage and fuel his hatred of all things Western, specifically the United States and its infidel soldiers.

Khalid's most recent assignment with ISIS had brought him to Nigeria and Boko Haram. Since 2011, Boko Haram—one of the largest Islamist militant groups in Africa—had conducted terrorist attacks on religious and political groups, local police, and the military, as well as indiscriminately attacking civilians in busy markets and villages. The kidnapping of over two hundred girls from their school in April 2014 drew international attention to the ongoing threat from Boko Haram, as well as the government's inability to contain it.

Boko Haram was based in Nigeria's northeast. Mohammed Yusuf, an influential Islamist cleric from the Borno State, created the group in 2002. The primary aim of the group, which began as an offshoot of the Salafi movement, a branch of Sunni Islam, was to establish a fundamentalist Islamic state with sharia criminal courts. The group's leader, Abubakar Shekau, had pledged his allegiance to Abu Bakr al-Baghdadi, the self-proclaimed caliph and leader of the Islamic State, or ISIS. Both these men were claimed to have been killed by government authorities, but they continued to be seen on videos, making most experts believe that they were still alive.

Khalid had been sent to meet Shekau to discuss the state of current affairs of Boko Haram's jihad. Specifically, Khalid was there to discuss different terrorist strategies besides the kidnapping of young women. Boko Haram's goal was to bring back a strict interpretation of early Islam, which included the belief that women were inferior to men. There was no place for women obtaining higher education in Nigeria. While al-Baghdadi shared the view of Islamic extremism, he wanted Shekau to focus on other targets as well, and Khalid had been tasked with helping to guide these efforts.

"As-salamu alaikum," Khalid greeted Shekau.

"Wa alaikum assalaam," replied Shekau. "We have much to discuss, my friend."

"Indeed. Caliph Ibrahim (al-Baghdadi) sends peace as well. He has asked me to share some ideas for your jihad."

"We feel we are already doing well, but I will gladly listen."

"We would like to see more attacks against U.S. targets. The killing of four American soldiers that took place in Niger is an example of the kind of attacks the Caliph would like to deliver to the infidels. Also, there are many Western businesses that could be targeted," said Khalid.

"Those are indeed worthy targets, but would require many things we do not have."

"Ah, but that is why I am here," beamed Khalid. "I can help you acquire what you need."

Over the next several weeks, Shekau and Khalid met to discuss the details of this strategy. And all the while, Boko Haram continued to harass the Nigerian government and military with focused, random attacks.

Chapter 26

Sam settled into his post-deployment routine at home and at work, including the daily briefings with D/NCS Royster and other members of the National Clandestine Service. He would train and work out, and often have lunch with Mariah as she was working in downtown D.C. at the Red Cross Headquarters. Most of their social activities revolved around Gracie, which included meeting the parents of her friends.

It seemed that Sam had improved his ability to transition back into day-to-day life better than when he had been in the Navy. He felt that parenthood had probably been the main reason for this change. Mariah had helped him before with this transition, but the added responsibility of being a father was even more help. The ability to "turn on and turn off" the focus necessary to be a tier one operator, as well as leave the horrors of human cruelty behind after returning home, was not an easy task.

Sam was fortunate to have the ability to clear his mind with Mariah, and he had always made it a point to make sure his team members had someone they could confide in as well. It was part of what made him a good leader, and one of the many reasons he commanded loyalty and respect from his team.

"We've identified a new priority mission in Africa," began Royster at one morning briefing. "We have excellent Intel that Khalid Ali is in Nigeria, meeting with Abubakar Shekau, the leader of the largest faction of Boko Haram. Khalid is apparently there on behalf of Abu Bakr al-Baghdadi. As you know, both Shekau and al-Baghdadi were thought to have been killed, but have shown up on recent videos, which we have verified as being current and authentic. It's safe to assume that those two dirtbags are still out there."

"Where did the intel come from? And is it solid?" asked Sam.

"We have several good agents in Nigeria who uncovered rumblings of a major meeting, and ultimately one of their major assets found out the particulars," responded Royster's assistant. "We have a very high confidence in its accuracy."

"The intel is too good to ignore. At worst, it's false information and we've wasted time checking it out. At best, we have two high value targets (HVTs) on our kill list together in one place," added Royster. "Sam, you and whoever you need will meet up with the Nigerian agents, and see if you can get eyes on these two. Of course, elimination protocol will be the order of the day."

"Copy that," said Sam.

"For those of you who don't know, Sam took out Faheem Ali while he was on a senior college humanitarian trip to Afghanistan."

Sam glanced at Marv with an uneasy expression.

"That was you?" said several members of the briefing simultaneously.

"He saved Lt. Commander Hughes' life. Helluva senior project!" was Royster's comment.

"Whoa, everybody, I was just a dumb kid who fortunately reacted the way I did." Sam was embarrassed by the attention. "Although the events of that day were responsible for my career choice. I was a Philosophy and Religious Studies major," he laughed. "My mom was okay with that; my doctor dad never said so, but I know he thought it was a worthless degree. Now they're okay because they think I'm making big money as a security consultant! They were both proud that I chose to become a SEAL, but boy, you can imagine their worry. At least not knowing the truth about what I do eliminates their worrying."

"I'm sure glad you made that choice, Sam," Royster commented after a prolonged silence had filled the room. "It's sad that we can't acknowledge individuals and their outstanding achievements, but every operator knows anonymity is for the safety of their friends and family."

"Without question," Sam quickly said. "I have no need for the limelight. Trying to rid the world of scum and those who are hell-bent on the destruction of this country and its ideals is reward enough for me."

"There's our next recruiting tape, Marv!" his assistant yelled.

The room laughed.

"Bottom line, I would rather have your statistics than any superstar athlete we see on TV," was Royster's response. "The difference is everybody in the country can look up their statistics, but your performances are classified."

"Okay, okay, that's enough," said a flustered Sam. "Let's work out the details of this mission."

"Absolutely, but I'm just pointing out who true heroes are," replied the D/NCS with a wink.

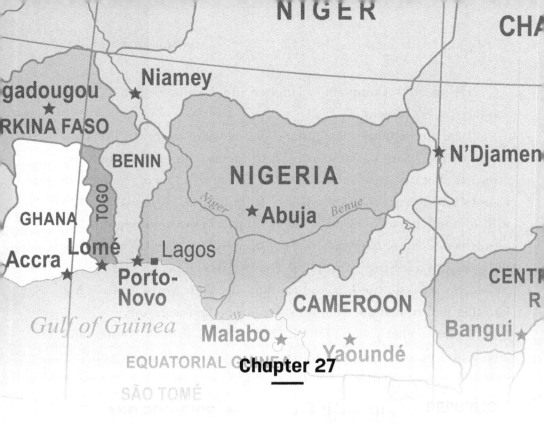

Chapter 27

After the discussion with Royster, Sam reviewed some basic facts about the region as he planned the mission for his team. Boko Haram was based in the Borno State of Nigeria, in the northeastern part of the country, bordering Niger and Chad. The capital of the Borno State was Maiduguri, with a population of nearly two million people. The Sambisa forest south of the city was the hideout for Boko Haram, and a place of fear for the people of the Borno state—the location where 230 schoolgirls had been taken and held. The geography made it extremely difficult, if not impossible, to deploy organized troops to attempt to find Boko Haram's main bases.

Sam had chosen his reliable buddies Durrant and Kerney for this mission. They had rotated out of the Venezuela trafficking mission, and were always ready for a new mission. Paul, Steve, and Sam had been close since their SEAL days, and had easily rekindled their friendship when they arrived in the Washington D.C. area. Their families were inseparable much of the time, alternating barbecues and play dates at one another's homes.

The three of them arrived in the city of Kano, the capital of Kano state, and planned to drive the 300-plus miles to Maiduguri. The drive would avoid any spotters at the Maiduguri airport who might be looking for any white Westerners. Fellow CIA agent Torin Blount, an African-American who had vast experience on the continent of Africa, drove them. He was the individual responsible for uncovering the intel regarding the upcoming meeting of Khalid and Shekau.

"Torin, how good is your intel?" Asked Sam.

"I would say it's 100%. My asset can be trusted. He's had family members butchered by Boko Haram, and he wants nothing but revenge."

"Perfect," Sam replied.

"We have about a six-hour drive ahead of us to the safe house in Maiduguri," said Blount. "There aren't many whites in the area, just those associated with aid groups, so we'll have to do our reconnaissance very carefully. Thank God for night-vision goggles. They'll enable us to see insurgents as well as the wild beasts of the Sambisa Forest."

He turned around to sneak a glance at Kerney and Durrant, whose eyes enlarged at that comment.

"Insurgents are not an issue, but beasts?" exclaimed Durrant. "I don't really do beasts."

Blount chuckled. "I'm messing with you. There are some beasts, but most scattered as Boko Haram has moved in. My guess is they know dirtbags when they see them and have no desire to be near them."

"Copy that. See big guy? It's all good."

Durrant rolled his eyes at Kerney's reply.

"Speaking of aid workers, what's the latest on the six who were recently kidnapped?" asked Sam.

"A recent video surfaced showing them alive and well, but for how long is anyone's guess. They work for Action Against Hunger, and their only 'crime' was feeding starving people. That shit is messed up. It seems that most of the world is either blind to the fact that these extremist groups prey on fellow Muslims with their jihads, or they just don't care," reported Blount.

"Probably a little of both," was Sam's reply. "The saga of man's inhumanity to man continues. Well, hopefully we can do some small act to disrupt that."

"Amen to that, brother," commented Blount.

They arrived at their destination and settled in. They spent the next day listening to Blount's team report everything they knew about possible meeting locations the terrorists might use. They were very thorough and professional, and it was obvious they were very experienced. They, too, were black. That was how it had to be in the world of clandestine service; just like you wouldn't send a team of African-American spies into White Russia, Caucasian spies roaming around Nigeria wouldn't be very smart. Therefore, Richards, Kerney, and Durrant were confined to the safe house during daylight hours.

Blount explained that his intel had revealed there were three main hideouts possible for the meeting location. Their source was trying to pin down which spot, but so far he had been unable to produce the exact location. However, he did know that the meeting was scheduled in two days' time. Blount's source had reported increased rumblings and heightened excitement in the terrorists' ranks. When Sam asked the asset why that was, the man said that he had no idea.

The three known terrorist hideouts ranged from being two to four miles apart from one another. If they couldn't obtain the exact site, then they would have to split the team up to cover all three locations. In addition to the six American CIA agents, Blount had six Nigerians he had trained and whom he trusted to help with the mission. Each Nigerian had lost loved ones to Boko Haram and desired vengeance.

"Okay, here's the plan," started Sam. "Since there's some distance between the sites, let's initially put each team of four about a mile apart from one another, but close to their assigned site. Torin, when your source confirms which of the three locations is having the meeting, we'll all converge on that spot.

"Sounds good. That strategy will cut down on the distance to travel to the site, once it's confirmed."

"Exactly," replied Sam. "Everyone will haul ass to the determined location."

"What happens if the source can't confirm the location?" asked Kerney.

"Well, that will suck a little. In that case, each four-man team will have to take their assigned location. Remember, the goal is not to take out the entire group, just the HVTs. We'll let the Nigerian Army come in and deal with the rest."

"How do you want to split up the groups?" asked Blount.

"We need a sniper in each group. I was thinking you and Durrant along with two of your locals, Kerney and I with two locals, your two fellow CIA guys with two locals."

"I like it. I'll set up my guys, and especially remind the locals that their job is to protect the sniper's perimeter and only kill any terrorists they see, no advancing. The Army could use a victory—they can come in and engage the terrorists."

"Perfect. It would be nice to get the exact location, though. I'd rather have all three snipers available in one place."

"My source will come through for us."

"Why doesn't Royster take them out with a drone?" asked Durrant.

"That's exactly what I asked him," replied Sam. "He told me that they wanted definitive evidence of the HVTs' demise without a spectacle. And like Torin said, the Nigerians could use a confidence boost and some good press. They haven't fared so well against Boko Haram."

"You can say that again," remarked Blount. "Their performance has been dismal to date."

"Makes sense," replied Durrant. "Hopefully we can set things up nicely for them and they can get some glory."

"Copy that, but I'm not holding my breath. I've seen them work, fellas," Blount added.

Later that evening, the three teams made their way through the forest to their respective positions under the cover of darkness.

"Comms check, Alpha 1 in position, status?" Sam spoke to the other two teams.

"Alpha 2 in position," was Blount's reply.

"Alpha 3 in position," came from one of Blount's men leading the third group.

"Alpha 2 reports very few tangoes in this camp; I only see 4 men."

"Alpha 3 has same situation here."

"Alpha 2, any word from your asset?" replied Sam.

"No contact so far," responded Blount.

"No problem. The meeting site has to be the camp where Paul and I are, because I'm looking at about 100 tangoes sitting and facing what looks like a makeshift stage. I'm calling this the site. Alpha 2 and 3, start getting your teams in position around this camp. As per plan, Alpha 2, you're closest to northwest side of camp, Alpha 3 you have northeast side. We'll stay in the north location. Check in when your snipers are positioned and the team is ready. It looks like the guests of honor are currently backstage. Alpha 2, inform your Army liaison of our locations so they don't shoot us as they advance and when we're getting the hell out of here."

"Roger that," Alpha 2 and 3 responded.

The teams were positioned under cover about 25 meters away from the meeting site, and now it was simply a waiting game. The snipers had secured high ground about 500 meters away. Each sniper had the McMillan TAC-50, U.S. military designation MK 15, the preferred rifle of the US Navy SEALs. The distance was not an issue, as a Canadian Joint Task Force 2 sniper had used this same type of rifle to record the longest sniper kill during the Iraq War—a distance of no less than 3,540m. The rest of the teams were using the Heckler & Koch MP5SD 9mm integrally suppressed submachine gun, a quiet weapon with a minimal muzzle flash, which was extremely important in giving them the ability to hide their locations when firing. Its peculiar sound also allowed for team members to identify the shots from their fellow team members.

They continued to wait several hours, and watched the Boko Haram soldiers growing restless. Many had gotten up and were milling around, but they made no moves to leave the camp. Sam was confident that this was the time, and the place, for the meeting.

Then, suddenly, someone appeared on the stage and simply stood there without speaking. The man commanded respect, or fear, as the terrorists became immediately quiet, and went back to sitting. Sam checked the man through a riflescope lens and immediately recognized him as Shekau.

"Snipers, confirm that you agree that this target is Shekau, and that you have him locked in your sights," Sam said softly.

"Copy that," came from all three.

"Standby," was Sam's reply.

Soon thereafter, Shekau was joined by another figure, but Shekau's gesticulating hands blocked Sam's line of sight. Once the terrorist leader calmed down, Sam was staring at the brother of the man he had killed and who had kidnapped his college classmates—Khalid Ali. The players were now in place, and it was time to put these scumbags down. As Sam was about to deliver the order, Khalid began speaking to the men. Sam watched the reaction from Khalid's words, noting an increased excitement in the mood of the terrorists, who were now up and cheering, and this made Sam wait to give the kill order. Khalid had stopped talking, and both he and Shekau turned to the rear to welcome a third figure to the stage.

Kerney, looking through his sniper scope, was the first to speak. "Fuckin-A, that's al-Baghdadi!"

"Affirmative," echoed Durrant.

"Holy shit," added Blount.

"Wow. All right, it's time to get this party started," Sam said rapidly. "Kerney, you take out Baghdadi, Durrant take Shekau, Alpha 2, your sniper has Khalid. Call it back to me as I said it. Understood?"

All three responded with an affirmative, then the name of their target.

"Fire on my count... ready, 3-2-1," Sam called out. As he hit 1, an artillery shell had struck behind the group. He saw the sniper shots strike true to the foreheads of Shekau and al-Baghdadi, and no doubt this time they were dead. However, Khalid's instincts had caused him to turn, and Sam saw the terrorist's left arm turn red as he fell.

"What the hell?" Blount yelled. "The fucking Nigerian Army must have started firing.

He then immediately confirmed this as he spoke to the Nigerian commander.

"That's confirmed—the Army commander thought the loud cheering was gunshots. That dumbass! The Nigerian troops are advancing."

Sam was trying to see the status of Khalid; the shot he had he taken to the arm would kill him only if he bled out. He no longer could positively ID him, but he did see a man being helped and taken away. That had to be Khalid. More artillery started to hit close to their position, so Sam told his team to head out of harm's way. Blount reminded the Army commander that the 12 men retreating would have a blinking green strobe on their helmets as they ran toward them, and "not to fucking shoot them."

Chaos ensued as the terrorists tried to regroup to defend themselves against the advancing Nigerian Army. When it was over, more than 50 terrorists had been killed, along with two Nigerian Army personnel. DNA would confirm Shekau and al-Baghdadi, but even with the damage from the headshots, it was obvious it was them. The mission had been to kill two HVTs, and they had done just that. Only dumb luck had allowed Khalid to escape wounded. Putting down the number one ISIS terrorist, this time for certain, was a huge victory. If al-Baghdadi or Shekau showed up on any videos again, the world would know that they were pre-recorded.

Sam would have to just wait and see if Khalid survived his wound.

Chapter 28

Sam returned to D.C., and as always, was met at the airport by Gracie and Mariah. He was noticeably different this time from when he'd returned from Venezuela. He had not personally witnessed the human suffering of the locals in Nigeria as he had in Venezuela, so he was all smiles as he saw his two favorite girls.

"Daddy!" Gracie yelled. "I missed you to the moon and back."

Sam scooped her up and squeezed her.

"You're not sad like after your last trip."

Recently turned four, Gracie continually displayed an amazing attention to detail. Sam was laughing to himself as he was thinking that this was a trait Gracie had picked up from him, since Mariah's style was a controlled chaos that always came together at the end.

"Gracie, you are so right!" said Mariah. "We would like to see Daddy this way every time we meet him at the airport."

"It was a very... satisfying trip. Who's hungry? I'm starving. Let's grab a burger on the way home!"

"Yay! Let's do it," replied Gracie.

They enjoyed their lunch, cherishing the time together. Sam and Mariah then watched Gracie wear herself out on the playground. Sam told Mariah, as he always did, the results of the mission.

"I watched their heads explode and really didn't feel anything. I felt more emotion when I didn't see Khalid's head explode. Kind of crazy, really."

"You think? You're glad the two are dead because of what they did to so many. You don't celebrate it, you acknowledge it. And you're pissed that you missed Khalid. Makes sense to me."

Sam appreciated his debriefings with Mariah, which were always helpful to process his emotions and evaluate the status of his soul. He did not want to turn into a robotic killing machine, like he'd seen some people become after years of this type of work. He led by example, and constantly stressed to all of his team members the importance of discussing their emotions by talking to someone close and trustworthy.

"You do remember that I'm telling you classified material, and by doing so, I'm essentially committing a crime."

Mariah laughed. "Who am I going to tell? Besides, I never ask you for details."

"I know, but I value your opinion, and I don't ever want any secrets between us. I told you everything when I was a SEAL, and I'm not stopping now."

"I'm glad, Sam, because knowing your mission and its location helps me manage my fears better. I hope you never stop sharing."

"No worries there, babe. So, what do you think?"

"I think you and your colleagues are heroes and a national treasure. The work you do saves lives, helps oppressed people, and eliminates terrible people. We've discussed this before, Sam. I believe there are instances when killing is justified. There's a huge difference between killing and murder. You have to keep that difference in the front of your mind when you and your team are out there doing what needs to be done. The people you kill are murderers, who kill indiscriminately in the name of a religion they've twisted to suit their needs. Or they're evil people taking advantage of the helpless."

"I know we've been talked about it before, but I appreciate the reminder. I couldn't have said it better myself," he replied. "As a matter of fact, that sounds very similar to the wisdom I poured upon you after I took down those four douchebags in Haiti."

She looked over at him, and noting his shit-eating grin, delivered an elbow to his ribs while she was driving.

"Wow, really? I don't remember your speech being as eloquent as mine."

Sam looked at the woman he loved, and she had a big, cheesy grin on her face. "Okay, okay, what do you say that I let you punish me for that remark when we get home?" Sam said as he stroked her inner thigh.

"Well, that was gonna happen anyway. How about you close your eyes and relax for the ride? Just visualize what's going to happen."

Sam closed his eyes and gave thanks for having Mariah as his wife. He was incredibly fatigued from the long flight home as well as from the deep contentment that settled through his body after seeing Mariah and Gracie. The cheeseburger in his belly added to his sleepiness. He rode the rest of the way with his eyes closed, but he went back through Mariah's comments, as well as their previous discussions on killing. It helped him to revisit his core beliefs; it kept his moral compass appropriately calibrated.

He thought again about killing versus murder. Like a lot of debates, the answer depended on one's interpretation of Scriptures, assuming one was Christian. Sam had been a Religion major, and so he was familiar with the arguments. He was also a Christian, so the Bible was his sole source for what mattered. Sam believed that murder was the unlawful taking of a life, while killing could be either lawful or unlawful.

In cases outlined in Scripture, taking the life of another in the name of justice was not murder. The question posed a false dilemma whereby killing did not have to be always right or always wrong—God provided qualifications. In the laws given to Israel through Moses, those sins that were worthy of death were detailed. Leviticus 19 was one such place where those commands were given. Since those commands came directly from God, and since Sam believed that God could not lie, then there must be no contradiction in the commands. The Old Testament had many other instances where people were killed. David slew the giant Goliath, Joshua led the children of Israel into the Promised Land, and God commanded the Israelites to utterly destroy the idolatrous people who inhabited the land; those are only a few of the many examples available for this argument of justified killing. Then Exodus 22 spoke of killing for self-defense as being justified.

The New Testament had Paul talk about government in Romans 13, and said that government was "God's servant for your good. But if you do wrong, be afraid, for he does not bear the sword in vain. For he is the servant of God, an avenger who carries out God's wrath on the wrongdoer." This was the argument to validate killing at least while serving in the capacity of a soldier and/or police officer.

What Sam believed for sure was that God hated sin, especially those sins that led to situations where a human life was lost. God's holy nature and subsequent hatred of sin made the taking of a life acceptable only in the rarest of cases, and that taking a life for justifiable reasons was only necessary because people lived in a world of sin. Sam did not believe that all Christians should be pacifists and always turn the other cheek. He was certainly not perfect like God's son, but even Jesus forgave the prostitute, and then rebuked and provoked the religious leaders of the day until they wanted to murder Him. Sam had faith that what he was doing was justified in God's eyes, but he wouldn't know the right answer until he met God. No one would know for sure until that time.

He also thought about Muslims and their faith. Again, there were arguments that Islam called for the eradication of all non-believers. This argument was the right wing's battle cry when discussing Muslims in general. The most common verse used to support this view was 9:5 from the Quran: "Kill the infidels (polytheist, pagans) wherever you find them, capture them, besiege them, and lie in wait for them at every ambush." Sam believed that most Muslims would say that real Islam denounced all violence, and that Islam meant peace, or tolerance. But other verses did say "not to make friendship with Jews and Christians" (5:51), "kill the disbelievers wherever we find them" (2:191), "murder them and treat them harshly" (9:123). There were arguments that those quotes were taken out of context and/or were "cherry-picked" by anti-Islam pundits and ISIS extremists. Many Muslim intellectuals said that the Quran permitted killing terrorists in self-defense, because they had waged pre-emptive war against other Muslims, or against Christians, Jews, or people of any faith. Yet even then, if terrorists desisted from war, the Quran forbade aggression against them. Those intellectuals claimed misconceptions about Islam abounded because people learn about the faith from headline news reporting terrorist acts, rather than from the Quran and the Prophet Muhammad.

Even from Sam's own studies, like a lot of Americans, he was wary of the Islam faith. He was not as sure as Mariah regarding the peacefulness of the Muslim religion. What he did know was that any belief system was open to interpretation. The Bible and the Quran had been written many centuries in the past, making it easy to support many different arguments about their contents. All faiths had extremists among them. The missions that Sam carried out were so far on the right side of morality that it really did not matter what group was carrying out the atrocities. Evil was evil, no matter what faith or group tried to justify their actions by their beliefs. If it were a radical extremist Christian group killing innocents, then Sam would want to apply his skills to stopping them. Was it ever right to traffic humans, to kidnap and rape young children, to throw people off the roof because of their sexual orientation, to indiscriminately kill innocents? Of course not. Sam would wage war against any religion or belief that felt those actions were permissible. That was what allowed Sam to sleep well at night and continue his missions. He just sometimes needed reminding by his beautiful wife.

Chapter 29

D/NCS Royster and his team continued to gain positive notoriety within the military and intelligence communities because they were affecting real change. Sam and his team of operators were also becoming well known within the cadre of men and women who were devoting their lives to protecting the United States from enemies, both home and abroad. The general public, however, was clueless about the actions of the National Clandestine Service of the Central Intelligence Agency. These warriors are the unsung, silent, American heroes whose acts of bravery were rarely known to the rest of the world.

"It's been a helluva month, Sam," commented Marv.

"Truly. Libya is a messed up country. Hopefully our actions there will improve the situation."

Sam was referring to the struggle for power in that country. There were three main players struggling for power and rule: the U.N. supported the Government of National Accord; their opposition was a general from Muammar Gaddafi's brutal regime, and then there was ISIS. The Libyans had failed on many occasions to take out the local ISIS commander, yet Sam and his team had eliminated him in short order.

"No doubt you helped the country. Letting ISIS have a shot at leadership in Libya is not acceptable."

The success came so quickly that they then traveled to Somalia to help US interests in that country. Al-Shabab, or "the Youth," was an Islamic insurgent group based in Somalia, which worked to destabilize the Somali government. They'd also been responsible for the death of a U.S. Special Operations soldier in June 2018. In 2014, the U.S. had eliminated their leader Ahmed Abdi Godane in an air strike. The primary ongoing U.S. objective in Somalia was now to minimize the ability of al-Shabab and other violent groups to destabilize Somalia and its neighbors, and harm the United States or its allies.

Al-Shabab's continued attacks degraded the Somali government's ability to provide security and to alleviate the dire humanitarian situation in the country. This was the common thread in the countries they went to—terrorists attacked and undermined the governments of the country. The citizens of that country were always collateral damage. Al-Shabab's influence in Somalia also undermined the United States' efforts to prevent the use of Somalia as a refuge for international terrorists.

Their new leader, Omar Sadiq, had been listed by the State Department as a Specially Designated Global Terrorist, and was the target of Sam's team. He hid amongst populations of innocents when not terrorizing the government and its supporters. Because of this, a drone strike would result in significant collateral damage. Unlike terrorist groups, the U.S. did everything that it could to avoid collateral damage.

"The ISIS hit was relatively easy, Marv. It really didn't take much help from your local assets to accomplish the mission. Now taking out Sadiq in Somalia, that was tougher."

"Copy that, Sam. That action took the 'three amigos' to whole new level."

"'Three amigos?'"

"You, Kerney, and Durrant. The Director coined that after I briefed him on your success. He says you guys have reached legendary status."

"Shit, Marv, we have a long way to go for that. The real credit should go to your agents and their local assets. Without their help and distractions, we wouldn't have been able to do it in such a pinpoint fashion."

"That's very gracious of you. Anyway, those two missions by the three of you eliminated two of the top terrorists on the African continent. At least for some period of time, those two countries are better off now than they were before the 'three amigos' arrived."

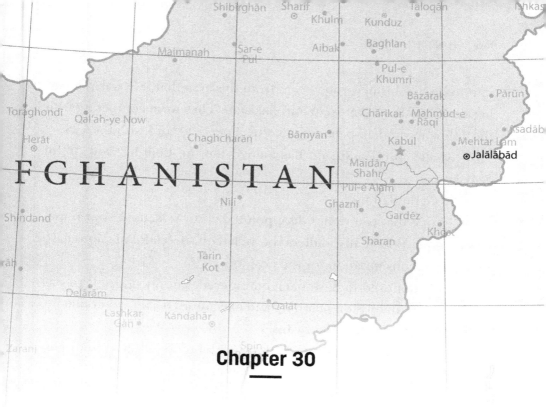

FGHANISTAN

Chapter 30

Khalid Ali had indeed made it out of Nigeria after receiving emergency medical care by surgeons loyal to Boko Haram. The treatment he received was enough to prevent him from dying, and he was then able to make it to Syria to obtain more definitive evaluation and care. He would never have full use of his left arm, but he was at least alive to continue his campaign of terror.

With the death of al-Baghdadi, there was a void at the top of the Islamic State. Many of the young fighters wanted to see Khalid ascend to that role, as he had been responsible for the planning and execution of many attacks on the West and other infidels in the local region. Al-Baghdadi's direct underlings felt that Khalid was too young and too focused on the American military as his only targets.

He had been summoned to appear at a rare meeting of the leadership in Jalalabad, the capital of Nangarhar province, adjacent to Pakistan to discuss his new role. It was from this area that ISIS was refocusing its efforts in Afghanistan and Pakistan. They were competing with the Taliban, who had been negotiating a peace accord with the U.S.

"Khalid, the leadership has named me the Caliph," said Abdul El-Bakri.

"Congratulations."

"I hope that you're not disappointed at my selection. Your popularity amongst the many soldiers you've led on successful missions gave you serious consideration for the position."

"I am honored to have been considered, but my desire is to stay directly active in mission planning and execution. It's no secret that my primary targets are the Americans."

"Sometimes we think to a fault, Khalid, but we all share your passion. My hope is that you convey your support of me to your troops, so that there is continued harmony in our ranks."

This old man was tiresome, thought Khalid. But he needed his support in order to accomplish his goals. The Caliph could provide funds, soldiers, and perhaps most importantly, the intel of the ISIS network. Their U.S.-based sources consisted of clerics, students on visas, and in some cases, Muslim-Americans sympathetic to the cause. Sure, 9/11 had made it more difficult to get into the United States, but the porous southern border of the U.S. was a nightly topic on the evening news. Khalid had developed some of his own channels into the West, but nothing like ISIS's reach. Lost in these thoughts, Khalid did not immediately respond to the man.

Al-Ameri continued, "We're elevating you to a position on the Shura Council, and you'll report directly to me. You'll be able to continue your missions as you see fit, but we'll provide broader resources."

"Excellent, Caliph. I will do as you ask."

"And I want you to know that we're actively pursuing the identity of the man who killed your brother. We've learned that he works for the CIA, and we'll continue to use our sources to uncover his identity."

"Thank you."

"Khalid, we would like you to shift your activities to Afghanistan. Do you have any thoughts?"

"Absolutely, I have many. And I'm prepared to begin," was his reply.

Khalid started his violence in Afghanistan with a renewed rage. ISIS had made their presence known in 2014, and battled the Taliban for footholds in the country. Khalid ratcheted up these clashes, attacking both the Taliban and urban centers of Afghanistan.

His soldiers established a reputation for unusual cruelty, even by the standards of the Afghan conflict. Afghanis caught in the crossfire could often only flee from the fighting with the few possessions they could carry. The Afghan Army and police force were ineffectual most of the time against these groups.

A recent orchestrated attack against a construction company had resulted in 16 deaths, including a military intelligence officer. The U.S military had been called in to assist Afghan forces during the five-hour battle. Khalid coordinated attacks on the Afghanistan military academy, killing at least 11 soldiers. He coordinated the slaughter of 48 recent Shiite high school graduates who were taking University entrance exams, simply because Shiites were considered to be heretics by the Sunni Islamic State. Similarly, Khalid coordinated an attack on a Shia mosque, killing at least 30. He was also able to send the British charity, Save the Children, back to the United Kingdom after 5 people were killed in one of his attacks. Khalid had discovered that these types of attacks were easy to execute, since the U.S. continued to withdraw troops and the Afghani army was easy to avoid and offered little resistance.

If America completely withdrew from the area, ISIS would battle the Taliban and the Afghan government for control.

However, Khalid longed to take the attack to America like bin Laden had on 9/11/2001.

Chapter 31

Sam's morning meetings with D/NCS Royster had become centered on the increasing violence in Afghanistan. Attacks on government facilities and civilian gatherings, as well as on the military, had become a daily occurrence. During the previous presidency, troop withdrawal had begun and was continuing. The current administration had continued this withdrawal, and had promised during its campaign that it wanted to end America's presence there altogether. However, the President had become frustrated with Afghanistan since taking office because of the lack of progress. The continued American "blood and treasure" lost in the ongoing conflict was unacceptable. Those frustrations peaked when a high-ranking member of the military commented that the Taliban might not be exactly winning, but they certainly weren't losing the war. The President had repeatedly threatened to close the American Embassy in Kabul as well. He felt that without a military presence, the Embassy and its staff would be in danger.

"As you may or may not know," began Royster, "the U.S. has been negotiating with the Taliban for some time. It's simply amazing to me that after running them out of the country, we're now trying to make a deal with them."

"The enemy of my enemy is my friend," replied Sam.

"Exactly. Most senior U.S. military and intelligence officials disagree that the Islamic State in Afghanistan poses a threat to the West. The military commanders say that ISIS is capable of inspiring and directing attacks in Western countries, contrary to the beliefs of many U.S. intelligence officials, who feel that ISIS is a regional issue and more of a threat to the Taliban. However, there are some of us in the intelligence community, myself included, who disagree that ISIS is only a local threat and not a threat to Western countries abroad. They continue to exhibit increasingly sophisticated military capabilities, along with a strategy of targeting civilians. So, yes, our enemy, the Taliban, who has had many skirmishes with ISIS, could be a potential partner in containing ISIS.

"I read the memo by our station chief in Kabul, who feels the recent wave of attacks by ISIS in Kabul are practice runs for attacks in Europe and the United States. He went on to say that the core of the ISIS mandate is to conduct external attacks."

"So, the Director agrees that without an aggressive, counterterrorist strategy against ISIS in Afghanistan, they'll possibly be able to carry out a large-scale attack in Europe or the US in the next year or two. We've found that ISIS fighters captured in Afghanistan have had contact with fellow militants in other countries."

Royster went on to explain on why he and the Director felt that placing too much emphasis on a relationship with the Taliban was misplaced. The Taliban viewed the Afghan government as a "puppet regime" of the West. Both the U.S. and the Taliban wanted a withdrawal of foreign forces. The Taliban had agreed to prevent Afghanistan from being used by terrorist groups; however, the definition of a 'terrorist' seemed to differ for each side. The Taliban would not start discussions with the Afghan government until they reached a deal with the U.S. The U.S. wanted an immediate cease-fire, but the Taliban wouldn't agree to one until U.S. troops were withdrawn. The U.S. wanted the protection of women's rights, and the Taliban said fine—as long as they were consistent with Islamic principles. The Taliban's Islamic principles differed from the U.S.'s interpretation, meaning that there would be fewer rights for women. Many in the U.S. government felt that the Taliban would rescind the agreement as soon as American troops were gone. A recent meeting, scheduled between the President and the Taliban at Camp David, had been canceled due to a recent bombing of a U.S. military vehicle that resulted in the death of an American soldier. Not included in these peace talks was the Islamic State.

ISIS was dug deep in the Nangarhar province of Afghanistan, a very rugged region along the border with Pakistan. U.S. forces struggled for years to hold high-altitude outposts there, before all but surrendering the region to the Taliban. They, in turn, struggled to hold the area as ISIS continued to push for control. The neighboring provinces of Nuristan, Kunar, and Lagham had also fallen to ISIS. This gave ISIS a large, remote, area to conduct training and acquire resources.

"The Director and I have convinced the President for a joint CIA-Special Ops mission in the Nandahar province. We convinced him that attacking ISIS will please the Taliban, perhaps helping with negotiations."

"Marv, you clever man," replied Sam.

"Why, thank you, Sam. This mission will be one of the largest offensives in recent years. Lately, every engagement with ISIS has either been a reaction to an attack or an attempt to try to contain them where they are. Not this time; we want to push them out."

Royster continued, "We need to go about this offensive with a very careful strategy. I think we need to have Special Forces advance from their current outposts to engage ISIS troops. Currently, they only engage in a defensive posture. I'm talking about an advance that would eliminate any fighters in the area. Any other thoughts?"

"Yes," Sam replied. "While they won't suspect the advance from below, I think that the terrain makes it easy for ISIS to respond to our ground forces."

"Okay, maybe. What's your idea?"

"We need to put some boots on the ground behind them. Not many; just a few good men to wreak havoc from their backside."

"Please, enlighten us on how you would do that."

Sam then conveyed his plan in an articulate fashion to the group sitting there. He had strong rebuttals to every question that was aimed at poking holes in his plan. After about 30 minutes of question and answer, there was silence.

"Sam, that's daring, but your defense of the plan is flawless. Let's run it by the Director."

Chapter 32

Sam would be taking a team of six hand-picked CIA operators from D.C. and would join another team of six in Jalalabad. He had his stalwart buddies, Paul Kerney and Steve Durrant, along with three former military special operators, Mike Hubbard, Sherwin Zenon, and Robert Enke.

One of the members of the team joining them in-country was a former Navy SEAL, Brad Heath, who was now a CIA operator in eastern Afghanistan. He and his other agents had a group of assets in Jalalabad, as well as in local villages that had been liberated in the 2016 offensive. ISIS had since retaken these villages, but Heath's assets remained loyal. The locals called the terrorists "Daesh" instead of ISIS, to separate them from their Muslim faith. The word had no other meaning in Arabic but was similar to the Arabic word "Daes," which meant, "one who crushes underfoot." The name had been given because ISIS soldiers did not differentiate between the elderly, the young, or women when they attacked villages. Their brand of cruelty was indiscriminate.

Several of these locals had become assets of Heath because of the cruelty displayed by the Daesh. They remembered the carnage wreaked on their villages, and were willing to do anything to eliminate the presence of these barbarians. Heath had established an excellent relationship with several villagers who continued to act as if they were sympathetic toward ISIS. By helping with supplies, these villagers often delivered items to ISIS camps. They would gather intel and, if possible, take photos of individuals who appeared to be part of the leadership. They were putting their lives on the line every time they did this, but they wanted their country back from these murderous extremists who twisted Islam to support their actions.

One of the biggest risk takers, as well as the best intelligence gatherer for Heath, was a fifty-year-old man named Dadvar Barakzai.

"*As-Salaam-Alaikum*, Bradley," said Dadvar to Heath.

"*Wa-Alaikum-Salaam*," he replied.

"There is much activity in several camps I take supplies to. Many meetings and many guards around special homes where these happen. I think something big planned. One camp seems more special than others."

"Any new faces, Dadvar?" asked Heath.

"Yes, only few, I see them in passing, but no pictures yet."

"Okay, that's great info, but don't take any chances with the pictures. Stay safe," Heath implored.

"I do, but something big going on, I go back in 4 days."

"Outstanding, Dadvar! How about you use the satellite phone when you return safely to your home after your next trip and update me? Remember, don't get caught with it. And *jazak allahabad khayran*."

This was an expression often used by Muslims meaning "things that one cannot repay a person enough."

Dadvar was moved by Heath's use of this thank-you expression. "*Afwan*, Bradley. I will call you."

Sam and his team were leaving the next day for Jalalabad to join Heath and the others. That night, he told Mariah about this mission.

"I thought ISIS had been kicked out of Afghanistan. Weren't there headlines in the *Post* saying 'ISIS Defeated?'" said Mariah.

"There were headlines like that because they were pushed back. They're like cockroaches—they scatter, but come back after you think Orkin has killed them all," was his reply.

"This mission is a lot different than any other you've told me about," Mariah commented. "It sounds more like a pure military mission than a covert CIA action."

"My, my, pretty and smart. You've learned so much over the years that I should have you listen in on our meetings via my phone," Sam said with a wink. "The problem with that is you would start shouting instructions! That would get me thrown in jail!"

"Don't be a patronizing asshole!" was her smiling response, as she lightly smacked him on the side of his head. "I'm serious. I don't like it."

She playfully tried to smack him again, but Sam avoided it and put his arms around her from behind, giving her a nice bear hug.

Standing behind her, Sam kissed her neck and said, "I agree with you. It is different, but this an extremely important mission. Just like I have you now, we want to trap those bastards."

"Oh, you think I'm trapped?" Mariah laughed, as she stomped on his foot and then elbowed his ribs as Sam was caught by surprise.

She spun around and said, "I hope you do better than that over there in Afghanistan."

Their eyes met, and then Mariah took off running down the hall with Sam in quick pursuit. They jumped on the bed laughing.

"Shhh, you'll wake Gracie," Mariah whispered.

"Me? You started it, you big bully! But I still love you!"

"And I love you." Mariah responded with a smile and a passionate kiss. Then nonchalantly she softly said, "I'm pregnant."

"Yes!" Sam yelled, then cringed.

"You dumbass!" Mariah whispered to him with a smirk.

Sure enough, the sound of Gracie's feet could be heard as she ran down the hall to her parents' bedroom. She came into the room with a look of concern.

"What's wrong? I heard Daddy scream. Are you okay?"

The look of concern on her face melted Sam's heart. Sam held his arms open, and she jumped into them for a hug with both of her parents.

"I'm sorry, sweetie. Daddy screamed because Mommy told me some happy news."

"You're going to have a baby, aren't you, Mommy?"

Sam's mouth dropped open and Mariah just laughed.

"Bingo," said Mariah.

"Yes, I knew it," responded Gracie as she hugged her mother.

"How did she know, and I didn't?" said Sam. "I've been home for a while, and I had no clue."

"Girls are smarter than boys, Daddy." Gracie winked at her Dad, although her wink consisted of quickly opening and closing both eyes.

"It's all she talks and asks me about when you're at work, Sam," was Mariah's reply. "She's so ready to have a sibling."

"I don't want a sibling, Mommy," Gracie said with furrowed brows. "I want a little brother or sister!"

Sam and Mariah laughed as they grabbed Gracie and hugged again.

Chapter 33

The team landed in Jalalabad and was met by Brad Heath and his two CIA colleagues, Charlie Edwards and Shane Fitzgerald, both former Delta Force. After introductions, they jumped into a modified Humvee and made their way to the CIA site.

"Wait for it," said Kerney.

Sam smiled while the others looked at Paul with a confused expression.

"Brad, I have an urgent question," Durrant said with a worried look on his face.

"Shoot," said Heath, waiting attentively for the question.

"How can you stand working with fake operators like these Delta guys?" Durrant's face was as serious as could be.

The four former SEALs all laughed, while the former Delta boys looked as if they were ready to slit Durrant's throat.

"He's just joshing ya," Kerney quickly said. "He really needs some new material because I have heard that like thirty times. It's a good icebreaker, though."

The expression on Edwards and Fitzgerald's faces was a "fuck you" look, and the former Delta boys remained quiet. There was an awkward silence for about thirty seconds.

"I'm sorry, did I hear you say something?" deadpanned Fitzgerald to Edwards. "I didn't know that squids could talk."

Now it was the former Deltas turn to laugh and fist bump each other.

"Hardy har har," was Durrant's reply, as he stuck his fist out for a bump from Edwards and Fitzgerald. They reciprocated fist-bumps with him, but with a little more oomph than usual.

"Okay, then, we got that out of the way," said Sam. "Now let's play nice together."

They settled into their quarters after a brief tour of the facilities, and were able to grab some food and shut-eye before their briefing by the mission commander. They were scheduled to deploy into the heart of the enemy the following evening. The Special Forces team consisting of 100 soldiers would leave as soon as it was dark. Heath's intel had revealed that several main ISIS strongholds were not that far away as the crow flies, but due to the rugged terrain, it would be an uphill climb for those troops. However, they had all done it before on normal patrols. The Special Forces troops were actually glad that this was a clear, offensive mission, not just the typical patrol of tracking the enemy, and that they would be able to take the offensive, not having to wait to be fired upon to engage the enemy. The rules of engagement would be modified; anyone walking around in the dark who was armed would be considered an enemy combatant.

The twelve-man team going behind enemy lines was in the briefing room, waiting on the commander and his staff. They came to attention as the man who had inspired Sam to join the Navy walked to the front of the room. Sam had kept track of Captain Patrick Hughes' career when he joined the Navy, but had lost sight of him over the years after he joined the CIA. D/NCS Royster had failed to mention to Sam that the mission commander was Hughes. He would have to ask him why that was when he returned.

"Gentlemen, your portion of this mission will be the most dangerous, and the most difficult, that I have ever heard of in my 18 years of service in the Special Forces," the Captain began. "I want you to know that putting you 12 men directly and immediately into harm's way was the vision of the National Clandestine Service, not the Special Forces Command. I know all of you in this room, either personally or from your service records. As you know, all of you are prior Special Forces. We have two former Air Force Tactical Air Control Party and two former Deltas as well as former SEALs on this team. You've participated in many game-changing missions during your careers, but none like this. You'll be led by one of the finest operators I've ever seen, Sam Richards. I'm sure you're all well aware of his reputation since he joined the CIA. His Naval career was just as distinguished, and the Navy lost a fine asset the day he left. Richards, I respected the reasons you had for your separation; you made the right choice on your last Navy mission to take out Kony." Those in the room looked at Sam with even more respect.

"Thank you, sir."

"By the way, was this 'behind enemy lines' thing your idea?"

"Yessir."

"Thought so. Only an operator would come up with such a brazen plan."

"Thank you… I think?"

The room chuckled.

Hughes went on. "What many of you don't know is that I'm standing here today only because of Sam's bravery when he was a college senior. Sorry, Sam, but I want them to know their leader, and I know you don't talk about yourself. You see, a bunch of college students were on a volunteer mission in a Shia-controlled region of Afghanistan, far from the violence, when a group of assholes decided to take them hostage. My boys and I were in the area, and we were tasked with rescuing them. Now, Sam, I don't think you know this, but the plan we were given by Command had come from a civilian fucktard sitting next to the President. I, like you, chose a different path, but the difference was I had a Commander who backed me. Yours should have done the same."

Even though Hughes was focusing on Sam more than Sam could hardly stand, this was a fact that he had not known. He had the deepest respect for Hughes, and now he had become aware of an instance when they both had disobeyed a direct command that they felt was idiotic. They had both made a decision based on the information they had in the field, rather than listening to someone sitting at a desk.

"Anyway, we had rescued those young Americans, a highlight for all of us on that team, when a terrorist who was hidden under a dead body was about to take me out. Sam had the wherewithal and bravery to shoot the motherfucker."

The room broke out with a smattering of "hooah," "hooyah," and "fuckin-a's."

"I had no clue. I just grabbed the gun and squeezed the trigger," Sam said. "It was just plain, dumb luck."

"In my experience, there's no such thing as luck," was Captain Hughes' reply. "Anyway, fellas, he saved my life; and me, my wife, and my children are sure glad he was there."

"Copy that, Captain, and likewise, I'm glad that your team was in the area to save us."

"Okay, gosh darn it, this fucking talk is going to make me all misty-eyed," said Hughes with a smirk. "Let's get this briefing going."

Captain Hughes relayed to them the intelligence obtained by Heath's asset, and confirmed by other sources, which indicated three main villages in the Pachir Aw Agam District were being used by ISIS for staging terrorist acts throughout eastern Afghanistan. This area included Tora Bora, a cave complex 31 miles west of the Khyber Pass and 6 miles north of the Pakistani border, just south and slightly west of Jalalabad. The Khyber Pass included the N-5 National Highway and had been important throughout the history of conflict in the region. It crossed a portion of the Spin Ghar Mountains and facilitated easier passage to and from Pakistan. Tora Bora was a complex that had been used by the Taliban and al- Qaeda. The CIA had financed an expansion of the area for the Mujahedeen when they were fighting the Soviet Union.

Hughes continued his briefing by giving the some history of the region. The area had been a hiding place for Osama bin Laden and was felt to be an impenetrable fortress. However, in December 2001, an elaborate military operation using CIA-US Special Operations Forces overtook the area, and no traces of any 'advanced fortress' were found. Instead, it was a system of small, natural caves, probably housing at most 200 fighters. The captured al-Qaeda soldiers confirmed that bin Laden had been there, but had escaped into Pakistan. In 2017, ISIS took the area from the Taliban, who then lost it to Afghan Forces. ISIS then re-acquired the area, and this was the target area for the current mission.

In the past, this area had reached by helicopters or off-road vehicles. Previous attacks had involved troops engaging any enemy they encountered, then calling in air strikes when appropriate. Two thousand troops had been used in the battle of Tora Bora with this strategy, and al-Qaeda had been pushed out. The total U.S. troop level presently in Afghanistan was around 10,000, so a force that size would not be available to use for this mission.

The goal of this mission was to have Special Forces engage combatants as they usually did on patrols, but with a slightly larger force and increased aggressiveness, making their way up the mountain to the villages occupied by ISIS. This engagement would occupy ISIS forces, while Sam and his team dropped in just behind these villages, and then engage the enemy in a guerrilla fashion from the opposite side. They were hopeful that Heath's asset would have more information regarding the identities of the new individuals that he had seen in the village during his resupply missions. It sounded as if those individuals probably represented significant ISIS leadership in the region. It would be outstanding if they could be eliminated.

Insertion of Sam's team was arguably the most dangerous part of the mission. To avoid detection, and to keep the element of surprise that would be lost by helicopter use, they would use the HALO technique for insertion—high-altitude, low-opening parachuting; essentially jumping out of an airplane with full combat gear and oxygen at 30,000 feet, reaching terminal velocity during free fall until the parachute was opened about 3,000 feet above ground level. Any mistake, such as loose equipment, the loss of one's oxygen mask, a tangled parachute deployment, was amplified with this insertion technique and could be deadly. Not to mention the risk of landing in a mountainous area. The normal injury rate with military jumps was about 10%, with about 4% being unable to continue the mission due to injury.

Sam and his troops knew the risks, but the reward of inserting behind enemy lines undetected would be huge. The threat of ISIS staging another 9/11 attack was becoming a heightened concern. If the leadership planning these potential attacks were in this area, then Sam and his group were ready to take the risk of a HALO insertion in order to eliminate those bastards.

"Godspeed and good luck, gentleman."

As nightfall and the ensuing darkness commenced, the 100 US Special Forces began their patrol and advancement toward the target area. Unlike previous patrols, this time they had air support from both the ageless B-52 and the new F-35. The old bomber was still very useful for large payload drops over appropriate areas, and the newest fighter could target via laser sighting delivered by ground forces. If that were not enough, drones were available for pinpoint strikes in order to reduce collateral damage. They were pulling no punches with this assault on ISIS. The lack of a desired number of ground forces would be bolstered by significant aerial support.

Chapter 34

Khalid was meeting with the ISIS leadership of Afghanistan to discuss continued acts of violence against the Afghan government as well as the Taliban. He was listening to Farrukh Saidov, a charismatic soldier from Tajikistan, discuss current operations. Saidov was describing ISIS expansion into neighboring provinces. He showed Khalid the areas where they had already been successful defeating the Taliban. If the Americans made peace with the Taliban, then ISIS would have a greater ability to expand in the area, becoming much more influential.

"We hope for the peace talks to succeed," stated Saidov. "That would weaken the government forces and allow us to focus more on displacing the Taliban."

"Exactly," agreed Ali. "With these successes, I would now like to focus more resources to attack the heart of the infidels in their homeland. It's been far too long since they've directly felt the pain of our Holy Jihad."

"I understand your feelings, Emir, but an attack on their home-land might change their minds about leaving this region. Surely we can afford to wait. I know that the resources are in place, but why not wait until after the Americans leave and after we acquire more villages and men here?"

"It's not a discussion, my Tajik brother. I'm here to tell you what I need from you to carry out my plans."

❈ ❈ ❈

It was Richards' and his team's turn to jump into the action. The ground troops had begun their ascent to the ISIS villages. His group was designated Alpha team for this mission. He had reports that the boots on the ground were making great progress and were about two-thirds of the way to the villages. Ground troop engagement with the enemy had been about as expected, with minimal resistance lower in the mountains. ISIS was overconfident; they felt the U.S. was no longer interested in attacking them. As a consequence, their patrol of the low-er region was sparse.

As of yet, the Special Forces had not needed any aerial support as they progressed up the mountain. Sam was pleased to hear that, because once the bombs dropped, the Special Forces would lose their element of surprise, and the ISIS fighters would realize that this was not a routine patrol.

The closer to the villages they advanced, the more intense the fighting would become. That was the intention—the Special Forces would dig in, hopefully engage large numbers of the enemy, and use air support as necessary to kill the bastards. Sam's team would then hopefully meet minimal resistance on ISIS's backside, and would be able to assassinate any leadership they encountered. His team would deliver a pinpoint blow.

They were now cruising above the Afghan mountains, enjoying the C-130 ride. The loadmaster had informed Sam that they were three minutes from target.

"All right, gentlemen, lets get locked and loaded. Check your buddy for secure gear and ensure that their O2 is good to go," said Sam. "Remember, the site we're landing is at 9,000 feet, so ensure chutes are set to deploy no lower than 12,000. That gives us a nice 18,000-foot free-fall. I'm not too proud to say that I've got a few goosebumps. It's been a while!"

"Roger that," was the response.

"Two minutes," the loadmaster said.

"I just got a report from my asset, who called in about 10 minutes ago," reported Heath to Sam. "He sent pictures of individuals from the village, and Command confirms that Khalid Ali is onsite, as well as all suspected ISIS leadership here in Afghanistan. He also estimates a total of 300 fighters in the three villages."

"Better late than never," was Durrant's reply.

"Outstanding," added Sam.

"One minute," from the loadmaster.

"Fuckin-A, let's go change the world," Kerney replied.

"Copy that. Prepare to jump on loadmaster's command. Happy hunting," said Sam.

They left the plane one by one and started their descent with speeds reaching 100 mph. Sam could not see the lead jumpers, but those he did see were looking good. He could also begin to see flashes down the mountain below his team's target. The Special Forces boys must have started to call in some air strikes on the enemy. As soon as that thought registered, a tremendous light show erupted across a large horizontal area of the mountain. This was unmistakably the result of a B-52 bombing run. Unless the drop was an "air ball," it had to have taken out a considerable number of terrorists, along with clearing a path of advancement for the good guys.

❄ ❄ ❄

About thirty seconds after hearing the bombs drop, a terrorist ran into the meeting place of the ISIS leadership.

"Farrukh, we're under attack," he screamed. "We've been engaging with American troops all night, but we thought it was just another typical patrol."

"Obviously, it's more than that," was his reply. "That was a significant bombing run. It would seem that this is a larger effort by the Americans. Probably to help their efforts for peace with the Taliban infidels. What's their number?"

"We estimate 50-75 men. We think they're all American Special Forces."

Saidov responded, "We have close to four hundred fighters. Leave about 30 here with me, and tell our leaders to engage them with the rest. Remember, the closer they are to us, the less effective the American air support becomes."

Ali spoke. "We should consider scattering our troops and reorganizing elsewhere. An air strike on us has to be imminent."

"You may flee if you want to, but I believe we'll be able to repel them. So, tell us of your plan to attack the Americans on their soil."

Chapter 34

Alpha team now had their chutes deployed and were all sequentially landing at their desired locations. Sam switched on his night-vision goggles after he began his glide, and could see hundreds of terrorist soldiers heading down the mountain to engage his brothers-in-arms. The American plan was unfolding as they had hoped—more men running down the mountain meant fewer guards left for Sam's team to engage at the top.

Sam was the last to hit the ground and saw his men already in defensive positions. He noticed two men on the ground being attended to by Edwards, a former Delta medic. One was holding his ankle, the other was holding his head. They had landed probably less than 2 kilometers from the target that intel had provided as the location where ISIS leadership were having their meeting. They were also about the same distance from the Pakistan border.

"Status?" asked Sam.

"Wilhelm has a broken ankle," replied Edwards, "and Glaser has at least a concussion, maybe a skull fracture. See the blood coming from his ear? He was the second to land; he got flipped around and landed on his head. He'd be dead, but his helmet saved his life. He was out cold for close to two minutes. Can't remember a thing."

"Damn it," Sam replied.

"I can still go," said Wilhelm. He tried to stand but immediately collapsed.

"You're a no-go." Sam smiled as he responded to Wilhelm's attempt to stand. "But I need you to hang here and protect Glaser. I don't believe there are any *hadjis* on this side of the village. We'll pass this way to get to our exfiltration site and pick you up. Stay on Comms, and shout if you need help."

"Copy that," replied Wilhelm. "I'm sorry, gentlemen."

Each man fist-bumped Wilhelm as they passed by. They knew that parachute landing injuries could occur to any of them.

"OK, let's get going. I want an advance formation. When we get a visual on the target, I want my Air Force boys to find locations on either side to lock in on targets for laser ordnance from our friends in the sky. You know the plan—call in strikes if there's a retreat by the assholes engaging our troops coming up the mountain. We won't take out the leadership group with an air strike; the rest of us will hit that and see who we can kill, and see if there's any evidence of attack plans on us or our allies."

Richards checked with Captain Hughes to give an update on his plan, as well as inform him of his two injured men. He was told that the Special Forces were "spanking" the enemy as they engaged them while pushing up the mountain.

"Alpha one, we copy and see your two team members' positions. We have an exfil chopper ready and waiting," Captain Hughes said. "You might see a whole bunch of *hadjis* running back up the mountain after these bomb runs. I recommend you expedite your assault. Hope you can get us some good intel."

"Copy that," replied Sam. "I got my Air Force boys painting the front of the mountain, ready to pinpoint laser bombs from the F-35s if the enemy comes back this way. We are set to engage."

Chapter 37

"And that's the plan," finished Khalid. "These attacks will strike at America's heart. The details have been coordinated, and most of the recruitment is completed. What I need from you, Farrukh, is some of the ordnance and cash you've acquired from your successful attacks."

Just then, another close explosion occurred. It seemed to be right outside their position. Ali could hear the advancing gun battle. He felt that this position was going to be overrun, and his intuition told him that a drone strike was imminent. Of course, he knew that this would be a blow to ISIS in Afghanistan, but his mission to strike abroad was more important to him.

"It's time. Let us escape and live to fight another day," Khalid said.

"Go, if you want. I'm sure reinforcements are on the way. I'll give you what you need for your jihad abroad, but I'm staying here to fight," was Farrukh's reply. "You how know to contact my group if I'm martyred here today."

Khalid had his men grab their weapons as he took the laptop. There was no other evidence of his plan left in the camp. As he headed toward the tunnel escape path in the back of the building, gunshots erupted throughout the house. He turned and saw the face whose image had been burned into his memory—the man who had killed his brother had entered the room. Khalid started to turn toward Sam, but one of his men pushed him into the tunnel, bringing him back to the present. Khalid and his men were on their way out, and after getting to a safe distance, they blew the tunnel so that they could not be easily followed.

"Kerney, Durrant, Heath, with me," barked Sam. "The rest of you look for any intel here. Check in with the ground force Commander to get the current location of our troops. We're heading back to Wilhelm and Glaser. I saw Khalid and a few men head out through what looked like a tunnel entrance."

Just then an explosion rocked the mountaintop right outside the house, nearly knocking the team off of their feet. There was silence; no gunfire.

"Alpha Team leader, this is ground force Commander. Your Air Force boys called in the F-35s, and you heard the result. We're heading to your position, will engage any enemy survivors. Advise your team to hold position, take out any runners, wait until we arrive."

"Copy that, Commander. Edwards, you take control here," added Sam.

As Sam and his three team members were heading out the tunnel to Wilhelm and Glaser, they quickly noticed it was impassable.

"Fuck," exclaimed Durrant.

They retraced their steps and hurried back the way they'd originally come into the building. The four of them were spread about 15 yards apart side by side, and were gracefully moving in complete harmony in pursuit of Khalid and back towards Wilhelm and Glaser.

"Alpha team, this is Wilhelm. I have six to eight tangoes coming toward my position approximately 400 meters away; say again, six to eight tangoes my way 400 meters out, advancing quickly. They look single file, so exact number hard to say. Correction, add four more, probably 400 meters behind front eight. They're spread out. Hey, please tell me that's you guys!"

"Copy that, Wilhelm," replied Sam. "We're in pursuit. We're the four you see behind the front group, probably less than two minutes behind them. Hang in there, brother. How's Glaser?"

"Awake, but clueless. He thinks he's back in training."

"Can you trust him to point his gun at the bad guys and shoot?" Sam asked. Talking and running was tough to do; just another reason special operators conditioned religiously. "If they don't see you, do not engage—repeat, only engage if they see you."

"Copy that," said Wilhelm.

Sam's group was closing the gap on the terrorists. He could detect eight tangoes, and he could now see Wilhelm's position. If the enemy continued their path, they would miss Wilhelm by about 20 meters.

"Alpha team leader," said Hughes, "we see four team members heading back to Wilhelm and Glaser. All good?"

Sam responded, "We're in pursuit of eight tangoes running toward them, heading to Pakistan. Looks like they won't see our boys if they stay on their current path. One of them is Khalid."

"Copy that," Hughes replied. "Put that bastard down!"

Immediately following those words, a cacophony of rifle fire came from the terrorists. Sam saw one his team members fall to the ground in his peripheral vision, followed by the unmistakable voice of his long-time friend, Paul Kerney. "Shit," Sam heard. At the same time, he saw the terrorists scatter like cockroaches.

"Paul, do you copy?" Sam asked as he slowed to a stop. "Status?"

"Hit in the thigh. Don't think it hit the bone, but I can't stand. Gonna put a tourniquet on."

Sam replied, "I'll be right there."

"No fucking way, Sam. I'm good. Go get those assholes."

Durrant, Paul's best friend, chimed in, "Sam, if PK says he's good, he's good."

"Copy that, you tough bastard. I'll get Edwards to you ASAP."

The rest of Sam's team, who were waiting at the building for the Special Forces soldiers, had heard all of Sam's transmissions. There had been a few terrorists running back up the mountain after the bomb run, but none in the last two minutes. After talking with the ground force commander over his Comms, Edwards felt comfortable leaving one man to meet the Special Forces on their way up the mountain, while the others high-tailed it to help Sam and the others.

Sam, Durrant, and Heath were now returning fire at the fleeing terrorists. The enemy had chosen to scatter, but the Americans' training and technology gave them the advantage. Heath and Durrant had each taken down one bad guy. Sam could see three more running together, only two carrying rifles and returning fire at his team. The third guy had to be Khalid; he appeared to have a bad arm.

"Heath, head towards Wilhelm and Glaser—they have tangoes heading their way. Durrant and I are heading toward that group of three running toward Pakistan."

"Roger that," was his reply.

As Heath was converging on Wilhelm and Glaser, he saw his two wounded colleagues engage the three terrorists heading their way.

Heath was behind the terrorists, so he had to be careful to not become stuck in a crossfire with Wilhelm and Glaser. He also could see that one of the two was firing without much purpose. That had to be poor Glaser. Wilhelm picked off one of the terrorists right before the enemy could take cover behind some rocks just 10 meters away from them. Heath was advancing, and saw a place to take refuge. Unfortunately, the two remaining terrorists both sent a volley of gunfire towards him, and he felt a crushing sensation in his chest as he was thrown off his feet. Wilhelm had seen the whole exchange. He glanced over at Glaser, whose eyes were closed; he was either dead or out cold again. Wilhelm was improving his position, raised to shoot, and saw one of the terrorists three meters away. Wilhelm saw the terrorist fall from his chest shot, at the same time he felt a hot, burning sensation in his right shoulder. The gunshot to his arm spun him around onto his back. He was staring at the terrorist who'd shot him, just a few feet away. The terrorist quickly glanced at Glaser, saw that he was no threat, and returned his gaze on Wilhelm.

"*Allahu akbar*, infidel pig," he said as he raised his rifle.

With his weapon out of reach and one arm useless, Wilhelm raised the middle finger of his left hand and yelled, "Fuck you, asshole!"

The terrorist smiled, but then the side of his head disappeared. Wilhelm looked over at Glaser, who was calmly blowing the smoke from the barrel of his handgun, like you might see in a cowboy movie, and he had a big grin on his face.

"Bye, bye, motherfucker," he said. He then looked over at Wilhelm and said, "This ain't no training mission, but I'll be damned if I know where the hell I am!"

Glaser crawled over to Wilhelm and put his head down beside him.

"Don't shoot, it's Heath," Brad said as he came around the rocks.

Heath saw his brothers and quickly assessed Wilhelm's shoulder.

"Body armor saved my ass," Heath said.

Pointing at Glaser, Wilhelm said, "My man woke up just in time to smoke that guy, or I was gone. But don't tell him," he said with a wink. "He won't remember a thing. I don't need him holding that over my head."

They both chuckled as Heath bandaged Wilhelm's shoulder.

Richards and Durrant were in hot pursuit of Khalid and his two guards. It was clear they were running for Pakistan, and they were very near.

"Alpha leader, I show that you're very close to the border," relayed Captain Hughes. "We've got an F-35 in the area who sees you as well. The pilot says that he could vaporize the three ahead of you."

"Negative," replied Sam. "We want a chance to capture and interrogate."

"Copy that," responded Hughes, "but it'll get dicey if they reach the border. The law and diplomacy both get a whole lot murkier at that point."

Captain Hughes was referring to the complicated relationship between the U.S. and Pakistan. During his tenure in the military, Hughes had seen Pakistan both bring some benefits as well as throw up some obstacles to U.S. interests in the region. The convoluted relationship was in the forefront of Hughes's mind as Sam chased Khalid to the border.

Chapter 38

Richards and Durrant were closing the gap on Khalid. Durrant had managed to take out one guard. Sam, in turn, had put a bullet in Khalid's torso area, but instead of taking Khalid down, the bullet appeared to hit whatever he had been carrying. Khalid hesitated and tried to pick the object off the ground with his one good arm, but his guard pulled him away.

As they approached the Pakistani border, the two CIA agents ran into a significant pocket of resistance. There were more terrorists at the border waiting for Khalid. Sam looked closely at the individuals firing at him. These were not raggedly dressed terrorists; they were wearing Pakistani Army uniforms. Surely, there couldn't be Pakistani troops out here supporting Khalid and ISIS! But whoever they were, they had Sam and Steve pinned down, and their only option was to take cover behind rocks. They were now on the defensive.

"Alpha leader, I'm heading your way with four other team members. Status," said Edwards.

"We've got at least 15 tangoes pinning us down. We've crossed the border into Pakistan. We could use some help," replied Sam. "Mission Commander, these guys are wearing regular Pakistani Army uniforms. That can't be for real, can it? I was going to ask for air support to take them out."

"Say again, Alpha leader?" replied a puzzled Hughes.

He then yelled for two of his staff to get D/NCS Royster on the phone, as well as their Pakistani Army liaison, who had been made aware that there would be a U.S. mission on the border, but not when or where. Sam repeated what he had said to his commander. "Standby," was Hughes' response.

"Roger that, but please expedite. Reinforcements in the same uniforms have arrived," Sam responded. "Every minute we waste, Khalid gets farther from us."

The rules of engagement for this mission had predicted this scenario might occur, and had allowed for incursion by U.S. ground forces into Pakistan, but prior approval for a missile strike in Pakistan had not been predicted. Possible Pakistani Army troops helping Khalid had not been part of their mission planning. Pakistan had been more cooperative since the President had threatened to stop financial aid, but allowing a missile strike into their country as part of a U.S. counterterrorist operation would test their cooperation.

Drone strikes into that area of Pakistan had started under George W. Bush and continued under subsequent administrations. However, the current President had become more aggressive in his strategy, ramping up strikes there and across the Middle East, so there was significant precedent for using a drone missile strike. However, the F-35s supporting this mission were not drones.

ANONYMOUS HEROES | **189**

Captain Hughes felt that by extrapolation, using the F-35 would be acceptable to his superiors. One plane was deployed in stealth mode, with four air-to-air missiles to protect the other fighter, which was deployed in beast mode, sacrificing stealth for more armament-carrying capacity, namely 22,000 pounds of ordnance. That amount would deliver a significant blow to whoever was on the receiving end. Hughes felt that the troops Sam was engaging had to be terrorists dressed as Pakistani Army, but this was not a tactic by ISIS that had been encountered before, so he had to be sure.

As Hughes was waiting, his ground Commander reported that they had overrun all resistance and could continue toward Pakistan to support Sam's team. Richards reported that Edwards and company had joined him, helping their situation significantly. American troops in Pakistan had rarely occurred. In 2010, the U.S. had about 200 troops in Pakistan, but eventually withdrew those forces. SEAL Team Six had gone into Pakistan to take out bin Laden without the knowledge of the Pakistani government, but a group of 100 troops pursuing ISIS terrorists into Pakistan would be a lot different than that. The Pakistanis would probably be upset about such a large ground force entering their country, but Hughes really didn't care. He gave the go-ahead for the Special Forces troops to join Sam and hold position with him. They would dig in defensively until he could get some clarification about the possibility of Pakistani Army personnel engaging Richards and his team.

The Pakistani Army liaison was of little help. He told Hughes that there were regular Pakistani army troops at locations along the massive border with Afghanistan, working along with the ISI (Pakistani intelligence), battling insurgents. The liaison said he just didn't know where those troops were located, and Hughes could not believe his ears. He asked the army officer to hold, as Deputy Director Royster was now available. Royster had been getting updates of the mission through Hughes' staff, as well as by satellite imaging.

"Looks like things are going well, Captain," said Royster.

"They have so far, but we have a potential problem," replied Hughes.

He then explained the situation to Royster as well as the Pakistani Army liaison's response to his inquiry.

"That's bullshit," responded Royster. "I know where all of my assets are located at all times. Let me try my ISI contact. I understand the situation is fluid and won't waste any time. Give me five minutes, tops."

Hughes passed this on to Richards and the Special Forces commander.

"Sir, with all due respect, if these are Pakistani soldiers, then they're aiding and abetting terrorists," replied Sam. "That makes them enemy combatants, and we should push through. Although personally, I think they're imposters."

"I agree," was Hughes response, "but Royster needs to make that call before I unleash the bombs and send you boys in. This is a CIA mission. If I haven't heard from him in five minutes, I'll make a decision. I won't leave you hanging. "

Royster called back within two minutes and was beside himself. He had obtained neither a denial nor a confirmation from his ISI counterpart. The ISI had told Royster that the CIA didn't exchange information with the ISI willingly, so they would reciprocate and not share their information.

"What an idiot," said Royster. "I asked him if he understood what could happen, and he was just silent. There's no way those guys are regular army, and there's no way that Pakistan wants to goad us into war. Therefore, Captain Hughes, do what you need to do to catch that Khalid bastard."

"Yes, sir. I take it you are looking at the satellite?" said Hughes.

"You're talking about the influx of more enemy troops?" replied Royster.

"Exactly," was Hughes' response.

By satellite, there now appeared to be close to 400 troops amassed along the area, heading toward the Americans.

"I think that's more proof they're imposters. That, plus our Pakistani counterparts have no friggin' clue. I recommend that you go big in your response, Captain."

"Aye, aye," responded the Navy Captain.

"Tell your troops to hunker down, Sam. Your forward position is about to get lit up," Hughes relayed.

Sam passed the info through his Comms to the rest of his team. By now, Khalid had been running for ten minutes. Was that enough of a head start to escape the bombing about to take place? A line of six explosions interrupted Sam's thoughts as the GBU-31 bombs found their targets. Having a heads-up about the attack, the U.S. troops were able to protect their ears. After the bombs were dropped, the gunfire had stopped, except from the few terrorists who were directly in front of them who had been in that safe zone from the U.S. bombs. The Special Forces unit dispatched them to "paradise," and then the area was eerily quiet. Sam ran to the object Khalid had dropped and discovered that it was a laptop. Unfortunately, there was a large bullet hole where Sam had hit it when Khalid had been holding it against his chest.

The Special Forces advanced, securing the area, taking pictures of any faces that were left, and looking for any useful intelligence. The front group of terrorists was wearing Pakistani Army uniforms. As Sam and his team advanced, it was evident that the soldiers not vaporized by the bombs looked like any other terrorist. So, as expected, the uniforms had been a ruse. He looked at every face, hoping to find Khalid, but he was not seeing him amongst the dead, and there were far too many human remains to take for DNA analysis. Unfortunately, Khalid had either been vaporized or his body was unrecognizable; neither outcome generated a gratifying sensation for Sam. And then there was a third possibility: that he had managed to escape the bombing. Sam wanted conclusive evidence, but it just wasn't possible. Overall, the mission had been successful, and a lot of bad guys had been eliminated. The mission had been well worth it.

Chapter 39

The first mission debriefing occurred in Jalalabad with Captain Hughes. A replay of the mission was reviewed, and as always, lessons to be learned were extrapolated and discussed. Sam likened this process to watching game films after lacrosse games in high school with coaches and teammates. After they completed the routine elements of the debriefing, Hughes excused the rest of Sam's team so that the two of them could discuss something in private.

"I want to give you a heads-up that Royster and I are getting some shit about our decisions," stated Hughes. "Apparently, the House Intelligence Committee is up in arms over our bombing and entry into Pakistan. It's basically a political issue now. Some House Committee members are pissed about the President's current drone war, his suspension of drone reports, the color of his tie, his hairstyle, yadda, yadda, yadda. I've dealt with political prima donnas a long time now, but with this

President in the White House, the relationship between the two parties is more hateful and juvenile than I have ever seen."

"I don't get it, Captain. They knew of the mission, they knew the importance of finding Khalid Ali and any possible indications for plans of terrorist acts on our homeland. What did they think would happen—we would waltz up the fucking mountain and they would just hand over stuff?"

"I get it, Sam," replied Hughes. "You know the constraints that were placed on you as a SEAL. They're much tighter now than when I was an operator. That's why I enjoy these joint missions with the CIA; there are fewer constraints. However, when the military is involved, there's more oversight than if it's solely a CIA mission. Marv Royster tells me this has been happening constantly since the current administration took over the White House. Marv sarcastically tells the Committee to 'keep his seat warm' after he finishes a session, because he knows he'll be back time and time again. However, he did say that this time it feels different. He wants you to call him on the way back. And Sam, you executed a flawless mission, put ISIS on the run from Afghanistan, and gathered much needed intel. Helluva job!"

"Copy that, and thanks, Captain Hughes," Sam said.

"Brother, you earned the right to call me Pat a long time ago. Remember, the only easy day was yesterday."

"Hooyah," replied Sam.

❊ ❊ ❊

Sam and his team always enjoyed the Gulfstream 550 flights to and from some of their missions. It sure did have better seats than the military transport planes. It was also usually stocked with an assortment of beer and bourbon. Sam spent about an hour on the phone with D/NCS Royster on his return flight. Marv recounted to him what Hughes had already passed on, but with more specifics. Both the Senate and the House Intelligence Committees had been formed to "provide vigilant oversight over the intelligence activities of the United States, to assure that such activities are in conformity with the Constitution and laws of the United States."

Sam didn't need a civics lesson, he thought, as he continued to listen to Royster. Every CIA agent knew the role of Congress in providing oversight. Royster told Sam that he had met separately with the House and Senate Chairs. Both expressed significant concern with the recent operation, however, and the House Chair had demanded a joint hearing to discuss the mission and it was scheduled to commence in two days. Sam had been listening to Royster, but only half-heartedly as he fought not to daydream.

He came to full attention when he heard Royster say, "Captain Hughes' and your presence are required at the hearing."

"Say what?" Sam spontaneously replied. "You've got to be shitting me."

"Afraid not," Marv responded. "Its unusual, but not unprecedented to call an operator in front of the committee. When they do, the party who's pissed will try to fluster and embarrass the individual. I want you prepared, so we should meet the morning of, and I'll give you some tips. This circus is routine for me."

Sam replied, "That's what Hughes said. But he also said you thought this occasion seemed different."

"It is different. Calling home a commander in the field and the lead operator on the ground is something I've not seen in my time here. But I'm not surprised, as the country has become so split down party lines for far too long The current President has made the divide as bad as it's ever been. The opposition can't believe he won, so they do nothing but obstruct any of his ideas. Even his own party can't believe he won; they mostly like his ideas, but would like to blow up his Twitter account. But something about him appealed to voters, and so here we are. As far as I'm concerned, he's allowed the CIA to do a ton of stuff to help U.S. interests that the public doesn't know about."

"Yeah, I voted for him because he was different. I support most of his ideas, but I gotta say, I cringe when he tweets. He could be more popular with 'using a little honey,'" Sam said. "He's definitely not a politician, he's a rich businessman used to getting whatever he wants and acts out when he doesn't.

"I would agree with that assessment. He's so polarizing, people either seem to love him or hate him. Anyway, the day after tomorrow, my office, 8 a.m. If nothing else, Sam, you're in for a real eye opener and an education! It really is a swamp here in D.C., and you'll want to take a shower soon after you sit down before the committee, because the atmosphere is filthy."

"I can't fucking wait," Sam said sarcastically.

Chapter 40

One of the sure things in Sam's life was knowing that his beautiful wife would be waiting for him at the airport when he returned from a mission. Even when he was a SEAL, she would make her way to the base with the other wives or girlfriends of the team members in time for their arrival. As a SEAL, he would break the rules and contact her on the satellite phone as they were heading home; he had always thought it was a stupid rule. Wives and girlfriends always knew when their men were leaving; why not their return? It was the duration of the mission that was the unknown. The rules were less strict in the CIA. When he was in a CIA office abroad, or similar area while on a mission, communication was possible with Mariah. This allowed wives to have a heads up from their husbands regarding their status, so Paul Kerney, Robert Glaser, and David Wilhelm had been able to tell their significant others about their injuries.

Kerney had a through and through gunshot wound of his thigh that was debrided in Jalalabad by an American surgeon working for the CIA. Glaser did indeed have a nondisplaced skull fracture, and the surgeon in Jalalabad had facilitated a video consultation with a neurosurgeon in the U.S. to assist in treatment. Glaser had actually recovered significantly in the last 24 hours, but he had no memory of saving Wilhelm's life. Wilhelm was still pissed at Brad Heath for telling Glaser the details. Glaser was going around telling everyone that he was a badass even when he was concussed. And poor Wilhelm—he needed surgery for his ankle along with his right humerus, which had been fractured by the gunshot. Glaser insisted that he push Wilhelm in his wheelchair when he reached the tarmac, even though his head was pounding. He told Wilhelm that they now had a special, mystical bond since he had saved his life. Wilhelm responded by telling Glaser he must still be mentally fucked up from his concussion. Glaser, Kerney, and Wilhelm would be going straight to the hospital for further treatment.

It was always a special feeling to see warriors return to their loved ones, thought D/NCS Royster as he watched the hugs and kisses of lovers and families reunited. These anonymous heroes took so much risk in order to protect their country from those dead-set on her destruction. Their recognition was limited to those in the intelligence committee with a high enough security clearance to know of their accomplishments. Of course, there are many men and women who take risks in service of their country in order to allow its citizens to keep the freedoms that they often take for granted. Royster wished that the political buffoons from the Intelligence Committee whom they would be spending most of tomorrow with could also see this reunion. It might humanize the job that these warriors performed for their country. As the group appeared to be moving away from the plane, Royster went over to them. He usually didn't show up on the tarmac when a team returned.

"Congratulations on a job well done, gentlemen. Your country owes you a great debt of honor," he said.

The group stopped, surprised to see their boss meeting them.

"The honor is all ours, sir," replied Sam. "Thanks for your confidence in us and supporting us to do the job... and thanks for coming to meet us."

The group echoed those sentiments, and Sam noticed his boss tilt his head, giving a signal to Sam that he wanted to talk alone.

"Excuse me for a minute, babe," Sam said to Mariah.

He joined his boss off to the side, and Royster gave Sam an update regarding tomorrow's hearing before the Congressional committee.

"One of the aides to the Senate Chair gave me a heads-up about tomorrow. He says some members of Congress are on the warpath, especially after Pakistan filed a complaint with the United Nations. That complaint isn't unexpected, of course. I brought you a little reading material before we meet tomorrow at 8 am. Don't sweat it; the truth will prevail. See you then, Sam," Royster said, who then shook Sam's hand and left.

His team knew that Sam had this meeting tomorrow, and Durrant had suggested they all escort Sam to the room with their full battle gear on, as if on a mission. Sam had laughed and said he'd be fine, but had to admit he was more worried about this hearing than he was before any mission. He just didn't want to say anything stupid or let his emotions get the best of him. The group gave each other hugs and said their goodbyes.

※ ※ ※

Gracie, Mariah, and Sam spent the afternoon playing in the back yard, enjoying the swing set, and throwing the ball to their black Lab, Bella. Sheesh, Sam thought, even the dog is a girl. He didn't really care if their next child were a boy or a girl; a healthy child was all that mattered. However, Sam chuckled to himself as he thought that it would be nice if they could have another male presence in the house.

He and Mariah put Gracie down for her nap, and then they had some alone time. Sam was so relaxed, and was always amazed how he could easily transition back into this sweet, sweet life when he returned home. Mariah was his soul mate, and she alone was the reason for this phenomenon. It had started with the trip as students, and had only grown stronger and stronger. It was as if she had a direct line of communication with God, and knew that Sam would be safe on his missions. She was always so optimistic. He always joked that he would have to be concerned the first time she displayed any worry before a mission. The rest of the evening was perfect—playing with Gracie while Mariah made dinner, later a bath and a bedtime story, and then time with Mariah.

Sam told Mariah about the mission, how his buddies had sustained their injuries, even Glaser's crazy response after he had saved Wilhelm's life. He talked about seeing Khalid, and his ability to slip away once again. He voiced his frustration about having to wait on approval to engage the terrorists in Pakistan. Because of that delay, Khalid could still be alive. He told her that tomorrow's hearing would probably focus primarily on the issue of entering Pakistan, and, he had to admit, that he was nervous about testifying.

"They'll dissect the entire op," said Sam, "and because they have no clue about battlefield decisions, their perspective will have no basis in reality."

"Sam, I know it's a cliché, but just be yourself," she offered. "If you relate your experience in a calm, soft manner, I think you'll impress the hell out of them. Many politicians have a misconception that soldiers are robots and killers. I think it's an opportunity for you to show them some reality."

"Hmm, I never thought of it that way, babe."

"Well, as Gracie says, that's because girls are smarter than boys," said Mariah, as she winked with both her eyes, exactly like their daughter winked.

"Ouch, damn. That's funny, because I was thinking earlier when we were in the backyard that even my sweet dog is a girl. I need another penis around here to help me out!"

"Well, I had an ultrasound last week, if you want to see it," Mariah said with a smile.

"Sure. It can't be any harder to understand than infrared imaging or satellite pictures," Sam joked.

"Here you go, big boy," Mariah responded.

Sam opened the scan and exclaimed, "Holy shit, our kid's got three legs!"

Mariah was belly laughing. "Yo genius, that's his penis!"

Sam was laughing as well and replied, "Wow, I will not be taking showers with him. Talk about feeling inadequate. Wait—are you sure I'm the father?"

Mariah playfully smacked his shoulder and said, "You asshole!"

Sam grabbed her and rolled her so they were both on their sides, face to face. "Such a naughty mouth," he said to her.

She slipped her hand down his pants and felt his excitement. "If you think this is inadequate, than woe to the girl who meets our son."

"Mariah, that's terrible," Sam said with a chuckle. "Who knows? Maybe he'll grow into it."

"Maybe," was her response, right before she took him into her mouth.

Chapter 41

Sam was punctual as usual, arriving at Royster's office promptly at 8 am. The two of them reviewed the mission again for the umpteenth time, focusing on the decisions that had been made and on the results.

Marv had some new information to share with Sam—a small amount of intelligence had been recovered from the laptop that Khalid had dropped. The bullet had caused significant internal damage to the hard drive, but experts at the CIA had gleaned some intel from the recovered files. It was clear that Khalid Ali had plans to strike the United States. The files showed more than wishful thinking; there were enough specifics to conclude that ISIS had probably already set something in motion.

Joining Marv and Sam for the pre-hearing meeting was Captain Patrick Hughes, and the CIA Director, Robert "Buck" Ritchie. Director Ritchie had handpicked Royster for the NCS directorship, and was to date well pleased with his performance. Royster, Hughes, and Richards had the Director's full support.

Hughes shared the final mission statistics with them: over 700 terrorists dead, 23 killed civilian villagers, 12 liberated villages, and the Afghani Army now in control of the regained territories. The majority of the civilians killed had died at the hands of ISIS. The few that had been killed by U.S. Special Forces had been used as human shields by ISIS soldiers. There had been no civilian casualties resulting from the American bombing, a tremendous feat considering the amount of munitions used.

The Pakistan government denied any involvement with ISIS and was embarrassed that the conversations during the mission with the Army and Intelligence liaisons had been unhelpful and caused a delay for advancing US troops. If Khalid had escaped, that delay had given him the necessary time. Both the Director and Royster tended to believe Pakistan's sincerity, as they had become more cooperative since the President had reduced American aid. Pakistan wanted that money back, and any involvement with ISIS would be the end to any effort to regain any U.S. dollars.

"Gentlemen, the facts are on our side, the results are on our side, and the President is on our side," stated Director Ritchie. "However, that don't mean shit in these hearings. The politicians will try to spin the facts to their beliefs, losing the truth. I was just informed before this meeting that the *Washington Post* is planning a story about this mission. We know that it was leaked by the office of a House Representative, but we haven't pinned down the source. I'm sure the House Chair orchestrated this whole thing—called for a hearing, then leaked the mission to the press. We'll see what the article says, and perhaps respond to it with our own article, including the true statistics. I have no problem with telling the American public that over 700 ISIS soldiers were killed.

This hearing will be a shit show no matter what, and we'll get covered by some of the splatter, but we'll survive."

Royster shared the Director's enthusiasm, but Hughes and Richards were both a little unsettled. This was way out of their comfort zone. Taking down bad guys was easy—make a plan, then execute it. Of course, unforeseen events always occurred, but experience allowed for appropriate adjustments. One of Sam's favorite instructors had always said that "a mission plan is often a list of things that won't happen, so always be ready to improvise."

Testifying before the Senate was uncharted territory. They were reminded by Royster to remain calm, answer the questions as they came, and tell the truth. The truth was on their side. He told both Hughes and Richards that there would be showmanship and grandstanding by the politicians, and to remember that they were smarter than most of them. Royster told both men that he had a theory about politicians that might help them during their questioning.

"I've met a lot of politicians over the years at various functions. I always make it a point to ask about their background, mainly their middle and high school years. I quickly observed that most of them were far from being the 'cool kids' growing up. Most of them have spent a lifetime compensating for that."

Both Hughes and Richards laughed.

"Okay, boys, time to play ball," Royster said. "No worries!"

They made their way to the Capitol building and were escorted to the closed-door location of the hearing. They entered the building through an underground entrance that provided anonymity when entering. They were escorted to the meeting room, and Sam was surprised at the number of people present. The House and Senate Intelligence committees accounted for nearly 40 people. But the total number of people in the room was easily close to 50, and Sam wondered how the contents of any hearing could be kept secret. No wonder there were always leaks to the press. There was an elevated desk at the front of the room, similar to that for a judge, but this desk had six seats. Sam saw the name tags in front of each chair. The Senate Chair and House Chair were seated in the middle. Flanking each Chair were two Congressmen of the same party that each had chosen, giving three Democrats and three Republicans.

The three men who had been called to testify made their way to the front, and D/NCS Royster sat between Hughes and Richards. Seated behind them in the audience were the other members of the committee. Of course, they were sitting in a way split exactly down party lines, with no mingling between the two political parties. Sam's stomach was in knots despite Royster leaning over to him and telling him that he looked calm and collected. At least his outward appearance did not reveal his inward emotions.

The six interrogators walked in and took their seats. Since the House Chair had called the hearing, he would be directing the event. He introduced the members in front and thanked Royster, Hughes, and Richards for coming; as if they had a choice, thought Sam. The House Chair, Representative Adam Smith, told them that he suspected the hearing would take the rest of the day and probably most of the next morning. He would have members from the Senate Chair's party ask questions first, followed by members of his own party whom he had chosen. Smith assured them that this was a closed hearing, and that their testimonies would be anonymous.

The Senate Chairman, Senator Richard Bates, began by thanking the trio for their service and asked questions that were simple and straightforward. The questions were essentially "chip shots" that were easy to answer. His line of questioning essentially took each of the three through their job description and duties. Following his questions, Senator Roy Sharp's questions allowed a walk-through of the mission from each of them. Again, very easy, thought Sam. Finally, Senator Marco Rodriguez asked questions that enabled the specific facts of the mission to be elucidated.

"So, about 110 US soldiers were able to kill over 700 ISIS soldiers, Mr. Richards?," Rodriguez asked.

"Yes sir, that is correct. But with the help of air strikes by our colleagues in the sky," was Sam's reply.

"I get that they helped, but was their accuracy dependent on your team being in position to locate those targets to ensure greater accuracy to minimize collateral damage?"

"Yes, sir," Sam answered. "And Captain Hughes' men confirmed that no civilians were killed during the air strikes."

Rodriguez then asked Director Royster and Captain Hughes questions about their phone calls made to their counterparts during the battle regarding information about the presence of Pakistani Army troops. He asked their opinion regarding the effect of the delay on the ability to capture or kill Khalid Ali, as well as their decision to go ahead and call in air strikes without definitive proof that those were not Pakistani soldiers. Each, in turn, gave his answer supporting their decision to bomb the hell out of them. They both stated that the delay had prevented the possible capture of Khalid Ali.

More importantly, Rodriguez asked about the intel obtained as a result of their efforts.

"Director Royster, can you summarize the intelligence obtained from this mission."

Royster replied, "We obtained a laptop Ali dropped while fleeing from Sam and his men. It was severely damaged, but our computer experts were able to obtain enough evidence to show that ISIS is well underway to strike the American homeland, on a scale like 9/11. Recovered data doesn't give us the where and when, but there are enough significant details to leave no doubt that Khalid is on his way here. The acquisition of that intelligence alone is a great win; the loss of 700 ISIS soldiers obtaining it was icing on the cake. We're continuing to work on the laptop for more specifics about their plans."

Rodriguez informed the Chairman that he was finished with his questions. Chairman Smith called for a short recess in the proceedings, as it was nearing 4 p.m.

Director Ritchie met his men outside the room and they sat in a conference room to talk. "OK, gentleman, you hit those change-up pitches out of the park, but now the heat is about to come," he commented. "Buckle up, stay calm, and don't let these political pricks get under your skin."

Royster was well aware that some in the room would be nasty and sarcastic. The divisiveness between the political parties seemed to be at an all-time high. Royster's previous testimony experience had shown the extensiveness of this division, and he knew how to handle it, but he was a little worried about how the two men sitting with him would respond to the vitriol. Hughes was a former operator who had no time for bullshit. Richards was perhaps the best Tier 1 operator this country currently had, maybe of all time, who might just let his emotions get the best of him. Their reaction to the next barrage of questions worried Royster as they took their seats.

Chairman Smith brought the hearing to order and had Rep. Joaquin Castillo begin his questioning. He started with Captain Hughes, asking questions regarding mission planning. Hughes answered his questions without any emotion in a slow, steady voice. This was difficult, as the Congressman questioned Hughes' competence throughout the mission. Through it all, the Navy SEAL Captain was calm and collected. Royster was impressed.

Castillo then turned his focus on Sam. "It seems, Mr. Richards, that you have been chasing Khalid Ali ever since you killed his brother."

There was silence. Sam stared at the Congressman with cold, focused eyes.

"I'm waiting," said Castillo.

"I didn't hear a question, just a statement," was Sam's reply.

"Don't be insolent. You know what I meant."

"Again, that's not a question, but I will say that circumstances have made our paths cross. I have no personal issue with anyone I pursue other than to eliminate them for the injustices they cause and to protect this country."

"Yes, we all acknowledge your service and the risks that you take, but couldn't a personal vendetta against someone lead to poor judgment on your part?"

Sam replied, "Once again, I have no personal vendetta against Khalid. Perhaps he does against me. But, in general, I would agree that making things personal could lead to mistakes. If you're accusing me of poor judgment on this mission, please point it out."

"Okay, since you asked—how about following Khalid into Pakistan with only one other man by your side, resulting in the two of you being pinned down by overwhelming forces?"

"My colleague and I were chasing three men, and only two were returning fire. We managed to improve those odds, and had it not been for Khalid holding the laptop across his chest, he'd be dead from my rifle shot. When we pursued them into Pakistan, we were indeed met by about 12-15 troops in Pakistani Army uniforms. We had men who were on their way to join us, so we held our position. We did not meet 'overwhelming' resistance."

The Congressman didn't let up, "15 to 2 is not overwhelming? I think it shows poor judgment and arrogance."

Royster tensed his muscles at this exchange. He sensed Hughes to his right, clearing his throat as if about to speak, and the D/NCS yanked Hughes' uniform jacket below table level to stop him.

"Confidence is different from arrogance, Congressman. I have the former. In the heat of battle, one has to make decisions on a split-second basis. I would do it again exactly the same way, as I think that my judgment was sound. An example of bad judgment might be something like tweeting the names of our Presidents' financial donors and their places of employment, potentially endangering a person just because they're practicing one of their democratic rights to vote the way they want. A right that I and others fight to defend."

Sam was referring to a tweet that Castillo had recently made. Even many members of his own party felt his tweet crossed the line and made for a bad precedent. The room was electric; murmurings and laughter abounded.

"You arrogant prick," replied Castillo.

Royster leapt to his feet shouting, "Out of order! The Congressman is out of order."

"Sit down, Mr. Royster," shouted Chairman Smith.

"He has no right to speak that way to Mr. Richards," Royster went on. "The three of us will walk out of here if the name-calling continues."

"Please sit down," was Smith's sarcastic reply.

Royster sat down, but was still screaming at Castillo and Smith about how the hearing was total bullshit. Richards and Hughes maintained their same posture throughout the exchange, the two of them placing their steely gaze squarely on Castillo. The Congressman saw their look and was clearly unsettled. It was like they were committing his face to memory. Chairman Smith restored order, and asked Congressman Castillo if he had any other questions.

"No," he replied shakily. He avoided looking at the three men sitting in front of him.

"Senator Harrison, you have the floor," Smith announced.

More of the same ensued. The Senator tried to trip up Hughes and Royster but was unable to elicit any reaction from them with her questions and barbs. She then turned her attention to Sam. She started off with praise, thanking him for his service.

"Mr. Richards, what would you have done if you caught Khalid?"

"The same thing we do when we capture any enemy combatant. I would have interrogated him."

"Right there, on the mountain?" she asked. "Is that usually productive?"

"It can be," replied Sam. "Often the shock and fear of being captured loosens the tongue of a combatant."

"Would you have tortured him?"

"I would have intensely questioned him."

"That sounds like you are implying torture, Mr. Richards," replied the Senator.

Sam wanted tear into the Senator, but contained himself and showed no change in his appearance.

"Information is crucial, especially in the heat of battle," he said. "We had been informed that 400 ISIS soldiers had gathered. If I'd captured him, I would have obtained information from him any way I could, short of killing him."

"Torture was abolished in 2006, by President Bush, Mr. Richards."

"You're correct, Senator, he did indeed. But that was torture performed by the U.S. military. I work for the Central Intelligence Agency. But to your point, ma'am, as I trust you to do your job, you'll have to trust me when I tell you that my techniques do not meet the definition of torture."

More laughter and murmuring occurred. Royster and Hughes exchanged smiles.

"Order," screamed Smith.

Senator Harrison would not let up. "Maybe I don't understand your definition of torture, Mr. Richards. Please, enlighten me."

"The definition is broad. A legal definition calls torture 'any act by which severe pain or suffering, physical or mental, is intentionally inflicted on a person for information.' An example of physical torture would be water-boarding. Today's hearing might be an example of mental torture."

Again, the room exploded with shouts and laughter. Senator Smith was not amused with Sam, but Senator Harrison was actually smiling.

"Continue, Senator," said Smith.

"Just one more question, Chairman. Mr. Richards, do you think it was necessary for Director Royster and Captain Hughes to call their counterparts regarding the Pakistani Army uniforms before the bombing?"

"I don't think that my opinion matters, as it was not my call to make. It's a tough call. If those guys were Pakistani Army, then they deserved to die because they were supporting ISIS. But then we would be criticized for killing 400 soldiers and be called war criminals. They weren't Pakistani Army, we bombed them, they're dead, and Khalid, in my mind, probably escaped. It's an example of how people who have no military experience influence decisions made in battle—every decision is scrutinized to the point of nausea. Soldiers have been threatened prosecution for murder when fighting a war because of ignorant policies. Don't get me wrong—I'm not against Congressional oversight or the prosecution of soldiers who knowingly murder civilians—but I *am* against people with no real knowledge of what needs to be done in the field making policy decisions for operators like me."

Some sitting in the audience clapped after Sam's answer.

"That's enough," cried Smith. "I will have people removed from this hearing if these outbursts continue."

"So, Mr. Richards, that means Congress is stupid?" asked Harrison.

"That's not what I said, Senator. Ignorance is the lack of knowledge; stupidity is the repeated mistakes once that knowledge is obtained. Come to think of it, Congress is probably both when it comes to making policy decisions for rules of engagement. I think that they sometimes allow politics to hamper their decisions about how to fight our enemies."

The room was deadly silent.

"No more questions, Mr. Chairman," replied the Senator.

"We will adjourn and reconvene at 8 a.m. I'll ask my questions, then give each of you the opportunity for follow-up questions."

Royster quickly ushered Hughes and Richards out of the hearing room and back to his office. Many Congressmen wanted to speak to Sam personally, but Royster would have none of that. Once back in Royster's office, they were joined by CIA Director Ritchie, who poured a couple of fingers of Blanton's bourbon for each of them, and they then unwound from the hearing while they sipped the smooth Kentucky liquor.

"Wow," said Royster, "you both were amazing. I don't think Smith has anything he can ask that will hurt us."

"I just don't get it," said Sam. "What are they trying to prove?"

"It's political posturing," said Ritchie. "They hate this President so much that they try to dampen any success with the question of immorality or wrongdoing. They might even completely approve of your actions. It's insane. I concur with Marv—outstanding performance. Sam, you poked the bear several times."

"Sorry, sir. I was getting tired of their 'holier than thou' attitude. I was tired of playing defense, so I thought a little subtle offense was called for."

"No need to be sorry. I thought it was perfect. I'm not so sure it was so subtle, though," laughed the Director.

Chapter 42

They met the next morning in Royster's office. As the CIA Director had warned, the *Post* did report about an American mission that started in Afghanistan and went into Pakistan. The report discussed the death of 700 ISIS soldiers, but inferred that there was more civilian loss of life than what had actually occurred. The article was critical of the President's "secret war" that was occurring without oversight. It was just about what one might expect from the *Washington Post*, a well-respected newspaper that had been given a left-leaning bias by numerous legitimate evaluators. However, the article did have an element that was different from a normal story: it named names. It mentioned Captain Hughes by name as well as a CIA agent named Sam Richards. The CIA Director was beyond angry; this was an act of treason in his mind, and he would demand a criminal investigation.

The CIA had previously had Valerie Plame identified as a covert officer in 2003 by journalist Robert Novak. She was not an operator like Richards. Differing opinions existed as to the damage done to the CIA and potential risk to others by reporting her as an agent. The identification of Richards was arguably worse, as he was an active operator. If Sam could be conclusively identified, it put both him and his family at risk from anyone trying to get leverage against Sam, potentially forcing Sam to forfeit his job as an operator for the Special Activities Division.

The CIA had managed to identify the source of the leak: a burner cell phone that had been used to make numerous calls to a *Post* reporter from the Capitol building. Furthermore, they had traced the phone to a batch of burners made available to the House Intelligence Committee. The CIA didn't know who took which burner phone from the batch, as the Committee didn't track that information. That meant one of the 22 Representatives on the House Intelligence Committee had leaked the identity of a covert CIA operator to the *Washington Post*. A quick check of the D.C. white pages showed 4,000 people with the last name Richards, six with the first name Sam, and only three of those six less than 40 years of age. That would assume that any other country's intelligence service looking for Sam's identity felt that the *Post* had used his real last name. It would certainly be easy to confirm Captain Hughes' identity, as his military life was more public than Sam's CIA history.

"Inform Smith that we'll be late," bellowed Ritchie to his assistant.

He then told them of his plan for the hearing.

The Committee and its six questioners were waiting in their seats when Royster, Hughes, and Richards entered. They took their seats as before and waited.

Smith began. "We've been waiting over an hour for the three of you; I could charge you with contempt. This hearing is important—the

Committee needs to ensure that this mission did not hurt our relationship with Pakistan, and that your forces caused no civilian harm."

"This hearing is bullshit," bellowed the CIA Director as he came in the door. "You have the Operation Report outlining all statistics and forensics. This hearing is a partisan political circus. Furthermore, one of you serving on the House side of the Committee leaked the identity of Captain Hughes and Mr. Richards to the *Washington Post.*"

Shouting and finger pointing began immediately throughout the room. Again, Royster, Hughes, and Richards sat impassively, unfazed by Director Ritchie's interruption.

"Everyone sit down and shut up," Chairman Smith bellowed through his microphone. "Director, you are out of order."

"No, Smith, you and this Committee are out of order. One of the 22 members of the House Intelligence Committee used a burner phone to talk to the *Post* reporter. We have the transcripts of the calls, and when I find that phone, heads are going to roll. Oh, and the hearing is over. My men are coming with me."

"You have no authority over this hearing," Smith was screaming, "and the CIA is not permitted to operate on US soil."

"Right, we don't operate in the U.S.," the Director said with a sarcastic smirk. "Let's go gentlemen," he said to the three men sitting up front.

The four of them were walking out the door as everyone was screaming, the Director escorting them from behind. Smith was yelling from the podium, calling for them to get back to their seats.

Ritchie turned to Smith and said, "Call the President, Chairman, he's excited to talk to you about the leak. Oh, and these gentlemen want a word with you."

The FBI Director and two agents entered the room and walked up to Smith, presenting warrants permitting them to obtain all cell phones from the members, as well as to search all offices belonging to members of the House Intelligence Committee.

❄ ❄ ❄

Six months passed quickly for Sam. Royster kept him inconspicuous, working on mission planning and analysis until the backlash from the hearing settled down. The FBI had investigated the *Washington Post* leak thoroughly and found that the phone used to call the reporter appeared to trace back to Representative Castillo. However, they could not say with 100% certainty. He, of course, denied the claim that he'd talked to the *Post*. Like a true politician, he placed the blame elsewhere and said that all of his staff had access to the phone. The reporter could or would not confirm the identity of his source. Investigations and hearings were taking place. Criminal charges by the government were levied against the *Post*, its editor, and the reporter.

Sam thought to himself, "same old swamp," referring to the ongoing filth of American politics. During the last six months, the highlight had been welcoming the birth of his son, Joshua Joseph (J.J.) Richards. Mariah was well, Gracie loved her brother, and Sam was both restless and content. Mariah had returned to work at the Red Cross Headquarters in Washington D.C., placing both Gracie and J.J. in onsite daycare. Their CIA-owned townhome was in Georgetown, making it a short commute to work for both Mariah and Sam. The location was nice, but they eventually wanted to get an affordable home with a big yard for the kids and Bella the dog.

During this time, the CIA had stepped up their efforts in pursuing any and all leads regarding Khalid and the gathered intelligence from his laptop. He had reached the same level of notoriety as Osama bin Laden for the CIA as well as the American people. He was number one on the CIA kill list. They had discovered, working with Pakistani intelligence, that he had gone through Islamabad, taken the Karakoram Highway to the Khunjerab Pass, and crossed into the Xinjiang province in Western China. There, it was assumed, he joined with Uyghur Muslims sympathetic to ISIS. Some Uyghur Muslims performed terrorist acts against the Chinese government, as they were a horribly persecuted minority group that was being forced to change culturally by Communist government. The Chinese government had established "re-education camps," estimated to hold hundreds of thousands of Uyghurs and other Muslim minorities. The CIA was still waiting to obtain certain confirmation of Khalid's presence in this region.

Chapter 43

Khalid and his plans for attacking the U.S. had gathered significant momentum and were progressing nicely. ISIS recruitment in Western China had been productive. The Uyghur militants were hungry for help against the Chinese government. They really didn't care about what was happening in the Middle East, as they were fighting a battle for their own survival. They had welcomed Khalid, and he was hidden outside the village of Tashkurgan, about 130 km from the Pakistani border. He had set up a very nice communications network, enabling him to get messages out of China into Pakistan. No electronic communications were used in China, as government surveillance was everywhere. But as ISIS regrouped, communications from Pakistan had become easier.

Khalid had started the process of acquiring the necessary materials for his plan to strike the U.S. about six months before the American attack on the mountain that had forced him to flee into China. His plan was not on the level of 9/11, but he was going to remind the Americans that after spending trillions of dollars and losing thousands of their sons and daughters to the wars in Iraq and Afghanistan, they still were not safe in their homeland.

Recruitment of ISIS sympathizers in the U.S. had proven to be easy. The Muslim extremists were hidden in college faculties and mosques. Khalid had sent close friends to Washington D.C. a year before to assist in his plan to attack the targets responsible for his brother's death: the CIA headquarters in McLean, Virginia and the headquarters of SEAL Team 6, located at Virginia Beach. These attacks were personal. Other ISIS leaders wanted easier targets to hit that would maximize loss of civilian life. Khalid had those targets as well, but he would attack those civilian-rich targets only after enough explosives were acquired for his personal targets.

Procurement of the materials needed for the attacks was not difficult in the U.S. Decades earlier, Timothy McVeigh and Terry Nichols had purchased or stole the necessary items they needed to manufacture the 7,000-pound bomb they placed in a Ryder rental truck outside the Alfred P. Murrah Federal Building. That bomb had consisted of forty 50 lb. bags of ammonium nitrate fertilizer, 1200 lbs. of nitromethane, and 350 lbs. of Tovex. Placing these components in 13 barrels and detonating it in front of the building destroyed one third of the building, killed 168 innocent lives, caused $650 million in damage, and was heard or felt up to 55 miles away. The bomb had only cost $5000 to make.

Khalid had his people procuring these same materials over a larger area of the U.S., little by little, so as not raise suspicion. What they couldn't buy, they stole. The process had been going on for nearly a year; supply levels accumulated to date had surpassed his highest hopes, and he now had about two and a half times the amount of explosives that McVeigh had used in Oklahoma City.

Security around government buildings and bases had become tighter after the Oklahoma City bombing and 9/11, however. It would be difficult to park a Ryder truck anywhere near a government building these days. Therefore, Khalid's plan primarily called for the use of cars, each carrying 1000 lbs. of bomb material. Several larger vehicles would be outfitted with explosives as well. His plan called for the vehicles to park close to their targets. Unlike McVeigh, who wanted to live after his bombing, his terrorist act was dependent on fuses. Khalid had the advantage of using individuals who were prepared to martyr themselves for the cause. They would have the ability to detonate at any time if an issue presented itself, but the goal was to park the vehicle and leave. Inflicting damage and death on the United States was the primary objective; but more importantly, these attacks would have a tremendous psychological effect on the American people.

With a year of planning, practice runs could occur with little risk, other than the individuals who were testing security being told they had to park their vehicle somewhere else. These simulations enabled his people to get a sense of security, as well as to note specific traffic patterns.

Khalid's plan was really simple in design. The largest vehicle was a cargo van that would hold 4,000 lbs. There was also a minivan for 3,000 lbs. and 10 cars each outfitted with a 1,000-lb. bomb. Obtaining access to the SEAL Navy Base and Langley was also relatively easy to accomplish. Both facilities used stickers on the front of the vehicles that gate guards would see in order to allow entrance. His people had followed individuals home from the base and practiced stealing the stickers from cars. They needed three stickers for Naval Air Station Oceana, and five for Langley. The remaining targets required only the address, and parking at those locations would be simple.

In the last six months, Khalid had also been trying to precisely identify the person who had killed his brother and who had also tried to kill him on several occasions. He had seen his face on two occasions: back in Afghanistan with the student kidnapping attempt, and again with the recent debacle outside of Tora Bora. The U.S. newspaper had given his name, and Khalid's computer experts had hacked into the Department of Motor Vehicles to obtain information on the three Sam Richards under forty. The hackers were able to obtain addresses for two of the three potentials, but the pictures of these individuals were unobtainable. The unlisted address was probably blocked by the government, and that was the Sam Richards that Khalid was pursuing. Khalid now had the addresses of two people who *might* be the elusive soldier who was wreaking havoc on the Muslim world, and more importantly, his brother's killer. *Allahu akbar*, thought Khalid. His plan was ready; his soldiers were waiting on his orders.

Chapter 44

Sam was growing antsier every day. This had been the longest period of his career between operations. He continued to work with analysts, as well as helped in planning missions. He would train with his buddies—at first only Durrant, and then Kerney too once his leg healed. Just recently, the three of them had been helping Wilhelm with his rehab in the gym. Their families spent a lot of time together, it was great to unwind and be relatively normal.

The expulsion of ISIS from western Afghanistan had continued to hold. The Afghan Army and local village militias were working together to keep them from retaking territory. The action had also pushed the U.S.-Taliban peace talks closer to a successful outcome. However, Sam and any other operator you talked to believed that it would be impossible for the Taliban to abide by any terms of peace. It was wishful thinking on the part of the U.S. to think that the Taliban wouldn't return to what they had been before 9/11. Hopefully, the Afghan government could consolidate power and enforce the terms of the agreement, but that was a tall order.

"Sam, I've got news on Khalid," Royster said one day as he waved him into his office. "The ISI—Pakistan's CIA—has been sending undercover agents into Chinese villages and obtained pictures of him in Tashkurgan, a village about 130 km from the border. We've verified this intel ourselves through satellites and local assets."

"We have assets in Tashkurgan?" Sam said. "Shit, Marv. Where don't we have assets?"

Marv laughed. "Uh, nearly everywhere, my friend. I don't know if you've noticed, but the world is on fire! Bad people are everywhere, most of them wanting a piece of the U.S."

"My team's ready. We're tired of sitting around. Let's go get him and put out some of those fires," Sam replied. "We know he's trying to hit us; let's get to him first."

"Copy that, Sam. But I don't think a covert assault into China would go over well with Beijing. You go ahead and plan it, but don't get your hopes up. Meanwhile, I'll talk to the boss and see if we can convince the President."

Sam was pumped. He would come up with a stealthy plan that would succeed right under the noses of the Chinese. He might just get another chance to put down the elusive Khalid after all. They needed to move quickly, though, as there had been a significant spike in chatter about upcoming terrorist attacks, with most analysts feeling that Europe was the target. After six months of trying to squeeze anything else out of the laptop they'd acquired from Khalid, the CIA had still not gotten any further information on specific targets or methods. Sam hoped that the analysts were right, and that the chatter wasn't about attacks on the U.S.

The response from the President was bittersweet. CIA Director Ritchie and D/NCS Royster had made a gallant effort, presenting the tremendous benefits of a successful mission to take out the world's number one terrorist. The presentation had been made first to the entire cabinet, then they'd had time with the President alone. Most Cabinet members were afraid of China's response should the mission be compromised. Similarly, if the mission were successful, and they announced to the world Khalid was dead, would the world's positive response outweigh the Chinese response of finding out their sovereignty had been violated by the U.S.? If they were successful, they debated claiming complete denial that the killing had taken place in China. The debate included a scenario where the U.S. briefed China and asked for permission to go after Khalid. When all was said and done, there was no consensus, but there were more no's than yes's on pursuing the mission into China.

When they met with the President alone, Ritchie and Royster thought they almost had him convinced. They were playing to his ego, reminding him that it took 10 years to kill bin Laden after 9/11. To be able to kill Khalid Ali just six months after the mission that drove ISIS out of Afghanistan would perhaps be one of the best wins ever for the CIA. It would show the world that the U.S. was still the world's dominant superpower, and they implied to the President that it would be a huge positive for his re-election campaign. They reminded him of the increased chatter involving ISIS that assets were reporting, and that this type of activity almost always occurred shortly before an attempted attack. The world didn't know about the many attacks that had been prevented by the CIA based on listening and responding to this chatter. Unfortunately, this time, they just couldn't get anything specific from the noise.

"So, Mr. President, what do you think?" asked Ritchie.

"What percentage do you put getting in and out without detection?" the President asked.

"Ninety percent confidence, if there are no major snags."

"How often is there a major snag during a mission?" he asked.

"Ten percent of the time there's a major snag; half the time the operators have to make changes based on minor issues."

"I've read a lot about Richards. He's a real star. I'm glad he's one of ours," said the President.

"Yes sir, he's the best," replied Royster.

The President asked some more thoughtful questions, and seemed to be really wrestling with the decision. He discussed the current trade war with China and how this mission could be a disaster for the U.S. if China detected their excursion. He suggested that they involve the Chinese, alert them to Khalid's presence, and see how they responded.

"I would advise against that, Mr. President," replied Ritchie. "They may already know he's there, and they're turning a blind eye to his presence. If that's the case, they may warn him. Then he moves, and we've lost him again. If they don't know he's there, they might want to go it alone after we tell them his location, and they could easily screw it up. China doesn't give a shit about possible attacks on the West. I don't see an upside for them."

"I want to get that bastard, I really do. A positive outcome would be huge!" the President replied. "But going into Pakistan to kill bin Laden without telling the Pakistanis is different than this mission. At that time, we were giving Pakistan huge amounts of money. If they'd raised a stink, they would have been cut off. The stakes here are exponentially higher."

"Yes, sir," the Director replied.

"Tell you what—keep gathering intel and watching Khalid. I want you to have everything you need in place to go after him two weeks from today. Come to me directly if anything changes. In the meantime, I really think that we should give the Chinese a chance to do the right thing."

Royster was replaying the meeting with Richards.

"I don't doubt the President's desire to get Khalid," Royster commented. "Drone attacks have been occurring now more than ever with this administration. His desire to defeat ISIS is higher than the previous administration. These stakes are high. It's more than the trade war; there's the Hong Kong protests, China's expansion into the South China Sea, and the ongoing China-Taiwan saber-rattling. If we go in and get detected, then the Chinese have a precedent to justify going into another country unannounced. Therefore, talking to the Chinese first does make sense, but only if they don't know he's there. Otherwise, we tip our hand, they tell Khalid, and we may lose him."

"Nothing's ever crystal clear, except for when you're operating the mission," Sam replied. "I don't think it would start World War III if we accomplished the mission and happened to be detected going into China."

"I concur, but we're just players in the game. The President said two weeks. I want your team in eastern Pakistan in one week, ready to go if we get the green light."

"Copy that," Sam replied.

Chapter 45

Sam filled Mariah in on the decisions regarding the mission to get Khalid. As usual, his wife was very insightful and understanding of the implications of entering China. In anticipation that Sam would be in Pakistan a week from now, they made plans to spend the time they had together as a family as much as possible. They visited the zoo, walked around the D.C. monuments, and had lunch together everyday. Sam would make the short drive from Langley, pick up Mariah from work along with the kids from the Red Cross daycare, and they would walk somewhere for lunch.

It was a nice spring day in D.C. The cherry blossoms were out, and the Washington Nationals had started their season. Today, lunch was going to be a picnic in front of the Lincoln Memorial with both the Kerney and Durrant families. The men would drive down from Langley to meet their wives and children. It would be good to unwind from the repetitive grind of mission preparation. His friends dropped Sam off at the beautiful, historic Red Cross building, and he went straight to the daycare. He placed J.J. in the stroller so Gracie could push it to Mariah's office.

"Mommy!" yelled Gracie when she saw her Mom, who was talking on the phone.

"Shh, Gracie, Mommy's on the phone," said Sam smiling.

J.J. started gurgling as soon as he saw his mother. Gracie ran over to her mom, throwing herself into her arms. Mariah was squeezing her with one arm, stroking J.J.'s head with the other, while cradling the phone against her neck. She finished her call and looked at Gracie.

"Are you excited about lunch?" Mariah asked Gracie. "This will be a treat to picnic with all of our friends."

"Yes, yes, yes," said Gracie, pulling her Mother's arm.

"Hold on, sweetie. Mommy needs 15 minutes to talk to someone about that phone call. How about you, J.J., and Daddy go ahead of me so you can get to your friends? I'll be right behind you!"

"We can wait, babe," Sam said.

"No, no, no, let's go Daddy!" Gracie exclaimed.

"It's less than a mile. I'll put on my running shoes and run like the wind over to you as soon as I'm done," said Mariah.

"Ok, sweetie. But if you're not there in 25 minutes, my team and I will come rescue you!"

"You're so chivalrous," she said. "But I don't think it will take that long. Gracie's pumped; get her over there so she can burn some energy."

"Copy that," was Sam's response.

Sam and his kids made the 15-minute walk with Gracie pushing J.J.'s stroller the entire way. When Gracie saw the other families, she broke into a sprint. Sam was concerned that the stroller would tip over or J.J. would begin to wail, but as he picked up his pace to run beside them and steady the stroller, he noted that his son was squealing with a smile on his face.

"Damn, Sam, did you make that girl double-time over here the whole way?" laughed Durrant.

"Hell yes," Sam replied. "You have to start young and hard if you want to be the first female Navy SEAL!"

"Stop," said Kerney's wife. "No, she won't be! We won't allow that."

"Hey, you're singing to the choir, but how do you tell a four-year-old she can't be something? Don't worry, Mariah and I will point her in another direction."

"That would be kick-ass," Kerney replied.

"You shut your mouth," his wife responded.

The group burst out laughing.

"Mariah needed 15 minutes, but she should be here soon," Sam said.

They gathered the kids to get them eating, the adults cracked open some beers, and they were enjoying the beautiful day sitting on the lawn in front of the Lincoln Memorial. And then... all hell broke loose.

Mariah had finished her conversation with her boss and was on her way to meet the group. She had exited the building, rounded the corner on to D Street, and started jogging toward Eighteenth Street. She was smiling, thinking about how fun their friends were, when she was knocked to her feet. She struggled to sit up, but then her world went dark.

Sam's phone buzzed, and he noted a text from his wife. He laughed.

"Mariah said she was running a four-minute mile, and would be here in three minutes."

Durrant's wife responded, "I hope she has on a good sports bra to support her milk-filled jugs."

That elicited laughter from the group just as all three of the CIA agents' phones buzzed together.

They looked down and almost simultaneously each let out a curse word. They had just been informed of a probable terrorist attack at Naval Air Station Oceana, Virginia Beach, the home of SEAL Team 6. They had each been part of that team in the past and were intimately familiar with the facility. They were being recalled to Langley immediately. As they raised their heads to look at each other, the ground rocked below them. Instinctively, the three agents looked toward the source of the explosion. Sam almost went to his knees as he registered the location.

"That's the Red Cross building," he screamed. "No, no, no." He broke into a sprint as his friends yelled at him to wait.

"Babe, get the kids and get to the cars. Can you do that?" Kerney asked his wife.

She was crying, but looked at her husband with steely resolve and responded, "Absolutely—go with Sam!"

Durrant and Kerney sprinted after Sam. Sam was running faster than they had ever seen him. As they were making their way, their phones buzzed again. Durrant looked down and couldn't believe his eyes.

"Fuck me, Paul, Langley's been hit!"

"Shit, we gotta get to Mariah now, that's all we can do," responded Paul.

They saw Sam kneeling over a body. Ashes were falling to the ground, and debris from building fragments was all around them. The sounds of sirens from first-responders were already beginning to be heard. When Steve and Paul got to Sam, they noted blood coming from Mariah's ears, her left leg was deformed below the knee, and her face was bluish. The three of them immediately went to work, their medic training and experience with battle injuries taking over. Sam was assessing Mariah for any wounds to her chest and abdomen; Kerney had straightened her left leg, applied his belt as a tourniquet, and covered the wound, while Durrant was stabilizing her neck and assessing her airway.

"Trachea is midline," commented Durrant. "Respirations are shallow, but she's moving air. I don't feel any gross deformities of her neck. Her pupils look normal."

Those findings ruled against Mariah having a tension pneumothorax, a large bleed in the brain, or an unstable cervical spine injury.

"She's got an open tibia fracture. It's not gushing blood without a tourniquet, and she has slow but good pulses," said Kerney.

An open tibia fracture occurs when the bone between the knee and the ankle breaks and comes out through the skin. It would bleed, but the lack of profuse bleeding and the presence of good pulses suggested that there was no arterial injury. A slow pulse along with her loss of consciousness was consistent with a significant head injury. Kerney speculated that she had been thrown into a nearby sidewalk bench, hitting her leg.

Steve Durrant softly said to Sam, "Hey, buddy, what did you find?"

When Sam looked up, Steve saw an expression that he had never seen before. It was like a movie was being displayed on Sam's face; expressions shifting from fear to rage to focus to concern, switching second by second.

"Um," Sam began, "no chest or abdominal entry wounds, no rib crepitus. Abdomen is soft."

Those findings suggested that there were no rib fractures and no current evidence of an abdominal organ injury.

Ambulances were making their way everywhere along downtown D.C., and Kerney flagged one over and quickly relayed their findings to the EMT.

"Are you a doctor?" asked the EMT.

"No," said Paul, "we're all former Navy SEALs." Pointing to Sam, he continued, "And she's his wife."

They would be taking her to George Washington University (GWU) Hospital, which was not far from their location. As they were getting her into the ambulance, another explosion occurred southeast of them.

"Fuck, there's a Nationals day game today, isn't there?" asked Kerney.

"Yes," said Sam softly. "This has to be Khalid. We should have chased his ass through Pakistan instead of assuming he was dead. They've hit the Annex (SEAL Team 6 headquarters), the Red Cross, and a baseball stadium! This is 9/11 all over again, for fuck's sake."

"Sam, they've also hit Langley," said Durrant. "That came over our phones while we were running to Mariah."

"Shit, you guys gotta go before they shut down the area. No, wait— our families! My kids!"

"Sam, don't worry. Nancy's got them, and they're in a safe place," replied Kerney. "You're right, we should get back to Langley. But you need to be with your wife."

Sam did not object. He rode the ambulance with Mariah, but once they arrived, he was escorted to a waiting area. The emergency room was already beginning to be swamped with injuries from the explosion at the Red Cross. The physicians and nurses were so busy that no one was available to talk to Sam about his wife. He was finally told to go and wait in the surgery waiting room. He felt helpless. He tried to reach Nancy Kerney to check on his kids, but his cell phone could not connect, and the same result occurred with his attempts to reach D/NCS Royster and Langley. The cell towers had to be overwhelmed. Landlines were helpful, but Langley had probably shut down all communication except for secure lines.

Unable to reach anyone by phone, all he could do was pace the hall. It was the worst feeling that he had ever experienced—total lack of control over every facet of his life, and tremendous helplessness. Almost three hours later, someone finally came out and pointed him in the direction of the Intensive Care Unit. He was informed by the unit secretary that a nurse would be out to talk to him. He asked the secretary about his wife, but she replied that she was not a medical person and had no information for him. He was near to losing it completely when a nice, concerned face tapped his shoulder.

"I'm Emily, the ICU charge nurse. Are you Mr. Richards?"

"Yes, yes. Call me Sam. How's my wife?"

"She's stable. I'm sorry the surgeon can't talk to you right now, but we're all overwhelmed, and he had to get back to the OR. Your wife sustained a subdural hematoma and a broken leg. A subdural..."

"I know what it is. How big was it, and what did they do?"

"The doctor said it was small, but he felt it was best to drain it and put a pressure monitor in her head to be able to address any possible fluctuations in intracranial pressure."

"OK, I know about that," replied Sam. "Did they put a rod down her tibia?"

"Why, yes. Are you a doctor?" asked Nurse Emily.

"No, I've just seen too many injuries. Can I see her?"

"Of course. Follow me. Now, she's not awake, and she has a breathing tube in place," said Emily.

Sam turned the corner into the ICU room, and his knees almost gave out when he saw the love of his life lying there unresponsive on a ventilator. He gathered himself as best he could and took Mariah's hand in his own. Mariah's nurse introduced herself to Sam, checked her ventilator and IV's, and then gave Sam some privacy. That was when he lost it. He leaned over her and sobbed like he never had before.

Chapter 46

It wasn't until 8 p.m. that Sam was able to get through on the phone to anyone. He spoke to Gracie and told her Mommy was okay but needed to stay in the hospital. Nancy Kerney had smartly made sure that the children avoided the television. She had told Gracie that her mommy had taken a bad fall.

He reached Royster shortly thereafter. Since 9/11, all government agencies had been much better at sharing information. Royster told Sam that the FBI had reported that the initial attack at Naval Air Station (NAS) Oceana could have been worse than it was. Three cars were able to get through the gates, but an alert gate guard sensed that three unfamiliar cars entering the facility all in a row was concerning. It was rare to see any unfamiliar vehicles, period. He had alerted the Master-at-Arms, who followed the vehicles. The cars had accelerated to try to collide into buildings. However, Navy police were able to converge and stop one vehicle before detonation. SEAL Team members who fortuitously happened to be training using live fire nearby took out another vehicle. The third vehicle was able to strike a barracks building, but fortunately, since it was near lunchtime, it had been empty. It was really pure luck that there was no loss of life from the three attacks.

Similar to NAS Oceana, damage at Langley could have been much worse. The parking lots were well away from the main building and access by vehicles was restricted by well-placed obstructions. Attentive guards had noticed several vehicles roaming around the grounds without displaying any purpose. Five vehicles had attempted to drive up on sidewalks in order to run into the building; all five exploded at different locations. Three detonated before getting close to the building after they were engaged by police vehicles who were able to shoot the drivers. Two vehicles had managed to strike the building and detonate; however, the ground obstructions prevented the attacks from occurring to populous areas of the building. The attacks did injure several CIA employees, but there were no fatalities.

The Red Cross attack followed next and had the worst outcome. In this attack, a van had been parked at the front of the building and had been detonated, which resulted in the destruction of the front half of the National Landmark Building. The early death toll was approaching fifty innocent souls, including some children who were in the daycare. If it weren't for the daycare being located in the back of the building, the number of deaths would have been much higher.

The attack on the Washington Nationals baseball stadium was also thwarted by the quick dissemination of information to local police, who were immediately placed on high alert after word of possible terrorist attacks was broadcasted over police radios. Two alert and brave Washington, D.C. policemen had noticed a cargo van trying to get into a restricted parking area. They confronted the vehicle, which then tried to reverse out in the same direction it came in. Unable to do so, the vehicle accelerated toward the stadium. The police officers engaged the speeding vehicle, and it was detonated before hitting the stadium. The two officers and 13 people in the vicinity were killed. It was no consolation that only slight structural damage had occurred to the stadium.

"Four targets hit in or around our Nation's Capital. It's unbelievable," said Sam.

"Actually, Sam, you haven't heard about two others from an hour ago," replied Royster.

"What?" said Sam. "Please, God, no."

"They were private homes, Sam."

"You've gotta be kidding, Marv. What's the connection?" Sam asked.

"The owners were named Samuel Richards," was Royster's response.

Sam was silent. Khalid had obtained Sam's name after someone associated with the House Intelligence Committee had leaked it and the *Washington Post* had printed it. Was that also the reason that the Red Cross had been hit? The CIA had ensured him that it was impossible to find his address through Internet searches, even when using a paid service to try to find an address. Hell, the CIA had even kept his address off of his license and other government identification. He had personally tried and failed to find his home address on the Internet; but some searches did show spouses' names. After he had made his search attempts, Sam had made a note to inform the CIA computer people that Mariah's name needed to be invisible as well. He had simply forgotten to follow through. Had he done so, the Red Cross probably would not have been targeted. He was riddled with guilt.

There were three Sam Richards under the age of 40 in D.C. Khalid had targeted the two addresses easy to find and the workplace of the third unlisted Sam Richards' wife. The prolonged silence led Royster to

238 | JOSEPH R. RITCHIE

believe that even in his current state of mind, Sam was processing this information and coming to the conclusion that he was about to tell him.

Sam spoke before Royster could. "He's made this personal. He hit the Red Cross because he somehow found out my wife works there! He hit the homes of people with the same name as me. All because some fucktard politician leaked my name!" he yelled.

Sam then asked about the status of the two other Sam Richards.

"One house was empty except for the two family dogs. The other killed a family of five while they were eating dinner," replied Royster.

Sam was crushed. Four attacks where innocent people were killed, simply for being at the wrong place at the wrong time. Along with that, an entire family and two loved pets had been killed only because they had the same name he did. It was a fucking nightmare. The extent of Khalid's drive for revenge for his brother's death all those years ago was unending. As quickly as Sam thought that, he understood the hatred and desire to have vengeance. Throughout all of his missions, justice had driven Sam. It was justified to kill Kony's men, the corrupt Haitians, the sex traffickers, the terrorists in Nigeria, al-Shabab leaders, ISIS soldiers, and others. He did it to make a difference, hopefully reducing pain and suffering for the people these scumbags preyed upon. But now, he was the victim of the world's number one terrorist.

"When do we go?" asked Sam with detached coolness.

"They've already gone," responded Marv. "Agent Heath is capable, and he's leading a team that we had training locally who have been standing ready. They'll be executing your plan, Sam. After today, the President doesn't care what the Chinese think."

"Khalid won't be there," Sam responded. "I'm sure the Chinese warned him. I gotta go, Marv. My family needs me, and Khalid's gone again."

The phone went dead before Royster could say anything else. The U.S had been rocked mightily, but none more than the day's victims, their families, and friends. The nearly two decades of preventing organized terrorist attacks on U.S. soil was over.

Chapter 47

Khalid Ali had been viewing the coverage of the attacks on satellite TV from his new location in Kashgar, China, located 290 km north of Tashkurgan. He and his small group had left Tashkurgan the day of the attacks, just in case his position had been jeopardized and the Americans were thinking of coming after him. The attacks had gone decently, even though some vehicles had been stopped before completing their missions. The death toll would be close to 100 infidels; not as many as he'd hoped for, but the psychological trauma of another attack on their country would ripple across the United States. Khalid had proven that soft civilian targets were relatively easy to attack. It was ironic that he had used the technique of Timothy McVeigh, an American, and that it had proven an effective and easy method to coordinate.

Buying supplies for the attacks over the course of a year had made it unlikely to set off any alarms used by law enforcement to find suspicious purchases. There were enough ISIS contacts in the U.S. to proceed with the same style throughout the country. Continued success would bring more recruits, who in turn would hopefully break the spirit of the infidels, and they would finally leave the Middle East. Their departure would then make Israel vulnerable to destruction. The result of this mission had also solidified Khalid's chances of becoming the next leader of ISIS.

Reports from his commanders were also optimistic.

"Emir, we're already seeing hundreds of men going to training camps to be a part of our cause."

"I suspected that would be the case, with more recruits, we'll be able to head back into eastern Afghanistan, displace the Taliban, and move across the country. If the Americans choose to stay, we'll be an enemy with increased strength and morale," replied Khalid."

"Do you think that this will increase aid from Iran and other countries that hate America?"

"Absolutely."

Khalid was extremely happy with the overall situation while he was able to stay safe at a location far from Western forces. In exchange for negotiating a truce between the local Muslims and the Chinese government, the Chinese government was willing to look the other way and allow his presence.

Khalid had also learned that the attacks had killed one of the Sam Richards and his family, though the other home had been empty. He had not known the third Sam Richards' home address, and he suspected that it was probably the home of the one who had killed his brother. His people had easily been able to find out that the wife linked to the third address worked at the Red Cross headquarters. Attacking an aid group in the heart of Washington D.C. had to further humiliate the Americans. Also, attacking the homes of its private citizens would give all Americans a new, heightened fear of attacks that could occur any-where. No one would feel safe.

❈ ❈ ❈

Royster received news from Heath that Khalid was no longer in Tashkurgan. The mission had gone flawlessly, the team entering the country via farm trucks and rendezvousing with their local asset there. But a nighttime sweep of the small village had come up empty. Ques-tioning locals revealed that the terrorist had probably left the same day that the attacks on the U.S. were executed. The hope of quickly capturing and killing Khalid to reduce the sting of the attacks was not going to happen. It had taken ten years to get bin Laden after 9/11; the U.S. could not allow the same amount of time to pass before getting to Khalid. The D/NCS would step up efforts to locate Khalid, who he felt was still in western China.

The current President, like President George W. Bush, was now stigmatized with having been commander-in-chief during an attack on American soil. He went before the nation to try to reassure them, to tell them that the FBI was feverishly working on leads in the United States while the CIA was doing the same abroad. The American military was poised to deliver retaliatory attacks wherever necessary. He still felt that the war in Afghanistan was too great a burden for the United States financially, and more importantly, no more sons and daughters should give their lives to this cause. He called these attacks another wake-up call to tighten the homeland security of America.

The President reiterated that enforcing the current laws regard-ing illegal immigration and completing a border wall were now more important than ever. He outlined a new plan to account for all people in the country in order to enforce visas that had expired and deport those without documentation. However, he did not simply call for de-portation across the board for all illegal immigrants. Like Reagan had done in the 1980's, the President was willing to give amnesty to those who had put down roots in America and who were productive assets to the country. Reagan had felt that "anybody who's here illegally is going to be abused in some way, financially or physically, they have no rights." His amnesty program had three million people come forward for legal immigration. The current President was willing to do the same in exchange for funding to complete the wall, because without tight border security, more people would come illegally, even after giving amnesty to those already in the U.S. who were deserving.

The President's plan would demand that continued determination of potential illegals would be necessary after giving amnesty. It would consist of active, continued monitoring for illegals. Those opposed to racial profiling by law enforcement would have to accept a measure of it to find those individuals who did not come forward with the offer of amnesty. Checkpoints and random pullovers to verify identification were two of the ways that people who refused the chance for amnesty could be found. These activities would allow determination of individual's immigration status in the U.S. The President articulated that he knew that there would be opposition, with many of his opponents making comparisons to Nazi Germany, the Soviet Union, etc. He argued that border security had been a problem in the U.S. for over 50 years, and that this policy would ensure that the U.S. eliminated undeserving illegals, but more importantly, it would also account for and deport anyone who was felt to be a threat.

The President called it a "filtering" of the country, giving amnesty for law-abiding, productive, illegals and deportation of "bad" illegals. He emphasized that the country had become great because of immigration and this policy would enhance that effect. The President's new policy did not stop there. To stop attacks on the U.S., he said that the country would have to eliminate the enemy from the Homeland.

To do so, the government would have to stop the political correctness and begin to racially profile. He bluntly said that if a radical faction of Muslims wanted to destroy America, then all Muslims needed to be evaluated for their loyalty. Unfortunately for Muslims living in America, there would be some early pain as they were subjected to background investigations. However, he argued that the process would be quick and easy for the majority of Muslims. People of Muslim faith who have been in the U.S. for years would be the easiest to confirm. He stated to the country, "Wouldn't any Muslim-American who loves this country be okay with confirming their status? If radical Christians or radical Jews were driving car bombs into buildings, than we'd target them for their status. Whoever is responsible for the threat, steps have to be taken to eliminate the risk of further attacks on America."

Many of the techniques the President was pushing for had been implemented in Israel, including the use of a wall. Since employing these methods, the incidence of terrorist attacks and loss of innocent lives had dropped drastically in Israel. The President knew that he would be accused of politicizing the recent attacks, but the status quo was not acceptable. He assured the American people that the goal was not to eliminate people of a certain religious belief but to eliminate un-productive non-citizens and anyone with confirmed ties to terrorism. He proposed involving Muslim leaders to help with oversight of the process, even though, in his mind, they had not been vocal enough in their condemnation of Muslim radicals.

Most of law enforcement, the FBI, and the CIA tended to agree with the President's new policies. Royster marveled how the President could take a horrific set of circumstances and turn it into a battle cry for his new policy—amnesty for appropriate illegals, deportation for others, and screening/removal of Muslims and anyone else with prov-en ties to terrorism. The country had united after 9/11, and as a consequence, President Bush had been given carte blanche to destroy the enemy. The current President was asking the question, "Doesn't every American want to be safe?" His new policy was rallying many people, even those outside of his base supporters. He was saying and implementing what many people had wanted to articulate for years, but hadn't because of fear of being called a racist. Even the opposing political party leadership had been silent from dissenting against his new policy for fear of alienating their supporters. This policy and its increasing popularity could deliver a huge blow to the President's opponents in the upcoming elections.

Chapter 48

Sam was distraught. He had never felt like this in his life. Immediately following the attacks, he had become withdrawn from his friends and from his employer. These days, he sat next to Mariah, never leaving her bedside, holding her hand. The nurses would bring him food, but he barely ate. Both his and Mariah's parents had come as soon as they could to be with their children and grandchildren. They were shocked to see Sam's mental state, and they did everything they could to help him. They would bring Gracie and Joshua in to visit Mariah, and only then did they see some flicker of his normal self.

"Daddy, when are you coming home?" Gracie would ask.

"When Mommy wakes up," he would say. "Your grandparents will be with you and J.J. while I wait for her to wake up."

This conversation would be repeated every time Gracie came to see Mariah. After ten days of the same, she asked another question.

"What if she doesn't wake up?"

Silence ensued in the ICU bay, except for the ventilator assisting Mariah with her breathing. Sam's mother leaned down and hugged Gracie. Sam's eyes closed, his head and heart feeling as if they would burst. He waited until the feeling passed, then thought hard about what his sweet daughter had just said. He felt a sense of calmness for the first time since the attacks. He realized that Mariah must always have had feelings of helplessness about his own fate whenever he went away. He thought of how, despite that feeling, Mariah had to carry on for her children in a normal fashion. Even though she worried about her husband and what he was doing when he was in harm's way, she was always able to be upbeat and positive. Sam was suddenly ashamed of his behavior, and he knew that Mariah would not approve. She was the mentally tougher one. Sam needed to reach down inside and come back emotionally for his family. He let go of Mariah's hand, turned to his daughter, took her into his arms, and hugged her tightly.

"She'll wake up soon, sweetie, I know it. She's my Sleeping Beauty. I kiss her all the time, and soon one of my kisses will wake her up! I'm so sorry I haven't been there for you. I promise, that's not happening any more. I'll be home tonight to put you and J.J. to bed. Okay?"

"Ok, Daddy. I love you."

"I love you too, Gracie."

Both sets of grandparents were in tears.

Just then, the neurosurgeon walked in to speak to them. He told Sam that her brain activity was normal and that they were going to pull her breathing tube, as she hadn't been using the ventilator for the last 24 hours. He told them that he was sure that Mariah's brain was responding to their presence and conversations. He felt that she would awaken soon, and that they should continue to keep the faith.

Sam did go home that night and put his children to sleep for the first time since the attacks. He returned to the hospital after spending a few hours talking to his in-laws and his parents. He apologized for his aloofness and expressed how thankful he was for their presence.

"Gracie's question about whether Mariah would wake up flipped a switch in my brain. I suddenly realized that I withdrew so much into myself that I wasn't there for J.J. and her. Hell, for that matter, I haven't been there for you guys. After Gracie's comment, it's like I could hear Mariah telling me to snap out of it and get a grip! That girl is the strongest person I know. She's my anchor, my best friend, and my therapist," he laughed.

"Are you kidding?" her father replied. "Don't be so hard on yourself—your response has been natural."

They took turns hugging, and then Sam said, "There's something I want to tell the four of you, but it can't leave this room. Mariah knows what I'm going to tell you."

They looked at him with a concerned expression. He then proceeded to open up about what he'd been doing since leaving the SEALs. He then told them about his line of work with the CIA.

His dad and father-in-law turned to their respective wives and both said, "I told you!"

His dad went on to tell Sam that he and Mariah's father had never believed that he worked for a security company. It was easy to connect the dots, because whenever Sam left home, something big was reported in the news while he was gone or shortly after he got back.

"You're kidding me," said Sam. "You know, if you'd asked me about what I was doing, I wouldn't have been able to lie to you."

"That's why I never asked," replied his father. "I didn't want to put you in a tough situation. What happens now, Sam?"

"Great question, Dad. I haven't heard from my boss. I suppose he's giving me some time."

"The President is really pushing an agenda," said Mariah's father, a staunch opponent of the current administration. He and Sam had a great relationship, but never discussed politics because they rarely agreed.

Her father continued, "Even though I don't like his politics, I have to agree with most of his new plan to give citizenship to the worthy and try to weed out the bad guys."

"Listen, I'm going back to the hospital and sit with her. Thank you again for your love and help. I'll call if anything changes."

Sam returned to the hospital, showered and refreshed. He took his usual place and held Mariah's hand. However, instead of brooding, he started telling Mariah about the status of their children and what he had told their parents about his work. He was back; he felt energized and optimistic. He continued to rattle on with conversation, holding her hand, his eyes closed and head down on the bed nestled against Mariah's side. He continued talking for hours, recounting the early years of their relationship and his hopes for their future. He had lost track of time when suddenly, he heard a voice in his ear.

"Can you please be quiet? My head is killing me!"

He lifted his head and saw an angel with tired eyes and a beautiful smile.

"Come over here, handsome, and give me a kiss before my husband comes back," said Mariah.

Sam leaned over, and then had a look of confusion. *Oh my God*, he thought, *she doesn't recognize me!*

"Sam, I'm kidding," she laughed.

"Not funny," he replied as he leaned over to kiss her.

Sam told Mariah of the bombings and the carnage involved. She had lost a lot of friends at the Red Cross, and she and the kids might also have died if it hadn't been for their lunch date as a family. Sam told her that he felt at fault because he'd been unable to eliminate Khalid on that mountain in Afghanistan as well as his guilt for potentially allowing their relationship to be identified by Khalid's people. He was also upset at the CIA brass for not allowing them to pursue Khalid into Pakistan, to either confirm that Khalid was dead or to finish the job.

He told Mariah that he had been worthless the whole time that she was in a coma, as well as purposeless and helpless. The last ten days he had been withdrawn from everyone, spending every moment at her bedside until Gracie had flipped a switch in his head. He wasn't proud of his behavior.

"I was lost without you, babe. I thought I was going to lose you, and I just fell apart. Gracie pulled me back by asking what would happen if you never woke up."

He was crying, telling Mariah their daughter's words.

"I knew then that I had to stop being selfish, be strong for our children, and get back into life. It's been the hardest time of my life."

"Sam, I get it, but your behavior sounds normal. It's a terrible feeling to have no control. That's when you need to depend on love and faith," said Mariah.

Sam held her tight, thanking God for bringing her back to him. "These last ten days have given me a glimpse of what you must go through every time I leave. I don't know how you do it, babe."

"Again, sweetie, it's all about love and faith. Anytime I start to worry about you and what you're doing, those two simple words and what they mean to me get you back to me unharmed."

"God, I love you so much, Mariah!"

Sam called their parents and told them of the news. They brought Gracie and J.J. as soon as they awoke the next morning. Gracie refused breakfast; she wanted to go immediately to see her parents. The reunion was epic, involving hugs and tears, crying and laughing. Mariah was transferred out of the ICU and allowed to go home after several days of physical therapy.

The reunions continued with visits from the Team and their families, as well as from survivors who had been in the Red Cross building. Mariah continued to get stronger every day, confirming what Sam already knew about his wife—she was a badass!

Chapter 49

Sam returned to work, where he quickly caught up on the latest intelligence reports and current missions. There had been no confirmed sightings of Khalid in Afghanistan or western China. They put assets in Kashgar, China, as they felt that this was probably where he had gone. So far, no sightings.

"Sam, I gotta tell you, the Director and I were upset that we couldn't get a hold of you," Royster said. "We could have used your help."

"I get it, Marv. I know I lost it there for about 10 days. I felt helpless, but all I knew is that I needed to be there for Mariah. I'm sorry."

"I get that, but..."

Sam interrupted, "No offense, Marv, but what could I have done? You had sent Heath to Tashkurgan, you haven't seen Khalid since then, and all we've been doing is a few missions here and there to make us feel like we're doing something. My wife was in critical condition, and

I needed to be with her. I'm an operator, and you weren't sending any-one on significant missions."

"Your first commitment is to this country and the CIA."

"Are you fucking kidding me right now? You want to talk about duty? I've put my life on the line far too many times for this country to have you lecture me about duty. There's not a better team than mine. We have delivered more wins for the CIA than the other teams com-bined. You're really going to bust my balls for being with my family after an attack on this country by Muslim terrorists? If I had been away on a mission when the attacks occurred, I would have fulfilled my duty. But I was here, I was the first person to my wife, and I wasn't going to leave her side!"

"It was all hands on deck, Sam," replied Royster. "You were a no-show. As you said, you were completely out of it for 10 days or so."

"Let me ask you something, Director," said Sam. "When was the last time you were in harm's way? Oh, wait, that would be forever ago. You spent almost your entire SEAL career in Intelligence, not Opera-tions. You think you know what it feels like? You have no fucking clue what we see or do. When my wife became part of the story, I did lose it. But I'm back, maybe better than ever."

"We're not so sure, Sam."

"Who the fuck is 'we'?" replied Sam.

"The Director and I think that you might need some time to get your head straight, maybe see someone that you can talk to openly. Say, maybe for a couple of months. We think this has become too per-sonal for you. Believe me, we're only thinking of your best interest. Besides that, we need to be sure that you haven't been compromised, that you're not a target."

"Are you kidding me? Of course I'm a target, thanks to the Con-gressman and the *Washington Post*. They targeted my wife, Marv."

"I know, Sam. You need some time to process what's happened."

"Wow, this is surreal," said Sam. "First, you bust my balls for not being around, and now, when I'm ready to go, you tell me I need time. Tell me that's not schizophrenic. I appreciate your concern, but I don't fucking need it. I can take care of myself. Let me change the subject for a second and ask you a question. What's the plan when a positive ID on Khalid comes through?"

"We won't be going into China for him. We thought we hadn't been detected when Heath went in, but the Chinese sent us photographs of our men in Tashkurgan two days after they came back. They said that invading their territory without consent is an act of war, and that next time, there would be consequences. The President has too many other things taking priority right now to worry about the Chinese."

"So the mastermind of these attacks walks. He's the single most dangerous terrorist in the world, and he *will* try again," Sam said.

"We think so, too, but we feel the changes that are being made to border security and the profiling of Muslims to look for terrorists will help stop future attacks. In line with the President's policies of isolationism, operations will be put on hold for now."

"You really can't believe that bullshit. Implementing a new policy here in the U.S. is going to stop Khalid's attacks against our troops abroad and further attempts on our homeland? You and the Director are insane if you believe that. Fuck this shit. You know what, Marv? You're right, you chickenshits don't need me if that's the plan. Consider this my resignation from the CIA."

"C'mon, Sam, we still need you. Just take some time. Let things settle down. You don't want to quit again."

"Fuck you, Marv! I didn't quit the SEALs, I quit a system that has rules of engagement that impede soldiers from doing their job, making missions more dangerous than they need to be. I seem to remember you telling me that you agreed with me, and that being in the CIA would change that. And, you know what, for the most part, it did. But now, when it's more important than ever to act, we're just going to sit tight and hope Khalid stumbles into an area where we have a drone and then kill him? The bastard needs to die now!"

"Sam, you're making this personal. That's not good. Take some time and get your perspective back."

"You're fucking right it's personal. He tried to kill my wife and family along with anyone else unfortunate enough to share my name. It's been personal for him; now it is for me as well, and the only way 'that's not good' is for that asshole. I will find him and I will kill him. Somehow, some fucking way, but I guess without your help. So long, sir, thanks for the memories," were perhaps the last words Sam would ever say to D/NCS Marvin Royster.

"I don't accept your resignation, Sam. I'll call you in a couple of months," Marv shouted as Sam was out the door.

❈ ❈ ❈

"Hey, honey, I'm home," Sam yelled as he entered his house.

Their parents had left, and their friends were helping Mariah during the day, although she was improving rapidly.

"Hey babe, you're home early. Everything okay?"

"Funny you should ask," was his response. "I was told I should take a few months to get my head together. As I told you, I shut down after you were hurt; I went to a place that I've never been to in my life, and it took Gracie to pull me back. Like mother, like daughter. They're pissed that I wasn't back at Langley the next day, business as usual. If I'd been deployed when you were hurt, I would have detached from the information and finished the mission. But I wasn't deployed—instead, I was the first person to get to you after you were hurt. There's a huge fucking difference."

"You're right," was Mariah's reply. "Thank God for you, Steve, and Paul. No one received better first aid care that day than me. Maybe Marv is right, though. Take some time for yourself and for us. I'm sure he's thinking of what's best for you."

"Mariah, do you really think Khalid is taking time off? That asshole is planning his next attack, maybe on our family. How do we know that he's not going to find out our address? We need to remove his ass from this planet. But Royster and the Director don't have the balls to go after him." Sam was shaking with rage.

"Sweetie, I think it's a little more complicated than that."

"It's fucking simple," Sam yelled as he put his fist through the drywall.

"Jesus, Sam, get a grip."

"That's just it, Mariah. I feel like I'm losing my grip."

"Come here, Sam, and sit with me."

Sam went over to his wife and laid his head down on her lap while she stroked his head. Sam thought to himself, *This woman is my life, and she was nearly taken from me. If it's between putting my family at risk or killing terrorists, I choose family. Maybe it's time to put the guns away.* He thought of the Bob Dylan song, "Knockin' on Heaven's Door." He was tense, edgy, restless, and dark, a mixture of emotions he had never had all at the same time before. He felt that he was ready to explode.

The next month was a blur to Sam. He couldn't focus. He felt like he was just going through the motions with family, friends, and life in general. He was having trouble sleeping, and at times would awaken with his heart pounding. He often felt as if he were going to jump out of his skin. He couldn't comprehend what was happening, and was afraid to tell anyone what he was feeling, even Mariah. And he always told her everything.

His emotions reached a crescendo while he and his family were at a Saturday morning farmer's market. It was a spectacular day, Mariah had been cleared to weight-bear as tolerated on her left leg, so she wanted to get outside and walk. Sam was pushing J.J. in his stroller while Mariah and Gracie went from vendor to vendor, oohing and ahh-ing over goods at each little shop. Sam could feel himself revving up—a need to be somewhere else, doing something else. It was all he could do to stay there, yet he had no idea where else to go. He was restless, but had no clue what he needed to do to get rid of the feeling.

Mariah came up to him, and she noticed a pained look on his face. He was pale, sweaty, and constantly looking around.

"Sam, what's wrong? You look terrible."

Sam was hyperventilating, trying to get control, but felt like the world was closing in on him.

"I don't know. I feel shitty. Where's Gracie?" Sam said anxiously, as he scanned the crowd for his daughter.

Everyone he saw looked like a threat.

"Relax. I sent her ahead to the ice cream truck."

But as Mariah was speaking, Sam spotted his 5-year-old daughter. A man Sam did not recognize was facing her, kneeling down in front of her, and had his hands on her shoulders, talking to her. Mariah had just seen the interaction between Gracie and the man when Sam bolted off in their direction. Mariah watched in horror as Sam took the man down onto his stomach and wrenched his arm upward behind his back.

Sam screamed at him, "Get your fucking hands off my daughter, asshole."

He was about to deliver a blow to his head when Mariah limped over and grabbed Sam's arm with all of her strength.

"Stop, Sam, stop! He's Gracie's preschool principal! We know him."

Sam let go, sank to the ground, and sat there with his knees up to his chest, face buried in his hands, and began to silently sob. Mariah helped the man to his feet, apologized profusely, and told her that her husband had been on edge since the terrorist attacks. The man had known Mariah was a victim of the attacks. Remarkably, she thought, he was very understanding, but he did say, "He needs to get some help."

A crowd had gathered, pointing and murmuring, but eventually it started to thin out as Sam continued sitting on the ground with his face in his hands. Gracie was crying, and Mariah tried to console her.

She then went to Sam, placed her hands on his face, looked him in the eye, and said, "I love you Sam, and we're safe. Let's go home."

They returned home, put J.J. down for a nap, arranged for Gracie to go to a friend's house, and the two of them talked. Mariah said that she was sorry, she had seen that Sam was upset, and that she should have done more to figure out why. Sam, in turn, apologized for internalizing his feelings, letting them get to the point where he'd almost done significant bodily harm to someone. He was a "tough guy," impervious to bullshit emotions such as fear and anxiety—or so he'd always thought. They laughed, they cried, and hugged each other.

"Sam, you have PTSD," said Mariah.

"Post-traumatic stress disorder? Please. Don't label me," he replied.

"I'm not. It's not a weakness, babe. It can happen to anyone after a hellish incident. I think seeing me hurt and being powerless to do anything fits the bill as an inciting event. It's been festering to the point of today's outburst. Sounds like you've been having panic attacks, from what you just described to me, and from what I witnessed today.."

"Mariah, I'm a Tier 1 operator. That shouldn't happen to me."

"Sam, you're human first. Only a sociopathic robot would lack emotion and not have to deal with feelings. It's never bothered you operating, because that's second nature to you. You always decompress by telling me about your missions in detail, and that's helped you process your emotions. This time, however, you weren't operating, and I was hurt. You had no control like you do when you're operating. You went on instinct to help me the day of the attacks, and then you essentially were at my bedside constantly for 10 days. You didn't talk to anybody. That's a huge difference."

"I guess you're right," Sam replied. "It just makes me feel so weak."

"Oh Sam, you silly man. If being sensitive and caring means you're weak, then that's what I want," Mariah said. "You've always been those things. It's just that the perfect storm tipped you over the edge."

"Ok, maybe… but what's next?" he replied.

"Now we start getting better. Understanding the cause and accepting its affect on you opens the door for healing."

"How did you get so damn smart?" Sam said with a smile.

"I think I've just always been like this—smart as hell," she replied straight-faced.

She looked at Sam, and they both started laughing.

"Wow, humility didn't come with those smarts. Now, it's time to rehab that leg, if you know what I mean," Sam said with a wink.

Chapter 50

Mariah had contacts in the mental health field, and she devoted the next several days to finding someone for Sam to see. The two of them kept up their own 'therapy,' and that was helping Sam with his moods. Sam also got back into a routine of physical activity, and renewing his running and weight room regimen helped tremendously. He tried to avoid watching the news, other than 10 minutes a day for a summary of anything important. He wanted to separate himself from thinking about potential missions and what he would do. He remained vigilant, but not paranoid, regarding any potential threats to him or his family. He had always been that way—it was his training—but it was now more heightened than ever. It had to be expected, considering the events of the bombings. His family had been targeted, and seeing your wife hurt by a terrorist attack will do that to a man. Sam resumed contact with his buddies on the team, working out together and socializing. He seemed to notice that Paul Kerney behaved a little differently when they got together. Paul was watching Sam more than usual, almost hovering at times. Finally, Sam couldn't take it any longer.

"Paul, what is your deal?" Sam asked.

"What do you mean?" Kerney replied.

"You've been watching me like a mother hen. You hover around me like I'm a kid just learning how to walk!"

"Really?" Paul answered. "I hadn't noticed."

"Shut the hell up and tell me why."

"I'm worried about you, Sam. You seem better, but you were in a bad place after the attacks. Do you even remember seeing team members while Mariah was in the ICU?"

Sam looked at him and said, "I don't remember much of that time."

Paul replied, "You're my friend for life, Sam, but I have to wonder if you've properly processed the day of the attack."

"Shit, you sound just like Mariah. I'm doing my best, man."

Paul then went on to tell Sam that there was a time at the beginning of his career that had been very difficult. He related feelings and experiences that Sam was now familiar with from the past six weeks. He opened up to Sam in a way that was comfortable because someone else knew exactly how he had been feeling… and had survived. Paul was a grade A badass. He told Sam that he'd seen a therapist who dragged him out of his anxiety and depression. At first, he'd been hesitant to see the guy, but he respected his credentials and made the appointment.

"What's so special about his guy?"

"He's one of us, Sam, a former SEAL, with multiple deployments to a lot of bad places. He gets it, he's been there, and he knows how to help. It's no bullshit; the man is skilled."

"Paul… I never knew."

"It happened before I met you. It's been all good since then. Your policy about having one person to talk to before and after a mission is smart. It's exactly the same advice that my guy gave me. I know that advice has helped a lot of guys," said Paul.

"Yeah, well, my strategy didn't help this time."

"That's because your "therapist" was in a coma, bro. You needed someone else—Steve and I should've seen it."

" I probably would've shut you guys out."

"Maybe, but go see my guy."

'I'll check him out, Paul, I promise."

❖ ❖ ❖

Sam met former Commander Chris Key the following week at his office. They acquainted themselves through small talk, but more importantly, through sharing stories of missions that had occurred during their time as SEALs. It wasn't a "who's the bigger badass" competition, but a series of stories about shared experiences. Chris told his own story—his struggle with PTSD and his comeback through Cognitive Behavioral Therapy. He was a fascinating storyteller and an even better listener. Sam was thankful to Paul for his recommendation.

"I think your wife hit the nail on the head, Sam. You have a very strong mechanism in place—talking with your wife to help deal with the mental aspect of the job—and that's always helped you process your missions. However, her injuries, and the inability to talk to her, led you to internalize this event. It snowballed, got out of control, and you beat up your daughter's principal," Chris said with a smile.

"Can't wait to tell her she was right," Sam responded with sarcasm.

"You're going to be fine. Let me give you a few things to work on, and then let's get together next week. You've made the turn and are on the road to recovery, but I think a few meetings together will expose you to some other defense mechanisms to have handy if you need them. We all need methods to put things in perspective and stop ourselves from having our thoughts run rampant and take over our mind."

They met over the next month, Sam getting the help he needed, and he made a new friend in Chris. As he was feeling better, sleeping better, and eating better, he was also increasing his conditioning and putting some time in at the shooting range. He felt that he was back to his normal self, mentally and physically. Mariah and Gracie were glad to have Sam back to his usual state of mind.

Mariah recovered quickly as well and was aching to return to work. She genuinely loved what she did for the Red Cross and wanted to be there to help in the rebuilding process. Sam went back to the role of Mr. Mom, enjoying every second of his time with his children. He continued to train with his buddies when they were available. Both Paul Kerney and Steve Durrant had become frustrated with the CIA's agenda. Currently, there wasn't much need for operators, as it was mostly spy work. They felt like they were sitting on the sidelines when they knew that if deployed appropriately, they could make a huge difference.

Sam was very sympathetic to them and explained to them that what they had just told him was the main reason that Sam had told Royster he was done with the CIA. Maybe he had made the decision while he was in a bad place, but if his skills weren't going to be used appropriately, then why stay? The three friends would work out, train like they were still SEALs, and long for the days of missions. They had been a great team and knew that their skills were as sharp as ever.

Sam shared his friends' opinions with Mariah, trying to convey the frustration they had in their voices.

"I sense some frustration in your voice as well," she said after listening to him. "Do you want to go back out there?"

Sam hesitated, not sure what to say. He was torn because he knew that he wanted to, but he just wasn't sure how Mariah would take it.

"It's okay if you want to," she said. "It's your calling, Sam, to deliver justice against those that take advantage of others. Lord knows, there's plenty of those assholes around."

"You're not opposed to that?" asked Sam.

"No, I'm not. I think at some point you'll carry on that fight but in a different way, such as planning or teaching. But you're not ready for that yet. You're a Tier 1 Operator, a grade A badass," Mariah said, and then giggled.

"Easy, girl, you're riling me up in a major way."

"Oh, my. Well, come on over and let me help you with your situation," she said.

Chapter 50

It was now six months after the attacks on D.C., and Sam was in the best shape of his life, and he yearned to get back into the game. Missions in the CIA were far and few between, so he couldn't even live vicariously through his friends' stories because they were basically stagnant. He had left countless messages with CIA Director Ritchie and D/ NCS Royster, but neither had called back. Sam was certain that he had probably burned that bridge. However, he was surprised at the lack of decency on their part—surely they could simply call back and tell him his status.

Sam worked out in the morning by himself, and then usually joined Kerney and Durrant when they were done with work. His morning workout enabled him to get his focus for the entire day. Rarely was anyone else around when he was working out, but he had recently noticed a gentleman in his mid-fifties hanging around whom he had

266 | JOSEPH R. RITCHIE

never seen before. He appeared to be in good shape and had a decent bench press for his age. He would ask Sam to spot him occasionally, but they never spoke more than necessary to one another. This went on for about two weeks, with no changes to either Sam's or the older man's routine. Then one day, the man looked at him and spoke.

"Sam, you look great. But how are you feeling?" he asked.

"I'm sorry, do I know you?" Sam responded.

"No, but I know everything about you through some mutual friends. They speak of you in the highest regard. More so than anyone else they've ever talked to me about."

"Is that so?" Sam laughed. "It would depend on who you talk to. I have some pretty stupid friends."

"Well, I assure you that these friends aren't stupid," the man said. "I won't reveal them to you until you agree to talk with me."

"Wait a minute—who the hell are you?"

"I'm a very good friend of some important people who have a lot of common interests. Call me Mr. Steen," he said as he reached out his hand to shake.

"Just Mr. Steen?" said Sam. "Sounds a little cryptic. So, is this the place you usually work out, or have you been stalking me?"

"Not stalking, Sam—*observing* is a better word. A friend called me about a month ago and told me about you. He went on and on about your skills and successes, so I figured that I would see for myself."

"Very mysterious, Mr. Steen. To what end?" Sam asked.

"I'd like to offer you a job," Steen answered. "A job that our mutual friend thought you would be perfect for."

"I'm intrigued, but I'm not a hit man for some private matter."

"No, nothing like that," Steen responded. "Why don't you and your lovely wife join me for dinner tonight? And I'll tell you everything, and answer any questions."

"I don't know about tonight; we'd have to get a babysitter, and I'm not sure about my wife's plans."

"I took the liberty several days ago to set up your usual babysitter. I also had the restaurant call your wife yesterday to confirm your reservation tonight," replied Mr. Steen. "She thinks that you made it."

"Wow, now I'm beyond intrigued. You're pretty slick, Mr. Steen," Sam said. "But when I tell her we were both tricked into a dinner with a stranger…"

"Tell her the whole story. From what I hear about her, she'll be just as intrigued as you."

"Damn, you are well informed," replied Sam. "Where and when?"

"I'll have a car pick you and your wife up around 7 p.m. No jacket required, Sam," said Mr. Steen as he left the weight room.

Sam kept thinking, *Who the hell is this guy?*

He had to be some intelligence guy, but with what agency? Sam had Top Secret clearance and had run missions with every agency that existed. Perhaps there was a government entity that he was not aware of; there had always been rumors of shadow government agencies, but that seemed very far-fetched. But he had also invited Mariah! What government group invited spouses to dinner? Especially those tasked with killing the enemy. None, of course. That meant he was probably some private security contractor or a mercenary recruiter. Well, after he had a conversation with Mariah, Sam was sure that they would cancel the dinner.

However, she surprised Sam, and was excited to meet this mystery man and hear his sales pitch. She told Sam that anyone who would include the spouse couldn't be all bad; it was almost like what happened in the real world when someone was looking at a job possibility.

Sam didn't know what to make of it. He knew Mr. Steen was interested in him for his skillset, but whom did he work for? And why include Mariah? Well, if nothing else, they could cut the dinner short and enjoy a night out together.

They pulled into Fiola Mare, an Italian seafood restaurant on the Washington harbor. They were escorted to a table outside, where Mr. Steen and a woman were already seated. Mr. Steen had secured an outside table away from other patrons; it seemed that he was well known to the concierge and wait staff. Introductions were made, cocktail orders were completed, and small talk proceeded. They asked about Mariah's recovery, about their children, and how they had met. None of their answers seemed surprising to Mr. Steen; it was as if he already knew all about them. He revealed to Sam and Mariah that he to, was from Ohio and had gone to The Ohio State University. He also was a member of the Sigma Chi fraternity.

"Are you making that up?" asked Sam. "That seems too perfect."

"Seriously—I grew up in Fremont, Ohio. Check the fraternity records. I'm in there," said Steen.

"Mr. Steen, what's your first name?" asked Mariah.

"Great question," his guest, Cathy Patrick, said quickly.

"My first name is Mr.," Steen replied, smiling.

Mariah gave him a sideways glance and responded, "I call bullshit, but if you don't want to tell us, that's your business. But it's very weird."

Ms. Patrick laughed and said, "I like you, Mariah. You don't hold back."

"Seriously, my Momma named me Mr. It was a bitch through school, let me tell you."

"Whatever," responded Mariah with a mischievous grin.

Mr. Steen just looked at Mariah with a shit-eating grin.

"You do know, Mr. Steen, that in some circles, 'whatever' has the same meaning as 'fuck you.'"

He just shook his head, reached into his pocket and showed Mariah his license. The name on it was Mr. Steen.

"That doesn't prove anything. A shady guy like you could have fake IDs made," said Mariah with a smile.

Sam was grinning from ear to ear. He hadn't done so for a while and it felt good. He was also used to seeing his wife casually interrogate people who made her suspicious. She was not one to back down or be intimidated.

"You go, girl," said Ms. Patrick. "She certainly has you pegged, Mr."

"You might be sorry you invited me, Mr. Steen," said Mariah with a chuckle.

"On the contrary, Mrs. Richards, I wanted you here for exactly that reason—so you could use your marvelous intuition to evaluate me," responded Mr. Steen sincerely. "I want you to know everything, and ask any questions about the opportunity I'm going to present to your husband."

"Well, I am impressed with that—no one invited me to dinner before Sam became a SEAL or joined the CIA. Oh, and Mariah is fine. That's what's on my license," Mariah said with a wink.

"Touché, Mariah," Steen responded.

They all genuinely laughed at the exchange. Their meals arrived, and their conversation centered on the food and wine. They behaved like old friends, passing their plates to share their orders, telling stories about one another, being at ease, and genuinely enjoying one another's company. Their plates were cleared, desserts arrived, and as if by design, no one came near their table.

"That was excellent," Sam said, breaking the silence, "both the food and your company…"

"But its time for business," interrupted Mr. Steen. "First of all, Ms. Patrick is a dear friend of mine, but also my lawyer and a lawyer for the group I represent. I apologize, but she needs these documents signed before I can tell you more. I assure you that they are standard non-disclosure agreements. The information that I want to share with you is such that we need assurances that people's names and our activities won't be revealed, especially if you decide not to come on board."

Sam wasn't surprised at the request, having worked in secrecy his entire adult life. He nodded to Mariah, they read through them, and signed the documents.

For the next 20 minutes, Mr. Steen detailed the organization that he directed. He described being the Chairman of the Board, with the Board consisting of a group of powerful men and women, whose names were well known to both Mariah and Sam. They were CEOs of different companies, a former Joint Chief of Staff, several former Senators from both sides of the aisle, a prominent theologian, and a former Attorney General. The group had diverse political views, had both men and women, and was a cross-section of successful Americans. These people, in turn, had connections with people in every aspect of American commerce and government, as well as the everyday American.

Mr. Steen explained that they were patriots who loved their country, but were often disillusioned with some of its decisions regarding its actions in various parts of the world. The fundamental rule of the group was to not do anything intentionally against the best interests of the U.S. Sometimes they exercised influence in locations that were the same as the U.S. government, using money when necessary or coordinating aid, and at times, using their power to coerce others to do the right thing. Sometimes the group tried to exert influence in areas where the U.S. government didn't want to go. They had limitless financial resources and connections, but they lacked manpower to physically fight the true evil of the world. There were times when money and influence weren't enough. They had discovered that an operational division was needed to occasionally bring wrath down upon those who were responsible for problems that could not be solved with money and aid.

"It sounds like a shadow government agency that wants a hired gun for the vigilante division," said Sam after Steen had finished.

"I can see where you might think that. But we exert no influence over government officials, and we don't make policy—that's for the politicians. We let our government system run normally. Lobbyists try to influence politicians,; we don't do that. We're more like an aid group such as the Red Cross, Amnesty international, etc. But we see an increasing need for using violence in certain cases to improve the conditions of the people we help. It's no different than the American government when they send in troops or CIA operators to try to balance the playing field. That's what you've done your whole career, Sam."

"There's one big difference," said Sam. "Those are sanctioned missions backed by the government. You're proposing vigilantism, which in essence is criminal. While it may be morally justified to provide order in circumstances being ignored by law enforcement or governments, it's still illegal, and that means potential consequences."

"Yes, I see your point. It's a fine line, isn't it? But that's where the connections of our Board members are so important. They have connections to every government agency as well as to their counterparts across the world, who would help with the legal ramifications of your work," replied Mr. Steen.

"What does that even mean?" asked Mariah.

Sam knew what it meant but wanted to see how transparent Mr. Steen really was.

"It means our influence is not limited to within the U.S. alone; we have influential friends everywhere who are sympathetic to our cause. Those friends include individuals in governments that can be of benefit when law enforcement might be involved. Let me give you an example of our government connections. Sam, how do you think I got your name?"

"I assume from contacts you have in the government, or hell, after the leak to the press that revealed my name, simply from reading the newspapers that discussed the other Sam Richards who were targeted in the attacks on D.C."

"Those articles didn't give much detail on you, Sam," said Mr. Steen. "No, I got your name and info from one of our CIA connections, D/NCS Royster. Maybe you've heard of him?"

Sam was shocked. He had been calling Royster for a month but had not received any return calls. He had wanted to apologize to Marv and consider asking him if there was room for him back at the CIA.

"Marv's been watching you, Sam, from afar. He wanted to give you space and all the time you needed. He knew from your last conversation that he wouldn't hear from you until you were ready to get busy. He's purposely not returned your calls, as he wanted us to have a conversation first. He told me to tell you he's sorry for the deception, and that if you turn me down, there's a job waiting for you at the CIA. He knows how you think, knows you like your independence, and knows that you are a patriot like he is. He still needs you, but he wants what's best for you. He also currently has his hands tied and can't do much about providing the type of operations that he knows you want."

Mariah reached out and took Sam's hand. He looked at Mariah and shook his head.

"Wow. I said some nasty things to him, and have been cursing his name because I haven't heard from him. Marv sure displayed the difference between a spy and an operator; spies are good liars and manipulators. I'm just an operator."

"And what are operators?" asked Ms. Patrick.

Sam hesitated, but both Mariah and Mr. Steen nodded to him.

"We're the ones who get things done. We're the tip of the spear. We deliver justice to those who are deserving, eliminating them as a problem and showing likeminded individuals to be very careful."

"Ooh," she said, "he does sound perfect for the job, Mr. Steen!"

"Yes, he does, Cathy," replied Mr. Steen. "Sam, Marv knows where you were coming from when you said those things to him. You can apologize to him whether you're with us or go back to the CIA. But, here's the deal—you would lead a team of special operators into missions agreed upon by you, the Board, and me. You would have free rein when it comes to planning and necessary resources. You fill out a shopping list, I'll get the items. You, and you alone, have full autonomy over mission specifics. Furthermore, the mission is a no-go if you disagree with the objectives. You have total control once the decision to go is made. Again, Marv would love you to come back to the CIA, but he thinks this is an option you should hear about. He told me that it's the next evolution for you—complete input into targets, complete autonomy on the missions, no political bullshit tying you down. He wants you to call him sometime after this meeting."

"Sounds too good to be true," Sam said.

"Agreed," added Mariah. "And what kind of missions are you talking about?"

"It's all true, no hidden agenda. The missions would be no different than what you're used to. Nothing like your last one in Afghanistan, but similar to your forays into Nigeria, Somalia, and Haiti," answered Mr. Steen.

"Haiti?" Said Sam. "I haven't operated there." He winked at Mariah.

"Right," was Steen's response. "And my Momma named me Mr.!"

Mariah and Steen pointed at each other, smiling like people do when they knew that the other person had been bullshitting.

"I knew it!" said Mariah. "You big liar. You, too, Cathy."

"Mariah, I swear, all of his legal documents say Mr. He's been lying to me too!"

"Ok, Mr. Steen, spill it. Your secret is safe with us. Add it to the NDA," said a smiling Sam.

"Only if you'll consider my offer after I tell you more about our group."

"Deal," said Mariah quickly. "By the way, does your group have a name or is it just 'group'?"

"We're called the Trust," he answered. "As in, you can trust us."

"Interesting. Mr., what's your first name?" prodded Mariah.

"Cowan," Steen answered.

There was about 10 seconds of silence, then all four burst out laughing. "As in Thomas Cowan Bell, of Sigma Chi founder fame?," asked Sam.

Mariah and Cathy exchanged glances, their expression displaying *Who?*

"No, as in my mom's maiden name. See why I don't use it? It's a terrible first name. There's no good short nickname—'Hey, cow' or 'Hey, wan'. That's top secret, by the way, and if it gets out, I'll know who leaked it!"

They teased Mr. Cowan Steen for a while longer, then the rest of the evening centered on answering any and all questions. Sam and Mariah were satisfied with Mr. Steen's answers—he answered promptly and didn't display any deceit that they could sense.

It was Mr. Steen who brought up the subject of compensation. Sam had obviously never asked as a SEAL or CIA agent what his salary would be, as salaries were established by government pay scales. Also, his motivation had never been money, and that hadn't changed. He felt uncomfortable discussing the financials, but it was important to

Mr. Steen. Instead of saying the amount out loud, he slipped Sam his business card with the amount written on it. Sam looked, and almost snorted brandy out the front of his nose. He showed the number to Mariah, who was more controlled when she saw it.

"Too low?" asked Steen seriously. "Private security contractors pay much more than the government, so we thought we'd compensate our people significantly more than they do. Along with that comes full benefits and a life insurance policy that would negate any need for money should the unfortunate occur."

"So it's a little more than the $400,000 Soldier's Guaranteed Life Insurance benefit from the military?" asked Sam.

"Uh, yeah, 25 times more, if my math is correct," replied Steen.

"Everything is more than generous. Again, almost too good to be true. I know it's a cliché, but if I had wanted to be rich, I would have never become a SEAL. I've always just wanted to help those who can't help themselves, and try to make the world a better place. It sounds sappy, but it's the truth."

"And you have, Sam. And if you want, you still can," was Steen's response. "I just hope that it's with us. Okay, we've taken enough of your evening. It was a pleasure meeting you, Mariah. I didn't want to start another conversation tonight, but your expertise from working with the Red Cross is something the Trust could use as well."

"That's very flattering, Cow... I mean Mr.," she said with a smile. "But lets think about one family member joining at a time."

"Deal," he answered. "Take all the time you need, Sam. Again, it's been a pleasure, and I hope you come on board."

Sam and Mariah sat quietly in the back of the car for the trip home, their driver respecting their silence. Not a word was spoken between them; they held hands, and each was deep in thought. They went straight to sleep when they got to their home.

The next morning, after they had gotten the kids moving, they rehashed the discussion, each asking the other questions, playing devil's advocate, trying to find something negative about the offer. They couldn't. Sam needed to talk to Marv and get his opinion of Mr. Steen as well as apologize to him. Unless he had a lot of negative things to say, Sam was on board with giving the Trust a shot.

Chapter 51

Sam called and spoke to Marv's secretary to set up an appointment for lunch. She laughed and said Marv was expecting Sam's call and had cleared his lunch schedule for the next week. Sam laughed, got caught up with the happenings in the NCS, and told her to say "Hey" to everyone.

"You're dearly missed by everyone, Samuel, but those two friends of yours just mope around and say, 'I wish Sam was here.' They really miss you."

Of course, she was talking about Kerney and Durrant.

"Don't pity them too much," he answered. "I work out with them all the time, and our families hang out together most weekends. We may not be working together, but we see each other an awful lot."

"Sam," she said, "they mean the missions."

"Ah," he answered. "Yeah, me too."

They said their good-byes and promised to stay in touch.

Sam met Marv at their favorite lunch spot, exchanged classic "bro" hugs—no frontal waist touching. Sam quickly began, and apologized for their last interaction and the things he'd said. Marv countered, and said he felt terrible about being passive-aggressive in forcing him to take time off, as well as waiting for him to call when he was ready instead of calling Sam to see how he was doing.

"You don't know how many times I wanted to call you, Sam. So, instead, I relied on intel from Kerney and Durrant. After a while, they told me to mind my own business and call you myself," Royster laughed. "I was worried about your mental state. I knew that we were changing our tactics and reducing operations. I thought that it would kill you to be doing nothing. I was wrong; you should have been able to do what you wanted. I truly had your best interests in mind, but my execution was terrible. For that I am truly sorry."

"Same on my side, Marv. It was the toughest period of my life, and you were right that I needed time. Thank you. I found a great person to talk to besides Mariah, and together, the two of them brought me back. I think I'm stronger than ever."

"Chris Key is a magician, is he not?" replied Marv.

Sam was a little taken aback, thinking Marv must have surveilled him.

Marv sensed Sam's wariness and quickly said, "Kerney told me he gave you his name. He thought it was okay to tell me since I had given him Key's name years ago. I know he's good because I've seen him too. It's nothing to be ashamed about, Sam."

"You're right, although I have to admit that I was ashamed at first. But then, talking to him was such a relief."

"I get it," Marv replied. "But now, you want to hear about my man Cowan."

"Ha, you know his first name too? That liar said we were the first to know," laughed Sam.

"You truly are one of few to know; he's obsessed with keeping it secret. But honestly, the guy has never lied to me, besides his name obsession. You can believe what he says to you. I hope you don't mind, but I gave him your name a couple of months ago. I've known him a long time."

Marv went on to explain that Steen had been a deep, dark agent of the CIA going back to the 90's. He had operated on every continent and executed countless successful, covert missions that changed the political landscape in the favor of the West. He was a national treasure that very few, even in the government, knew about. To use a title from a Steven Seagal movie, he was the original "Glimmer Man." He was absolutely ghostly about how he accomplished his missions; his adversaries could only ever catch a glimmer of his presence, and by then it would be too late. He finished his CIA career with distinction and was a living legend within the intelligence community. He had moved off the grid somewhere out west, and did occasional consulting work for Royster and others.

Mr. Steen had taken Marv into his confidence a year ago and told him about a group of powerful people who had approached him and described their desire to do their part in righting wrongs and protecting the United States. Royster had vetted the individuals and found no wrongdoings or alternative agenda. Steen took the job and had worked in partnership with Royster, sharing the Trust's interests and activities. Mr. Steen had told Marv that he wanted the Trust to have the ability to use more than money and aid to improve people's lives. He wanted to have a group of operators who could level playing fields for oppressed people, as well as effect U.S. policy in a positive way when the government felt too handcuffed to act.

"I knew I couldn't stop him from doing that, Sam. So, I asked to be kept in the loop, and said I'd offer intel as necessary in exchange. Of course, that's not common knowledge. I think that there may be times that he and I can help each other. When he said that he wanted an operations unit, I told him that the job sounded perfect for you. With you having the final say and the ability to give the go/no-go on missions, I know that everything will be legitimate. Your moral compass is beyond reproach. In summary, I say give it a shot; I'll be in your corner unofficially. If you don't like it, as long as I'm in the CIA, you'll always have a home here."

"I can't be a one-man show. I'll need to ensure that I have good people working as a team," said Sam.

"I'm sure there are already; Steen doesn't just settle. I guarantee that the men he's approached are top-notch," said Marv. "There's also your two mopey friends, Kerney and Durrant."

"You'd let me talk to them?" asked Sam.

"Absolutely," he replied. "I've known the three of you for a long time, the finest trio of operators that I've ever seen. If they're interested, go for it. My only condition is that if I need the three of you in the future for 'consulting work,' you'll help me. It's perfect for the three of you because we're at a real standstill in the CIA."

"You have my word—I'll be there if you need me," replied Sam.

"Your word is better than a contract," Marv answered.

Sam departed from lunch on cloud nine. He was pumped up for the first time in a long time. A man whom he trusted implicitly had told him to go for it, and approved the recruitment of his best friends. Sam decided that he would give it a go with the Trust, feel it out before trying to recruit Paul and Steve. The next step was to tell Mariah he was saying yes to Mr. Steen, and then call him to accept the offer. Life was good!

Chapter 52

Sam made the call to Mr. Steen, who was ecstatic that Sam had accepted. The two of them met, and Sam was introduced to the Board members through videoconference. The Board members knew about his exploits, as Mr. Steen had briefed them. They shared their excitement with Sam and assured him that he had their full support. They seemed transparent with their ideals, telling Sam reasons that they needed to be able to do more than give money and supplies. They saw a need for pinpoint operations to improve the situations of certain groups of people as well as bring justice where others could not. It reminded Sam a lot of what he had done in Haiti and Venezuela—eliminating the corruption so that the aid groups could get their jobs done.

Sam then met two gentlemen that Steen had recruited to be part of the team. Randy Bury and David Woprice were both former Delta Force. Mr. Steen had shared their resumes with Sam, noting the missions they had done were very similar to Sam's SEAL days. They were very accomplished Tier 1 Operators. The two Deltas had gone through training together, and like Sam, Paul, and Steve, were best of friends. Mr. Steen told Sam that they had similar ideals and, like Sam, were morally beyond reproach.

There had always been a friendly competition between America's best of the best Special Forces operators.

"You have any problems with SEALs?" asked Sam.

"Not at all—we love going to Sea World to see them do tricks," said Bury, chuckling.

"Good one, Randy," said Woprice, rolling his eyes.

"C'mon, it's an oldie but a goody!" he responded. "No, really, Sam, we've done many joint missions with you guys, and your training seems adequate." He delivered this statement with a shit-eating grin.

Both he and Woprice were now laughing.

They looked at Sam, who turned toward Mr. Steen and remarked, "They'll probably be adequate for the B team that we want to put together."

Nothing but silence followed.

Then it was Sam's turn to laugh. "Lighten up, boys," said Sam, "if you're going to give shit, be ready to take it. Besides, I've got a few training exercises picked out to see if you boys are squared away."

"Copy that," they both said.

Over the next two weeks, the three of them trained together on the road, in the gym, and with exercise scenarios that Sam had created. Both Bury and Woprice were impressed with the slightly older man's stamina and skills. By the end of that time, they told Sam that they had never worked with a better operator. Likewise, Sam respected their skills and knew that they would make a great team.

"Tomorrow, we're meeting with Steen to discuss several mission options," said Sam. "It's been six months for me, so I'm beyond ready."

"You wouldn't know it from the training exercises, Sam. And okay, I admit it, SEALs are badasses," said Randy.

"We're all badasses, brother," replied Sam with a fist bump to Randy.

Mr. Steen and the team met the following morning to discuss the inaugural mission of the Trust's new Operations Division. Since the terrorist attacks, the President had gained significant support regarding amnesty for illegals when appropriate and deportation when they were found inappropriate. The wall on the southern border was still being built, but not quickly enough. There was still a significant number of people finding ways across the border undetected.

Almost all of these were people were of illicit background, such as MS-13 gang members. Currently, there were about 8-10 thousand MS-13 gang members in the U.S. Many were being deported under the new policy, but many were still streaming across areas of the unsecured southern border. The National Guard and Border Patrol were struggling to cover this vast area. It had been discovered that these groups were crossing in large groups, they were coming well-armed, and they were overwhelming the National Guard and Border Patrol troops.

"This is a great first mission," said Mr. Steen. "We have intel that shows that the most common entry points for these gang members. Satellite info from my CIA friend shows 50-100-man groups traveling together in Mexico before they cross. The Mexican police and army show no interest in taking them out before the border. That's where we come in. The geography of the area forces them to go through a narrow pass before it opens up to a wider area where they can spread themselves out. The pass would be a perfect place to take them out, while they're still in Mexico. What do you say, Sam?"

Sam studied the maps and satellite images. Steen was correct in his assessment; some well-placed explosives and snipers should be able to prevent the group from wasting any more oxygen that was meant for good people. It was a slam dunk mission, even one he could probably do solo.

"No problem," said Sam. "But are we sure that they travel alone and not with innocents as well?"

"Great question," replied Steen. "The National Guard and Border Patrol report no civilians were present when they had up-close skirmishes with these assholes. We would certainly need to personally verify that information. What do you think, fellas?" he asked. "Any problems with taking out gang members before they reach the U.S.?"

The three operators exchanged glances with one another, giving each other a barely perceptible nod.

"No issues. Seems like a good policy to us," Sam answered for the three of them.

Over the next three weeks, the three-man team took out four groups of gang members along different routes of possible entry into the U.S. Sam assumed that the satellite coverage they were using was from Royster, and by passing this information along, Sam's team could do what the American Government would not: hit these guys within Mexico. It was perfect deniability for the government. The word seemed to be spreading, because after the successes of Sam's team, satellites had not picked up any more groups trying to cross for the last several months. A simple but effective, solution had succeeded. The Border Patrol was now no longer overwhelmed and could now more effectively do their job. To avoid any link to the American government, a disinformation campaign had followed each attack, pointing blame on rival gangs in Mexico. The Mexican government and the media had bought the campaign, accepting it as criminal-on-criminal violence.

Chapter 53

Over the next six months, the three men helped with other causes requiring their expertise. Very similar to what Sam had done in Haiti, they protected several aid groups in volatile areas while the groups distributed goods to the poor. They spent time in Syria, helping to keep Doctors Without Borders safe as they cared for the many refugees affected by that conflict. These were rewarding missions with good outcomes, but not the real game-changers that the team desired. Sam expressed this to Mr. Steen at one of their routine meetings where they would evaluate areas in the world that might require their service.

"Is it not our purpose to affect positive change in the world that is in the best interest of not only the United States but also the people of that region?" asked Sam.

"It is," replied Mr. Steen. "But remember, we're more of an adjunct to the CIA, not a branch. They should be dealing with the bigger problems. You know that Marv would give us a mission that he felt needed to be done, but for some reason the Government wouldn't do."

"Exactly—sometimes go to places and do things that the US government refuses or can't do," replied Sam.

"Again, yes, Sam. Sounds like you have something in mind."

"Bingo," was Sam's response. "You're aware that I operated in Venezuela, helping to eliminate several large sex trafficking rings preying on the many Venezuelan refugees leaving the country. It was rewarding, but the country continues to be in free fall because of the current President's ruling clique. Having badly mismanaged the economy, he now refuses to admit his contribution to the depth of Venezuela's agony or accept most humanitarian relief from other countries. He's the biggest obstacle to peace, social reform, and economic stability for the country. The CIA has been supporting the opposition and trying to destabilize his government, with apparently minimal success."

"All true, Sam, but what can the three of you do?" asked Steen.

"We can take the motherfucker out," Bury quickly answered.

"Exactly," said Sam. "Carefully, and in a way that neither the opposition nor the U.S. can be accused of being responsible for the assassination."

"Wow," was Steen's reply. "I'm going to have to hear your plan and see what the Board thinks."

Chapter 54

Sam began his plan's description by giving a short history lesson about Russia and Venezuela's relationship. Russia had been increasing its ties to Venezuela since the early 2000s, extending loans to the country as well as providing military equipment. In fact, in 2006 and 2013, Venezuela was one of the top four purchasers of Russian military hardware in the world. Russia wanted a foothold close to the U.S., much like they'd had with Cuba before the fall of the Soviet Union. Recently, about 100 Russian personnel had arrived in Caracas. The Kremlin claimed that they were part of a maintenance team sent to work on equipment. The U.S. and others didn't believe that explanation for a second. The relationship between the two countries had certainly become closer as the current President's opposition continued to gain momentum. There had been recent reports that the President had been ready to flee Venezuela, but the promise of Russian support convinced him to stay. Besides having his normal group of bodyguards, there were always several Russians around his home, the Miraflores Palace in Caracas.

CIA intelligence revealed that the President made very few trips outside of the palace without significant escort. The exception to this was the weekly visit to his mistress. Those excursions were always the same; dine at the same restaurant, stay the night in the same hotel suite, and head back to the palace by the following midday. In the past year, there had been no deviation from this schedule. The Venezuelan President would travel in a convoy of three vehicles, with two of his personal guards in the first vehicle, he and two more of his guards in the second, and two Russian bodyguards trailing in the third. The CIA had been able to eavesdrop on the communications between the cars and had noted the man's many comments regarding his distaste of the Russians, as well as promises to his bodyguards that he would reward them if he decided to leave the country with their protection. He had made many comments regarding the leader of Russia that were far from flattering.

Sam and his team arrived in Caracas and were able to verify the CIA intelligence over a two-week period. The President did indeed follow the same routine when it came to his mistress. Sam had also received tapes from the CIA that contained the leader's rants against Russia and its leadership. Sam and his two new friends had finalized their plan and were ready to act.

The next evening was the scheduled visit with his mistress, and Sam and his team would be finally able to attempt a game-changing mission. The trio had secured entry the evening before into the suite regularly used for the rendezvous. It was easy to do in a country so corrupt and with opposition sentiment to the leader so high. A few well-placed bribes had allowed them to gather access to the suite. Recording devices and cameras had been planted to assist for use in the evening's activities.

The President's convoy arrived at the hotel, and the group did what it always did. The Russians stayed in their vehicle, parked across the street from the hotel and hidden within a small wooded park. The bodyguards from the lead car would inspect the premises and then return to escort the leader and his mistress up to the suite, along with the two bodyguards in his vehicle. The lead car's bodyguards would then return to their vehicle, on watch at the front of the hotel, while the two from the President's car stayed inside the hotel, close to him. The opposition players were all in position.

At 3 a.m., Sam, who was 20 feet from the Russians' vehicle, noticed that one of the Russians got out of the car to relieve his bladder; the other was sleeping. A silenced 9mm double-tap to the head put the Russian to the ground. Sam then returned to the vehicle, got in, sat in the passenger seat as if he were the other bodyguard, and quietly disposed of the second Russian.

"Russian guards neutralized; proceed with caution."

"Copy that," replied Woprice.

He and Bury then made their way to the President's suite and proceeded to quietly eliminate the two bodyguards positioned outside the door. Four guards had now been eliminated, leaving only the two at the front of the building.

They entered the suite without making a sound and stood before the bed, watching the snoring Venezuelan leader and his mistress sleeping. Sam could also see the scene playing out through the cameras they'd positioned earlier. Woprice gently awakened the President, who expectedly startled when he did not see the faces of his personal bodyguards. His mistress began screaming, but was quickly quieted by Bury via duct-tape to her mouth.

"What is the meaning of this? Where are my guards?" bellowed the President.

"Shut up and listen," responded Woprice in Russian-accented Spanish. He then played a compilation of recordings consisting of the Venezuelan leader's rants against Russia and its President, along with his comments about leaving the country.

"My superiors are not very happy with you," said Woprice. "We have stood by your side, yet you disparage us and plan to humiliate us by leaving."

The President began pleading, offering excuses and apologies for his comments. His mistress was attentively listening to the conversation with eyes full of fear.

"I'm feeling the stress and was just ranting," he said. "I meant none of it. Please, tell your superiors that I'm very sorry."

"Do you understand that if you leave, you make us look weak?" replied Woprice.

Before he could respond, Bury put a bullet in the man's forehead. Woprice then told the mistress that no harm would come to her, and he gently blindfolded and restrained her. Sam, sitting in the Russian's car, remotely turned off the cameras; Woprice then retrieved them before he and Bury quietly left the scene. Sam waited a few more hours after they had left, then drove off with the dead Russian sitting beside him, the other having been placed in the trunk by Woprice and Bury before they departed.

"Damn, your accent was spot on," Randy said to Dave. "Where the hell did you pick that up?"

"Cuba," replied Woprice.

"When the hell were you in Cuba?" asked Bury. "You never told me about Cuba."

"Bro, I am a man of mystery," Woprice replied as he shrugged his shoulders and grinned at Bury.

An anonymous call to the Caracas police about a shooting at the hotel started the ensuing chaos. The two bodyguards left at the front of the hotel were clueless about what had happened to their boss and were still outside. They were unsure why the police arrived with sirens blaring and assumed it was a potential coup to take out the President. They began firing on the police and were killed in the gunfight. Thereafter, the police found the Venezuelan leader dead, along with a hysterical naked woman bound and blindfolded beside him.

One of the policemen was a supporter of the opposition, and he made a call to the group. They, in turn, obtained a copy of the interview with the President's mistress, who had recounted the entire incident to the police. She explicitly stated that a Russian had killed the Venezuelan leader. In turn, an anonymous leak of the conversation between this "Russian" and the President made its way to the press. The two Russian bodyguards and their vehicle were never found. Russia, of course, denied the entire event, blaming the CIA for the assassination. The U.S. President, along with the CIA, vehemently denied any involvement; however, the President did tweet that whoever had done it had sure executed "a damn good plan."

The fallout from the event was immediate. The Venezuelan military leaders, who had backed the President, did not believe the Russians and felt betrayed by them. Now that they threw their support behind the opposition leader, the healing of the people and the country of Venezuela could now begin. It was a huge win for the Trust as well as for the United States. The three operators had favorably changed the political and social landscape of this South American region.

❈ ❈ ❈

Upon returning home, Sam was greeted by Mariah and the kids at the airport. The reunion was perhaps the best one yet. Sam, Dave, and Randy had executed the plan flawlessly and had eliminated a tyrant responsible for the tremendous misery of millions. It was exactly the fulfilling mission Sam had needed.

The fallout from the Venezuelan President's death had been minimal. Russia had backed off their continued denial of their involvement because the evidence was overwhelming. With a history of numerous poisonings of political rivals approved by its leadership, it was it credible that the Russians had killed him.

Marv had already called to give his congratulations to the group during the return flight. Of course, Sam had jokingly denied his involvement, but had heard that the critical intelligence that helped with the mission's success had come from the CIA. Marv likewise denied giving any intelligence to anyone. All of Sam's previous accomplishments were unknown to the public; now even fewer people knew about his operations. This was fine with Sam. He had never wanted fame and glory, just a better world.

"What did I tell you, Sam? Your idea, your planning, your mission. You're at the top of your game and right where you need to be!"

"It does feel damn good, Marv. I'd been toying with a plan to eliminate that Venezuelan dictator ever since you sent me there for my first CIA mission. I'm grateful to you for hooking me up with your boy Steen."

"Are you kidding, Sam? The Director and I are grateful to you for cleaning up a major problem that has consumed countless U.S. resources. You can't begin to understand how much easier you have made things for us. And per your wishes, he and I are the only ones who know that it was you. Not even the President heard it from us, although he has asked about you."

"Really? I'm sure it'll get back to him somehow, probably from someone on the Trust's Board who won't be able to keep his or her mouth shut. Doesn't matter, though. I plan to stay under the radar."

"Anonymous heroes," replied Royster.

"Copy that," was Sam's reply.

Chapter 55

Since the attacks on the United States, Khalid Ali and ISIS had been very busy. While the U.S. and the Taliban continued their negotiations, ISIS had been steadily creeping back into eastern Afghanistan, retaking many of the villages that Sam and his team had liberated. The Afghan Army was still not strong enough to hold them off, and for about the tenth time, the area changed hands again. The reduction in American troop presence was making it easier for ISIS to also push back the Taliban. All in all, Khalid was quite pleased with their progress. However, he wanted to reactivate his people in the U.S. for more attacks.

"Do we have any new information on Sam Richards?" Khalid asked his second, Jamal.

"I'm afraid not, Emir. We can't confirm if we succeeded in killing him during the bombings of the private homes. Not much in the way of description of any victims appeared in the news."

"We have to assume that he's still alive. I still have hope that I can kill him and avenge my brother's death."

"Of course, Emir, but we've lost numerous assets due to the American president's new policy of racial profiling. We're trying to find new sympathizers every day."

"I'm surprised that America didn't initiate such a policy after 9/11. If we wanted to eliminate our homeland of infidels, I would do the same if I were in charge. Their open society and political correctness will be their undoing."

"Perhaps we should turn our attention to Europe. They haven't followed the lead of the American president. I also find the American response to our bombings to be unusual."

"How so?" asked Khalid.

After 9/11, the infidel Bush attacked al-Qaeda and the Taliban with gusto; this time the U.S. retaliation has been minimal."

"That's true. Instead, they're 'retaliating' in their homeland by using the new policy to dispose of anyone that they feel is a threat to them. It actually may be more rewarding for them, when you think about it."

"Maybe, Emir, but I'm fearful of a major response from them."

"That won't happen, Jamal. They're scaling down here, and we are succeeding in out-waiting them, like the mujahedeen did the Russians in the 1980's."

"I hope you're right."

"That's why I want to hit them again in their homeland."

"We do have a tremendous amount of material left over from our first attack. Assets have kept it well hidden."

"How much exactly?"

"About 15,000 pounds, Emir."

"Excellent. That's almost as much as we used in the D.C. attacks. I want to hit similar targets as before. They aren't guarded like government buildings."

"Do you have some in mind?"

"Yes. When my family lived in the U.S., it was clear that Americans love festivals, concerts, and sporting events. A coordinated attack on a number of these types of targets so soon would be monumental and show the world that the Caliphate is unstoppable."

"Won't that be difficult with the American president's new policy?," asked Jamal. "Our people might be stopped before they even get close to a target."

"Don't we have some radicalized white Muslims in America?"

"Yes," responded Jamal.

"We'll use their own people that we've converted to get past the profiling and deliver the bombs to their targets. It will be added insult and show their President that the enemy also looks like him. Jamal, let's set the plan in motion."

❄ ❄ ❄

Khalid's relationship with China continued to be helpful, as the Chinese government turned a blind eye to him as long as he kept the local Muslims tamed. Khalid lied to the locals, telling them that in due time he would help them fight back against the Chinese. He had to be sure that he had reestablished a base of operations in eastern Afghanistan before doing so, because he wanted to be out of China before the local Muslims caught on to his deceit.

The Americans had already attempted to dispose of him in China but had failed. After finding this out, the Chinese government had proclaimed that this was an act of war, and repercussions would be severe if it occurred again. The Chinese had also responded with major crackdowns against protesters in western China, as well as in Hong Kong, using the American excursion into their country as leverage. For these reasons, Khalid felt extremely safe in Kashgar. He would continue to use it as his base of operations while he planned new attacks on the U.S. homeland.

Chapter 56

The Trust continued to help people internationally via aid organizations throughout different regions of conflict and human suffering. There was certainly no shortage of locations meeting these criteria existing on the globe. It was a job security that Sam wished would go away. He and his two teammates supported these missions utilizing violence only when necessary.

Sam continued to tell Mariah every aspect of his missions. This habit, along with the techniques that he picked up from Chris Key, continued to keep him mentally on track. Mariah had returned to work for the Red Cross, and her injuries had healed very well. Sam continued to be connected to his former team colleagues at the CIA and had begun recent discussions with Paul Kerney and Steve Durrant about the Trust and the work that they were accomplishing. Sam had shared the details of his missions with Paul and Steve, who were impressed with his autonomy in choosing and planning missions. The three of them were talking in Sam's basement while their wives and children were outside.

"How can you work with two Delta pukes?" Durrant asked with a smile. "What you've done is even more impressive, since you've had second-team quality partners helping you."

"What is your deal with Delta?" asked Paul. "I know we all give each other shit, but you seem to pick on them endlessly." Kerney chuckled, then continued, "Did a Delta hurt you in the past, big guy?"

Both Sam and Paul were belly laughing. They began to stop as Steve stood up, stretching his 6'5" frame to its fullest extent while staring down at his two friends. They were concerned they had pushed their friend a little too far. He was a formidable man.

"As a matter of fact, yes, but not how you think," said Steve. "Before we all hooked up as teammates on SEAL Team 6, I had my worst day as a SEAL working jointly with a Delta team in Fallujah. It was my first deployment; I was fresh out of training. I was partnered with an older Delta guy, who constantly gave me shit for being a SEAL. He constantly called me 'second teamer.' But, it was all good, we became great friends, and he taught me so much. He saved my life in Fallujah, pushing me to safety as an RPG hit our position. As he was dying, and as I was holding him, he told me I had made the first team. I'll never forget it."

There was nothing but silence. Then both Sam and Paul put a hand on Steve's shoulders, saying they were really sorry.

"So, I guess you're kind of paying his harassment forward, so to speak, to honor your fallen friend?" asked Sam.

"Or maybe it's a coping mechanism?" asked Paul.

Again, there was an awkward silence as Steve had his hands on his face, letting out a subdued sob. Sam and Paul exchanged glances, giving each other the "What do we do now?" look.

After a second sob, Durrant said, "No, that's not why."

"Why, then?" asked Paul.

With his hands still on his face, Steve responded, "I just hate those arrogant fuckers." He then started laughing.

"You asshole," was Sam and Paul's simultaneous response as they pummeled him with friendly smacks.

"You made that all up?" asked Paul.

"Not all of it—just him dying. He did save my life, though, we're still great friends. You guys are gullible idiots."

"And you're such a dick," yelled Sam.

Sam and Paul both tackled Steve and pummeled him some more. They were wrestling hard, knocking furniture and toys over, when all of a sudden a loud whistle shrilled. They turned to see their families staring at them from the stairs, Paul's wife Nancy with a whistle in her mouth.

"What the fuck is going on?" yelled Durrant's wife. Her statement was met with eight kids murmuring, "Uh oh, she said fuck." That put all of the adults in hysterics as the kids jumped on their dads.

❖ ❖ ❖

Durrant and Kerney integrated into the team seamlessly. The five men trained hard, pushing each other, trying to outdo one another. The machismo was on display full force during the first week they trained together. They harassed one another in a friendly way, all the while gaining trust in one another's abilities.

"Okay, I admit, you guys are good," said Durrant. "But it's a good thing there's three SEALs on the team to make it special."

"Yeah," responded Woprice, "that's about right—two Deltas equals three SEALs."

The five-man team never passed up an opportunity to give each other shit. Sam was never as confident in a group of men as he was with this one. Sam was excited to see how well they would perform under live-fire conditions. It wouldn't take too long for him to get his wish.

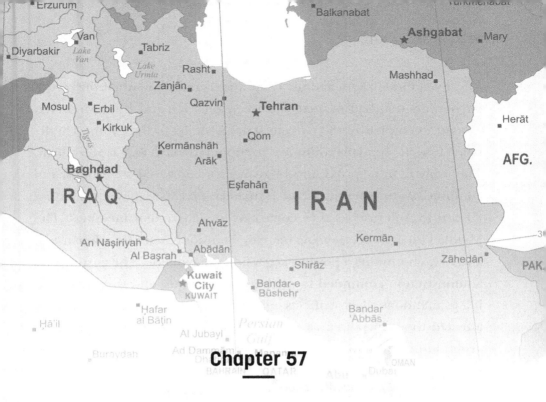

Chapter 57

Recently, the Strait of Hormuz had become the most dangerous waters on the planet. The U.S. and Iran had shot down each other's drones, and Iran had seized two British oil tankers. They had returned one, but continued to hold one tanker and its crew at an undisclosed location. Neither the U.S. nor Great Britain seemed to be interested in a military solution to reacquire the tanker and its crew, relying on increased sanctions to bring the Iranians to the negotiation table. Iranian tankers trying to get oil to Syria had been seized and then later released. During these incidents, the Iranian President had pledged to continue uranium enrichment unless sanctions were lifted and Iran was allowed to sell their oil abroad. He also wanted the U.S. President to get back into compliance with the nuclear agreement made by his predecessor.

Even though Sam and the team were certainly aware of the recent encounters that had occurred between the U.S. and Iran, Mr. Steen wanted to emphasize the current state of affairs to the group. He detailed how the Iranians continued to support Syria as well as Hezbollah. They were fighting proxy wars by giving assistance to these groups, and continuously threatening Israel. Iranian lawmakers were seen chanting "Death to America" as they convened for Parliament meetings. The Middle East was experiencing increased tension, even more than usual, and it was becoming a powder keg waiting to explode. The current U.S administration continued to ratchet up sanctions, and they were having tremendous adverse affects on the Iranian people. Sanctions never affected those in power, as the elite continued to eat well and drive around in chauffeured Mercedes. The National Council of Resistance of Iran (NCRI), along with other sector's of Iran's society, continued to pursue a free and democratic Iran, trying to improve the 80% poverty rate of its people. These groups, along with the citizens of Iran, were not interested in wasting money on a nuclear program or financially supporting the export of terrorism to Syria, Iraq, Yemen, and Lebanon. It was these groups that the U.S. hoped would be able to initiate positive change for the country. The Iran-U.S. relationship was tenuous at best, on opposite sides of about everything there was.

With the volatility between the U.S. and Iran, Sam and Mr. Steen had been having discussions about whether there was a role for the Trust to offer any help to ease the increasing tensions between the two countries.

"Something's gotta give, don't you think, Mr. Steen?"

"I do. The Iranian government is being backed to the wall by sanctions. It's only a matter of time before they lash out again."

"Marv have any ideas?"

"No, Sam, I think that it's so volatile right now that he doesn't want to risk escalation. Plus it's not an area easy to operate in. The CIA doesn't have a ton of assets in positions to offer help."

"Agreed. I've given thought to hostage rescuing, but we don't know where they're being held. Getting rid of their leadership would probably be a suicide mission."

"I've got some contacts in Iran. Let me see if they have any ideas."

"I hope they do," replied Sam.

Mr. Steen had developed a fairly decent intelligence network of his own during his long service to the U.S. government. He had also been able to cultivate relationships in many countries, one of those being Iran. His contact was with the National Council of Resistance of Iran (NCRI), and the individual was a former asset of Steen's. Farzad Ghorbani had been instrumental in helping Mr. Steen achieve success twenty years ago when he was an operator in Iran. Over the years, Steen had helped Farzad as well.

"Farzad, my old friend. How are things in your world?"

"It's funny that you ask," said Farzad. "It seems you always know when to call."

"I have a new employer who is eager to help improve the situation between the U.S. and Iran, as well as do anything they can to improve the state of the Iranian people."

"You're no longer with the CIA?"

"I left them several years ago. Think of my new employer as a powerful NGO with its own Special Ops team who has the ability to offer more than material aid."

"Sounds intriguing. Tomorrow, I'm meeting with someone who says he has evidence of a nuclear facility that's unknown to the world."

"Really? Seems that would be hard to hide."

"I agree. But if it's true, perhaps you could put that information to good use.

"Maybe," replied Steen. "I'd have to hear the specifics first."

"But of course," replied Ghorbani. "I'll let you know."

Steen and Sam began planning for a possible mission to Iran. Despite relations between the two countries, U.S. citizens were permitted to visit by the Iranian government. The Iranian people had always been described as very friendly, and the country had beautiful ancient ruins and religious sites. It wouldn't be difficult to obtain standard tourist entry into the country. The difficulty would be operating covertly once there. Until they received more information from Farzad, they had no clue as to what type of mission would be helpful, and more importantly, if it was even possible to successively accomplish.

Sam read a memo on the nuclear program in Iran that had been provided by Royster. The known nuclear facilities in Iran had been identified by the recent inspections performed by the International Atomic Energy Agency (IAEA) as part of the Joint Comprehensive Plan of Action (JCPOA) agreed upon by Iran and the P5+1 countries. These countries were the permanent members of the U.N. Security Council (U.S., Russia, U.K., France, China) plus Germany.

The main facilities for uranium enrichment in Iran were located in Fordow and Natanz, the latter facility having more advanced centrifuges. The agreement was supposed to give the IAEA unfettered access to these facilities for "continuous monitoring." After the U.S. withdrawal from the agreement, Iran began exceeding its agreed-upon stockpile of low-enriched uranium. In the past, Iran had enriched uranium to a level of 20%, far below the weapons grade of 90%, but once a country was able to achieve the level of 20%, production of weapons grade uranium, from there it was fairly straight forward to reach weapons grade. The technical difficulty and the expense required for the enrichment process was the main barrier to producing weapons grade uranium. Opinions varied on Iran's ability to produce a nuclear weapon or the timeframe required for its production. However, it had to be remembered that those opinions were based on the IAEA's findings and Iran being honest. There were some experts who believed Iran was much closer than previously thought to reaching its goal of producing a nuclear weapon.

"Wow, that's some scary shit in that memo, Mr. Steen. I hope your buddy has some actionable intel, and we can think of a way to help."

"Agreed. I expect a call any time."

Farzad relayed information to Steen the following day.

"Mr. Steen, I have some disturbing news. It's not a new facility that the Iranian government is hiding. They're hiding a stockpile of highly enriched uranium."

"HEU? Holy shit, that is disturbing. Does your source know where it is? Or how much they have?"

"Not yet. He's working on it. Only 35 pounds is needed to make a significant weapon. And since HEU only emits alpha radiation, it doesn't need a large storage site to hide."

"Thank you Farzad, keep me posted. Let me know if your source can find out the location."

"Will do, my friend. I hope you can help. This regime is killing my country."

❖ ❖ ❖

Sam and Steen debated what to do with this information.

"Should we tell Marv, Sam?" asked Mr. Steen.

"That's a tough question. Probably; but without proof, the U.S. government can't just announce to the world that the Iranian government has been lying about its nuclear capabilities."

"True. And if they tip their hand that they know, the Iranians will be more vigilant in hiding the material."

"Right now, the P5 + 1 countries think Iran can only enrich uranium to 5%. we just found out that's false. We don't know how fast they can enrich, we just know they can. There's only one solution."

"We need proof of their deception."

"Exactly," replied Sam. "We have to find proof and bring it back."

"Getting proof would change the relationship between Iran and the rest of the world. If they've been lying about the ability to produce HEU, along with the drone attacks on Saudi Arabia, shooting down a U.S. drone, pirating tankers in the Strait of Hormuz—I mean, the list just continues—the world might just isolate them completely."

"That might just get them to play nicer with others," said Sam.

"I wouldn't hold your breath, but yeah, maybe."

Chapter 58

Farzad took one variable out of the equation when he informed Mr. Steen that his source had revealed the location of the HEU. Steen asked Farzad about the background of his source and was told he was a high-level scientist involved in the nuclear program, working at the Natanz facility. This scientist and his group were opposed to Iran developing nuclear weapons while its citizens starved and lived in poverty. He was opposed to the cleric-based government of the current leader and his zealot colleagues. He was eager to do anything to help facilitate change.

The storage site was located at a small village between the Natanz and Fordow facilities called Hoseynabad-e Mish Mast. It consisted of a very small population of around 300 families, and was a two-hour drive south of Tehran. Farzad's contact traveled to the location weekly, accompanied by several Revolutionary Guards, to check on the stockpile and place more HEU, if any was available. The scientist told Farzad that the enrichment had been going on for many years, allowing a slow but steady accumulation of material. It had been a very well kept secret.

"Okay, I have a plan. Let me run it by all of you," Sam told Steen and the team.

He then spent the next 20 uninterrupted minutes laying out his plan to the group.

"That's intense," replied Kerney.

"Probably insane," added Bury.

"Suicidal," said Woprice and Durrant at about the same time.

"It's a covert mission in a country where we have no real assets for support, where you'll have no weapons, and no method for a rapid exfiltration," said Steen.

"It's a voluntary mission, gentleman, not an order, not mandatory," replied Sam. "We don't need all five of us, although more would be better. You're the bravest men I know, whether you choose to go or not. I don't want peer pressure to persuade anyone, so just write yes or no on the piece of paper in front of you and give it to Mr. Steen on your way out. I'll meet you all in about ten minutes for a cold one at Papa Joe's."

It took about five seconds for the papers to be filled out and handed to Mr. Steen as the Team exited. Sam waited about five minutes, trying to point out any faults in the plan with Mr. Steen, then asked him for the results.

"All yes," said Steen. "I would have expected nothing less from this group."

"Me too," replied Sam, "but they needed to have a choice. This mission is unlike any other."

"Without question," was Mr. Steen's response.

Sam met the group for a beer and told them that four of the five had agreed to go. They all looked at each other, wondering who had responded with a no.

"So, I'll be sure to look after your wives while you're all gone," said Sam. "When I'm through with them, though, they won't want you guys back."

Sam was the only one laughing at his own joke.

Without so much as a grunt from any of them, he was pelted with a barrage of peanuts.

"We knew you'd pull some bullshit," said Woprice.

"You don't think we all told each other our vote before we ordered our beers?" echoed Durrant.

"You're still an asshole," said Bury.

"Wow," replied Sam. "I've become that predictable. Tell your babes the plan, and make sure you tell them I said you didn't have to go. I don't want them pissed at me."

❖ ❖ ❖

Kerney and Durrant would leave for Iran from London with U.K. passports. Woprice, Bury, and Richards would depart from Montreal with Canadian passports, all of them undercover as journalists writing articles about Iran. One article was for *National Geographic* and the other for the Canadian journal, *Peace Magazine.* They were able to smuggle a hand-held laser spectroscopy device inside a false compartment of a news camera bag that had been recently developed by the U.S Atomic Agency Commission. This device could detect highly enriched uranium as well as determine the percentage of enrichment. It was a smaller version of those used to detect HEU from a distance. It was a fantastic development designed for fast identification and determination of any uranium they would encounter.

310 | JOSEPH R. RITCHIE

They arrived in Tehran and checked into separate hotels. They had acquired the proper credentials for journalists through the Trust's contacts at the two different magazines. The credentials would identify them as well as the reason they were taking pictures and video, and give them the ability to travel through most of Iran. They were reminded that Iran was an Islamic country and they should respect its rules, as not doing so could lead to significant consequences. Pictures of mosques were allowed, but non-Muslims were not permitted to enter the buildings.

Through Farzad Ghorbani, each group was provided with a car and driver loyal to the NCRI. This was a mission where Sam and his team were depending greatly on assets they didn't know, something that left them all a little uneasy. It was not the norm, but this entire mission was far from ordinary for them. The drivers were very familiar with the area that they would be traveling to, and one of the drivers, Ashkan, was the son of Ghorbani.

They spent the first several days playing their parts—sightseeing through Tehran, taking pictures and video, talking to locals. Both groups of men had detected surveillance as they roamed the city. Ashkan told them that this was typical; that the government would usually follow Western visitors for a short time, and then stop the surveillance.

Kerney and Durrant headed south to Eslamshahr on the third day, a city only 12 km away. They noted new surveillance picking them up there. Bury, Woprice, and Richards traveled a little farther south to Defa'e Moghaddas Cinema Town, a small community founded by the Basij Resistance Force to support films featuring revolutionary themes and sacred defense, an ironic location to be visiting for an article that was supposed to appear in *Peace Magazine*. They were guided through the city by government officials the entire visit. Both groups continued their journey south, stopping at various villages, until arriving at Qom, the seventh largest city in Iran, with over a million inhabitants, and a significant city of pilgrimage for Shia Muslims. It was also an important petroleum city, with a direct pipeline to a refinery on the Persian Gulf.

In Qom, they stayed at two different hotels several blocks apart, the Laleh Hotel and Fadak Hotel. They separately roamed the city, again noting surveillance by the Iranians. They met at the Jazire Café, just down from their hotels, allowing for the appearance of a happenstance gathering of Western journalists far from home, who appeared to be comparing notes on Iran. It was here that they would coordinate the operational part of the mission.

"Okay, we've both noted surveillance along the way. We haven't noticed anyone following us the last 12 hours," said Sam.

"Copy that," replied Durrant. "We had a tail coming here, but I notice that he's left us. We'll do some counter surveillance moves when we leave here to see if he's gone or not."

Sam responded, "Sounds good. Tomorrow, we'll head to Jannatabad in a two-car convoy. It's about seven miles from Hoseynabad-e Mish Mast, which I'll call "HMM" from now on. It won't be suspicious that two Western groups join up and share the journey together. We'll separately roam the area for a couple of hours; it's a small village. We'll check for surveillance, and if there's none, then we can make our way to HMM. If we're followed, then we'll have to address that. Ashkan will take us on a tour through HMM, and leisurely take us by the HEU storage location. We'll get into position tomorrow night. Ashkan and his friend have brought sleeping bags and some camping equipment."

"How unusual is it for people to camp in these small villages?" asked Bury.

"Ashkan says it's rare for locals and most tourists, but fairly common for journalists," replied Richards. "He says you usually lose surveillance by camping because most of the tails don't want to sleep in their car. He said that they'd probably go back to Qom for the night and return in the morning."

"That would work perfectly," replied Woprice.

Chapter 59

They set out as planned the following morning in their two vehicles, and they noted that a vehicle was tailing each of them. They leisurely went through Jannatabad, doing what journalists do, then met at a café. After lunch, they made their way to HMM, now noting only one car surveilling them. They repeated the process around the small village, noting the HEU storage building in the southwest area of the village, just off the road leading to Kashan. They saw only one guard outside the storage building, though Ashkan was not sure if there would be more inside.

They found a location to make camp about 500m from the building. They left their vehicles, and then Ashkan bartered with locals for dinner. The villagers were very friendly to the Westerners, always smiling. It seemed to Sam that this was the case almost wherever he went in the world, the locals being friendly toward Westerners even though their own governments oppressed them and hated the West. They enjoyed the company of the villagers, taking their pictures, singing songs, and answering questions by way of Ashkan's translation. Several villagers offered them a place to sleep, but they kindly turned them down. They needed to be away from other people to carry out their plans that evening. Saying goodnight, they made their back to their camp and settled in for the evening. Their surveillance did not leave, but parked about 200m to the east.

"Well, that's a small glitch in our plans," said Kerney.

"For sure, but not a huge issue," replied Sam. "Randy and I will go to the building instead of all five of us. We'll stuff our sleeping bags to look like we're still here."

"None of the surveillance has ever confronted us," commented Woprice. "We'll deal with it if he does tonight."

At 3 a.m., Randy and Sam made their way to the facility. There was no guard evident on the exterior of the building. They probably assumed that with the remoteness of the location and the authoritarian government of Iran, there was no need to worry about trespassers. The local population would be too fearful to approach a government building.

Entry into the facility wasn't difficult either, and a quick, silent walk through the small building revealed a single, sleeping guard. Sam doubted that he even knew what he was guarding. They found the highly enriched uranium in a simple, unmarked lead container. They estimated that there was about 20-25 lbs. of material. Randy was filming the entire encounter, having started during their approach to the building. He continued to film, showing the use of the handheld device to confirm that the enrichment level of the uranium was 90%. Placing the HEU into his protective backpack, he and Randy left the building after spending a total time onsite of just 15 minutes.

Meanwhile, Steve Durrant woke the others and pointed to the approaching figure of the government individual who had been following them. He reminded Ashkan of the plan, and then they all went back to the appearance of sleeping.

"Wake up, wake up now!" the Iranian screamed in Farsi.

The group acted startled, but remained lying down. They couldn't help but notice the pistol that he was waving around in his hand as he stopped ten feet from Durrant, the closest of the group.

"On your feet now!" he screamed.

Ashkan had started speaking to the man, and then translated to the group to stand up. They complied with his request, but Sam and Randy's bags didn't move. More screaming ensued from the Iranian as he alternated pointing his gun at Ashkan and the empty sleeping bags. The conversation seemed to be escalating, and the three special operators were exchanging glances. Durrant had seen enough; he was going to disarm this guy and put him down. He conveyed his intentions to his teammates with his eyes, they nodded back in response. He was counting it down when all of a sudden he heard Randy's voice.

"What's all the racket about?" Randy yelled.

Everyone turned to see him, and the Iranian swung his gun around, pointing it at Randy.

"Whoa," he said, raising his hands. "I was just taking a piss."

Ashkan quickly translated as Durrant edged a little closer to the Iranian.

"Where's the other one?" the Iranian asked Ashkan.

Ashkan shrugged his shoulders, and trying to buy time, he said, "How should I know? I've been asleep."

The Iranian responded with a tirade, now pointing his weapon at Ashkan while talking so fast and angrily that spittle was flying from his mouth. Durrant was ready to move on the guy. However, the Iranian's shouting was again interrupted, but this time by Sam.

"What's going on?"

As before, the Iranian swung around, now screaming at Sam and shaking his weapon. Sam could see that Durrant was about ready to deliver a blow to the man, but he told him to stand down with a slight side-to-side nod of his head.

"Ashkan, tell him that I was taking a dump. That's why I'm holding a shovel—I didn't want to leave my smelly shit on this beautiful countryside."

Sam gave a big smile to the Iranian.

The shovel had actually been used to uncover the top of a dried well they had previously located, so that the lead box containing the HEU could be carefully lowered down, then the top covered again. Sam had put a GPS locator in the box, just in case. It was not an ideal solution, but smuggling 20 lbs. of HEU out of the country on a commercial flight was not feasible. The odds of it being found in the future where Sam had ditched it were astronomical, as this area of Iran was certainly not going to be developed any time soon, if ever. The depth of the old well was over 200 meters. The lead box would keep the radioactive signal hidden from any searches that utilized detection devices.

Sam's answer and his smile seemed to completely defuse the situation. The Iranian dropped his weapon down to his side and started laughing. The rest of the group began fake-laughing as well. The Iranian then began speaking and gesturing to Ashkan, who translated.

"He's asking about our plans," said Ashkan.

Sam responded, "We're leaving at first light back to Tehran. We'll stay there for a few days before our flight leaves. Tell him, that if he wants to, we'd be happy to have him join us for breakfast when we make our first stop. It's the least we can do for getting him all fired up."

Sam delivered another big smile.

Ashkan translated Sam's offer to the man, who politely declined. He then made his way to his car and drove away. They then settled back into their bags for a few hours of sleep, or tried to, anyway.

The following morning, they made their way back to Tehran, but instead of hanging around like Sam had told the Iranian tail, they got their asses on the first flights they could. The journey home was a re-tracing of their entry into Iran. Their equipment was searched going through security—always a moment of trepidation—but once again, the secret compartment went unnoticed. The HEU was well protected, and the Iranian airport security had no clue what they had allowed to leave their country. Mr. Steen, who had arranged a bypass of Customs on entry into London and Montreal, would meet Sam's team in Canada.

After arrival in D.C., they met to plan their next course of action and how to use the damning evidence they now possessed. They also arranged for testing to confirm the quality of the HEU from the minuscule sample they had brought back.

"What an incredible mission, Sam," said Mr. Steen. "Five Americans, no support, no weapons, in and out without notice. Fucking spectacular."

"I agree, truly special. We can't get cocky, though; we still have to talk to the Iranians," replied Sam.

"I'm on it," replied Mr. Steen. "I have a plan for that."

❈ ❈ ❈

The Iranian President had just received word from his Defense Minister that the highly enriched uranium was gone. Cameras at the storage building had confirmed entry by two individuals. Their entire time in the building was documented, including the testing of the uranium with a small handheld device. A delay in finding out about the theft was the result of having no scheduled checks of the material. The onsite guard didn't know what was at the facility. Only a handful of people knew what was stored in the building, so discovery of the missing material only became evident when one of the scientists made his weekly check. The authorities soon discovered that a group of Western "journalists" had traveled through the area, and the Iranians rightly concluded that they had to be the individuals responsible for this debacle.

"Do you realize how many years it took us to procure that amount?" the President asked his Minister. "How did they get it out of the country?"

"I don't know the answer to those questions," replied the Minister.

"The United States will confront us with this information on the world stage, their President will be vindicated for pulling out of the nuclear deal, and our deceit will be confirmed," the Iranian leader went on.

"They have no proof," stated the Minister. "We'll just deny it."

At that moment, the Iranian President's secretary informed him of a call from the Iranian ambassador in Australia. He informed the President that he had received a package addressed to him. The Ambassador was not sure of its origin. It contained a single page letter and a USB drive. The ambassador was forwarding the material through encrypted email to the President.

Once received, he and his Minister viewed the contents of the USB drive together. It showed a video that was unmistakably the storage facility, the storage box, and a device that read 90% after being pointed at the HEU. The picture was much better quality than the Iranians' security tape showing the same event. The video also showed the perpetrators turning on a GPS that showed their location. There was no denying this evidence; the Americans had caught them red-handed.

Surprisingly, the narrator of the video said that he was not aligned with any country or terrorist group. His organization was willing to keep silent about the HEU in exchange for the Iranian government going forward with the Trust's requests. Failure to do so would result in the U.N. Security Council receiving a copy of the tape. The narrator said that meeting these requests would, in the end, help Iran recover economically and improve their credibility on the world stage by taking the higher ground. The world didn't have to know that blackmail was the impetus for Iran's actions.

The Iranian President made a statement to the world the following morning. Iran would pay Saudi Arabia reparations for the damage done by its recent drone attacks, they would release the British tanker they had captured, they would release all Western hostages, they would welcome back IAEA inspectors and reduce their number of centrifuges, they would cease support of terrorist groups, and they would hold democratic elections to be monitored by the U.N. The Trust's wish list had been long, and all of it was being fulfilled.

The world was stunned. The network news pundits all speculated why there was a 180-degree turn by the Iranian government. The Iranian people responded with cheering on the streets. In response, the U.S. President announced an ease in sanctions and requested a meeting between he and the Iranian President.

It was a total victory for the Trust.

❖ ❖ ❖

"Well, Sam, the Dream Team wins again! You gentlemen outdid yourself this time," said Mariah. "Just remember, though—you guys aren't invincible."

"We're pretty damn close," Sam replied with a cocky smile. "No, you're right, Mariah, we were extremely blessed to succeed. But it does feel good to pull off a mission that will make a positive change in the world, at least for the time being."

"And you didn't tell the U.S. government about the uranium?" asked Mariah.

"We told Marv," Sam said. "He understands that it's a better scenario if Iran appears to do this on their own rather than it being the U.S. forcing them to do so. Neither country's president wants a war—somebody just needed to blink, and we made Iran blink. The negative is that the Iranian president may stay in power, especially if he cheats in the next election. The everyday Iranian thinks that he's responsible for the shift in beliefs. Hopefully, they'll remember the years of shitty existence under the cleric regime when they go to the voting booth. However, if he doesn't stop the continued oppression, we'll have to talk to him again."

"I don't think you boys will ever be able to top that operation," said Mariah. "Now, come on over here and let me reward my hero," she said, grinning.

"Yes, ma'am!"

PART FOUR:

Three Months Later

Chapter 59

The team returned from Central America feeling an incredible sense of achievement. Taking out the cartel leaders felt damn good. A disruption of the drug cartels to this extent would allow local authorities to get ahead of the drug kingpins, at least for a while, hopefully reducing drug distributions for quite some time. At the very least, the Trust had eliminated a large number of shitty humans from the planet with one fell swoop.

Sam, as usual, filled Mariah in on the results of the mission. He had shared the plan with her before he had left. It felt good to settle into their routine, spending their down time in the usual way, together as a family, as much as possible. They were even able to enjoy a two-week vacation, splitting time with grandparents for a week, then a beach vacation together with the Kerneys and Durrants. The world continued to spin with all its problems during their holiday, but they were all able to enjoy this time of isolation, avoiding news programs and leaving their work behind.

The three dads were enjoying the beach, sipping beers and building sandcastles with their children.

It was Kerney who first spoke about work. "I've been thinking."

"Bad idea," said Durrant.

"Shut up and listen, and try to keep up with me if you can," replied Paul.

Durrant's response was the middle finger.

"Every target we've hit has been abroad. The first mission we did as a five-man group in Iran was huge, and the one we just got back from smoked a lot of bad hombres. But, there are also a shit-ton of issues in the good ol' U.S. of A. that the five of us could improve or eliminate."

Sam responded, "You're exactly right, Paul. I think targeting criminal elements in the U.S. would allow the police to work more effectively. Let's talk to Steen about that when we get back."

"Sounds good," agreed Durrant. "But I have this paranoia that there's going to be another attack on the homeland."

"Damn, we spend too much time together. I share your paranoia," replied Sam. "But the landscape has changed with the President's policy of amnesty for the worthy and deportation of expired visa holders. That's had to have had an effect on reducing potential threats here in the States."

"I hope you're right, my friend," said Durrant. "I just wish we could have gotten that bastard Khalid."

"Amen to that," said Sam. "However, I fear we may never get another chance."

The three men returned to D.C. well rested and ready to present their ideas about missions in the U.S. to Mr. Steen. They met the next morning to find a hyped-up Mr. Steen at the office. However, they never had a chance to tell him of their new ideas.

"Gentlemen, I hope you enjoyed your time away," he said. "I'd love to hear about it, but I can hardly contain myself because of our next opportunity."

"You do seem a little more stoked than usual," commented Bury.

"Why don't you take a couple of deep breaths, sit yourself down, and tell us?" said Woprice.

"Easy, smart ass," was Steen's reply. "As you know, the CIA and the military have scaled down their involvement in Afghanistan. The President wants to end the loss of American lives along with the bottomless money pit that the war has become. His more isolationist philosophy may be what this country needs, but I think there's some unresolved business over there." He made his last statement with his eyes solely focused on Sam.

"Khalid," said Sam. "But he's in China."

"He sure is," replied Steen. "We have confirmed intelligence that identifies his exact location in Kashgar."

"That's where we suspected him to be, and it's even further inside of China than where the last attempt to find him was," said Sam.

"True, but this time we have inside help—a Chinese dissident group led by a man named Kong Chiang Kei. The Trust has been working with him to get humanitarian aid into the country. In exchange, he has fed us, and the CIA, very valuable information."

"I don't like it," said Durrant. "That's a huge risk."

"Agreed," said Sam. "Why do we even need this source?"

"Because he knows exactly where Khalid is located, and more importantly, he routinely travels across the Pakistan/China border in a truck. If you haven't noticed, none of you look Chinese or Middle Eastern," replied Steen. "You need this guy's help."

"Give us a minute alone, Mr. Steen. The five of us need to talk. No offense," said Sam.

"None taken, Sam."

The five of them debated Steen's information. They spent close to an hour outlining options with and without the help of the Chinese dissident. They all five agreed with going forward, but they were mostly favoring an approach to do it on their own. However, their experience in Iran showed that assistance from motivated locals could be a great help.

"Okay, Mr. Steen," said Sam. "We're not convinced that we can trust your guy, so we're going to hammer out some plans with and without him. I propose that after we finalize our plans, we meet this guy in Pakistan. Depending on my read of him, we either tell him no thanks or go with him. We trusted your contact in Iran and it went well, but this time I want to meet the guy in advance."

"Perfect. I'll arrange transportation and wait for your other requirements," was Steen's reply.

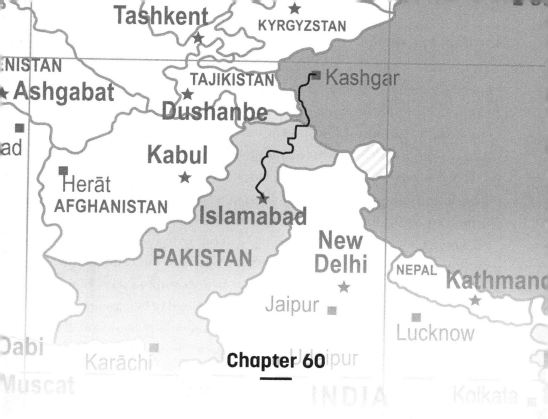

Chapter 60

Sam and his team proceeded to work out the details for the mission. Whether they used Kong Chiang Kei or not, they needed plans for infiltration and exfiltration. The staging point in Pakistan was an area that Sam, Paul, and Steve were familiar with from prior missions. However, the last time they'd been there, ISIS was on the run. The area was now back in the hands of the enemy, and getting to the Chinese border would require precision and detail. Sam still had trusted contacts in the region from his CIA days, but whether they were still located near the border and could help him remained to be seen.

The Karakoram Highway, or Friendship Highway, was the main route between Pakistan and China. It has often been called the eighth wonder of the world due to the difficult conditions that were encountered during its construction. It was the highest paved road in the world, with a maximum elevation of 15,466 ft. The crossing point into

JOSEPH R. RITCHIE

China was called the Khunjerab Pass and was known to have the highest ATM in the world. Pakistan and China issued renewable border passes to the local residents for easy transit through the pass, which allowed villagers from each country to market merchandise across the border. In 2006, bus service between Gilgit, Pakistan, and Kashgar, China, was established. Going into China legally required a Chinese visa, and it was mandatory for tourists to have a guide while in China.

The security at Khunjerab Pass had typically consisted of about 15 guards as well as elements of the Pakistani Army. On the Chinese side, local herdsmen also supplemented security by reporting to the Chinese guards. Sam's options for crossing the border consisted of being smuggled through by someone local, or covertly crossing somewhere away from the Pass. Sam and his team made contingency plans for both options.

Getting into Pakistan would not be difficult, as the government of Pakistan was making it easier for those holding U.S. passports to visit the country. Their motivation for this was simple: Pakistan wanted American aid to continue to flow into the country. The journey from Islamabad to Gilgit would be easy, but from Gilgit to the Pass and on to Kashgar would be the tricky part. Sam was hopeful that he would get good vibes from their Chinese connection, Kong Chiang Kei. Ex-filtration out of China involved the same complexity, but once back in Pakistan, Royster had arranged for transportation.

❁ ❁ ❁

"I need to talk to you about our next mission, babe," Sam said to Mariah. "This, without doubt, will be the most dangerous and difficult one to date, primarily because there are so many variables."

"I think I've heard you say that before. There are no easy missions, Sam."

"You're right, just some that are easier than others."

"Is the risk worth the reward?" she asked.

"Without question."

"Unlike before, as a SEAL or in the CIA, you have a choice about whether you do or don't choose a mission. Is the whole team on board?" she asked.

"Wholeheartedly," he responded.

"What's the target?" she asked almost nonchalantly, as these conversations had been occurring for years and become almost routine.

"Khalid Ali."

"Oh. Sam. Isn't he still in China?"

"Yes, but his exact location had been confirmed. The CIA won't go in because their prior excursion was discovered by the Chinese and because of the repercussions if they were found trying a second time."

"But Sam—all of you are obviously Americans. The Chinese's first thought if they discover your entry will be that it's the CIA. Who else would go into China?"

"Well, two things are different this time. One, *my team* is going in; and two, the Chinese know that Khalid is planning to head back to Afghanistan at some point. They won't know if he was snatched in China or if he left the country on his own," responded Sam. "It's Khalid, Mariah—the man who killed our friends when we were students, who killed your friends in the Red Cross, and who killed an innocent family because they had the same name as me. He's the new bin Laden, and he tried to kill our family."

"I know, Sam, but my concern is that this is the first time that a mission has become personal, and because of that, you might be taking too big a risk."

Sam responded, "It *is* personal, but not to the point I would throw my life away, I know our plan will work. Besides that, Royster tells me that there is increased chatter similar to several weeks before the attack on D.C. Now is the time to go!"

"Then go get him and deliver some justice."

"Copy that, babe."

Chapter 61

They flew into Islamabad posing as American journalists and not aid workers since Pakistan had expelled more than 18 international aid groups the year before. Thus was the schizophrenia of the Pakistan government: they cried for foreign aid, yet expelled humanitarian aid groups who were pouring millions into the country to help the average citizen. In Islamabad, a Pakistani asset working for the CIA gave them their required gear and weapons, along with transport to a safe house in Gilgit, 170 miles from the Chinese border.

The next day, Kong Chiang Kei was brought to the safe house to meet with Sam and the team. He was a small but rugged-looking man, who appeared to be around 60. He spoke English, a mandatory requirement while he was in the Chinese Army. The Team asked him questions about his past and learned that he had been a dissident since separating from the military, but the Chinese government did not know this. He explained that he was a Muslim, like many Chinese in the western part of the country, and that many Muslims had been placed into reeducation camps by the Chinese government.

He and others had been fighting a guerrilla war against the Chinese Army, albeit largely ineffectual. He did not subscribe to radical Muslim beliefs, but had hoped that the presence of Khalid in the area would help his group's cause. Instead, he told Sam's team, the Chinese government allowed Khalid free passage in the area because he was persuading the local Muslims to stand down from their protests. But Kong had found that Khalid was doing more than that—he was actually informing on Kong's fellow dissidents as he discovered them. Kong was seeing his friends being arrested, sometimes executed on the spot, or sent to the camps—all because of this "fellow" Muslim Khalid. Sam was convinced of Kong's genuine desire to help them when he shared the rest of his story.

"I was conscripted into the Army as an 18-year-old. My family were peasants, so being in the Army ensured three meals a day. After my training, I was sent to various assignments, all having in common the suppression of people's rights. I was then transferred to the Khunjerab Pass to be a border guard, an assignment I welcomed as it was close to home. I married and had three children. Our two families had known each other for many years. I had become an officer and was in charge of security at the Pass.

"Sounds like it was great," said Sam.

"It was—for a while. Then, in 2015, the Chinese Premier announced a crackdown on all religions in China, bringing religion under control of the atheist communist party. Shortly thereafter, over one million Muslims from western China were placed in internment camps, including my family. One day I was guarding the border, the next day I was beaten, thrown out of the Army, and placed in a camp. Simply because I was Muslim. I begged to be placed in the same camp with my family, but was denied even seeing them. Soon, I received word that our parents had died, then my children, then my wife and siblings. I'm 38 years old and have no one left.

The silence that followed was only disturbed by Kong's subdued sobs. The pain and suffering in this region was immense, with most of the world ignorant of its existence. This man looked 20 years older than he was; now Sam understood why.

"We're so sorry, Kong."

"So, you see, if I can help inflict even a little pain on the Chinese government or someone who uses religion to justify the killing of innocents, I will do it. That's why I want to help."

The team exchanged looks with Sam, and all gave a simple, affirmative nod. They would trust this guy.

Kong continued to explain to them that he came to Gilgit, Pakistan, 2-3 times a week from Kashgar, China. He still knew people whom he had formerly commanded who were stationed at the Khunjerab Pass and who were sympathetic to his past. Because of that, they never searched him when he crossed the border. His truck had been modified with hidden areas that accommodated transport of people who chose to flee China. This would be the first time he would be smuggling people *into* China, though. It had been his mission since his family died to help as many Muslims as he could leave the country.

The 450-mile trip would take close to 12 hours, but the Team would only need to be hidden for about 30 of those miles. Upon arrival back in Kashgar, Kong's two trusted colleagues would be waiting to report the latest on Khalid. Upon completion of the mission, they would exfiltrate almost the same way, the difference being that a CIA helicopter would be waiting close to the Khunjerab Pass in Pakistan, eliminating a significant portion of the return journey.

"Easy peasy," was Kerney's response to the plan.

"The only easy day was yesterday," replied Durrant.

"Make a simple plan, inform everyone involved, don't change it, and kick it in the ass," said Bury.

"Fuckin-A," responded Woprice.

Sam could see the confused look on Kong's face. The man had no clue what his team's comments meant.

Sam turned to Kong and said, "They all agree it's a great plan."

Chapter 62

Plans for another strike on the U.S. were coming together nicely. Khalid's contacts had found three American Muslim sympathizers who would drive and place the vans each containing 5000 pounds of explosives.

Khalid had the soft targets picked out that would maximize chaos and loss of life. One of the American drivers had actually suggested the targets and explained his rationale. Khalid had no idea what a football tailgate was until he had been enlightened by the recruit. He wasn't familiar with the concept of country clubs and professional golf tournaments until talking to the same young American recruit. And finally, the only parades he was familiar with until now involved the military. The carnage from these three very American activities would surely kill the spirit of the infidels. He could hardly wait.

❀ ❀ ❀

Sam and his team were on their own once again. It was the same when they worked for the CIA, but not having the American government behind them was a completely different feeling, and none of them had gotten used to that. Unlike their Iran mission, at least they would have weapons this time. This mission was different than previous ones for the Trust; they were covertly going into a country with nuclear weapons, and it was somewhat anxiety-provoking. With the prior CIA mission being discovered, Sam and the team knew that there would be no holding back by the Chinese if their mission were discovered while they were in country. They had discussed contingency plans if their capture was imminent.

Well, thought Sam, at least the scenery was fantastic; the Naltar Valley was one of the most beautiful areas he had ever experienced. The crossing of Khunjerab Pass went uneventfully, with barely a conversation between Kong and the guards. The vastness and desolation of the Chinese side of the border was overwhelming, but also gorgeous.

They arrived in Kashgar under cover of darkness, typical of Kong's previous trips to Pakistan. They were met by two of his friends who spoke no English, so they relied on Kong for introductions and translation of what they knew about Khalid. Both men were excited and eager to tell their stories to the Americans. Neither had nearly the anguish of Kong's story, but their stories also involved oppression and death. Sam and the others understood their motivation.

The five of them had been to a lot of shitty places and heard a lot of shitty stories, but this place was close to the top of the heap. People who bitched and moaned about their problems in the United States had no idea how fortunate they were. Everyone Sam had ever met who had served their country understood how good it was in the U.S., even with all its problems. Well, except for most of the politicians he had encountered over the years, but their service was different than that of those who risked their lives. That appreciation of the U.S. and all of her issues was the primary difference between the civilians and military personnel who served the country.

"Khalid is very lax in his security," reported Kong. "He has four guards with him, but he walks freely about the city."

"He's not afraid at all?" asked Sam.

"No. The city is made up primarily of Muslim Uyghurs, so he feels that sharing the same faith protects him."

"That's ballsy," commented Bury. "What's the population of Kashgar?"

"Around 500,000," answered Kong.

"Is there a curfew?" asked Woprice.

"Not as yet. why do you ask?"

Sam answered Kong, "The sizable population and lack of curfew will enable us to do reconnaissance at night with minimal risk. During the day, we'll stay inside."

Kong lived in what was left of the Old City, which, at its prime, had been one of the best-preserved examples of a traditional Islamic city. The majority of the beautiful old buildings had been destroyed by riots and Chinese modernization. The homes in this area were small dwellings built nearly on top of one another. Khalid was staying in a house about 500 meters away from Kong's home.

"While I was gone, my men saw Khalid on his satellite phone much more than usual," reported Kong. "He always used it outside at least once a day, but recently it's been at least six times a day. They also say that Khalid and his men are always laughing and smiling, behavior not seen before."

Sam and the Team exchanged glances with one another after hearing this, realizing this probably meant that there were imminent attacks scheduled abroad. They had known that there was urgency to this mission, but this information signaled the reality of the situation.

"That's great information, Kong. Tell your men that's great work."

Kong relayed the American's words to his men. They smiled and bowed in response to Sam's gratitude.

"What does that information tell you, Sam?"

"It tells us that we need to act very soon. Khalid has probably been talking to his followers. We're fairly certain that he's planning to hit the United States again. I can't tell you how much we appreciate you and your men."

Kong was smiling as he translated Sam's words to his men. The three Chinese then had a short, fast conversation with one another, occasionally pointing at Sam and the other Team members.

"What's so funny?" asked Sam when they stopped talking.

"Nothing's funny. We were just saying how nice you are. We've been taught since we were children that Americans are evil. We didn't expect your kindness."

The Team and the Chinese men nodded at one another. The Americans bowed in response to the Chinese, the Americans proceeded to teach the Chinese how to fist-bump. The tension in the men was relieved by this simple, human gesture.

"Hell, Kong, as Americans go, we aren't even close to being the nicest," said Sam with a wink.

Sam shared with Kong and his two men what their impact on the mission meant. As ballsy as it had seemed when they were planning it, the truth was that all of the risk involved the journey to and from Kashgar. Kong had made the trip easy for Sam and his men. Once they arrived, it had been far easier to lie low in this urban atmosphere than in the desert of Iraq or the mountains of Afghanistan. Similarly, they had been much more exposed in Iran than they were here. There were plenty of places in Kashgar to conceal themselves when they ventured out at night. Kong and his men had made reconnaissance so much simpler.

After he was finished praising the Chinese men, Sam announced, "Okay, gentlemen, it's time to act. We'll enter Khalid's residence the next morning, grab him and whatever intel we can find, then hit the road, returning the way we came."

"Copy that," was the group's response.

Chapter 63

Khalid had received an update from the U.S. The three vans were loaded with explosives and ready to be parked at each location. It had been somewhat difficult to get tailgate parking passes for the Saturday's football game between Ohio State and Michigan in Ann Arbor, but enough money had led to success. That same day was also the third round of the last PGA tournament of the year, taking place in Sea Island, Georgia. The Macy's Thanksgiving Day Parade was two days prior to these events, so it would be the first target. The security for that event would be much more stringent.

For the Parade, Khalid had narrowed down his attack options to parking the van in a garage close to the parade, using a suicide run from a neighboring street, or parking the van very close to the route early in the morning with the hope that it wouldn't be towed. He needed to make the decision soon, as New York City was 12 hours behind

Kashgar. It was now 8 a.m. in NYC, and the parade would be starting in roughly 24 hours.

Khalid was processing his final preparations when suddenly there was a loud knocking on the front door of the house. His men grabbed their weapons about the same time that armed men broke the door inward. Khalid and his men were staring at the rifles of four Chinese soldiers. He quickly told his men to stand down.

"Is there a problem?" asked Khalid in English.

A fifth soldier sauntered in with a cigarette between his lips and stars on his shoulder lapels. This was a high-ranking officer, more rank than the other Army officer with whom Khalid had dealt with to allow him to stay in China.

One of the officer's soldiers translated for him. "Let me see your satellite phone."

Khalid quickly complied.

The soldier asked the next question. "We've noticed an increased use of your phone and are concerned. Why is this?"

Khalid hesitated, unsure of how much to reveal to this man. Whether it was because of his hesitation, or it was going to happen anyway, the officer ordered his soldiers to bind Khalid and drag him away. He confiscated the weapons in the house and left two soldiers to watch Khalid's men. Khalid was hooded after being placed in a vehicle between two Chinese soldiers. The drive in silence seemed to take around 30 minutes. Upon arrival he was taken to a room, handcuffed to a table, and the hood was removed. He was staring at the officer who had abducted him, along with the colonel he knew that had helped Khalid arrange his stay in China.

"These calls are going to the United States," said the Colonel. "My superior wants to know why."

The Chinese had been able to pinpoint the origin and the end point of the calls, but not the encrypted content. Ironically, they'd obtained the call log information by hacking an American satellite. The new officer was concerned about Khalid being an American spy.

❀ ❀ ❀

Sam and his men had seen the army truck pass Kong's house and watched helplessly as it pulled up in front of Khalid's location. Kong had snuck up as close as he dared, trying to hear any conversation. They then saw Khalid handcuffed and escorted to the vehicle and taken away.

"Shit!," was Sam's exclamation. "What the hell just happened?"

Kong had returned and told them what he had heard.

"Has this ever happened before?" Sam asked.

"Never," was Kong's reply. "I know that general. He recently arrived in Kashgar and has been increasing crackdowns, taking people away who are never seen again."

A cacophony of curse words came out of the Americans' mouths.

"Sonuvabitch," said Woprice. "We're ready to go, and some new general has a hard-on for increased security!"

"Okay, here's the plan," said Sam. "We were going into Khalid's place tomorrow anyway. Our choices now are to stay the course and go in, or wait for Khalid to return. I feel we're pretty safe here. I don't want to miss another chance to get this bastard!"

"There is another option," said Kerney. "If Kong knows where they went, we could potentially go there."

The Team exchanged glances with one another. Finally, Randy Bury broke the silence.

"That's fucking suicide," responded Bury. "Even if we did get him, the Chinese would know quickly, and every vehicle on the road would be stopped."

"Yeah, that is a stupid idea, Paul," said a smiling Durrant. "I have to agree with my new Delta friend Randy."

Kerney shrugged his shoulders as Woprice gave him a gentle fist bump for trying.

Kong interjected, "The general left two soldiers in the house. They won't stay forever."

"He's right," said Richards. "That general wouldn't leave those guys here for days. If we go in tomorrow—or now, for that matter—their bodies would be discovered, and the border along with the roads would be immediately closed. Fellas, we gotta wait it out for now. But we go in as soon as we see Khalid. Hopefully, Khalid didn't activate any plans before he was taken, and he won't be able to do so while the Chinese are holding him."

Chapter 64

Khalid looked at the colonel who had enabled Kashgar to be his sanctuary.

"As I told you before, I'm organizing attacks on the U.S. As a matter of fact, it's urgent that I make a final call to set the plans in motion."

The two officers then had a conversation in Chinese. One didn't need to know Chinese to understand that the general was giving the colonel an ass-chewing. The general grabbed the phone from the colonel and they both left the room.

Khalid was growing weary; it had to have been at least four hours or more that he had been sitting in this room. He had dozed, he knew, but not for any appreciable time. There were no windows for reference to the time of day.

Suddenly, the door opened, and he was again hooded and walked out. He was hopeful that they were taking him back to his house, but he was sat down again. The hood came off and he was handcuffed to a bed. He was beginning to panic a little.

The Team took turns grabbing a few hours of sleep, but everyone would be ready to go at a moment's notice. They had now been in China over 24 hours, and Sam felt that they were beginning to push their luck a little. It was approaching 6 p.m. local time, and Sam felt that going in to gather intelligence from Khalid's house might be worth it, rather than waiting for his return. Who knew if he would ever return. Their goal was to capture Khalid, but obtaining any information they could to prevent possible upcoming attacks on the U.S. was more important. Sam, once again, might have to forsake the opportunity to deal with Khalid in order to get whatever information he could.

Khalid was hooded again and taken from his room. He was afraid to allow himself hope that he was going back to the house. He knew that for sure when he was pushed into a seat, although no handcuffs were placed this time. The hood was removed and he was staring at the colonel once again.

"My apologies," he said, "but my superior just recently arrived, and he seems eager to check everyone out. Last night, he considered you an American spy. He personally called the numbers on your satellite phone to verify with your people. I told him, of course, that they could be lying and that he might have been talking to the CIA. Because of my remark, you can see that I don't have as much rank on my shoulder. Anyway, here is your phone, and my men will take you back."

❀ ❀ ❀

Sam called his team together to discuss options. He was favoring hitting the house; checking for any intelligence about imminent attacks in the U.S., and taking their chances on getting the hell out of Dodge.

"Sam," Kong yelled, "there's a truck coming."

"Okay, boys, it's go time. As soon as we see that truck leave, we hit the house. With or without Khalid. If this is him returning, he'll be telling his men about his night, and that will present us the perfect opportunity to put their lights out."

Sam saw Khalid exiting the truck and noticed that he had his satellite phone in his hand. The two Chinese soldiers who had been guarding Khalid's men came out of the house and began conversing with their comrades in the truck. They sure were taking their sweet-ass time leaving, Sam thought, and he wondered if they were picking up Khalid's guys to move them. If that were the case, Sam was going to hit them all, no survivors.

"Yo," he said over comms. "If this is a pick-up of Khalid's men, and they're all driving away, we don't let that happen."

There was no debate, just a response of "Copy that."

Sam watched as Khalid had dialed his phone and appeared to be waiting for it to be answered. This phone call seemed to have a sense of urgency and was occurring at the same time the Chinese truck was driving off. Khalid's men went back into the house, leaving him alone outside.

"Now," Sam said.

Khalid turned toward Sam and they made eye contact just as the dart hit Khalid in the chest. Sam could see on Khalid's face that before he fell, he recognized Sam's face. The team made quick disposal of Khalid's men with a silenced headshot to each terrorist.

He heard Bury say, "That's fifty from each of you—my guy hit the ground first."

Talk about relaxed, Sam thought; those guys had bet on which guy would hit the ground first.

They secured Khalid and placed him in the truck. Sam grabbed the satellite phone while the others quickly went through the room. They were in the truck within three minutes and heading to Pakistan. It was 8:30 p.m. local time.

Chapter 65

Mohammed had been talking to Khalid when all of a sudden the line went dead. He'd never had problems with satellite connections before now. He and the American with him had been waiting in a parking garage to hear from Khalid regarding how to deliver their bomb. If they didn't hear from Khalid, the contingency plan was to try to drive through roadblocks into the Thanksgiving Parade and martyr themselves. Mohammed had been all for helping the cause, especially with the U.S. President's new policy of racial profiling, because many of his friends had been deported. However, if the truth be told, he wasn't real keen on dying. He had seen suicide bomber depictions on TV shows like "Homeland," where the martyr was fired up to meet 72 virgins in paradise. Mohammed wanted to meet a virgin while he was still alive, so he wasn't doing this for martyrdom. However, the American teamed with him was a psycho, and Mohammed was sure he believed all that shit about the virgins in paradise. Mohammed thought he could probably convince the American that he could give him his virgins, so he could have 144 when he martyred himself.

"What did Khalid say?" asked the American.

Mohammed answered, "He said we should park as close as we can, put the bomb on timer, and head home."

"What? That might not kill many people. I think we should drive through the roadblocks and blow it."

"Feel free to do that, but I'm not dying," answered Mohammed.

"Dude, you're a pussy," he answered.

"And you're a psycho, but hey, good luck," said Mohammed as he opened the passenger door.

"Hey, just one more thing," said the American. Mohammed turned to look back, and was on the receiving end of a 9 mm bullet to the face.

❧ ❧ ❧

Kong was driving the truck and Sam was on his satellite phone with Mr. Steen, while the others were trying to boot up the laptop from Khalid's house as well as look through the papers they had taken, searching for any clues to indicate attacks abroad.

"I have a satellite phone that's been used to call numbers in the U.S.," Sam told Steen. "One in particular has been called numerous times in the last 24 hours, and Khalid was talking to that number when we darted him."

"Okay, I'll get those numbers over to Royster ASAP. You guys otherwise good?"

"Just peachy," said Sam. "We got about 7 hours to the border. Khalid should be waking up shortly. I'm sure he won't give up anything, but I'll do the best I can in the back of this truck to interrogate him."

"Copy that. Sam, good luck," replied Steen.

Steen made the call to D/NCS Royster and gave him the phone numbers. Royster confirmed that there was a huge amount of chatter from their Afghanistan agents regarding something big about to occur. Security for everything in the U.S. was tighter than it had ever been in the past, due to the chatter and from the attacks just nine months ago. It was Thanksgiving Day, 9:30 a.m. in America, and Royster prayed that Sam's intelligence would be fruitful.

Khalid could feel the vibrations and knew he was in a vehicle. He realized that his hands and feet were bound. He felt incredibly weak, as if he were sick. It took significant focus just to move his head around. He could hear voices that sounded distant. Over the next minute, it was like his brain was coming into focus. He opened his eyes to see the man who had killed his brother.

"Welcome back, Khalid," said Sam.

"Samuel Richards, we meet again," replied Khalid. "We've been close before. I've hoped Allah would bring us together again."

"Well, you got your wish, and my prayers have been answered as well. Who knows, maybe it's the same God. One thing's for sure—God has to be crying about how his or her creations are treating one another in this world."

"There is no true God but Allah. And HE is on our side."

"I'm not going to argue your point, but, like you said, both of our prayers have been answered. However, your God has allowed you to be zip-tied, and I'm holding the gun this time. It would seem that my God is more in control."

Khalid looked away from Sam and closed his eyes. Sam's buddies were listening intently to the conversation while pouring over the materials they had recovered.

"We have a few hours to kill. Why don't we chat and get to know each other?"

"I don't want to know you. I want to hurt you and your country, then kill you," replied Khalid.

"I guess that means that you won't tell me about your upcoming plans?" said Sam.

"Burn in hell, infidel. Torture me all you want, but I would rather die."

"I'm not going to torture you, Khalid. I know it wouldn't work, although you deserve the pain because of all the things that you've done," said Sam.

"All that *I've* done? You hypocrite," replied Khalid.

Sam responded, "Everything that I've done has been either in self-defense or to stop the killings that you execute in the name of your twisted interpretation of Islam."

Khalid again broke eye contact with Sam at the same time that Sam's sat phone rang. It was D/NCS Royster calling with an update. He informed Sam that they had a location on the last number called by Khalid. There were FBI agents closing in as well as barricades being set up by police. They suspected the method of the upcoming attack would be something similar to the D.C. bombings.

"Khalid, you're a well-educated Muslim who was born into prosperity. You lived in the United States for years. Why the hatred? I don't buy the 'Islam must take over the world' shit as your reason. You sell that crap to your soldiers."

Khalid laughed. "My time in your country awakened my spirit. I was ridiculed by your people and treated as an outcast by the American Muslims. They're no better than someone like you."

"So, basically, you were bullied, and you turned the treatment you received from some stupid teenagers into a hatred of anyone like them. You've become just like Hitler or any other mass murderer, often a crybaby in their youth. You prey on other Muslims who are jobless, live in countries with poor economies, and are just angry and looking for someone to blame. They follow you like sheep. I killed your brother because you killed my friends while we were on a mission to help the less fortunate—in that case, your fellow Muslims. I went to Uganda to stop a man who was butchering people. I went to Nigeria because Boko Haram was killing aid workers and kidnapping young girls for slavery in the name of Islam. Libya, Somalia, Afghanistan—all for similar reasons.

The rest of the Team was exchanging glances. They couldn't believe the passion coming from Sam, usually a cool customer. But he didn't stop.

"Every mission was in response to atrocities committed on innocents by twisted people such as you, who pervert the Muslim faith. Tell me that there is a religion or belief system where helping others is a sin or a crime; it's certainly not a sin to help others in the true Muslim faith. You're simply evil; we're simply trying to help the oppressed. Every action I've undertaken has been a reaction and response to your actions against innocents."

"You're correct, Sam, my obsession to hurt you and the West comes from my experiences. But the West is not 'innocent,' as you say. I no longer have any beliefs except that obsession. I long ago gave up believing in a god; probably the day you killed my brother. I devoted myself to becoming powerful enough as a leader in ISIS to have command over the fanatics who would do my bidding. I don't think I'm any different than bin Laden or al-Baghdadi, who also wanted power. It's almost always about money or power, isn't it? If it weren't me in charge, it would be someone else doing the same. If my interests are the same as my soldiers' interests, but for different reasons, what does it matter?"

"So, again, your motivation has been personal, fueled by hatred from being bullied as a teenager and from the death of your brother, for the sole cause of exacting revenge. You're nothing but a hypocrite and a psychopath," said Sam.

"Maybe so, but my only regret is not having killed you," responded Khalid.

The other men continued to really focus on Sam, and Khalid was silent. Kerney nudged Sam, who saw the eyes of his friends looking at him with concern.

"I'm good, guys. I know I'm wasting my breath, but he's made this personal, and I've always wanted to confirm his motivation. He's just another power-hungry douchebag manipulating others for his cause."

Sam's phone rang. Royster reported to him that the FBI had taken down a van driven by an American citizen who had been planning to drive it into the Macy's Day Parade. A sniper had killed him before he could detonate. They were still trying to locate the other phones, but they were turned off, and the NSA had not found a way to turn them back on so they could be traced. Royster surmised that Khalid probably had a schedule to communicate with his people, and the phones would only be turned on at the appropriate time to receive his orders. Sam relayed the information to his team and told them to concentrate on locations or anything showing times in the laptop or confiscated papers.

"Your attempt to bomb the Macy's Thanksgiving Parade was just stopped."

Khalid looked away, hiding the disappointment in his eyes.

"There's another difference between you twisted fucks and us," Sam continued. "Our targets are terrorists or soldiers. Our laws will prosecute soldiers who knowingly kill non-combatants. You hide among innocents, usually fellow Muslims, and sometimes they get killed by our hands because you use them as shields. You primarily target innocents through cowardly acts."

Khalid stared at Sam with a hint of sadness that quickly turned into hatred. It was as if Sam had connected with some decency in him for just a moment, until the fanaticism returned.

"Yo, Sam, look at this," said Durrant, who showed him some scribbling. "I'm not an expert, but are those three dates written in the Islamic calendar?"

"Shit, Steve, I don't know. Why do you think that?" replied Sam.

"Uh, because I took some Islam classes in college and paid attention," said Durrant.

There was a murmuring of coughs mixed with "bullshit" from the group, then laughter.

"Let me shoot those three dates, or whatever they are, off to Royster," said Sam.

Bury had been closely watching Khalid throughout the exchange between Richards and Durrant.

"Durrant's right, Sam," said Randy.

"You took the same class, Randy?" replied a smiling Sam.

"No fucking way did I waste my time in a class like that, but I could see it in that shitbag's eyes."

"I hope you're right, Randy," replied Sam. "Keep looking for anything else."

They were making great time through the mountains and had seen only a few other vehicles. Kong had told them that there was nothing out of the ordinary on the roads. The group continued to hope that the Chinese soldiers would not return to the house and find the four dead terrorists before they reached the border. That could create problems if the Chinese found the soldiers and reacted by closing the roads or the border.

Chapter 66

The other two terrorist vans had arrived close to their locations in Michigan and Georgia. The drivers had communicated with each other through different burner cell phones along the way. They were confused that there was no news about the attack in New York City. But there was no news of an attack being stopped, either. They tried calling Mohammed to get an update on his efforts at the Parade, but were unable to reach him. They discussed calling Khalid, but decided against it, because the importance of adhering to the phone schedule had been drilled into their heads. In the end, they decided to stick to the plan, whether they received another call or not. They would lie low for two days, check in with Khalid at the appointed times, and stay prepared to execute their mission for Allah.

❀ ❀ ❀

"Your government will pay for taking me from China. The Chinese promised retaliation if you came back," said Khalid.

"We're not with the government, dickhead, we're free agents, making a citizen's arrest," responded Woprice.

Sam could see confusion on Khalid's face.

"He means we don't work for the U.S. government. I guess we're like vigilantes. Besides, the Chinese won't ever know, because you've just vanished. They'll think you ran back to Pakistan and got caught there."

"You're not planning on killing me?" asked Khalid.

"All of us would really like to," responded Sam, "but we've decided to give you to the CIA so you can have some rest and recreation at GIT-MO with other assholes like you. Besides, we may be killers, but we're not murderers like you bastards. There's a big difference."

Kong was listening to the conversation, waiting to give the soldiers an update. He was surprised at the continued conversation between Khalid and the American leader. He understood transporting him to Pakistan before announcing his capture, but why not just show his dead body in Pakistan? Why not kill him now? He was surprised at the Americans' restraint. Kong knew that he would gladly butcher anyone responsible for the death of his family.

"The border is close," said Kong. "We should stop and get everyone hidden."

"Sounds good, Kong. Sweet dreams, Khalid," said Sam, as he darted him again.

As before, the crossing at the Khunjerab Pass went uneventfully. They were now on their way to their exfiltration point in Sost, the first town inside of Pakistan. There were landmarks available at that location to help with the next part of Sam's plan.

Royster had called back to confirm that the pictures Sam had sent him did indeed represent dates. Of the three dates, one corresponded to that day's attempted attack and the other two were for Saturday, two days hence. However, the locations remained unknown. Sam told the D/NCS that they had been through all the intel and found no clues about possible targets. They had Khalid's laptop, though, and Sam would turn it over to the CIA when they were picked up. Perhaps it would enlighten them about target locations.

The assumption after stopping the attack on the Parade was that the targets would be similar—non-government buildings, and designed around some event. They also assumed it would be like D.C attacks, copying Timothy McVeigh with vehicle bombs, especially since this had been the design of the attack on the Thanksgiving Day parade. Royster said that they were putting efforts into obtaining the information on the thousands of rented vans across the country, and were continuing to monitor the phone numbers they had received from Sam.

"Do you think Khalid would give up the info if pressured?" asked Marv.

"I really don't," responded Sam. "Plus he could easily make up any location. I think the best bet is via the phones or laptop. You're okay with the next part of my plan? I think it's time we play by their rules."

"No problem at all. I doubt it will have any positive effect, but it sure can't hurt," said Royster.

"True that. If anything, it'll be unprecedented," said Sam.

"Copy that, Sam. But much of what you do lately is unprecedented."

"In part, thanks to you, Marv. Talk soon."

The Team arrived in the village of Sost. The location sat between the local mountains with the only main road through town being the Karakoram Highway. The buildings were drab, rectangular structures. Sost was the village where Pakistani and Chinese trucks exchanged their wares for transport to each other's country. The team's exfiltration would take place just outside the city.

Before leaving for exfiltration, Sam and the team were preparing the VSAT system (Very Small Aperture Terminal), to broadcast the capture of Khalid to the world. They would be filming in a position that unmistakably showed that their location was in Pakistan, ensuring that the Chinese had no proof that there had been an excursion into China. They planned to mimic ISIS, who made a point to live-stream executions for sheer horror. Video killings were disturbing, even though the killing was happening in a distant place—the fact that it was a live video was chilling to the observer.

The typical ISIS video showed masked terrorists making statements of hatred toward the West, calling for all jihadists to stand strong, etc. The propaganda delivered in the speech and the spectacle of an execution were not things that viewers could easily forget. The stage usually had the group's flag in the background, the victim bound and kneeling in the foreground, and the executioner behind him or her. Sam had prepared a banner showing a map of the world, and the National Security Agency had provided technology that not only masked voices but allowed various forms of accented English to be heard through the speaker. They had scripted their speaking parts, with each team member having a different accent to their English—Russian, Arabic, German, Asian. Sam would be the only one who sounded American. It really didn't matter if the world suspected the Americans of having Khalid, but the intention was to make people think that this had been a global effort.

They began the broadcast, all of them masked and standing side by side behind Khalid, each with their own part to say.

"Kneeling before you is Khalid Ali, a current leader of the terrorist group ISIS and the mastermind of many attacks on innocent people of all religions. He and his leadership, like all terrorist groups, have twisted and perverted a belief system in order to justify their actions. That religion's mainstream believers would call these actions blasphemy. He and his leadership have used radical religion to fight against the modern world, and to recruit alienated, young Muslims to participate in his actions. He's using his soldiers as pawns. If you don't believe us, watch and listen to this exchange."

Woprice had videotaped Sam's conversation with Khalid during the drive from China. The video showed Khalid's face, but not Sam's. Sam was playing the section when he and Khalid discussed the differences between the motivation for their actions, ending with Khalid stating that he no longer believed in Allah and that his efforts were personal. It showed his admission to gain power only so he could use others to fulfill his personal vendetta.

Khalid's mouth was currently duct-taped shut, so he could not respond to the video being shown. After that video finished and the broadcast went live again, there was terror in Khalid's eyes as he registered in his mind what his followers must be thinking.

The five men began again, each saying their part in accented English.

"We are individuals from different countries, representing all religions. We do not represent any particular country. We represent decency, and we stand for what is right. All religions have had pockets of extremists, but nothing like the radical Islamic terrorism of today. We argue that the Age of Enlightenment revealed to all people that rational thinking, not only religion, is reason enough for secular values we hold dear today: freedom to practice any religion, equal rights, freedom of speech, freedom of the press, civil liberties for all, equality for women and men. It seems that radical Muslims may be ignorant of these beliefs, and perhaps don't realize that the people they attack have these values. Perhaps many of you have had this knowledge suppressed from you. We plead with all of you watching to look within yourself and ask if you truly disagree with these principles. All people should challenge their leaders who are leading you astray. Ask them if they know what the rest of the world truly believes. They're lying to you if they tell you that the world wants to wipe out the Muslim faith, or any faith. We all want the same thing: a peaceful, happy life. Only when everyone understands this can there be hope that the world will become a better place."

After this live version, the message would be continuously replayed in Arabic, Farsi, and other major languages. They ended the broadcast with perfect timing. The pilot had notified Sam that his ETA was 10 minutes. As he was conversing with his team, the unexpected occurred. Kong had walked over to Khalid, and was screaming at him.

"My family was killed by my atheistic government because we are Muslims. Their prejudice is fueled by ignorance, but it's reinforced by your terrorist actions. They, like many, believe that all Muslims are bad because of people like you. They use people like you to justify their actions, but they kill *us*."

Sam and his team were listening, not sure where this was going, and were slowly moving closer to Kong.

He then said, "For this, you must go to Jahannam."

Kong then slit Khalid's throat from ear to ear.

This was followed by silence, then Kong Chiang Kei softly spoke.

"I am sorry if this is bad for your plans, and I don't care if you kill me for my actions." He dropped to his knees sobbing. "I have allowed my rage to take control. There has been so much death in my life, but that man deserved to die."

The team came over to Kong, and Sam helped him to his feet. They each told him that it was okay, that no harm had been done.

"We have no problem with what you did, Kong. He didn't deserve to be alive," said Sam. "He would have rotted at GITMO, or maybe stood trial. It would have been a waste of air and food for him to keep on living. We actually were going to have him 'slip' out of the chopper on the way to Islamabad. For him to hear what you said, and it coming from another Muslim, was perfect."

Kong continued to sob, but the team came over to him, each telling him again that it was okay. After several minutes of silence, Woprice spoke first.

"Wow, that was a perfect ending," said Woprice. "But what the hell is Jahannam?"

"That's Muslim hell," answered Bury.

"You know a fair amount of Muslim stuff—about their calendar, about their hell. You took a class like Durrant didn't you?" mocked Woprice.

Randy responded with his middle finger. "No, I'm just a knowledgeable guy."

"Bullshit," muttered the group.

"Okay, I dated a Muslim girl for a while. She wanted to get married, and I kind of blew her off."

Bury was the only one of the five who had remained a bachelor, and he was quite the ladies' man.

"What a surprise," replied Woprice.

"That's how I found out. She kept texting me that I was going to Jahannam. I finally googled it to see what the fuck she meant."

They all laughed, and even Kong was smiling now.

He asked Sam, "What will happen to me now?"

"That's up to you, Kong. I'm sure that we could get you asylum in the U.S., if that's what you want," answered Sam.

"I think I'll go back and continue to smuggle as many people out of China as I can. I have nothing else to live for."

"You could make a new life for yourself in America, Kong. We all agree that you deserve it," answered Sam.

"Thank you, Sam, but I'm staying."

"If you ever change your mind, you let me know."

Kong shook hands with the five Americans, got in to his truck, and headed back towards the Khunjerab Pass.

They threw Khalid into a body bag, loaded it onto the Blackhawk chopper, and headed towards Islamabad. It was now early Friday morning in D.C.

They boarded the Gulfstream 650ER in Islamabad, courtesy of the Trust. This plane would get them home traveling at Mach 0.85 in about 15.5 hours, getting them to D.C. in the middle of the night. This would allow the CIA to have about 5 hours with the computer before the sun came up on Saturday, the day that two more attacks were expected. Hopefully, the locations would be discovered from the laptop.

❀ ❀ ❀

Every television network in the world had been replaying the live stream video over and over. Commentary from political pundits was all over the spectrum, similar to any debate involving politics. The U.S. vehemently denied any involvement, as did other Western countries. Conjecture about who was responsible ranged from the comical to the scary. Most thought that the U.S. had to be the architect.

It was clear that there were very few who disagreed with the content of the message, however. It had said what a lot of people thought, but were reluctant to say, because of fear of being labeled Islamophobic. The message also gave hope that the extremists would know what the West really stood for, as many radical Muslims had been indoctrinated to think that the West persecuted people of their faith.

Chapter 67

On the flight home, each team member was able to talk with their significant other and assure them that they were safe. As Sam had always done, he encouraged his team to tell their significant other specifics, unless they thought it was better not to. He knew all too well how it had made his life easier.

Mariah and the kids were in Ann Arbor, Michigan, at her brother's house. Her brother's job had taken him there, and as an Ohio State alumnus, he hated living in the arch rival's back yard. Sam and Mariah coordinated their Thanksgiving at his home every odd year, when the Buckeyes traveled there to play the greatest college football rivalry game the Saturday after Thanksgiving.

"I guess you won't be here for the game?" said Mariah.

"I wouldn't hold out hope, babe. The earliest I could get in is probably by dinner. Take your dad to the game."

"We'll see. I love you, Sam, and I'm so proud of you for not murdering Khalid," she laughed.

"It might have been the hardest thing any of us ever had to do—not kill him," Sam replied. "I really thought someone was going to say, 'Ah fuck it,' and shoot him. I guarantee if someone had shot him, all five of us would have followed suit. Not only because it would have felt good, but also to put all five of us on the hook for any disciplinary action."

"You guys are unbelievable. Give my love to the others."

Sam had just ended his call to Mariah when Khalid's satellite phone rang.

"Hello," answered Sam.

"Who is this?" asked the caller. "Where is Khalid?"

"Did you not see the video, my friend? Khalid has been captured," said Sam. "He wanted you to stand down from any further attacks. You heard him say that he was not for the 'cause,' but was simply involved for selfish reasons."

"I must confirm that with him."

"That's impossible. Why listen to him anyway? By standing down and giving yourself up, you would be an example of wanting to start a dialogue towards peace and coexistence." There was no response; the line simply went dead.

Ahmed was confused. He was at his hotel with the American who had volunteered to drive the van, as security was profiling anyone who looked Muslim. The President's new policy was making it very difficult for Muslims in the U.S. They were constantly being stopped to ensure that they had been vetted. If not, they were detained until a thorough background check was conducted. Ahmed and his American partner were currently about ten miles from the PGA event.

Ahmed found the video online that the person who had answered Khalid's phone mentioned, and it was certainly distressing. Could the

Americans have faked the conversation between Khalid and the American he was heard speaking with? When he heard Khalid say that he no longer believed in Allah, and that he simply was doing this for revenge, Ahmed had nearly puked. But did it matter? This attack was what all Muslim terrorists wanted, wasn't it? Not ever having been to America before being sent to participate in this attack, he was exactly the type of person that the video had mentioned—no job, angry, and told that the West was to blame. His parents had both cried when he had told them that he was joining ISIS. Ahmed agreed with the video that we should all have freedoms. The call that he had just made to Khalid's phone had only confused him more.

❖ ❖ ❖

Hazim was blown away by the video of Khalid. He had expected him to be executed at the end like ISIS always did on their tapes. He felt no reason to call Khalid to check in because he believed what he had seen. He had lived in the U.S. for ten years now, having escaped Afghanistan and the Taliban with his family. He agreed with the comments regarding the Western secular beliefs of basic human rights. The Americans and Muslim Americans did not have a chip on their shoulder like Muslims at home. When he'd first come to the U.S., he was very wary of Americans, but he had been treated well. He could actually understand their fears of Muslims after 9/11, as he had been fearful when the U.S. rolled across Afghanistan. But they had helped his family and allowed them to come to America. Sure, they were still poor, but the opportunities for them here were endless, and the future was bright.

His cousin in Kabul, who had told him that the Americans were butchering Muslims there and that Khalid Ali was the next savior, had dragged Hazim into this mission. He had been told that it was his duty to help his Muslim brothers. When the President began his profiling of Muslims, Hazim had thought persecutions were beginning here in

America, and so he had agreed to participate in the attack. After the profiling began, he had gone to one of the centers and had his background check done. He had been vetted, so now when he was stopped, he was quickly thanked by law enforcement and then able to go his own way. Again, he really couldn't fault the American government, since people with his background and appearance were similar to that of the terrorists. It was an inconvenience to be stopped, but Hazim would rather be in the U.S.

Hazim had been partnered with a white kid who had swastika tattoos on each arm. When Hazim had asked him about it, he had told Hazim that he used to be in a gang, but had found Allah. He had actually said that he no longer hated sandniggers, spics, and regular niggers. Hazim thought that he might be crazy, like the recent white male individuals who had committed numerous mass shootings in America.

The two of them were scheduled to enter the tailgate parking lot at about 10 a.m. They would set the timer for 10:30, the peak tailgate time before the football game. Hazim had a problem with the target, because since relocating to Detroit, he had become partial to the University of Michigan basketball program. He was told that the football program had always been historically good, but since his arrival, they had not won a Big Ten Championship or beaten their arch rival Ohio State. He didn't feel right about bombing any American target. He now realized that he had been wrong to get involved with this plot and he wanted out. In fact, he didn't want to blow the bomb.

Chapter 68

Royster called Sam two minutes after Ahmed had ended the call with Sam.

"Sam, great job—we have a location on that phone you just spoke with," said Marv. "It came from the east coast of Georgia. The only big event nearby is the RSM Classic at Sea Island Resort. That has to be the target. The FBI is moving in."

"Anything on the third location?" Sam asked.

"Nothing," was Marv's response.

"I tried calling that phone; no pick up," said Sam. "I'll keep trying, and if he picks up, you can lock in on that one as well."

The team arrived in D.C. at 3:30 a.m., turned the laptop over to the computer nerds with the CIA, and went to eat breakfast at the Langley canteen. It was like old times for them; they had eaten many meals here together. Royster and Steen came down to congratulate them for a job well done. The Chinese had remained quiet, so they surely had no idea that they'd snatched Khalid. Marv told them that he was also impressed with their video performance.

"Outstanding job on the video, gentlemen. Especially since I wasn't sure any of you could still read."

This was met by a variety of responses ranging from "Hardy har har" to the "Old cough and fuck you" routine.

Steen then chimed in as well. "What did you do when Kong slit Khalid's throat?"

"We were silent. Kong thought we were going to kill him, and then we sang 'Hallelujah,'" was Kerney's description.

The group laughed.

"No, we told him that we understood his actions. That dude has had a hard life. I tried to get him to come with us," said Sam. "Seriously, though, I was thinking of killing Khalid myself. It took a lot of self-control not to."

Sam's admission was followed by each Team member revealing that they had had the same thoughts.

"Kong did us all a favor," remarked Mr. Steen. "Hey, I'm sure its only a coincidence, but the chatter in Afghanistan, Iraq, and Yemen has been reduced since your video. Who wrote the script?"

All fingers immediately pointed at Sam.

"He's the only one with a degree that required writing a lot of papers," said Bury. "The rest of us had majors that could have gotten us a real job."

He immediately received the middle finger from Sam.

"Speaking of college, don't you have to get to Ann Arbor for the game?" asked Mr. Steen.

"There's no way I can make it. I'll get there by dinner," replied Sam.

"Not acceptable, Sam. I have a light jet that can get you there in little over an hour. Call Mariah and tell her you're on the way. You deserve it."

"Wow, she already digs you, Mr. Steen, but now, no telling what she'll do when she sees you next."

❊ ❊ ❊

Ahmed was following the GPS coordinates to The Sea Island Resort in Georgia. The scenery was beautiful, as was the day. The American with him was driving, so people passing them would not see Ahmed's face. He was sure that if he were seen by law enforcement, he would be pulled over. There was a significant number of police cruisers on the road patrolling the highways, and security was significantly heightened. They saw several cars pulled over and the vehicles were being searched.

Ahmed continued to think about the video, and what the men holding Khalid had said. All he had ever known was what was told to him by his elders—that the West was evil and Muslims living there did not practice true Islam. Therefore, both Americans and western Muslims were infidels and deserved to die. The video spoke of rights that every person should have, and those rights made sense to Ahmed. His parents were religious people, but they did not share the sentiment of ISIS. They weren't zealots. The Islam they practiced did not involve hate and indiscriminate violence, and they had been distraught over Ahmed's decision to go to America and accept a part in these acts. His parents had always tried to be good, pious Muslims, staying away from radical teachings. Maybe they had been right all along. His thoughts were interrupted by the American, who told Ahmed the GPS showed that they would be arriving at their destination in an hour.

In Michigan, Hazim and the American were getting close, the ETA estimated to be 45 minutes to the parking area. As they drew near, he was really having second thoughts about killing people. The video with

Khalid was a reminder of what he had seen while living in the U.S. The people were mostly friendly, and he had made many friends. Religious background was never part of the conversation with his new friends. His favorite teacher had been doing all she could to help Hazim get into college, even though he had graduated high school three years ago. She still felt that Hazim had great potential.

Sure, the U.S. had its problems, but here, everyone had the right to say what they felt. People had been killed for free speech back in Afghanistan under the Taliban. He was starting to feel that if more Muslims could experience the U.S. the way he had, they would begin to feel as he did. As a matter of fact, he wondered why more prominent Muslims living in the U.S. didn't help get that message out. They could use their influence to teach Muslims abroad how life here really was for those of his faith.

As they continued to drive, Hazim noted that the American driver was getting more and more excited, working himself into a frenzy. He was really ready to kill innocent people. This further reinforced to Hazim that he was on the wrong side. This guy was going to kill for the sake of killing; he wasn't a Muslim, he was a neo-Nazi. Hazim had made up his mind. The two of them were now coming into town. He had decided to jump out of the vehicle at the next stop sign or light. He would take the phone and the suicide trigger so the American couldn't blow the bomb instantly. If the skinhead wanted to blow the bomb, then he would have to use the timer. Hazim didn't know enough about the explosive to stop the timer, so he would have to hope that he could get help in time to stop this maniac.

Chapter 69

Sam called Mariah and gave her the good news.

"Even though I'll get there in time, tell your dad he can still go to the game. I'll hang out with the kids. I don't want to ruin his excitement."

"I didn't ask anybody to go," said Mariah. "Somehow I expected you to make it. Mr. Steen gets a big kiss when I see him next!"

"Ha! I already warned him. I'll meet you at the tailgate."

"Can't wait, Sam. It'll be nice to enjoy the game together and have some quiet time together after," she said.

"Amen to that!" was Sam's response.

❊ ❊ ❊

In Georgia, Ahmed and his partner were turning into the parking area at the resort. The tournament had already started, but Ahmed was told that the crowds would steadily arrive throughout the late morning, since the tournament leaders teed off later in the day. Their bomb would certainly destroy a lot of vehicles, though maybe not as many people. He just wanted to get parked, set the timer, take the dead man's switch just in case, and get as far away as he could. He wanted to put this behind him and disappear, never to help ISIS again. He just wasn't completely sure about the video, and he was worried that if he aborted, his parents would suffer consequences.

The FBI was finally on the scene in Georgia. Local law enforcement had been stopping all vehicles after being notified of a terrorist threat. Officers were also doing a grid search to eliminate vehicles that had already parked. It was now 9:30 a.m.

Ahmed and the American found a spot to park that was surprisingly close to the front. He could actually see golfers on a practice green; it did pay to arrive early. When they had entered the parking area, there had been no search of the vehicle. Ahmed had hidden in the back with his hand on the suicide trigger in case the vehicle was stopped and searched. He set the timer for 30 minutes, firmly gripped the suicide trigger, and then they were ready to leave the van. The trigger had a range of three miles, so if Ahmed did not hear an explosion in 30 minutes, he could simply release his hand and the bomb would detonate.

Special Agent Thomas O'Connor was leading a group of three local police officers through their search area. They were making good progress through an area of cars that had been allowed to park before the search had begun. None of the parking attendants could recall anyone that appeared suspicious. As they were progressing, O'Connor happened to look up when he heard the crowd roar. Someone must have sunk a great putt, he thought to himself. Whether it was instinct or luck, he scanned the vehicles in his line of sight as he was looking up, and saw two young men exit a cargo van. One was a longhaired white kid, and the other had a baseball cap pulled low over his face and had his head turned down.

"Gentlemen," he said to the officers, "act normal and follow my direction, staying spaced apart."

They made their way toward the two men who were on a course approaching them. Ahmed made eye contact with Special Agent O'Connor; he then pulled his American partner's arm to change their direction.

"Control, this is O'Connor. We're pursuing two suspicious men in our area heading southwest. They came out of a white cargo van three rows from the front. I think it's our guys; they changed their direction when they saw us."

"Copy that," replied Control. "Bomb squad en route."

They were closing in, now about 25 yards behind them. O'Connor knew that the previous attacks on D.C. had timers for the bombs as well as dead-man switches. It was fair to say that one of the two young men was probably squeezing the switch right now. He was debating on starting to run at them when the decision was made for him. The white kid stopped, turned, and spun around.

Ahmed was panicking. He saw the officers and a blond guy wearing a golf shirt turn in their direction shortly after they left the vehicle. They changed direction after he and the blond guy had made eye contact. The American had noticed as well and told Ahmed to be ready to blow the van. Ahmed had never been this conflicted. He didn't want to die, but he didn't want his parents to suffer once ISIS discovered he had aborted. If he did fail to blow the bomb, he was sure that they would torture and behead his parents publicly to make an example of them. How could he have let himself become involved with such barbarians? Just then, he noticed that his American partner had stopped.

Special Agent O'Connor was staring down the barrel of the terrorist's gun. There was no fear in the eyes of the young man who held the weapon, and it was clear that he intended to use it. O'Connor had told the officers with him to keep their weapons holstered, but he had been holding his weapon down and at his side, unfortunately, giving the young man the drop on him.

Without hesitation, O'Connor raised his Glock 19 and fired a split second after the terrorist had shot his own gun. O'Connor immediately felt an intense burning in his left shoulder. He was able to continue standing as well as keep his senses; he was now depending on his training as well as the effects of the adrenaline coursing through him. His aim had been true: the shot had struck the terrorist between the eyes, dropping him to the ground immediately. O'Connor was now staring at the man in the baseball hat, who was holding a suicide trigger up in the air. The young man's eyes reflected panic.

"Stand down," O'Connor yelled to the officers, who complied and lowered their weapons down to their sides.

"Son, look at me. No one's going to shoot you. Just look at me," called O'Connor, who was trying to smile despite the pain in his shoulder.

Ahmed looked at the wounded man while continuing to hold a death grip on the suicide trigger.

"I really don't want to die today," said O'Connor. "You see, it's my wife's birthday, and I planned on taking her to dinner with our children."

Ahmed was struck by the seeming kindness in the man's eyes. It was almost as if he were reading Ahmed's mind because of what he said next.

"Don't you have somebody that you love and want to see again?"

Ahmed had tears rolling down his cheeks. "My mother and father," he responded in a subdued voice. "I never really wanted to do this, but they said that they would kill my family if I didn't carry out the attack."

O'Connor winced at the statement. He knew this was probably true; he had read reports of suicide bombers who had aborted their missions reporting the same thing.

"What's your name, son?"

"Ahmed."

"Ahmed, I'm Tom, and I'm sorry, Ahmed, I really am. They've put you in a terrible position. You can let go of the switch, killing yourself and many innocent people you don't know, or we can turn it off, perhaps causing your parents to die. I guess the only thing I could tell you is to ask yourself—what would your parents want you to do?"

"They're peaceful people," said Ahmed. "They believe in all of the ideas in that video. Most of the people I know back home agree with those ideas. But these evil men are all anyone in the world sees of Muslims."

"I know that, Ahmed. I have many Muslim friends who are embarrassed by the perversion of Islam. This is your chance to stop some of the violence."

"I want to," replied Ahmed, "but my parents will die."

"Maybe," said O'Connor, "but a part of them will die if you let that bomb go off. I think that they would want you to stop and make a stand against the terror."

He could see that Ahmed was about ready to give up, and he started walking toward him. Ahmed was not alarmed as he approached.

Now with his hand on Ahmed's shoulder, Special Agent O'Connor said, "No one needs to know you aborted. We can say the bomb failed to blow."

Ahmed showed O'Connor the trigger, put it in safe mode, handed it to him, and said, "No, I want the world to know that I could have done it, but I chose not to."

"Good for you, Ahmed, good for you," replied O'Connor.

Police officers and other FBI were rushing in towards Ahmed when O'Connor yelled for them to stand down. He was going to make sure that no asshole in their ranks tried to mistreat Ahmed.

Chapter 70

Sam arrived at the Stadium parking lot at about 9:30 a.m. Now all he had to do was find Mariah and her brother with their tailgating friends. He was getting his bearings on which direction to go when his cell phone buzzed.

"Sam, they got the van in Georgia," said Royster.

"Outstanding," Sam replied. "One more to go. Any news on that?"

"Yes, listen carefully," he said.

Sam broke out of his reverie concerning the news about Georgia just in time to hear Marv say more.

"We got a call from a Muslim kid saying that he was sorry, and that he left the van with the third bomb. It's heading to you, Sam. Scheduled to detonate at 10:30. The kid said the plan is to go in and park it with the tailgaters, set the timer, and leave. It's a recently poorly painted, navy blue cargo van with U of M magnets on the sides."

"For real, Marv? There's probably quite a few like that here," replied Sam.

"The kid remembers the parking ticket saying gate 1, hospitality A," continued Marv. "He said that there's only one person in the van, a skinhead-looking, white guy in a yellow hoodie. The Muslim kid also said that he took the suicide trigger with him, so the hoodie skinhead will have to set the timer. It has a 30-minute minimum set time."

"Yellow hoodie, navy blue van—those are just Michigan's frigging colors! I'm not far from there. Does local law enforcement know, and is there any FBI onsite?" asked Sam.

"Yes to local law enforcement and they have their bomb guy, the FBI is on the way. You're the only one there who doesn't look like a cop. You're our best shot, Sam."

"Shit, thanks for that Marv. You know I hate the pressure," he said with a chuckle. "Let law enforcement know I have on a red Ohio State hoodie, black jeans, and red tennis shoes. Oh, and I'll be running, so tell them not to shoot me."

"Copy that," replied Marv.

Sam looked at his phone and noticed a text from Mariah saying they were in hospitality A, the same section as the target van. Sam tried calling Mariah, but the cell towers must have been overwhelmed, and he couldn't get through. He noted the time to be 9:45 a.m.

He sprinted toward the hospitality A section along Stadium Boulevard, and all the while people were screaming at him and giving him shit because of his hoodie. All normal for this rivalry, but all Sam needed was for some Michigan fan to try and stop him. He arrived in the area and slowed his pace, scanning for the appropriate vehicle. This was a section with large vehicles, making it difficult to see more than the row in front of him.

Suddenly, he heard his name called out. "Sam, Sam."

He turned to see Mariah and her brother. He couldn't really stop and explain, so he shouted to her to stay there and that he would be right back.

"Maybe he's got to take a shit," said Mariah's brother.

She barely heard her brother as she took off after husband. She caught up to him and was right behind him when she said, "Hey handsome, where ya going?"

Sam was focused on his search. At exactly the same moment Mariah said something to him, he spotted a blue van with areas of white showing through the blue paint on the roof. A poor paint job was what Marv had said. Sitting in the passenger seat was a white guy with a shaved head who made eye contact with Sam and ducked into the back of the van. It had to be the guy. Sam sprinted toward the vehicle, yelling for Mariah to stay back. He was about 40 feet from the vehicle when the side door opened, and out came the skinhead with a gun in his right hand. He was squeezing something in his left hand.

"Back off motherfuckers, or I'll blow this place," he said.

The kid looked wired, from meth or something, and he was waving the gun while scanning the crowd. Sam was slowly moving forward toward him whenever the guy looked away. Some in the crowd were already a little drunk, typical for a game day tailgate, and they didn't show any fear in their eyes. Sam wasn't sure a lot of them were registering what was happening. The kid continued to back up against the van, waving the gun 180 degrees side to side, threatening to shoot. Sam was now about ten feet away. The skinhead focused on Sam and appeared ready to pull the trigger, when suddenly a blue and gold football came flying in and struck the side of the terrorist's head. A Michigan fan had delivered a perfect spiral. The skinhead turned toward the fan, fired one shot, and then went down from Sam's blow to his head. Sam saw that the kid had been holding a ball, not a trigger, and he thanked God that Marv's intel had been accurate about the suicide trigger.

Sam opened the side door of the van and saw the bomb barrels and the detonation wires, with the timer counting down. There were screams of "Oh shit" behind him when the crowd saw the van contents. Mariah had made her way up to Sam and grabbed his hand. The timer was at 7:15 and counting down.

Sam turned to Mariah, kissed her, and said, "Grab your brother, and start running. Don't stop, don't look back, run your fastest mile."

"Sam, you have to come with me."

"I can't, babe. I've got to see if I can stop this thing. Go, please. It'll be okay."

A group of police officers showed up while Sam was telling Mariah to go. She reluctantly left after kissing him quickly. They cuffed the skinhead, who was still unconscious.

"You must be Richards," one said. "You got here fast."

"Where's your bomb guy?" responded Sam.

"Right here," said a guy who looked about 20.

"The FBI bomb squad is about 20 minutes out," said the first police officer.

"Not going to work," said Sam pointing to the timer. It read 5:45.

"Oh shit," was the bomb guy's reply.

Sam and the demolition specialist went into the van and followed the wiring, noting the set-up. The young guy was talking out loud, and he sounded competent. The barrels were positioned in a way that tearing off the blasting caps would set off the bomb, so they were going to have to cut the wires at the timer. They traced the wires and noted that there were a total of four; two red, one yellow, and one blue.

"I've seen this configuration before," said the young bomb expert. "It's the second red one."

"Where have you seen this before?" asked Sam.

"During training," he answered. "In a four-wire configuration with two red, we were taught to cut the second red. The wires and their paths are identical to what I was taught. The second red also appears to be the 'hot' wire to the blasting caps."

"I agree," said Sam.

The bomb officer was ready to cut the second red wire when Sam stopped him. "Did your instructor teach you that jihadi terrorists know about that protocol, so they'll reverse it, meaning that you should cut the first red?" asked Sam. The timer was at 1:30.

"No, he didn't," the young, bomb expert responded. His hand was shaking. "Is that true? I'm sure it's the second red wire."

"No, man, I'm just messing with you; assessing your level of confidence. You passed. If you say second red, cut the second red. I trust you, and you should trust your training," said Sam.

The young expert quickly cut the second red and the timer stopped at :40. They had not blown up, and Sam high-fived the guy, who then turned his head and threw up his breakfast.

Sam could hear The Ohio State band playing in the distance, a reminder that the rest of the world had no clue what had just happened. He texted Mariah and said that he would meet her at their entrance gate. The return text was an emoji of a smiley face blowing a kiss, followed by "The only easy day was yesterday," a SEAL motto. God, he loved that girl.

Epilogue

The plots against the United States had been thwarted through the efforts of those acting behind the scenes. Americans took it for granted that these men and women would work tirelessly to keep the country safe. They didn't know about the many unpublicized attempts on the safety of Americans. Anonymously, these heroes went about their important work without due recognition and celebration.

Sam and his team met with Mr. Steen the week after Thanksgiving.

"Gentlemen, I want you all to take some well deserved rest and recreation until the New Year," said Steen. "The U.S. government can protect the country until then!"

"Wow, a whole month! You must still be drunk from our post-mission celebration," said Bury.

The rest of the group broke into hysterics.

"Funny, smart ass," replied Steen. "Seriously, enjoy your time. I'd like to hear about any new ideas at that time. I also want to say that it's an honor to work with you men."

"Confirmed," said Sam. "He's still drunk."

The group continued to laugh, and it only got louder as Mr. Steen gave them the middle finger.

The effect of the video recording of Khalid Ali continued to ripple across the world. Muslim-Americans were quick to agree with their belief of these secular values. Prominent Muslim clergyman were speaking out against extremist Islamic terrorists like never before. Many Muslims hiding in the shadows of the U.S. voluntarily came forward to be vetted under the President's new policy. They felt less fear than they had before the release of the video.

The effects were also seen across the Middle East. Muslims were questioning their leaders as to why a shared belief in secular values had not been emphasized before. Their opinion about the West seemed to be changing to a more favorable attitude. Unfortunately, violence between Muslim factions showed no change in behavior.

For the time being, Iran continued to behave and show improved behavior. A meeting between the two country's presidents had been set, and sanctions against Iran had been lessened. The world continued to spin, and war and oppression were still present in areas around the globe. But... what else could one expect in a "fallen" world?

Acknowledgments

I started writing a novel about seven years ago. I had written down ideas and storylines initially, then began to sit down and started the initial 30-40 pages. I would go back and reacquaint myself with these ideas and then perhaps write a few more pages. I was doing this while engaged in my busy Orthopedic Surgery practice; hence, I did not get very far. I have always liked to tell stories; as a kid, I made them up in my head and this would help me drift off to sleep. When I had children, I would make up stories to tell them at bedtime. Of course, these stories did not involve death and destruction!

I recently retired (I think) from medicine, and while I was cleaning out my desk at home, I came across my notes for this book. I then reread what I had started and periodically had reviewed over the years. I became more excited about something that involved "work" than I had for a long time. Having read a tremendous amount of thrillers over the years, I thought that I would give it a shot. My aspiration became to finish what I had started. I looked forward to it every morning and became immersed in research and writing. The story evolved over this period somewhat from my original notes, but that was okay. Prior to this, my writing had been limited to articles for medical journals and books chapters, so this was much more fun to have the story flow. I read an interview of David Baldacci, one of my favorites, who said that he pretty much made things up as he went. The story was in his head, but getting it to paper was a process of continued change and improvement of the story. I don't pretend to be anywhere near his ability, but it did reinforce to me that what I was doing to write this book had worked for someone who is so successful!

I enjoyed the solitary process of writing this book. I have enjoyed talking and listening to patients for many years, but I found the atmosphere of background music and writing to be equally enjoyable.

Without question, I could not have done this without the encouragement and support of my wonderful wife. I know it's a cliché, but seriously, she's the best part of me. She's also very liberal, certainly much more tolerant than me, and not a big fan of watching the news. She is a very spiritual being with an optimism and positivity that I admire greatly. As you might expect, she's not a great fan of my storyline!

Anyway, "it is what it is," and I hope that people enjoy reading it as much as I did writing my first novel. If you don't, well, thanks for giving it whatever chance you gave it!

About the Author

Joseph R. Ritchie, MD, is a son, brother, husband, father, military veteran, and recently retired Orthopedic Surgeon debuting his first novel. He was born and raised in the Midwest, completed undergraduate and Medical School at The Ohio State University. After finishing his specialty training in Orthopedics, he served in the United States Air Force. He was in private practice until he retired. His greatest passion is his family, but he also enjoys everything outdoors; especially sailing, snow skiing, and wake surfing.